THE GREATEST
HINDI STORIES
EVER TOLD

Also translated by Poonam Saxena

Scene: 75 (Novel) by Rahi Masoom Raza
Chander & Sudha (Novel) by Dharamvir Bharati

The
GREATEST
HINDI
STORIES
EVER TOLD

selected & translated by

POONAM SAXENA

ALEPH

ALEPH BOOK COMPANY
An independent publishing firm
promoted by *Rupa Publications India*

First published in India in 2020
by Aleph Book Company
7/16 Ansari Road, Daryaganj
New Delhi 110 002

ISBN: 978-81-947353-0-4

3 5 7 9 10 8 6 4

Printed in India

CONTENTS

INTRODUCTION

Bookshops have been my refuge for as long as I can remember. The comforting silence, broken only by the soft sound of pages being turned or of people talking in low voices, and the rows upon rows of books were a warm cocoon in which I was happy to lose myself. Leaving the bookshop was a disorienting experience as one adjusted to the noise, people, sunlight or, if it was evening, the gathering darkness. But the bundle of books that I hugged to myself promised many happy hours ahead. It was the same with libraries. As a schoolgirl, when I went to Mussoorie during my summer vacations, inordinately lengthy periods of time were spent borrowing books from its beautiful nineteenth-century public library, and sitting curled up in the hotel room reading them.

Finding bookshops was never a problem in Delhi, but finding bookshops that sold Hindi books was. For years I had a secret reading life no one knew about—I refer to my reading of Hindi novels and short stories. This love affair started when I was in college, and when I say it was a 'secret', I mean it was something I couldn't really share with my friends. Most of them were immersed in Camus, Shakespeare, Wodehouse. As was I, but I was also enamoured of Mannu Bhandari and Rajendra Yadav, Premchand and Usha Priyamvada. Perhaps it had to do with my family background—being from Uttar Pradesh, we spoke Hindi at home, there were Hindi books in the house, one of my aunts taught the subject in a college and wrote Hindi poetry. (A big reason I began translating from Hindi to English and why I remain a cheerleader of translation in general is because of this—it gives me an opportunity to share books I've read and enjoyed with people who can't read Hindi.)

I am not a scholar of Hindi literature (I studied History in St Stephen's College, and did an MPhil on women in the freedom movement in UP); I am a lover of Hindi fiction. So I would scour the city for Hindi bookstores, and eventually I found my havens: little (and sometimes not so little) shops tucked away in Connaught Place or Mandi House or Daryaganj. Some of them shut down, but new ones opened; annual book fairs were a godsend, as are online shopping platforms.

Years of buying books has meant overflowing bookshelves and tottering piles on the floor next to my bed. I've realized that it would take several lifetimes to read every short story and every novel that I want to.

And that is partly the story of this anthology. I wanted to include dozens of different authors, to put together not one but five volumes, and accommodate every short story I liked. But that was obviously impossible.

There are some short stories without which no anthology can be complete. Such as Chandradhar Sharma Guleri's 'Usne Kaha Tha' ('She Had Said So'), the impactful and touching 1915 tale about Indian soldiers in World War I. Though written more than a hundred years ago, it has not dated at all. A story about war, love, and sacrifice, 'Usne Kaha Tha' is rooted in historical reality—over a million Indian soldiers fought in the War, most of them from Punjab, like the characters in the story: Lahna Singh, Bodha Singh, Vajira Singh, and the Subedar. The story vividly recreates images of soldiers crouching in muddy trenches, frozen to the bone, facing booming shells that left shuddering aftershocks, fighting to the death in what was really someone else's war, and then, in the moments before death, yearning for the sweet mangoes from the tree in their village.

'Usne Kaha Tha' is widely regarded as the first modern Hindi short story—it was of its time, rooted in reality, and a pioneer in the use of colloquial words and phrases (in this case, Punjabi). However, the first clutch of Hindi short stories date back even earlier, to the beginning of the twentieth century. Before that, stories were more in the nature of mythological tales and adventurous yarns. But at the turn of the century we see stories with a conscious narrative, or foregrounding a particular incident or situation, or capturing a moment of emotional intensity.[1] Most of these early short stories were published in the Hindi monthly journal, *Saraswati*. Benaras-born Kishorilal Goswami's 'Indumati', loosely based on Shakespeare's *The Tempest*, was published in 1900. Madhavrao Sapre's 'Ek Tokri Bhar Mitti' was published in 1901 (not in *Saraswati*, but in a magazine called *Chattisgarh Mitra*), about a zamindar who turns out a defenceless widow from her hovel, only to realize the injustice of his action later. In terms of theme, it is markedly different to 'Indumati' and is considered the first genuine Hindi short story by writers like Kamleshwar.[2]

In 1902 came 'Plague ki Chudail' by Master Bhagwandas; in 1903, Hindi scholar and writer Ramchandra Shukla published his story, 'Gyarah Varsh ka Samay'. Also in 1903 came 'Pandit aur Panditani' by Girija Datta Bajpeyi. Rajendrabala Ghosh, who wrote under the pen name Bang Mahila, published 'Dulaiwala' in 1907. Though a Bengali, Bang Mahila, who was born in Benaras in 1882, wrote regularly in Hindi for several years (she also wrote in Bangla, under the name Pravasini).

The stories covered a variety of themes: Master Bhagwandas's dramatic tale centres around the wife of a notable zamindar in Prayag, who is believed to have died of the plague. She survives and is labelled a witch come back from the dead, till the truth is discovered and she is reunited with her husband and son. 'Gyarah Varsh ka Samay' is also about the reuniting of a young couple, separated for eleven years because of misfortune and fate. The thrilling reunion takes place in the crumbling ruins of a village just outside the city. In contrast, 'Pandit aur Panditani' is a humorous story of a squabble between a forty-five-year-old pandit and his twenty-year-old wife; the latter is desirous of getting a talking parrot, the husband is quite firmly opposed to it, but in the end has to give in to his

---

[1]Sisir Kumar Das, *A History of Indian Literature: 1800-1910: Western Impact: Indian Response,* New Delhi: Sahitya Akademi, 1991.
[2]Kamleshwar (ed.), *Beesveen Sadi ki Hindi Katha Yatra Volume 1,* New Delhi: Sahitya Akademi, 2016.

determined young wife. 'Dulaiwala' too is a light-hearted tale about
a trick played by one friend on another.

These early Hindi short stories[3] belong to what is often called
the 'Dwivedi Yug'—after Mahavir Prasad Dwivedi, the famously
austere legendary editor of *Saraswati* magazine for eighteen years
(1903–20). *Saraswati*, published from Allahabad, was started in 1900 by
the proprietor of Indian Press, Chintamani Ghosh, with the blessings
of the Nagari Pracharani Sabha (NPS). The NPS, founded in 1893 in
Benaras, stood for the propagation of the Devanagari script, and the
overall cause of Hindi. *Saraswati* became a prestigious and influential
journal of its time, with Dwivedi firmly laying down rules for the
standardization of the language. An important goal of the NPS was
to ensure that the language and script used in government (in courts,
in administration) changed from Urdu to Hindi. The history of Hindi
and Urdu, the debates, the politics, is long and complicated, and this
is not the place to go into the details. There are several excellent
books on the subject for those who are interested in further reading.[4]

But going back to our subject, that is, Hindi short stories—
the growth, development, dissemination and popularity of this
particular creative literary form owed much to the Hindi journals
that proliferated in north India at the time. There was *Saraswati* of
course. Then came the monthly *Madhuri*, launched in 1922, under
the editorship of Dularelal Bhargava, who was from a great Lucknow
family of publishers. It was less stringent than *Saraswati* in terms of
rules of language, published a vibrant variety of short stories from

[3]For more information on these, see: Vijayendra Snatak, *Hindi Sahitya ka Itihaas*, New
Delhi: Sahitya Akademi, 2018; K. B. Jindal, *A History of Hindi Literature*, New Delhi:
Munshiram Manoharlal Publishers, 1993; Neelabh (ed.), *Hindi ki Yaadgaar Kahaniyan*,
New Delhi: Orient Publishing, 2016; and Das, *A History of Indian Literature*.
[4]See Amrit Rai, *A House Divided: The Origin and Development of Hindi/Hindavi*, New
Delhi: Oxford University Press, 1984; Alok Rai, *Hindi Nationalism*, New Delhi: Orient
BlackSwan, 2001; Francesca Orsini, *The Hindi Public Sphere, 1920-1940: Language and
Literature in the Age of Nationalism*, New Delhi: Oxford University Press, 2009 (repr.);
and Christopher King, *One Language, Two Scripts: The Hindi Movement in Nineteenth
Century North India*, New Delhi: Oxford University Press, 1994.

well-known and new authors, and very soon established an enviable place for itself in the region.[5]

Jaishankar Prasad is another literary figure associated with early Hindi short stories—his story 'Grama' appeared in his monthly magazine *Indu* in 1911, about a zamindar who, when out on an inspection of his land, is suddenly confronted by his father's perfidy. But Prasad's fame rests more on his works of poetry and drama, often on historical and mythological themes. *Indu* was launched in Benaras in 1909, but couldn't scale the heights that *Saraswati* or *Madhuri* did.

Apart from these major publications, a profusion of smaller journals mushroomed. Journals were important avenues through which writers' works reached large swathes of readers. And among the writers, the single most important name was that of Premchand. Born in 1880 in Lamhi, a village near Benaras, this colossus of Hindi literature revolutionized the Hindi short story with his use of simple, everyday language and his powerful themes of social justice and exploitation set, more often than not, in the vast rural countryside. He wrote in both Urdu and Hindi, and can rightfully be claimed by both: there is an Urdu Premchand and a Hindi Premchand and they are but two sides of the same coin.

It was extraordinarily difficult to pick one among the dozens of unforgettable stories he wrote, but I have gone with 'Thakur ka Kuan' ('The Thakur's Well'). It is a remarkable story: in barely three pages, Premchand tells us a tale of unyielding caste discrimination, and the courage of a woman, Gangi, in a dangerous, desperate situation.

Premchand picked political themes, whether it was the suffering of the peasantry, deeply entrenched social inequalities, or communal harmony. In his prolific writing years—the 1920s and 30s—his own province, the United Provinces (present-day Uttar Pradesh), was convulsed with agrarian unrest. These were also the years when Mahatma Gandhi's mass movements took place—the Non-Cooperation movement in 1920, the Civil Disobedience movement

---

[5]For more on Hindi journals, see Orsini, *The Hindi Public Sphere*.

in 1930. Deeply affected by these events, and by the fight for India's independence, Premchand left his government job when Gandhi gave the call for non-cooperation. All this is reflected in his celebrated novels such as *Karmabhoomi* and *Premashram*, but also in his short stories, such as 'Samar Yatra', 'Juloos', 'Ahuti' and in his tales of rural distress and exploitation ('Sava Ser Gehun', 'Poos Ki Raat', 'Sadgati', and many others). In his historic presidential address to the All India Progressive Writers' Association in 1936, barely a few months before he died, Premchand offered his own philosophy of literature—that it was 'the criticism of life', and that it should be the mirror of its age; he spoke of the need to go beyond empty entertainment and to become socially responsible. [6]

Premchand's words have echoed through the ages and continue to do so till today. I do believe that the style and form may have changed, as also the sensibilities and the way of looking at characters and stories. The concerns may (or may not) have changed, the focus may have shifted from society to the individual, the emphasis on a 'higher purpose' may have gone out of vogue, but the truth is that the greatest Hindi short stories remain those that have held up a mirror to their time.

In the post-Premchand decades, the Hindi short story morphed. India became in many ways a new country in which a new generation of writers emerged. The country was grappling with the trauma of Partition, the shock of Gandhi's assassination, the euphoria of Independence, followed by the challenging post-Independence years.

No one knows the exact figures, but around half a million to one million people are believed to have been killed and a staggering 12 million estimated to have been displaced in the cataclysmic division of the country that tore Hindus and Muslims apart, leaving behind wounds that continue to fester today.[7]

---

[6]Full speech here: http://www.columbia.edu/itc/mealac/pritchett/00urdu/kafan/taraqqi_1936_speech/rahbar_trans_english.pdf

[7]Andrew Whitehead, 'Partition 70 Years On: The Turmoil, Trauma—and Legacy', BBC News, 27 July 2017.

But there was also freedom from a racist colonial government. With Independence, the task of nation-building began in right earnest. Literacy levels began going up.[8] The urban population increased.[9] Industrialization took off.[10] Employment opportunities began opening up slowly.[11] With the departure of an alien, imperial power, political activity entered a new phase.

Women had the vote, better literacy levels[12] and were starting to join the workforce. There were an increasing number of women in certain professions—teaching, medicine, bureaucracy. The Hindu Code Bill, violently opposed by conservative sections of society, introduced monogamy, gave women the right to inherit, the right to divorce, and the right to maintenance.[13] But these winds of change brought with them storms and intense social churn. It was also a time of daunting challenges for the young nation. It still had to combat poverty, economic inequalities, social injustice. And over everything lay the grim shadow of Partition, the bloody cost of the country's freedom.

All this concerned the newer generation of writers. The first few decades after Independence are particularly rich in terms of literary output and it's not a coincidence that some of the greatest Hindi

---

[8]From 18.33 per cent in 1951 to 28.3 in 1961 to 34.45 in 1971, Census of India 2011, https://censusindia.gov.in/2011-prov-results/data_files/india/Final_PPT_2011_chapter6.pdf

[9]From 44,153,297 in 1941 (13.9 per cent of the total population) to 109,113,977 in 1971 (19.9 per cent of the total population), http://censusindia.gov.in/Census_Data_2001/Census_Newsletters/Newsletter_Links/eci_3.htm

[10]There was a three-fold increase in aggregate index of industrial production between 1951 and 1969. For more on this, see A. Vaidyanathan, 'The Indian Economy Since Independence (1947-70)', in Dharma Kumar (ed.) *The Cambridge Economic History of India, Vol. 2 1757-1970,* Cambridge: Cambridge University Press, 1983.

[11]For example, India's scientific and technical manpower increased more than twelve times from 190,000 in 1949 to 2.32 million in 1977; Bipan Chandra, Mridula Mukherjee and Aditya Mukherjee (ed.), *India Since Independence*, New Delhi: Penguin Books, 2008.

[12]From 8.86 per cent in 1951 to 15.35 in 1961 to 21.97 in 1971, Census 2011, https://censusindia.gov.in/2011-prov-results/data_files/india/Final_PPT_2011_chapter6.pdf

[13]See Chandra et al, *India Since Independence.*

short stories were written in this period. As was the case earlier, literary journals—such as *Kahani*, *Dharmyug*, and *Sarika*, to name just three—played an important role in publishing short stories by new and established writers. Some of these magazines were helmed by great writers themselves—Dharamvir Bharati edited *Dharmyug* for over twenty years with enormous success and Kamleshwar took *Sarika* to new heights of prestige and popularity. And *Kahani*, dedicated to the short story, was brought out by Sripat Rai, the son of Premchand and an accomplished writer himself. After finding acclaim as a writer of short stories and novels, Rajendra Yadav found a new calling as the editor of *Hans*—a journal founded by Premchand—where he published a range of new writers who went on to achieve fame of their own. Yadav was one of the first to spot the talent of Dalit writer Omprakash Valmiki.

Inevitably, a large chunk of the stories featured in this volume belong to this era. One of the major literary movements, the Nayi Kahani movement, which began in the fifties, led by the celebrated trio of Rajendra Yadav, Kamleshwar, and Mohan Rakesh, brilliantly reflected the social churn. As migration to big cities took place, stories shifted away from rural to urban spaces. Writers turned their gaze to middle-class and lower middle-class life in cities and towns, to newly forged relationships between men and women, to the cracks in family life. The Indian family's default status as an ideal social construct came under the scanner and its uglier facets, particularly the oppression of women, were exposed. (Later, the Nayi Kahani movement would be criticized for not having paid enough attention to rural India or to marginalized communities. But the movement remained extremely influential, shaping future writers.) Rakesh spoke of the restlessness among writers, of the writer trying to alienate himself from the reality around him, even as he was part of it.[14]

The Mohan Rakesh story I have chosen for this volume is 'Malbe ka Malik' ('Lord of the Rubble'), which poignantly captures

---

[14]Interview with Mohan Rakesh—K. P. Singh, Asghar Wajahat, *Journal of South Asian Literature*, Vol. 9, No. 2/3, Mohan Rakesh Issue (1925-1972), Fall and Winter 1973.

the tragedy of Partition: An old Muslim man, Abdul Ghani, returns to Amritsar seven years after Partition, to the city where his son, daughter-in-law, and grandchildren were killed. It was a tough choice, because Rakesh has so many other memorable stories to his credit—from 'Suhagine', which explores the predicament of a financially independent married woman who yearns for marital closeness and children, both of which are denied to her, to 'Ek Aur Zindagi', which looks at the brittleness of a modern marriage and the male ego, from the loneliness of Miss Pal in the eponymous story, to the loneliness of Avinash, the narrator of 'Paanchve Maale ka Flat', who stares out of the window of his shabby Bombay flat at the dull sight of the same roofs with their drying clothes, broken toys, and empty bottles.

For Rajendra Yadav, I have selected his hair-raising story, the memorable 'Jahan Lakshmi Qaid Hai' ('Where Lakshmi is Held Captive'). And for Kamleshwar, I have included his bleak tale of a funeral in a big city, 'Dilli Mein Ek Maut' ('A Death in Delhi'). Both Yadav and Kamleshwar had many other compelling stories too, such as Yadav's stories of suffocating family life, where women's freedom and self-respect are ground to dust and where lack of money is a constant reality, where tradition still fights to keep its oppressive hold ('Biradari Bahu', 'Pass Fail', among others). I was also very tempted to include his unusual 1962 lesbian love story, 'Prateeksha', a rare story of queer love for the time. Kamleshwar has the ability to rip away the curtain of hypocrisy and respectability ('Ek Ashaleel Kahani'). His stories like 'Itne Achche Din' and 'Maas ka Dariya' hit you in the gut. And his 'Khoi Hui Dishayen', an exploration of urban isolation, is rightfully regarded as one of his best. This feeling of alienation in a cold, anonymous big city was but a reflection of what many writers themselves were going through when they left their small towns and districts in search of work. (Mohan Rakesh was from Amritsar, Rajendra Yadav grew up in Agra and Surir, a small qasbah near Mathura, and Kamleshwar was from Mainpuri in UP. All of them ended up in Delhi.) 'Trishanku', a short story by the gifted Mannu Bhandari, told simply and with humour, addressed this post-Partition generation, caught between tradition and modernity. Schoolgirl Tanu's mother is determined that her daughter should not grow up with the same restrictions that she faced as a young girl—but discovers that she can't quite let go of them either. The story is partly autobiographical. When Mannu Bhandari's daughter was in Class 9, some first-year college boys moved into the house opposite theirs. She called them home and encouraged her daughter to become friends with them, but then wondered, how would she react if her daughter developed romantic feelings for one of the boys?[15]

Over the years, there were other literary waves too—the Akahani, the Sachetan Kahani, the Samantar Kahani and so on. But this is not a history of the Hindi short story told through literary movements. This is a personal selection of stories that enthralled me, disturbed me, moved me, stories that stayed with me long after I finished reading them. I consulted fellow translators, Hindi writers and academics, knowledgeable friends and ended up with a formidable list of authors. But in the end, I chose the stories that I liked and the stories that—as mentioned earlier—best reflected their time.

One of the most persistent themes over the decades was Partition. The division of the country had a profound effect on writers, especially those who had themselves been uprooted from their homes. In Krishna Sobti's 'Sikka Badal Gaya' ('The Times Have Changed'), the matriarch Shahni bids a heartbreaking farewell to the village (now in Pakistan) where she has lived all her life. As Shahni takes her leave from the weeping villagers, there is a sense of people being swept away in the inexorable forward movement of history, as if they were little pieces of straw being carried off on an unstoppable current. Sobti, herself a victim of Partition, wrote movingly about it in her novels as well—such as in her autobiographical work, *Gujarat Pakistan Se Gujarat Hindustan*. Her robust use of idiomatic Punjabi gives her writing a distinct flavour. But there are many excellent

---

[15]Susham Bedi, Interview with Mannu Bhandari, Hindi Urdu Flagship Channel (YouTube), 31 May 2013, https://www.youtube.com/watch?v=WCOGVSXv2ag

stories written around Partition—stories of terrible violence, of what such a cataclysmic event can do to people, of the tragic Hindu-Muslim divide, of courage and humanity in the midst of death and hate or, simply, personal tales of loss and longing. There are stories by the great Bhisham Sahni—'Amritsar Aa Gaya Hai', 'Pali', 'Sardarni' and 'Veero'. One of my favourites is 'Pali', the story of the Hindu boy brought up by Muslim parents, then returned to his Hindu family: Who is he really? A Hindu? Or a Muslim? There's also Badiuzzaman's poignant 'Pardeshi' and 'Antim Ichcha' that talk about the yearning of displaced people for their homes and make many insightful observations; Agyeya's 'Sharandata', about a Hindu man who is helped by a young Muslim girl to escape certain death; or Rajee Seth's 'Thehro Intezar Husain', where Intezar Husain's novel *Basti* triggers the protagonist's memories of fleeing Lahore, forty years after Partition.

Stories also abound of women's battles for dignity, self-respect and happiness. In Krishna Baldev Vaid's 'Udaan', four women seize just one day for themselves before reality strikes. When I read the story, I was struck by how much and how often the women laugh on their escapade. The truth is that women were—are—not expected to laugh in such a wild, unrestrained fashion and Sheela, Vanti, Rani, and Veeran's laughter defines that one magical day of freedom for them. (In fact, this 'unladylike' behaviour makes people assume they are prostitutes.) In Doodhnath Singh's 'Napni' ('The Human Measure'), the freedom and assertion come at a different point in the story, but they come with the force of a thunderclap. Singh, an outstanding writer of short stories in the post-Nayi Kahani era ('Mai ka Shokgeet', 'Reech', 'Sapaat Chehere Wala Aadmi', among others) has given us a precious gift in 'Napni'. A fine story like Kamtanath's 'Saari Raat' ('All Night Long'), in the form of a conversation between a newly-married husband and wife lying in bed, tells us more about how a traditional Indian man viewed women's freedom, sexual and otherwise, than any number of newspaper articles or studies could. Yashpal's stories are known for their pointed targeting of traditional beliefs and established norms and 'Phoolo ka Kurta' ('Phoolo's Kurta') is justifiably one of his best-known: a sharp comment on child marriage and notions of female modesty, told with admirable brevity.

There are stories of ageing parents who find themselves tragically out of sync with the 'new' urban family, stories written with deep sympathy. This is a recurring theme and I think almost every Hindi author has attempted a story on the increasingly painful relationship that elderly parents have with their sons and daughters, particularly when they have to live under the same roof. The high ideal of selfless love for vulnerable, helpless dependents is long gone—if it ever was as widespread in practice as myth and tradition would have us believe. Bhisham Sahni's 'Chief ki Dawat' ('A Feast for the Boss') is arguably his most famous story: What should be done with old, rustic, timid Ma when the American boss comes home for dinner? In Usha Priyamvada's 'Vaapsi' ('The Homecoming'), Gajadhar babu comes home to his family after being away for years, but finds the reality quite different from his rosy post-retirement dream. The story has many layers and is a microcosm of middle-class life. (But there are other stories of ageing parents, with different nuances, and I wish I had been able to feature them. Swadesh Deepak's 'Bagugoshe' gives us a heart-warming portrait of the writer's mother as he visits her when she's on her deathbed. Geetanjali Shree's remarkable story, 'Iti', looks at the death of old man, a retired officer who has become eccentric and embarrassing in his old age. Another of Shree's stories, 'Bhitraag', features the seventy-plus Girdhari who has a constant, irrational fear of dying, but a ninety-three-year-old friend offers a valuable lesson. Gyan Ranjan's acclaimed story 'Pita' is a marvellous character sketch of a cantankerous old man who refuses to spend a penny on himself, much to the exasperation of his son.) And along with the stories on ageing, there is a tender tale of lost childhood, Shekhar Joshi's 'Dajyu', probably the writer's most renowned piece of short fiction.

If much of post-Independence Hindi fiction was urban-centric, there were writers like Phanishwarnath Renu who remained devoted to the village (his short story 'Teesri Kasam' was published in the *Nayi Kahani* magazine in the fifties; and in his later years Renu too introduced urban milieus in his work). 'Teesri Kasam' is steeped in the fragrance of the soil of Bihar. Renu's liberal use of lilting local idiom, folk tale, and folk song imparts a certain wistfulness to the story of the endearing bullock-cart driver Hiraman.

Hindi writer Shaani (the nom de plume of Gulsher Khan) once asked: 'is Hindi literature Hindu literature?' during a discussion with Hindi literature stalwarts—critic Namwar Singh, fiction writer Kashinath Singh and poet Vishwantah Tripathi. It was a valid question—where were the Muslim characters and stories in Hindi fiction? I want to direct readers to Shaani's brutally honest, unsettling story, 'Yuddh' ('War') believed to be autobiographical, about what it was like to be a Muslim in India at a time of war with Pakistan. And to the harrowing 'Shah Alam Camp ki Roohein' ('The Spirits of Shah Alam Camp') by Asghar Wajahat, about the aftermath of a communal riot. Wajahat is a major contemporary literary voice and has written some of the most gut-wrenching stories in recent times. Amarkant's 'Maut ka Nagar' ('City of Death') looks at the fragile thread that holds together communal peace and shows how easily it can snap. Yet the story is not without hope.

Shivani, a popular, pioneering woman writer with an assured command over language and portrayal of emotion, created many memorable characters. In her stories, the women dominate with their strength and their tenderness, their audacity and vulnerability: 'Kariye Chhima' ('Forgive Me'), set in her beloved Kumaon, is a prime example and I was delighted to discover that it was her favourite too.[16]

Choosing a story by Agyeya was exceptionally hard, given his wide-ranging oeuvre—from his stories set in the freedom movement to those about army life, particularly in the Northeast, to his Russian stories (with Russian characters)—but I settled for his famous

---

[16]Quoted in the Bhumika (Introduction), Shivani, *Meri Priya Kahaniyan*, New Delhi: Rajpal and Sons, 2016. Also told to me by her daughter, Mrinal Pande.

'Gangrene', a masterful look at the numbing monotony of middle-class life.

There is humour too, in Bhagwaticharan Verma's 'Prayshchit' ('Atonement'), and Harishankar Parsai's 'Bholaram ka Jeev' ('The Soul of Bholaram'). Verma is a self-confessed writer of the chutkula-as-story, literally the joke-as-story, but that 'joke' hides within it scathing satire, as 'Atonement' amply demonstrates. ('Do Baanke', 'Sauda Haath Se Nikal Gaya' are other excellent examples, though of course Verma wrote 'serious' stories too.) On his part, Parsai elevated satire to literary heights. His deceptively simple, fable-like story is sharp, cutting and also very funny. I wish I had been able to include one of Amritlal Nagar's humorous stories, especially his riotous parody of detective fiction, 'Kaaldand ki Chori', in which a bizarre cast of characters—Sherlock Holmes, Sexton Blake, Robert Blake, Inspector Mohammed Sarwar, Jameliya the female dacoit and many others—come together to solve a theft that involves no less a personage than the Yamraj.

The inclusion of writers from the earlier decades necessarily means it's been impossible to fit in as many contemporary authors as I would have liked to. In the limited space available, I have chosen a short story by the exceptional Uday Prakash, 'Tirich'. Prakash's surreal imagery coupled with a detached, almost clinical description of the nightmare that takes place in a city, make for an unforgettable tale. Prakash has written other extraordinary stories ('Dilli ki Deewar', 'Chappan Tole ka Kardhan', 'Hiralal ka Bhoot', 'Paul Gomra ka Scooter') too, and it was difficult to pick just one. Then there is Sara Rai's exquisite 'Bhool Bhulaiyan' ('The Labyrinth') that evocatively chronicles the now ancient but still spirited Kulsum Bano's memories of life in her ancestral home, Noor Mahal in Benaras. Once a grand haveli, it has crumbled into a dilapidated old ruin. Rai's writing has a mesmerizing quality, as 'Ababeel ki Udaan', a story of childhood and superstition, also demonstrates. Omprakash Valmiki, best known for his autobiography *Joothan*, a milestone in Dalit literature, wrote extremely stark and powerful short stories on caste discrimination.

Among them, 'Bhay' ('Fear') stands out. The writer chillingly depicts the sheer terror of the protagonist that he will be 'found out', that his upper-caste neighbours and friends will discover that he is 'SC'.

Apart from the writers I have already mentioned, I have had to leave out other wonderful writers too, such as Vinod Kumar Shukla, Kashinath Singh, Upendranath Ashk, Nirmal Verma, Mahendra Bhalla, Akhilesh, Mamta Kalia, Mridula Garg, Chitra Mudgal, and so many more. The sad truth is that in any anthology, it is impossible to include every writer you want to.

Hindi short stories have been part of decades-long ongoing debates, discussions, introspection and a search for the truth of the time they were written in. They shine a light on years of social change. This is their abiding strength and relevance. I hope that this collection of twenty-five stories will offer readers unfamiliar with Hindi fiction a glimpse into this rich world. There is so much more to discover.

SHE HAD SAID SO

CHANDRADHAR SHARMA GULERI

Residents of big cities, whose backs have been flayed and whose ears have turned sore from the whip-like tongues of ekka drivers, we entreat them to come and apply the soothing balm that is the speech of Amritsar's bamboo-cart drivers. On the wide roads of big cities, ekka drivers, while lashing the horses' backs with their whips, sometimes establish a close relationship with the maternal grandmother of the horse, sometimes express pity at the fact that pedestrians have no eyes, sometimes drive over the same pedestrians' toes and yet paint themselves as the wronged ones, the very avatars of the entire world's remorse, anguish, and despair as they move ahead. Their counterparts in Amritsar make their way along narrow, circular lanes through a jungle of white turbans, mules, ducks, sugarcane sellers, roadside vendors, labourers carrying loads, waiting for every cart driver to pass, displaying an overflowing sea of patience as they cry out, 'Watch it, Khalsaji', 'Make way, bhaiji', 'Wait, bhai', 'Make way, Lalaji', 'Move, child'. Catch anyone moving out of the way unless they hear a 'ji' or 'sahib'. It's not as if they don't know how to give a tongue lashing, they do, but it's more like a sweet, fine knife thrust. If an old woman doesn't move out of the way despite repeated warnings, they respond with such figures of speech—Move, you deserve to live; you're fortunate; you're beloved of your sons; save yourself, there's a long life ahead of you; why do you want to come under the wheels of my cart? Save yourself.

A young girl and boy made their way through these very bamboo-cart drivers and met at a shop in the marketplace. From his long hair and her loose pyjamas, it was clear that they were Sikhs. He had come to buy fresh curd for his uncle to wash his hair with and she had come to buy badiyan (spiced lentil balls) for the kitchen. The shopkeeper was bickering with a stranger who was

1

refusing to move until he had counted every papad in a one-kilo pile of wet papads.

'Where's your house?'

'In Magre, and yours?'

'In Manjhe, where do you stay in Magre?'

'With my mama. Atarsingh.'

'I'm also staying with my mama, his house is in Guru Bazaar.'

Meanwhile, the shopkeeper had finished with his customer and began attending to them. They made their purchases and left the shop together. After they had walked for a while, the boy asked with a smile, 'Are you engaged?'

At this, the girl's eyes flashed with anger and with a 'Dhat!' she ran away, leaving the boy staring after her.

Every other day, they ran into each other unexpectedly at the vegetable seller's or the milkman's. This went on for a month. The boy asked her the same question a few more times. The reply would always be 'Dhat!' One day, when the boy, teasing her good-humouredly, asked the same question, she said, 'Yes, it's done.'

'When?'

'Yesterday. Can't you see this shawl with silk embroidery?' The girl ran away. The boy set out for home. On the way, he pushed a boy into a drain, ensured a hawker lost a full day's earnings, hurled a stone at a dog and poured milk on a vegetable seller's cauliflower-laden cart. Colliding into a freshly bathed Vaishnav woman, he earned the epithet of 'blind'. Only then did he reach home.

ᔐ

'Ram, Ram, what kind of war is this? Sitting in these trenches night and day, my bones have become numb. It's ten times colder than Ludhiana, and on top of that, all this rain and snow. We're up to our calves in slush. Can't see the enemy, every couple of hours, there's an explosion that bursts your eardrums and with it, the whole trench shakes and the earth itself seems to shoot high up in the air. We can fight only if we escape from these hidden bombs. I had heard of the

Nagarkot earthquake. Here, there are twenty-five earthquakes a day. If by chance your turban or elbow pokes out of the bunker, you'll be instantly hit by a bullet. Who knows where those treacherous fellows are, lying in the mud or hiding in the grass.'

'Lahna Singh, there are just three days left. We've already spent four days in the trenches. "Relief" will turn up day after tomorrow and then seven days, leave. We'll kill a goat and eat and sleep to our hearts' content in that firangi woman's house—the grass there is like velvet. She literally showers you with milk and fruit. No matter how many times you ask her, she refuses to take any money. She says, "You're like kings, you've come to save my country".'

'Haven't slept a wink for four nights. You know the saying—a horse gets agitated if it's not exercised, it's the same for a soldier if he doesn't fight. If only I could get the order to strap on a bayonet and march. And if I don't return after killing seven Germans, let me never be lucky enough to touch my forehead at the threshold of Darbar Sahib. Scoundrels, the minute they see a bayonet, they clutch at your feet, begging for mercy. But at night they throw bombs weighing hundreds of kilos. In our attack the other day, we didn't leave a single German alive in four miles. The General sahib gave us the command to back off, otherwise....'

'Otherwise you would have reached Berlin straightaway, right?' Subedar Hazara Singh said with a smile. 'Matters of war are not decided by jamadars or naiks. The senior officers think long term. The front is 300 miles long. If we advance on one side, what will happen?'

'True, Subedarji,' said Lahna Singh, 'but what can one do? The chill has settled into our bones. The sun never comes out, and it's like the streams and wells of the Chamba keep pouring in from both sides of the trench. Just one attack would warm us up.'

'Udmi! Get up, put some coals into the brazier. Vajira, four of you throw the water out of the trench in buckets. Maha Singh, it's getting to be evening, change the guard at the entrance of the trench.' Saying this, the Subedar started doing his rounds.

Vajir Singh was the comedian of the regiment. Throwing the dirty water he had collected in buckets out of the trench, he said, 'I've become a priest. This is an offering to the German king.' At this, everyone burst out laughing and the clouds of gloom dispersed.

Lahna Singh filled a second bucket of water and, handing it to him, said, 'Pretend you're watering the melons in your field. You won't get such rich water in all of Punjab.'

'Yes, this is not a country, it's heaven. After the war I'm going to ask the government to give me ten ghumas of land and plant an orchard here.'

'Will you get your wife here too? Or that firangi mem who keeps offering milk....'

'Shut up. People here have no shame.'

'Every country has its own ways. To this day I haven't been able to explain to her that Sikhs don't smoke tobacco. She insists on giving me a cigarette, wants to put it between my lips, and when I step back, she thinks her raja has got offended and won't fight for her country anymore.'

'Achcha, how is Bodha Singh now?'

'He's all right.'

'As if I don't know. Every night, you cover him with both your blankets and you spend the night with just the brazier for warmth. You also do guard duty for him. You get him to sleep on your dry planks of wood, and lie in the slush yourself. What if you fall ill? It's not just cold, it's like death, and those who die of pneumonia don't even manage to get a square piece of land for themselves.'

'Don't worry about me. I'll die next to the pit in Bulel. My head will be in the lap of Bhai Kirat Singh, shaded by the mango tree I planted in the courtyard.'

Frowning, Vajir Singh said, 'What is all this talk of dying? Let the Germans and Turks die! Come on, brothers, sing something. Yes, like this....'

Who knew that these bearded, married Sikhs could sing such bawdy songs? But the entire trench resounded with the song and all the soldiers were refreshed, as if they'd had four days of rest and recreation.

It is late at night. It is dark. There is silence all around. Bodha Singh is sleeping on three empty biscuit tins covered with both his blankets, and he has two of Lahna Singh's blankets plus an overcoat spread over himself. Lahna Singh is standing guard. One eye is on the entrance to the bunker and the other on Bodha Singh's thin frame. Bodha Singh groans.

'What is it, Bodha Singh bhai?'

'Give me some water.'

Raising a tumbler of water to his mouth, Lahna Singh asked, 'How are you?' Drinking the water, Bodha said, 'I'm shivering. It's like there's an electric current running through my body. My teeth are chattering.'

'Achha, wear my jersey.'

'And you?'

'I have the brazier and I don't feel the cold, I'm sweating.'

'No, I won't wear it. For four days you've been doing so much for me....'

'Yes, I just remembered. I have another warm jersey. It came this morning. These foreign women keep knitting jerseys and sending them. May Guru bless them.' Saying this, Lahna removed his coat and began taking off his jersey.

'Are you telling the truth?'

'Of course, do you think I'm lying?' saying this, he forcibly put the jersey on the protesting Bodha and, wearing a khakhi coat and shirt himself, went to stand guard. The story of the foreign woman knitting a jersey was just that—a story.

Half an hour passed. A voice called out from outside the trench, 'Subedar Hazara Singh.'

'Who's that? Lieutenant sahib? Yes, sir.' Saying this, the Subedar presented himself in front of his officer, standing at attention and executing a military salute.

'Look, we have to mount an attack immediately. About a mile

from here, at the eastern end, is a German trench. There aren't more than fifty Germans there. Take the road below the trees, it cuts through two farms. There are three or four turnings. I've placed fifteen soldiers at every turning. Leave ten people here, take the rest and go meet them. Capture the trench and stay there until the next order. I will stay here.'

'Yes, sir.'

Everyone got ready in silence. Bodha also removed his blanket and prepared to leave. Lahna Singh stopped him. When Lahna Singh moved forward, Bodha's father, the Subedar, pointed towards Bodha with his finger. Lahna Singh understood and said nothing. An argument broke out over who was going to stay back. No one wanted to. Somehow the Subedar managed to convince ten men to stay back and set off on the march. The Lieutenant sahib, looking away, went and stood next to Lahna's brazier, took out a packet of cigarettes from his pocket and lit one. After ten minutes, he extended his hand towards Lahna, saying, 'Here, have one.'

In the blink of an eye, Lahna Singh understood everything. Keeping his face expressionless, he said, 'Here, give it to me, sahib.' As he put his hand out, he saw the sahib's face in the light of the brazier. He saw his hair, and the penny dropped. How had the Lieutenant sahib lost his sideburns overnight and acquired the close-cropped haircut of a prisoner?

Maybe the sahib was drunk and had had the opportunity to have his hair cut? Lahna Singh decided he had to investigate a little more. Lieutenant sahib had been in his regiment for five years.

'Well, sahib, when will we go back to Hindustan?'

'When the war ends. Why, don't you like this country?'

'No, sahib, the shikar here is not that much fun, is it? Do you remember, last year after the military exercises, you and I went to Jagadhari District for shikar? Yes, yes…where you rode a donkey and your khansama, Abdul, went to a temple to make an offering of water….'

'Yes, that scoundrel.'

'And a nilgai passed by in front of us, so big.... I'd never seen such a big one before. And your bullet hit the shoulder and came out of the rump. It was a pleasure hunting with an officer like you. Well, sahib, did the head of that nilgai come back from Shimla where it had gone to be stuffed? You'd said you'd mount it on the regiment's mess wall.'

'Yes, but I sent it abroad.'

'What big antlers! They must have been at least two feet big.'

'Yes, Lahna Singh, they were two feet four inches. You didn't smoke your cigarette?'

'I'll just smoke it, sahib, let me get a matchstick.' Saying this, Lahna Singh went into the bunker. Now he was in no doubt and he quickly decided what had to be done.

He collided with a sleeping form in the dark.

'Who's that, Vajira Singh?'

'Yes, what is it, Lahna? Has there been a calamity? You could've let me nap a little longer.'

'Wake up, the calamity is here and it's come wearing the Lieutenant sahib's uniform.'

'What?'

'Lieutenant sahib has either been killed or taken prisoner. This is some German wearing his uniform. The Subedar didn't see his face. But I did and spoke to him too. The bastard speaks Urdu fluently, but it's bookish Urdu, and he gave me a cigarette to smoke.'

'So now?'

'We're all dead. We've been deceived. The Subedar will be marching around in the slush and this bunker will come under attack. And they will be attacked in the open. Get up, do as I say. Run and follow the tracks of the regiment. They won't have reached far. Tell the Subedar to return immediately. That story about the bunker is a lie. Go, leave the trench from the back. Quietly, not even a leaf should move. Hurry.'

'But the order was to....'

'To hell with the order. This is my order—Jamadar Lahna Singh, who is, at this moment, the seniormost officer here, it is his order. Let me fix this Lieutenant sahib.'

'But there are just eight of you here.'

'Not eight, ten lakh. A single Akali Sikh is equal to one and a quarter lakh men. Go.'

Lahna Singh turned back and, at the entrance to the bunker, he flattened himself against the wall. He saw that the Lieutenant sahib had taken three explosives out of his pocket, each the size of a wood-apple. He stuck the three into different parts of the bunker, connecting them with a wire. At the end of the wire was a knotted string which he placed near the brazier. He moved towards the opening of the bunker and was going to light the fuse....

Moving like lightning, Lahna Singh hit the sahib's elbow with the butt of his rifle. There was a thud and the matchstick fell from the sahib's hand. Lahna Singh hit him again, this time on the neck and the sahib cried out, 'Ach mein got' and fell senseless to the ground. Lahna Singh picked up all three explosives and threw them out of the bunker. He dragged the sahib's body to the brazier and searched his pockets. Lahna Singh took out three or four envelopes and a diary and put them in his own pocket.

The sahib recovered consciousness. Lahna Singh laughed and said, 'So, Lieutenant sahib, how are you? Today, I learnt many things. I learnt that Sikhs smoke cigarettes. I learnt that there are nilgai in Jagadhari District with two-feet-four-inch antlers. I learnt that Muslim khansamas offer water to idols and Lieutenant sahibs ride donkeys. But how did you learn such good Urdu? Our Lieutenant sahib couldn't utter five words without saying "Damn".'

Lahna hadn't searched the trouser pockets. The sahib put both his hands in his pockets, as if to protect them from the cold.

Lahna Singh kept talking, 'You're very clever, but Lahna of Manjha has spent many years with his Lieutenant sahib. To fool him, you need four eyes. Three months ago, a Turkish maulvi had come to my village. He gave childless women amulets and distributed medicines among the kids. He would lie on a cot under the chowdhry's banyan tree smoking a hookah and tell us that the Germans were real pundits. They'd learnt how to fly planes by studying the Vedas. They didn't kill cows. If they came to India, they would end cow slaughter. He used to mislead the Baniyas by saying they should withdraw their money from the post office, as the British Raj was going to end. Polhuram, the postmaster, got quite scared. I shaved off the mullah's beard and threw him out of the village, warning him that if he ever set foot in the village again....'

The sahib fired the pistol in his pocket and the bullet hit Lahna's thigh. Lahna fired his Martini-Henry twice and smashed the man's skull. At the sound of the shots, everyone came running.

Bodha shouted, 'What happened?'

Lahna pacified him and asked him to go back to sleep, saying that 'a mad dog had come in, and he'd just shot him dead', but he explained the real situation to everybody else. They got ready with their guns. Lahna tore strips off his turban and tied them tightly around his wound. It was a flesh wound; the tightly bound strips would prevent any further blood loss.

At that moment, seventy screaming Germans stormed the bunker. A volley of fire from the Sikhs' rifles stopped the first attack. Then the second. But they were just eight (Lahna Sigh was firing accurately— he was standing, the others lying down) and the Germans seventy. The Germans kept coming in, climbing over the dead bodies of their fellow soldiers. In a few minutes, they would....

Suddenly, there was the war cry: 'Wahe Guruji ki fateh! Wahe Guruji ka khalsa!' and rapid fire from guns rained on the Germans' backs. They were caught in the middle of the fire. Subedar Hazara Singh's soldiers were firing from behind and in front, Lahna Singh's comrades were busy wielding their bayonets. As the soldiers at the back came closer, they too began attacking the Germans with their bayonets.

Another war cry: 'An army of Akal Sikhs is here! Wahe Guruji di fateh! Wahe Guruji da khalsa! Sat Shri Akal purukh!' And the fighting was over. Sixty-three Germans had either fallen in the fight or lay on the ground groaning. Fifteen Sikhs had lost their lives. A bullet had grazed past the Subedar's right shoulder. Lahna Singh had been hit in the rib. He filled the wound with the wet mud of the bunker and tied the rest of his turban tightly around his waist, like a cummerbund. No one knew that Lahna had been injured a second time—and more grievously.

As the battle was raging, the moon had risen. A moon, whose light had led Sanskrit poets to name it kshayi. And the light breeze would have been described as 'dantveenopdeshacharya' in Banabhatt's language. Vajira Singh was describing how kilos of French soil had stuck to his boots when he ran after the Subedar. The Subedar heard what had happened from Lahna Singh, looked at the papers he had seized, and praised his quick thinking—if he, Lahna, hadn't been there, they would have all died today.

The sound of the battle had been heard by the soldiers in the trench that was three miles away to the right. They had telephoned the base camp. Instantly, two doctors and two ambulances for the injured were dispatched; they arrived within an hour-and-a-half. The field hospital was close by. They would make it there by morning. The wounded, their injuries treated with simple bandages, were taken in one ambulance and the dead were placed in the other. The Subedar wanted Lahna Singh's thigh to be bandaged too. But he brushed it away, saying it was a minor injury; they would see to it in the morning. Bodha Singh was delirious with fever. He was made to lie down in the ambulance. The Subedar didn't want to leave Lahna behind.

Lahna said, 'For the sake of Bodha and the Subedarni, you have to go in the ambulance.'

'And you?'

'Send an ambulance for me when you reach. Anyway, the ambulances will be coming to take the German dead bodies too. I'm not in bad shape. Can't you see, I'm standing on my own two feet? Vajira Singh is with me.'

'All right, but—'

'Has Bodha got into the ambulance? Is he lying down? You too go, get inside the ambulance. And, listen, if you write a letter to the Subedarni, give her my respects. And when you go home, tell her that I did as she bid me.'

The vehicles started moving. As he was leaving, the Subedar caught Lahna's hand and said, 'You saved Bodha's and my life. Why the letter? We will go home together. You tell your Subedarni yourself. What did she say to you?'

'Now just get into the vehicle. Write and tell her what I said, and then tell her when you meet her too.'

As soon as the ambulance left, Lahna lay down. 'Vajira, give me some water and open my cummerbund. It is soaked.'

⌣

Memory becomes very sharp a few moments before death. All the events of your life flash before you, one after another. The colours of every scene become crystal clear, the fog of time lifts completely.

Lahna Singh is twelve years old. He has come to Amritsar to stay with his uncle. He keeps meeting an eight-year-old girl everywhere—at the vegetable seller's, the curd seller's, everywhere. When he asks her, 'Has your engagement happened?' she says 'Dhat!' and runs away. One day, when he asks her again, as is his habit, she replies, 'Yes, I got engaged yesterday, can't you see this fine red shawl with flowers embroidered in silk?' Lahna Singh feels unhappy when he hears this. Angry too. Why?

'Vajira Singh, give me some water.'

⌣

Twenty-five years have passed. Now Lahna Singh is a Jamadar with 77 Rifles. He doesn't remember the eight-year-old girl. Who knows when she met him, or whether they met at all. He has taken seven days' leave and come home in connection with a court case about a piece of land, when he receives a letter from his regiment's officer that he and Bodha Singh are going to the front too. 'On your way back, come visit us at our house. We'll go together.' The Subedar's village was on the way and the Subedar was very fond of him. And so Lahna Singh reached the Subedar's house.

As they were about to leave, the Subedar came out of the courtyard. He said, 'Lahna, the Subedarni knows you. She's asking for you, go and meet her.' Lahna Singh went inside. The Subedarni knows me? Since when? The Subedar's family had never stayed in the regiment quarters. At the door, he greeted her respectfully, and received a blessing in return. Lahna Singh stood silently.

'Do you recognize me?'

'No.'

'Has your engagement happened? Dhat, yes it happened yesterday—can't you see this fine red shawl with embroidered silk flowers—in Amritsar—'

His clashing emotions brought him back to consciousness. He turned on his side. The wound in his rib started bleeding gain.

'Vajira, give me some water.' She had said so.

⌣

He is still dreaming. The Subedarni is saying, 'I recognized you as soon as you came. I want you to do something for me. I am doomed. The government has awarded him for his bravery, given land in Lyallpur, and now it's time to repay all that with loyalty. But why didn't the government create a women's regiment so that I too could have gone with the Subedarji? I have one son. He joined the army just one year ago. Four came after him but not one survived.' The Subedarni started crying.

'Now both are going. This is my fate! Do you remember, one day, the tongawallah's horse went out of control near the curd seller's shop? You saved my life that day. You braved the horse's kicking legs, picked me up and stood me on the shop's wooden plank. Save these two like you saved me that day. I am begging you.'

Crying, the Subedarni went inside the women's quarters. Wiping his tears, Lahna came out.

'Vajira Singh, give me some water.' She had said so.

Vajira Singh was sitting with Lahna's head cradled in his lap. Whenever Lahna asked for water, he gave it to him.

Lahna was quiet for half an hour, then he said—

'Who's that? Kirat Singh?'

Vajira understood. He said, 'Yes.'

'Bhaiya, lift me a little. Put my head on your thigh.' Vajira did as he was told.

'Yes, now it's all right. Give me some water. Bas, this time in ashadh, the mangoes will be plentiful. Uncle and nephew will both sit there and eat the mangoes. The mango tree is as old as your nephew. I planted it the very month he was born.'

Vajira Singh's tears were flowing.

A few days later, people read in the newspapers—France and Belgium—68th list—Died of wounds on the front, 77 Sikh Rifles Jamadar Lahna Singh.

THE THAKUR'S WELL

PREMCHAND

Jokhu put the lota to his mouth—a vile stench came from the water. He said to Gangi, 'What kind of water is this? It's impossible to drink because of the smell. Here I am parched with thirst, and you're giving me this foul water to drink!'

Every evening Gangi would go and fetch water. The well was far; it was difficult to go again and again. When she'd brought the water yesterday, there had been no stink; how was it smelling so bad today! She brought the lota to her nose; yes, there really was a stench. Some animal must have fallen into the well and died. But where could she get some other water?

Who would allow her to go to Thakur's well? People would start yelling at her from far away itself. Sahu's well was on the other side of the village, but there, too, who would allow her to fill water? There was no other well in the village.

Jokhu had been ill for many days. For a while he lay quietly, enduring his thirst, then he said, 'I can't bear it any longer. Give me the water, I'll hold my nose and drink a little.'

But Gangi wouldn't give it to him. She knew that drinking the dirty water would make him more ill. But she didn't know that if you boiled the water, it would be safe to drink. She said, 'How can you drink this? Who knows what animal has died in it. I'll get some fresh water from the well.'

Jokhu looked at her in surprise and said, 'Where will you get some other water from?'

'Between Thakur and Sahu, they have two wells. Won't they let me fill one lota?'

'You'll get your hands and feet broken, that's all. Just sit quietly.... The Brahman-devtas will curse you, the Thakur will hit you with his lathi, Sahuji will ask for a whole lot of money. Who understands

14

the suffering of the poor! Nobody will look in even when we die, forget lending a shoulder for our funeral bier. You think these people will allow you to fill water from the well?'

This was the bitter truth. What could Gangi say in reply? But she wouldn't allow him to drink the stinking water.

It was nine o'clock at night. The exhausted labourers had already gone to sleep, but a handful of idlers had gathered outside the Thakur's door. This was not an age of valour, as in days past. Now they talked about valour in the law courts. How cleverly the Thakur bribed the Thanedar in a particular case and got off scot-free. How smartly he'd got a copy made of an important court judgment. Everyone—the court officer and other senior officials—said it couldn't be done, but he'd done it. Some asked for fifty, some demanded a hundred. One had to know the art of getting work done.

That was when Gangi arrived to draw water from the well.

It was lit by the dim, murky light from a small oil lamp. Crouching behind the platform of the well, Gangi waited for an opportune moment. The whole village drank water from this well. Nobody was prohibited from using it, except these unfortunate ones.

Gangi's rebellious heart struck at traditional restrictions and constraints—why are we low-born and why are they high-born? Because they tie a thread across their shoulder? All those gathered here, each is worse than the other, each one is a villain. They steal, cheat, indulge in false cases. The other day, this Thakur stole a sheep from the shepherd and later killed and ate it. The pandit over here, his house is a gambling den twelve months of the year. That sahu, he mixes oil in ghee and sells it. They get work done but when it comes to paying wages, it is as though doing so will put them in dire straits. In what way are they superior to us? Yes, they are higher than us when it comes to opening their mouths—we don't keep running through the streets, screaming we are superior, we are superior! When I come into the village sometimes, they look at me with lustful eyes; they're so burnt up with envy, but their arrogance, that they are superior, never goes away.

She heard the sound of footsteps approaching the well! Gangi's heart started pounding. If anyone saw her it would be catastrophic. She picked up the pot and rope and moved away in a crouch. She went and stood in the dark shadow of a tree. When have these people ever shown mercy to anyone! They thrashed poor Mehngu so badly that he spat blood for months. Just because he refused to work without payment! Does this make them superior to us?

Two women had come to the well to fill water. They were talking to each other.

'They decide to go and eat and order us to fill fresh water and bring it. But don't even have money to buy an extra pitcher.'

'Men can't bear to see us just sitting and relaxing.'

'Yes, they can't pick up a pitcher and fill water themselves. Just issue a command: go and fill fresh water, as if we are their servant girls!'

'What else are you if not a servant girl? Don't you get food to eat and clothes to wear? Somehow you manage to save five or ten rupees for yourself. That's what servant girls are like!'

'Don't shame me, Didi. I wish I could rest for just a second. If I worked so much in someone else's house, I would be far more comfortable. On top of that, he would have been grateful. Here you may die working but no one will appreciate you.'

After both of them had filled water and left, Gangi came out of the shadow of the tree and went close to the well. The idlers had left. The Thakur had also shut the door and was going to the courtyard to sleep. Gangi breathed a sigh of relief. Finally, the coast was clear. Even a prince on a mission to steal nectar from the gods couldn't have proceeded more cautiously and intelligently. Stealthily, Gangi climbed up on the platform of the well. She had never felt such a sensation of victory before.

She fitted the noose of the rope around the pitcher. Looking right and left, she was watchful and alert, like a soldier trying to find an opening in an enemy's fort at night. If she was caught now, there would be no forgiveness or leniency. Finally, praying to her gods, she steadied her heart and lowered the pot into the well.

The pot sank gently into the water. There was not a sound. Gangi quickly tugged at the rope two or three times. The pot came up to the mouth of the well. The strongest wrestler could not have pulled the pitcher up so fast.

Gangi bent to pick up the water pot and place it on the platform when suddenly Thakur sahib's door opened. Not even the open mouth of a lion could have been more terrifying.

The rope slipped from Gangi's hand. The rope and the pot of water fell into the water with a loud splash and the sound of the ripples in the water echoed for a few moments.

The Thakur walked towards the well, shouting, 'Who's there? Who's there?' Gangi jumped down from the platform of the well and ran.

When she reached home, she saw Jokhu drinking that same dirty, stinking water from the lota.

ATONEMENT

BHAGWATICHARAN VERMA

If there was anyone in the whole house that the spotted cat loved, it was Ramu's bride, and if there was anyone in the whole house that Ramu's bride loathed, it was the spotted cat. Ramu's fourteen-year-old bride, beloved of her husband, adored by her mother-in-law, had come from her maternal home to her husband's home for the first time. The storeroom key dangled at her waist; the servants obeyed her commands: she had become the most important person in the household. The mother-in-law took out her rosary and busied herself in prayer and worship.

But the bride, just a fourteen-year-old girl, would sometimes leave the storeroom door open, or fall asleep inside. Seizing the opportunity, the spotted cat would polish off the milk and ghee. Ramu's bride would be furious, but for the spotted cat, things couldn't have been better! She would doze off while ladling ghee into the big earthen pot; the leftover ghee would disappear in a trice into the spotted cat's stomach. When she'd cover the milk and go to the cook to give her some grain, the milk would vanish. If things had ended here, it wouldn't have mattered, but the spotted cat had become so familiar with Ramu's bride that the poor girl could not even eat or drink without some problem or the other! A bowlful of thick, sweet milk would be brought to her room, but by the time Ramu arrived, the bowl would have been licked clean. Cream would be bought from the bazaar, but by the time Ramu's bride prepared a paan, the cream would have disappeared.

Ramu's bride made a decision, only one of them could live in the house: either her or the spotted cat. Battle lines were drawn, both were alert. A big wooden cage to catch the cat arrived. It was stocked with milk, cream, mice, and various other delicacies that cats favour, but this particular cat didn't so much as glance in that direction. But now the spotted cat began displaying a certain amount of ardour; earlier she used to be scared of Ramu's bride, now she started following her around, though she prudently kept herself at arm's length.

The spotted cat's new brazenness meant that things became a tad difficult for Ramu's bride in the house. She had to suffer mild rebukes from her mother-in-law and, as a result, her husband had to suffer indifferently cooked food.

One day Ramu's bride made some kheer for her husband. Pistachio, almonds, fox nuts, and all kinds of dry fruits were simmered with the milk. When the kheer was ready, she covered it with light golden foil, filled a bowl to the brim, and placed it on a high ledge where the cat couldn't reach. Then she got busy preparing a paan.

Meanwhile, the cat entered the room, stood below the ledge, looked up at the bowl, sniffed—yes, it was excellent fare—sized up the height of the ledge—Ramu's bride was busy readying the paan. As soon as she left to give the paan to her mother-in-law, the spotted cat leapt, hit the bowl with its paw and the bowl fell to the ground with a loud crash!

Ramu's bride threw the paan in front of her mother-in-law and ran to the room only to find the bowl broken into tiny pieces, the kheer splattered on the floor, and the cat busy slurping away at it. The moment she saw Ramu's bride, the cat instantly made herself scarce!

Ramu's bride saw red. She was going to get rid of the cat once and for all. She couldn't sleep all night and kept thinking of what strategic move she should make, how she should attack the cat so that it wouldn't survive. When morning came, she saw the spotted cat sitting at the door, gazing at her lovingly.

Ramu's bride thought for a bit, then got up, smiling. As soon as she got up, the cat promptly slunk away. Ramu's bride filled a bowl with milk, left it at the doorstep, and went away. When she returned with a flat stone in her hand, she found the spotted cat devouring the milk. It was the perfect opportunity; Ramu's bride lifted the stone and hit the cat with all her might. The spotted cat didn't scream or shriek, just crumpled to the floor, still and unmoving.

Hearing the sound, the servant abandoned her broom, the cook abandoned her kitchen, the mother-in-law abandoned her prayers and all of them presented themselves forthwith at the scene of the crime. Ramu's bride stood, hanging her head guiltily.

Said the servant, 'Arre Ram! The cat is dead! Maaji, how terrible if the cat has been murdered by her!'

Said the cook, 'Maaji, the murder of a cat is as bad as the murder of a human being. I can't cook anything in the kitchen till this murder charge hangs over her head.'

Said the mother-in-law, 'Yes, you're right, until we remove the stain of this murder, no one can drink any water or eat any food. Bahu, what have you done!'

Said the servant, 'So what should we do? Should I call the panditji?'

The mother-in-law felt life ebbing back into her. 'Oh yes, quickly, run and get the panditji.'

The news of the cat's murder spread like lightning in the neighbourhood—women from nearby homes began queuing up at Ramu's house. There was a barrage of questions from all sides, while Ramu's bride sat, head bowed.

When Pandit Paramsukh got the news, he was in the middle of his prayers. But the moment he heard, he stood up and told his wife with a smile, 'Don't cook today, Lala Ghasiram's daughter-in-law has killed a cat, there will have to be atonement, there'll be plenty of delicious food to get our hands on.'

Pandit Paramsukh Chaubey was a short, corpulent man. His height was four feet ten inches and the girth of his paunch was fifty-eight inches! He was round of face, with big moustaches, fair-skinned, and his long plait hung all the way to his waist.

It was said that whenever there was a search for Mathura's pandits with a fondness for spicy food, Pandit Paramsukh's name would top the list.

Pandit Paramsukhji arrived and the quorum was complete. The jury sat down—the mother-in-law, the cook, Kisnu's mother, Channu's grandmother, and Pandit Paramsukh. The rest of the women expressed their sympathy for Ramu's bride.

Said Kisnu's mother, 'Panditji, which is the particular hell you go to if you murder a cat?'

Pandit Paramsukh consulted a page from his papers and said, 'A cat's murder by itself is not enough to find out the name of the hell, it is necessary to know the time the cat was killed, only then can I tell you.'

'Around seven in the morning!' said the cook.

Pandit Paramsukh turned the pages of his book, moved his fingers on the letters, and placed his hand on his forehead, looking thoughtful. His face became clouded, furrows appeared on his forehead, he wrinkled his nose, and his voice became grave, 'Hare Krishna! Hare Krishna! This is terrible! The murder of a cat early in the morning, moments before sunrise! Kumbhipaak, the hell of boiling oil, is ordained for that! Ramu's mother, what happened is terrible, terrible!'

Tears sprang to Ramu's mother's eyes, 'So, then, Panditji, what will happen now, please tell us.'

Pandit Paramsukh smiled, 'Ramu's mother, there's nothing to worry about, why are we priests here, after all, if not to help at such a time? The way to atone is prescribed in the scriptures. If you do penance, everything will become all right.'

Said Ramu's mother, 'Panditji, that's why we called you, please tell us, what do we have to do next?'

'What to do—get a cat made of gold and get the bride to donate it to charity. Till the cat of gold is not given away, the house will remain impure. After that, you should have recitations from sacred texts for twenty-one days.'

Channu's grandmother said, 'Yes, of course, Panditji is giving the correct advice. First the donation of the cat, followed by the recitation.'

Said Ramu's mother, 'So, Panditji, how many tolas of gold should the cat be?'

Pandit Paramsukh smiled. Stroking his paunch, he said, 'How many tolas of gold should the cat be? Arre, Ramu's mother, the scriptures say the gold should be equal to the actual weight of the cat; but this is Kalyug, virtue and duty are dead, no one has true faith. So, Ramu's mother, a cat made of as much gold as its weight is not possible, because the cat must easily weigh about twenty, twenty-one kilos. But the cat should at least be twenty-one tolas, though of course, it's up to you and how much piety you have.'

Ramu's mother stared at Pandit Paramsukh, her eyes almost popping out, 'Arre baap re, twenty-one tolas of gold! Panditji, this is too much, can't we make do with a cat of just one tola?'

Pandit Paramsukh laughed, 'Ramu's mother! A cat of one tola! Arre, is the greed for gold more important than your bride? She has such a terrible sin hanging over her head, should you be so greedy!'

Negotiations over the weight and cost ensued and the matter was settled at eleven tolas.

After this, talk turned to the prayers and rituals that would be required. Said Pandit Paramsukh, 'What is the problem? What are we here for, Ramu's mother? I'll do the recitation from the scriptures, you can send all the material for the rituals to my house.'

'What will you need?'

'Arre, we'll try and manage with the least. About ten maunds of grain, one maund of rice, one maund dal, one maund sesame seeds, five maunds barley, five maunds chickpeas, four paseri ghee and one maund salt too. That's it, I'll manage with this much.'

'Arre baap re, so many things! Panditji, all this will cost about 100–150 rupees....' Ramu's mother said tearfully.

'I can't manage with less. The murder of a cat is a grave sin, Ramu's mother! Before looking at the expenditure, look at the nature of the bahu's sin. This is penance, not a joke—and people should spend money commensurate with their belief in the penance. You aren't just anybody, arre, 100–150 rupees is nothing for you.'

The members of the jury were influenced by the words of Pandit Paramsukh. Kisnu's mother said, 'Panditji is right, a cat's murder is not some ordinary murder, it is a big sin for which you have to spend big money.'

Said Channu's grandmother, 'Exactly, giving alms and charitable donations reduces sin—and you can't be stingy in such matters.'

Said the cook, 'Maaji, you are well off. What is this expense for you?'

Ramu's mother looked at everyone. All the people on the jury were in agreement with Panditji. Pandit Paramsukh was smiling. He said, 'Ramu's mother! On the one hand is kumbhipaak, a special kind of hell for your daughter-in-law and on the other hand is a little bit of expense. Don't turn away from that.'

Taking a deep, resigned breath, Ramu's mother said, 'I have no choice now, I will have to dance to your tune.'

A little annoyed, Pandit Paramsukh said, 'Ramu's mother! This is something to be happy about—but if you don't like it, if you mind doing it, then don't do it, I'm off....'

Saying this, he started gathering his sacred leaves and papers.

'Arre Panditji, Ramu's mother doesn't mind at all. The poor thing is so upset...don't be annoyed!' chorused the cook, Channu's grandmother, and Kisnu's mother in one voice.

Ramu's mother fell at Panditji's feet—and Panditji sat down with renewed authority and purpose.

'What else?'

'You'll have to give twenty-one rupees for twenty-one days of recitation from the scriptures and you will also have to feed five Brahmins twice a day for twenty-one days.' After a pause, Panditji said, 'Actually don't worry about that. I will eat twice a day myself and that will suffice, you will get the same result as you would if you fed five Brahmins.'

'Panditji is right. Look at Panditji's paunch!' said the cook with a mocking smile.

'All right then, get the preparations for the atonement underway, Ramu's mother. Take out eleven tolas of gold, I'll go and get a cat made out of it—I'll get it made in two hours and be back, till then, get everything ready for the rituals—and make a note, for the prayers....'

Panditji had not finished his sentence when a servant girl ran into the room, panting, and everyone looked up. 'What happened?' asked Ramu's mother in some panic.

Stammering, she replied, 'Maaji, the cat got up and ran away!'

PHOOLO'S KURTA

YASHPAL

The villages in our parts are very small. In some areas, they're tiny, the number of houses ranges from about ten or twenty to five or six, and they're all set very close together. One village may be situated in a valley while another on a mountain slope.

Banku Sah's shop, shielded by a thatched roof, meets all the needs of the village. The veranda of his shop is like the village club. In front is a peepul tree where the children play and the cattle sit and chew their cud.

The rain, which had been falling since the morning, had stopped and the sun was out. We needed carom seeds for some medicine. I left home thinking I would pick them up from Banku Sah's.

Five to seven good men of the village were sitting in the veranda of Banku Sah's shop. They were smoking a hookah. In front of the veranda, the village children were playing hopscotch. Sah's five-year-old daughter, Phoolo, was also among them.

What can a five-year-old girl wear? A kurta hung down from her shoulders, that was it. Phoolo's engagement had been fixed with Santu from 'Chula' village, about a furlong away from our village.

Santu must have been around seven. What is a seven-year-old boy to do? There were two buffaloes, one cow, and two bullocks in his home. When the cattle went for grazing, Santu, stick in hand, would mind them and play alongside; why would the cattle go into someone else's field? At dusk, he would herd the cattle home.

Now that the rain had stopped, Santu was herding his cattle down the green slope. Spotting the children playing below the peepul tree in front of Banku Sah's shop, he made his way there.

Seeing Santu enter the game, Hariya, the six-year-old son of the local goldsmith, shouted—'Aha, Phoolo's bridegroom has come.'

The other children also started yelling.

Children learn and understand everything without adults and venerable elders having to explain anything to them, simply by observing. Phoolo was five years old, but so what? She knew that she must be shy and modest in front of her bridegroom. She had seen her mother and other respectable women in the village demurely cover their faces. The traditions taught to her had told her it was appropriate and fitting that she should cover her face modestly.

As the children screamed, Phoolo was overcome with shyness, but what could she do. All she was wearing was a kurta. She lifted the hem of her kurta with both hands and hid her face with it.

Seeing this display of shyness, the respectable middle-aged men sitting around the hookah in front of the hut burst into hearty laughter.

Kaka Ramsingh lovingly threatened her and told her to let go of her kurta.

The naughty little boys thought this was a joke and began going 'Ho ho.'

I had come to Banku Sah's shop to get some carom seeds for some medicine but seeing Phoolo's artlessness, I felt upset. I left empty-handed.

This is what happens when, even in changing times, you try to protect morality and modesty with established traditions.

GANGRENE

AGYEYA

As soon as I stepped into that deserted courtyard, I sensed a shadow of some curse hovering over it, something in the atmosphere that couldn't be expressed in words or touched, but it was burdensome, trembling, dense and it was spreading....

At the sound of my footsteps, Malti came out. She recognized me and her weary face lit up for a second with sweet surprise before returning to its original expression. 'Come!' she said, and then without waiting for an answer, turned to go inside. I followed her.

Once we were in, I asked her, 'He isn't here?'

'He hasn't come yet, he's in the office. He'll come in a little while. He usually comes at around 1.30-2.'

'When did he leave?'

'He leaves as soon as he gets up in the morning.'

After saying 'Huh,' I was about to ask, 'And what do you do in that time?' but then thought it was not appropriate to ask this question all of a sudden. I looked around the room.

Malti brought a fan and began to fan me with it. I objected, 'No, I don't want this.' But she wouldn't listen, and said, 'Wah! How can you not want it? You've come from outside and it's so hot and sunny. Here....'

I said, 'All right, give it to me.'

Perhaps she was about to say 'No' but, just then, a baby started crying in the next room and, quietly giving me the fan, she placed her hands on her knees and with a tired 'Huunh,' levered herself up and went inside.

I watched her leave and, looking at her thin body, kept thinking—what is this...what is this shadow that has settled over this house....

We were distantly related and by that connection, Malti was my sister, but it was more accurate to call her my friend, because we always had a relationship of mutual friendliness. Since our childhood, we had played together, fought together, been punished together and we'd studied together quite a bit too, and this was always because we wanted it to be so, never because we were tied by bonds of familial relationship....

I had come to see her after about four years. When I last saw her, she was still a girl, but now she was married, the mother of a child. I hadn't thought about whether this would have changed her and if so, how, but now, watching her receding back, I thought— what is this shadow over this house...and especially over Malti....

Malti came back with the baby and sat on a rug on the floor a little distance away from me. I turned my chair to face her and asked, 'What's his name?'

Malti looked at the baby and replied, 'We haven't decided on any name as yet, but we call him Titti.'

I called out to the child, 'Titti, Titti, come,' but he looked at me with his big eyes, then clung to his mother and cried out tearfully, 'Unnh-unnh-uunh-oon....'

Malti looked at him again, and then looked out towards the courtyard....

There was silence for some time. For a while, the silence was natural, during which I waited for Malti to ask me something, when all of a sudden I realized that Malti had said nothing at all...she had not even asked how I was, how come I was here...she was just sitting quietly, had she forgotten the days gone by in just two years of marriage? Or was it that she wanted to keep me at a distance? Was it because that free mutual friendship was no longer possible...even so, this kind of silence shouldn't be there even with a stranger....

A little aggrieved, I turned away and said, 'It seems to me you're not exactly happy that I've come....'

She started and said, 'Hunh?'

This 'Hunh' was in the form of a query, but not because Malti hadn't heard what I said, but because she was surprised. That's why I didn't repeat what I said but sat silently. Malti didn't say anything, so after a while I looked at her. She'd been staring at me unblinkingly but the moment I turned towards her, she lowered her eyes. But I saw that there was a strange emotion in those eyes, as if something inside Malti was trying to remember forgotten things, trying to awaken and set in motion once again a fragmented universe, to revive some broken thread of behaviour, and was failing in this effort...as if a person was suddenly trying to lift a limb that hadn't been used for a long time, as if it had died during a long period of forgetfulness...it could not be lifted with such feeble strength (though that strength was entirely obtainable).... I felt as if the yoke around a dead creature's neck had been put on a living human being and that being was trying to remove it and throw it away but was unable to....

Just then, someone knocked on the door. I looked at Malti but she hadn't moved. Only when there was a second knock did she put the baby aside and get up to answer the door.

It was he, that is, Malti's husband. I was seeing him for the first time but I recognized him from his photo. Introductions were made. Malti went into the courtyard to prepare lunch, and the two of us sat inside and began talking, about his job, about his life, about the place where they lived, and other such topics which usually crop up in an initial conversation after two people have just been introduced, like a sort of protective armour of expression....

Malti's husband's name is Maheshwar. He is a doctor in a dispensary in this mountain village, that's how he lives in these quarters. He goes to the dispensary every morning at seven o'clock and returns around one or one-thirty, after that he's free the whole afternoon, he just has to go in the evening for one or two hours, to see the patients in the small hospital attached to the dispensary and give them necessary instructions...his life too follows a fixed pattern, every day the same work, the same kind of patients, the same instructions, the same prescriptions, the same medicines. He himself is bored, and in addition, the fierce heat makes him listless even in his free time....

Malti brought food for both of us. I asked, 'Aren't you going to eat? Or have you already eaten?'

Maheshwar said with a little laugh, 'She eats later....'

The husband comes home to eat at two-thirty, so the wife stays hungry till three!

Maheshwar began eating, looked at me and said, 'You're unlikely to enjoy the food, given that we're eating at such an odd time.'

I replied, 'Wah! Eating late is better because one is hungrier, but perhaps we're putting Malti behen to trouble.'

Malti interjected, 'Uhh-huh, this is nothing new for me...this is an everyday affair....'

The baby was in Malti's lap. He was crying, but nobody paid any attention to him.

I asked, 'Why does he cry?'

Malti said, 'He's become like this, so irritable, he's always like this.'

Then she scolded the child, 'Be quiet.' Which led him to cry even more, she picked him up and put him on the floor. And said, 'Okay, cry.' After this, she went away towards the courtyard to fetch rotis.

By the time we finished our meal, it was almost three. Maheshwar said he had to leave for the hospital earlier than usual, there were a couple of worrisome cases that might need to be operated on...two of them may need their legs amputated, gangrene had set in...he left after a while. Malti closed the door and was about to sit down next to me when I said, 'Now go and eat, I'll play with Titti till then.'

She said, 'I'll eat, what's the fuss about my eating,' but she left. I started swinging Titti in my arms, which quietened him down for a while.

Far away...perhaps in the hospital itself, a clock struck three. Suddenly I was startled by Malti's voice from the courtyard saying, with a long, tired sigh, 'It's three o'clock....' As if some task had been accomplished after a great deal of austere and rigorous work.

After some time, when Malti returned, I asked, 'Was there anything left for you? Everything was....'

'There was plenty.'

'Yes, there was plenty, I ate up all the vegetables, there wouldn't have been any left, don't just say so authoritatively that there was plenty,' I said with a laugh.

Malti said, as if she was talking about some other topic, 'You don't get any vegetables here, if someone is coming or going, we manage to get them from below; I've been back for fifteen days, we're still using the vegetables I brought....'

I asked, 'There's no servant?'

'We haven't found anyone suitable, maybe in a couple of days we'll get someone.'

'Do you wash the dishes?'

'Who else?' said Malti, then went to the courtyard for a second and came back.

I asked, 'Where had you gone?'

'The water hasn't come today, how will I wash the dishes?'

'Why, what happened to the water?'

'This happens every day...it never comes on time, now it'll come at seven in the evening, the dishes can only be washed then.'

'Chalo, you'll be free till seven in the evening,' I said, but I was thinking, now she will have to work till eleven at night, she's hardly going to be free.

She said the same thing. I had no answer, but Titti came to my rescue, all of a sudden, he began crying and tried to go back to his mother. I handed him over.

There was silence for a while, I took out my notebook from my pocket and started looking at notes from the last few days, that's when Malti remembered that she had not asked me why I had come, and she said, 'What brings you here?'

I said, 'So you remembered only now? I came to meet you, what else?'

'You'll stay for a couple of days, won't you?'

'No, I'll go back tomorrow, I have to go.'

Malti didn't say anything, but looked a little upset. I began going through my notebook again.

After some time it struck me that I'd come to meet Malti, she was sitting here waiting to talk to me and I was busy reading, but what should one talk about? I felt as if the mysterious shadow over this house was beginning to exert its power over me too, I was also becoming as drab and lifeless as—yes, as this house was, as Malti was....

I asked, 'Don't you do any reading or writing?' I looked around to see if I could spot any books.

'Here?' Malti said, laughing a little. Her laughter implied, 'What is there to read here?'

I said, 'All right, I'll go back and send you some books....' And the conversation once again petered out....

After a while, Malti asked, 'How did you come? In a lorry?'

'I walked.'

'You walked so far? You have a lot of courage.'

'After all, I was coming to meet you.'

'You came just like that?'

'No, the coolie is following with my luggage. I thought, let me bring my bedding as well.'

'You did the right thing, here it's just....' She lapsed into silence, then said, 'You must be tired, why don't you lie down.'

'No, I'm not at all tired.'

'Don't say you're not tired, you must be.'

'And what will you do?'

'I'll scrub the dishes, and wash them later when the water comes.'

I said, 'Wah!' because I couldn't think of anything else to say....

After a while, Malti got up and left, taking Titti with her. I too lay down and began looking at the roof...my thoughts, combined with the khan-khan sound of the dishes being scrubbed, created a monotonous drone, because of which my limbs began feeling limp and I started feeling drowsy...

All of a sudden, the monotonous sound stopped. That's how I snapped out of my drowsiness and tried to listen in that silence....

The clock was striking four and Malti had stopped when she heard the first gong itself....

I saw the same reaction as when the clock had struck three, though this time it was more pronounced. I heard Malti say, in a dreary, involuntary, expressionless, mechanical—and that too, like a tired, exhausted machine—tone, 'It's four o clock,' as if her machine-like life was all about involuntarily counting the hours, the way a speedometer tracks the distance travelled, and in a languorous, programmed way, says (to whom!) that I have covered this much of the immense, empty road…. I don't know when and how I fell asleep.

It was well past six when the sound of someone coming in woke me up, and I saw that Maheshwar had returned and along with him came my coolie carrying my bedding. I was about to ask for water to wash my face when I remembered that there was no water. Wiping my face with my hands, I said to Maheshwar, 'You got quite late?'

He said in a slightly apologetic voice, 'Yes, I had to do that gangrene operation today, I did one and sent the other patient in an ambulance to the big hospital.'

I asked, 'How did the gangrene happen?'

'A thorn pierced the skin, that's how it happened, the people here are very careless….'

I asked, 'Do you get good cases here? Not in terms of income, but in terms of experience for a doctor?'

He said, 'Yes, I do get such cases, the same gangrene, every second day, fourth day, a case arrives, even in the big hospitals below….'

Malti, who had been listening from the courtyard, came in and said, 'Yes, how long does it take to make a case? A thorn pierced the skin, and so someone's leg had to be amputated, is this any kind of medical practice? Every other day, he cuts off someone's leg or arm, is this what is called good experience for a doctor!'

Maheshwar laughed and said, 'So we shouldn't amputate the limb and let him die?'

'Yes, were there no thorns in the world earlier? I'd never heard that one could die because of a thorn….'

Maheshwar didn't reply, just smiled. Malti looked at me and

said, 'This is what doctors are like, it's a government hospital, so who cares. I hear such things every day. Now if I hear of someone dying, I don't even think about it. Earlier I wouldn't be able to sleep all night.'

Just then the open tap in the courtyard went—tip-tip-tip-tip-tip-tip-tip....

Malti said, 'Water!' And got up and went away. From the clinking and clanking sounds, we could make out that the dishes were being washed....

Titti had been standing, holding on to Maheshwar's legs for support, and looking at me, but now suddenly he left his father and began crawling towards Malti. Maheshwar said, 'Don't go there!' He picked him up and Titti began squirming in his arms and crying loudly.

Maheshwar said, 'Now he'll cry himself to sleep, only then will there be any peace in the house.'

I asked, 'Do you sleep indoors? It must be very hot inside?'

'There are a lot of mosquitoes too, but who will carry these iron cots outside? Next time I go down, I'll bring up some charpoys.' Then, after a pause, he said, 'We'll sleep outside today. There should be some benefit to your coming here.'

Titti was still crying. As Maheshwar put him on the cot and began pulling it, I said, 'Let me help,' and, picking up the other end, helped carry it outside.

Now the three of us...Maheshwar, Titti, and I, sat on the two cots and, not finding any appropriate topic of conversation, we sought to cover that inadequacy by playing with Titti, he had quietened down after we came out but every now and then, as if remembering some forgotten duty he had to perform, he would start crying and then suddenly become quiet again...and sometimes we would laugh, or Maheshwar would say something about him....

Malti had finished washing the dishes. Now she was taking them to the kitchen in one corner of the courtyard, that's when Maheshwar said, 'I've brought some mangoes, wash those too.'

'Where are they?'

'They're on the brazier, wrapped in paper.'

Malti went inside, picked up the mangoes and put them in her pallu. They were wrapped in a torn piece of an old newspaper. Malti kept reading that newspaper in the feeble evening light as she walked...she reached the tap but kept standing and reading. Only when she had finished reading both sides of the paper did she draw in a long breath, throw it away, and begin washing the mangoes.

I suddenly remembered...it had happened a long time ago...when we had just got admitted to school. When our biggest happiness, biggest victory was slinking out of the class after marking our attendance, running to the mango orchard a little distance away, climbing the trees, plucking the small, half-ripe mangoes, and eating them. I remembered...sometimes when I'd run away and Malti wouldn't be able to come I would return in a very glum state of mind.

Malti never read anything, her parents were fed up, one day her father handed her a book and said she had to read twenty pages every day. After one week he'd check if she'd finished the book, and if she hadn't he would thrash her within an inch of her life. Malti quietly took the book, but did she read it? Every day she would tear off ten or twenty pages and throw them away, and continue to play as before. When, on the eighth day, her father asked her, 'Did you finish the book?' she replied, 'Yes, I did,' and when her father said, 'Bring the book, I'll ask you questions on it,' she stood there without saying a word. When her father asked her again, she replied defiantly, 'I tore the book and threw it away, I won't study.'

After that she was thrashed quite badly, but that's another matter. At this moment, all I could think was that that impertinent, playful Malti had become so subdued, so quiet, so desperate for a scrap from a newspaper...was this, this....

At that moment Maheshwar asked, 'When will you make the rotis?'

'I'm just going to make them.'

But this time when Malti set off for the kitchen, Titti's sense of duty became even more acute, he stretched out his hands towards

Malti and began crying and wouldn't stop till Malti lifted him in her arms, made him sit in the kitchen and patted him with one hand while picking up several small containers and placing them before her....

And both of us waited silently for the night, for the dinner, for a conversation with each other, and for numerous unknown voids to be filled.

We finished our meal, lay down on the bed and Titti went to sleep. Malti had spread an oilcloth on the bed and put him down on it. He had fallen asleep, but sometimes woke up with a start. Once he even sat up but then immediately lay down again.

I asked Maheshwar, 'You must be tired, go to sleep.'

He said, 'You must be more tired...you've walked eighteen miles to come here.' But it was as if he added the words, 'I am tired too.'

I was quiet and after a while, I sensed that he was dozing off.

It was around ten-thirty by then; Malti was eating dinner.

I looked at Malti for some time, she was lost in thought—not any deep thought, but still, lost in thought as she ate her food slowly, then I shifted my position to make myself comfortable and gazed up at the sky.

It was a full moon, the sky was cloudless.

I saw—that government quarter, whose slate roof looked so desolate and colourless during the day, appeared to shine in the moonlight, so cool and smooth, as if the moonbeams were flowing on it, cascading down....

I saw—the pine trees in the wind...pine trees that had turned dry and discoloured in the heat...had softly, slowly started singing... some raag that was gentle but not pitiful or sad, that was restless but not agitated....

I saw—even the bats, in their soundless flight at the edge of the murky blue sky, looked beautiful....

I saw—the day's burning heat, discomfort, fatigue rising like steam from the mountains, only to get lost in the atmosphere above, and the mountains, like little babies, raising their arms—like branches of a pine tree—towards the sky....

But I saw all this, I alone.... Maheshwar was dozing off and Malti, having finished her dinner, was washing a clay pot with warm water, so that she could set the curd, and saying...'I'll just be free.' And at my saying, 'It's going to be eleven o'clock,' shaking her head a little to indicate that it turned eleven every day.... Malti didn't see any of that, her life was flowing along at its own prescribed pace, not prepared to pause for the moonlight, or for a universe to unfold....

How does a baby look in the moonlight, I thought idly, and turned towards Titti, and he suddenly, out of some childlike perversity, woke up, shifted on the bed, fell off and began crying at the top of his voice. Maheshwar got up with a shock and said, 'What happened?' As I rushed to pick him up, Malti came out of the kitchen, remembering that 'khat' sound, I said softly, in a voice full of compassion, 'The poor thing must be badly hurt.'

All this had happened in a second, in one unbroken action.

Malti put out her arms to take the baby from me and said, 'He keeps getting hurt, he falls down every day.'

For a second I was stupefied, and then my mind, my entire being, rebelled—but only my mind, not a word actually came out—'Ma, you're a young mother, what has happened to your heart that you are saying this when your one and only child has fallen down—when your whole life is ahead of you!'

And then I suddenly knew that this feeling was not a lie, I saw that a deep, frightening shadow had made a home in this family, was eating away at this first youthful phase of their lives like a worm, had become such a part of them they couldn't see it for what it was, but continued to move within its perimeter. Not just this, I even saw that shadow....

By then, everything became peaceful, as it had been before. Maheshwar lay down again and began dozing off. Titti was clinging to Malti on the bed, he was quiet but occasionally his tiny little body would shake with a sob. I too felt that my bed was quite comfortable. Malti was looking silently at the sky, but was she looking at the moonlight or the stars?

The clock struck eleven, I lifted my heavy eyelids to abruptly look at Malti with an inarticulate expectation. As the first of the eleven gongs sounded, Malti's chest suddenly rose and then slowly fell, like a blister on the body, in unison with the sound, and then she said, in a voice that faded away into silence, 'It is eleven o'clock....'

A FEAST FOR THE BOSS

BHISHAM SAHNI

There was a feast for the boss in Mr Shamnath's house today. Shamnath and his wife didn't have a moment to even wipe away their perspiration. The wife, in a dressing gown, tangled hair scraped back into a bun, unmindful of the powder and rouge spread all over her face, and Mr Shamnath, smoking cigarette after cigarette, holding a checklist in his hand, were going in and out of rooms.

Finally, by five o'clock, the preparations started falling into place. Chairs, tables, stools, napkins, flowers, everything had been moved to the veranda. The drinks had been arranged in the sitting room. Now all the useless household things were being hidden behind the almirahs and under the beds. That's when an obstacle presented itself to Shamnath—what was to be done with Ma?

Neither he nor his accomplished housewife had given this matter any thought. Mr Shamnath turned to his wife and asked in English, 'What about Ma?'

His wife stopped her work and after thinking for a while, said, 'Send her to her friend's house, the one who stays in the house behind. She can even stay the night. She can return tomorrow.'

With his cigarette in mouth, Shamnath looked at his wife with narrowed eyes for a moment, then shook his head and said, 'No, I don't want that old woman to start visiting our house again. We stopped those visits with such difficulty in the first place. We should tell Ma to eat her dinner in the evening and then go to her room. The guests will come around eight. She should finish with everything before that.'

The suggestion was reasonable. Both liked it. Then his wife said, 'But if she falls asleep and begins snoring? The veranda where everyone will eat dinner is right next door.'

'So we'll tell her to close the door from inside. I'll put a lock on

39

the outside. Or I'll tell Ma not to sleep when she goes in, what else?'

'And if she falls asleep, what then? Who knows how late the dinner will go on? You keep drinking till eleven o'clock in any case.'

A bit irritated, Shamnath said, 'It was all set, she was going to my brother's place. But because you wanted to appear good and noble, you had to interfere.'

'Wah! Why should I become the villain between mother and son? Do what you want!'

Mr Shamnath was silent. This was not the time for an argument. A solution had to be found. He turned to look at Ma's little room. Its door opened onto the veranda. Looking at the veranda, he said quickly, 'I've figured it out,' and went and stood outside his mother's room. Ma was sitting on a low stool close to the wall, head and face wrapped in a dupatta, fingers moving over her prayer beads. Seeing all the preparations since the morning, she had been anxious and tense too. The bada sahib from her son's office is coming home, everything should go off satisfactorily.

'Ma, eat your dinner early today. The guests will come by seven-thirty.'

Ma slowly removed the dupatta from her mouth and, looking at her son, said, 'I'm not going to eat today. You know, beta, whenever meat or fish is cooked in the house, I don't eat anything.'

'Whatever it is, wrap up your routine early.'

'All right, beta.'

'And, Ma, we will first be in the sitting room. During that time, you stay in the veranda. Then when we leave, you go into the sitting room through the bathroom.'

Ma looked at her son, at a loss for words. Then she said slowly, 'All right, beta.'

'And, Ma, don't fall asleep early today. The sound of your snoring can be heard from far away.'

Shamefaced, she said, 'What can I do, beta? It's not in my control. Ever since I recovered from my illness, I can't breathe through my nose.'

Mr Shamnath had figured out the solution all right, but despite that, his dilemma persisted. What if the boss suddenly decided to come to this side of the house? There would be eight to ten guests, desi officers, and their wives. Anyone could go towards the bathroom. Anger and agitation sparked off his irritation all over again. Picking up a chair, he placed it in front of her room in the veranda and said, 'Come on, Ma, just sit here for a moment.'

Adjusting her pallu, carefully holding on to her beads, Ma got up, slowly went to the chair and sat down.

'Not like this, Ma, don't put your feet up. This is not a cot.'

Ma put her legs down.

'And, for God's sake, don't wander around with bare feet, and don't wear those wooden clogs. One day I'm going to throw them away.'

Ma kept quiet.

'What will you wear, Ma?'

'Whatever I have, beta. I'll wear whatever you tell me to wear.'

Cigarette in his mouth, Mr Shamnath looked at his mother through half-closed eyes and began to consider her clothes. He wanted everything to be just so. The supervision of the entire house was in his hands. Where should the wall pegs be placed in the rooms, where should the beds be placed, what should the colour of the curtains be, which sari his wife should wear, what should the size of the table should be…. Shamnath wanted to be sure that if Ma were to appear before the boss, he, Shamnath, shouldn't be embarrassed. Looking at his mother from head to toe, he said, 'Wear a white salwar and white kameez, Ma. Go put it on now, let me see.'

Ma got up slowly and went to her room to wear the clothes.

'This problem with Ma isn't going anywhere,' he said to his wife in English. 'If it was some reasonable issue, then one could do something about it, but this…. If something were to go wrong and upset the boss, then everything will be spoilt.'

Ma came out wearing a white kameez and salwar. With her tiny, shrivelled-up body wrapped in white clothes, eyes dim and cloudy, half of her sparse hair covered by her pallu, she looked only a little less unsightly than before.

'Well, it's all right. If you have any bangles, put them on too. There's no problem.'

'Where will I bring bangles from, beta? You know very well that all my jewellery was sold to pay for your education.'

This sentence pierced Shamnath like an arrow. Flaring up, he said, 'Why are you raking up this topic, Ma? Just say you don't have jewellery, that's all. What is the connection with education–veducation? The jewellery may have been sold, but I've made something of myself. I haven't come out a useless fellow. You can take back double of what you gave.'

'May my tongue burn, beta, will I take jewellery from you? It just slipped out. If I had any bangles, I'd wear them thousands of times.'

It was already five-thirty. Mr Shamnath had yet to bathe and get ready. His wife had gone to her room long ago. Before leaving, Shamnath gave instructions to his mother once again, 'Ma, don't sit all silent and lost like you do every day. If sahib happens to come this way and asks you something, answer his question properly.'

'I'm not literate, beta, I'm not educated, what will I say to him? You tell him that my mother is illiterate, she doesn't know or understand anything. He won't ask me anything then.'

As seven o'clock approached, Ma's heart started beating fast. If the boss came to her and asked her something, what would she say in reply? She panics when she sees an Englishman even from a distance, this man is an American. Who knows what he may ask her? What will she say? Ma wanted to quietly slip away to her widowed friend's house at the back. But how could she go against her son's diktat. Silently, legs dangling, she sat on the chair.

A successful party is one where the drinks flow. Shamnath's party was kissing the pinnacle of success. Conversation flowed in an unbroken stream, with the same fluidity with which the glasses were getting replenished. There were no stoppages, no obstructions. The sahib had liked the whisky. The memsahib had liked the curtains, the design of the sofa cover and the décor of the room. What more could one ask for? The sahib had started recounting humorous stories and anecdotes during the second round of drinks itself. He was as friendly here as he was intimidating in the office. And his wife, dressed in a black gown, a string of pearls around her neck, awash with the fragrance of scent and powder, had become the object of worship for all the desi women sitting in the room. She would laugh and shake her head at every comment and she chatted away with Shamnath's wife as if they were old friends.

And with all this conviviality and drinking, it was suddenly ten-thirty. No one realized where the time had flown.

Finally, everyone drained their glasses, got up for dinner and walked out of the sitting room. Shamnath was leading the way, followed by the boss and the other guests.

As they reached the veranda, Shamnath suddenly stopped. The sight that met his eyes caused his legs to totter and, in a flash, all his alcohol-induced intoxication began to evaporate. In the veranda in front of her room, Ma was sitting as she had been, but both her feet were resting on the seat of the chair, her head was rolling from side to side, and loud snores were emanating from her mouth. As and when her head stopped rolling for a bit, the snores would become louder. And when her sleep would break for a moment, her head would once again start rolling from right to left. Her pallu had slipped from her head and her scanty hair lay disordered over her balding scalp.

As soon as he saw her, Shamnath became enraged. He felt like pushing her awake and shoving her into her room, but it was not possible to do this. The boss and the other guests were standing just there.

Seeing Ma, some of the wives of the desi officers tittered but the boss said softly, 'Poor dear.'

Ma woke up with a start. Seeing so many people standing in front of her, she got so panicky that she couldn't say a word. Quickly covering her head with her pallu, she stood up and stared at the ground. Her feet felt unsteady and the fingers of her hands trembled and shook.

'Ma, go and sleep, why are you awake so late?' Shamnath looked at the boss with mortification.

There was a smile on the boss's face. Standing there, he said, 'Namaste.'

Timidly, shrinking within herself, Ma put her hands together but one hand was inside the dupatta, holding her beads, the other outside. She couldn't do a proper namaste. Shamnath got even more annoyed at this.

By then the boss had extended his right hand. Ma became more nervous.

'Ma, shake his hand.'

But how could she shake hands? Her right hand was clasped around her beads. In her nervousness, Ma placed her left hand in sahib's right hand. Shamnath burned inside. The desi women giggled.

'Not like this, Ma! You know you have to shake hands with the right hand. Do it with your right hand.'

But by then, the chief, repeatedly pumping her left hand, said, 'How do you do?'

'Say that I'm all right, Ma, say I'm doing well.'

Ma mumbled something.

'Ma says she's fine. Say how do you do, Ma.'

Slowly, hesitantly, Ma said, 'How do do....'

Once again, there was a loud burst of laughter.

The mood lightened. Sahib had saved the moment. People had started laughing and talking. Shamnath's agitation subsided a little.

Sahib was still holding Ma's hand in his own, and she was shrinking further into herself. She could smell the alcohol on sahib's breath.

Shamnath said in English, 'My mother is from the village. She's lived all her life in the village. That's why she's so shy in front of you.'

Sahib appeared pleased at this. He said, 'Really? I like people from villages very much. Your mother must surely know some village songs and dances?' Shaking his head with delight, the boss was gazing raptly at Ma.

'Ma, sahib is saying, sing him a song. Any old song, you must know so many.'

Ma whispered, 'What can I sing, beta. When have I ever sung?'

'Wah, Ma! Can one turn down a guest's request? Sahib has asked you so eagerly; if you don't sing he'll feel bad.'

'What can I sing, beta, what do I know?'

'Wah! Why don't you sing a nice tappa? Do pattar anaaran de....'

The desi officers and their wives clapped their hands at this suggestion. Ma looked miserably first at her son's face and then at the face of her daughter-in-law, who was standing nearby.

And the son, in a voice that brooked no disobedience, said, 'Ma.'

After this, there was no question of a yes or no. Ma sat down and in a weak, trembling voice, began singing an old wedding song:

Hariya ni maaye, harya nimainde
Hariya tain bhaagi bhariya hai!

(Oh mother of Hariya, sisters of Hariya
Hariya is blessed)

The desi women started giggling. After singing three lines, Ma fell silent.

The veranda resounded with the sound of applause. The sahib wouldn't stop clapping. Shamnath's vexation morphed into pride and pleasure. Ma had introduced a new mood into the party.

When the applause stopped, the sahib said, 'What is the craftsmanship in the villages of Punjab?'

Shamnath almost swayed with pleasure. He said, 'Oh, many things, sahib! I'll gift you with a set of all the things. You'll be thrilled when you see them.'

But the sahib shook his head and again asked in English, 'No, I don't want things from shops. What is made in the homes of Punjabis, what do the women make with their own hands?'

Shamnath thought for a while and said, 'Young girls make dolls, the women make phulkaris.'

'What is phulkari?'

After an unsuccessful attempt to explain what phulkari was,

Shamnath said to his mother, 'Ma, is there any old phulkari in the house?'

Ma went inside and came out carrying her phulkari.

The sahib looked at it with great interest. It was an old phulkari. The threads had come loose in many places and the cloth had started fraying. Noticing the sahib's look of interest, Shamnath said, 'This one is torn, sahib, I'll get a new one made for you. Ma will make it. Ma, sahib really liked the phulkari, you'll make one just like this for him, won't you?'

Ma was silent. Then, she said, her voice low and fearful, 'My eyes are not what they used to be, beta! What can these old eyes see now?'

But interrupting Ma mid-way, Shamnath said to the sahib, 'She'll definitely make it. You'll really like it.'

The sahib nodded, said thank you and then, lurching ever so slightly, moved towards the dining table. The other guests followed him.

When all the guests had sat down and their gaze had been averted from Ma, she slowly got up from the chair and, hiding from everyone's eyes, went into her room.

She had barely sat down in her room when the tears started flowing from her eyes. She wiped them with her dupatta, but they kept gushing out, as if they had burst through a dam that had held them in check for years. Ma tried again and again to calm her heart, she folded her hands, called out to God, prayed for her son's long life, but the tears, like the monsoon rain, would not be contained.

It was midnight. The guests had eaten and left. Sitting close to the wall, Ma kept staring at it with wide-open eyes. The tension in the house had lifted a little by now. The stillness in the rest of the neighbourhood had settled on Shamnath's house too. The only sounds, of plates clanking against each other, came from the kitchen. That's when the door to Ma's room started rattling loudly.

'Ma, open the door.'

Ma's heart sank. She got up in a panic. Did I make some other mistake? Ma had been cursing herself—why did she fall asleep, why had she started feeling drowsy? Had her son still not forgiven her? Ma got up and opened the door with trembling hands.

As soon as the door opened Shamnath swayed forward and caught her in an embrace. 'Oh, Ammi! You really set the mood today. Sahib was so happy with you that I don't know what to say! Oh, Ammi! Oh, Ammi!'

Ma's tiny form was lost in her son's embrace. Ma's eyes filled with tears again. Wiping them, she said hesitantly, 'Beta, send me to Haridwar. I've been telling you for so long.'

Shamnath's swaying stopped at once. His brow became furrowed with tension again. His hands fell from his mother's body.

'What did you say, Ma? What is this old story you've started again?' Shamnath's anger was rising, he said, 'You want to ruin my reputation so that the whole world can say that a son can't keep his mother with him.'

'No, beta, you can stay with your wife the way you would like to. I have lived my life. Now what will I do here? I will take God's name in the remaining days of my life. Send me to Haridwar!'

'If you go, who will make the phulkari? I agreed to give sahib the phulkari in front of you.'

'My eyes are not what they used to be, beta, that I can make phulkari. You can get it made from somewhere else. Get a ready-made one.'

'Ma, will you let me down and just go away like this? You'll ruin something that's working out so well for me? Don't you know, if the sahib is happy with me, I will get a promotion.'

Ma fell silent. Then, looking at her son's face, she said, 'Will you get promoted? Will your sahib give you a promotion? Has he said anything?'

'He hasn't said anything, but didn't you see how he went away so happy. He said, when your mother starts making the phulkari, I'll come and see how she makes it. If the sahib is pleased, I can get a bigger job than this one, I can become an important officer.'

The expression on Ma's face began changing. Gradually, her

wrinkled face brightened, her eyes started shining with a gentle light.

'So you will get a promotion, beta.'

'Will I be promoted just like that? I'll have to please the sahib, only then will he do something, otherwise there's no dearth of people eager to please him.'

'Then I'll make it, beta, however I can, I'll make it.'

And in her heart, Ma once again began praying for her son's bright future. And Mr Shamnath, stumbling a little, said to his mother, 'Now go to sleep, Ma,' and left the room.

THE THIRD VOW

PHANISHWARNATH RENU

A tingle ran up the spine of Hiraman the bullock-cart driver.... For the last twenty years, Hiraman had been driving his bullock cart. He had carried rice and wood from across the border, from Morung Raj in Nepal. In the era of control, he had ferried black-market goods from one side to the other. But never had he felt this tingling in his back!

The era of control! Hiraman could never forget those days! Once, after driving the cart laden with four consignments of cement and bales of cloth from Jogbani to Biratnagar, Hiraman had become fearless. Every black-market trader in Forbesganj regarded him as a pukka bullock-cart driver. His bullocks were praised by the big merchant, the sethji himself.

It was on the fifth trip that the cart was caught on the other side of the border in the terai. The merchant's clerk, the munim, was hiding, crouching silently in the midst of the bales of cloth. Hiraman knew how bright the light that shone from the daroga sahib's torch was, a torch as long as one-and-a-half hands. Even a single flash in your eyes could blind you for an hour! And with the bright light, came the crackling voice: 'Ai! Stop the cart! Saale, I'll shoot you!'

Twenty carts stopped all together in a chaotic mess. Hiraman had said earlier, 'No good will come of this!' Shining his light on the munimji crouching in his cart, the daroga sahib had laughed fiendishly: 'Ha-ha-ha! Munimji-i-i-i! Hee-hee-hee! Ai saala driver, what are you gawking at me for! Remove the blanket from above this sack!' Poking at the munimji's stomach with his short lathi, he had said, 'This sack! S-saala!'

There must have been an old hostility between the daroga sahib and the munimji. Otherwise, even after agreeing to so much money, why didn't the daroga relent! The munim was ready to give four thousand while he was sitting in the cart itself. Then the daroga stabbed him with his lathi a second time. 'Five thousand!' Another thrust. 'First get down....'

After the munim got down, the daroga shone the light in his eyes. Then, along with two police constables, took him to a bush away from the road, a distance of about twenty yards. Five more policemen with guns guarded the bullock carts and drivers! Hiraman understood there would be no reprieve this time.... Jail? Hiraman wasn't afraid of jail. But what about his bullocks? How long would they survive without water and fodder, thirsty and hungry, at a government office gate? Then they would be auctioned. He would never be able to show his face to his brother and sister-in-law.... The sound of bidding in an auction resounded in his ears—one-two-three! It didn't look like matters would get resolved between the daroga and the munim.

A constable on guard near Hiraman's bullock cart spoke to another constable in their dialect, his voice soft, 'What's happening? Is the matter getting sorted out or not?' Then, on the pretext of giving him some chewing tobacco, he moved closer to that constable....

One-two-three! Hidden by three or four bullock carts, Hiraman made his decision. Stealthily, he untied the ropes from around the necks of his bullocks. He tied the two together while sitting in the bullock cart. The bullocks understood what they had to do. Hiraman got down, wedged a bamboo pole to hold the cart up and freed the bullocks. He tickled both of them behind their ears and said softly, 'Chalo bhaiyan, if we escape with our lives, we will get many such carts.' One-two-three! Gone!

Screened by the bullock carts was a large, deep expanse of dense bushes on the edge of the road. Exercising the utmost control, all three crossed the bushes, noiselessly, fearlessly! And then they were moving at a quick trot! Both the bullocks stuck out their chests and plunged into the dense terai forest. Sniffing out a path, they ran, crossing rivers and water channels, their tails up in the air. Behind them was Hiraman. The three ran all night....

After reaching home, Hiraman lay senseless for two days. When he came to, he held his ears and swore he would never carry black-market goods. Tauba, tauba! God knows what had happened to the munimji! And God knows what had happened to his cart, which was in such good condition! It had an axle of real iron. One of the two wheels was brand new. The tassels of coloured thread decorating the cart had been strung with great care and love.

He had taken two vows. One, he wouldn't ferry black-market goods. Second—bamboo. He asked every contractor right in the beginning: 'These items are not stolen or smuggled, are they?' And bamboo? If someone gave him even fifty rupees to carry bamboo, Hiraman's bullock cart would not be available. They could look for another cart.

A cart laden with bamboo! The bamboo sticks out four hands in front and four hands at the back! The cart is always out of your control. The out-of-control cart and Khairhiya. The incident that happened in town! The stupid servant of the contractor who was walking, holding the front end of the bamboo, had been busy looking at the girls' school. That was it, he hit a horse-drawn buggy at the turn. By the time Hiraman pulled at the bullocks' ropes, the bamboo poking out in the front had pierced the covering of the buggy. The driver of the carriage cursed, lashing out with his whip!

Not just bamboo, after that Hiraman vowed never to pick up any load from Khairhiya. And then when he began going from Forbesganj to Morung, he lost his cart! For several years after that, Hiraman had worked his bullocks in a partnership. Half the earnings would go to the owner of the cart and the other to the owner of the bullocks, himself, that is. Isss! It was like driving the cart for free! The earnings from this arrangement weren't enough to feed the bullocks properly. He had finally got his own cart made just last year.

May the goddess give her blessings to the circus company's tiger. Last year, both the horses that pulled the fair's tiger trailer had died. When the mela had to travel from Champanagar to Forbesganj, the manager of the circus company proclaimed to the cart drivers:

'A hundred rupees will be given as fare!' A couple of bullock-cart drivers agreed. But their bullocks baulked in fear when they were ten hands in front of the tiger trailer. Baaan-aaan! They broke the rope that held them and bolted. Hiraman had stroked the backs of his own bullocks and said, 'Look, bhaiyan, we're not going to get such an opportunity again. This is the chance to get our cart made. Otherwise we'll be back to sharing.... Arre, what is there to fear from a caged tiger? You've seen the tigers roaring in the terai in Morung. And I'm right here with you....'

The group of bullock-cart drivers had broken into applause. Hiraman's bullocks had salvaged their pride. Bellowing, they moved ahead and were yoked to the tiger cart one by one. Only the bullock on the right, after being yoked, urinated profusely. Hiraman hadn't removed the piece of cloth he'd tied around his nose for two days. Without covering his nose, like the big sethji did, it had been impossible to bear the stench of a tiger.

Hiraman had been the driver for a tiger cart. But he'd never felt this kind of tingling in his back. But today, every now and then, the fragrance of the champa flower filled his cart. Whenever he felt the tingling in his back, he lightly rubbed his back with the shoulder cloth.

Hiraman felt as if the Champanagar mela's patron deity, Bhagwati maiyya, had been benevolent towards him for two years now. Last year he was able to manage the tiger cart. Apart from the hundred rupees he got as the fare, there were tea and biscuits, plus he got to see the spectacle of performing bears and monkeys and clowns for free!

And now, this female passenger. Was she a woman or a champa flower! The bullock cart had been suffused with this fragrance since she got on.

The right wheel of the bullock cart chose this inopportune moment to jolt the cart as it got momentarily stuck in a small pothole on the kachcha road. There was a soft sound, 'Siss,' from the back of the cart. Hiraman lashed the bullock on the right with his

whip and said, 'Saala! Do you think you're carrying a load of sacks?'
'Don't beat them.'

Hiraman felt surprise at the unseen woman's voice. It was as
thin and delicate as a child's, like the voice that comes out of a
gramophone!

Could anyone be unfamiliar with the name of Hirabai who played
Laila in the Mathuramohan Nautanki Company! But Hiraman's case
was unusual. For seven years, he had continuously ferried the loads
of country fairs but he'd never seen a nautanki-theatre performance,
or the bioscope-cinema. He had never even heard the name of
Hirabai or Laila, forget having watched her. So fifteen days before
the fair was to break up, when he saw the woman wrapped in a
black shawl, in the middle of the night, he felt uneasy. When the
servant carrying her trunk tried to haggle over the fare, she stopped
him with a shake of her head. Fastening the cart, Hiraman said,
'Why, brother, these are not stolen goods, are they?' The man who
had carried the trunk gestured to him to get the cart going and
disappeared into the darkness. Hiraman remembered the black sari
of the old woman who sold tobacco at the mela....

How could he drive the cart in such circumstances?

For one, he was feeling that tingling in the back. Second, a
champa flower seemed to be blossoming slowly in his cart. If he
scolded the bullocks, his passenger would start with her 'Isss-biss....'
His passenger! A woman alone, and not that old tobacco seller! After
he heard her voice, he kept glancing back at the canopy of his cart,
wiping his back with a piece of cloth.... God knows what was
written in his fate this time! When the bullock cart turned to the
east, a slice of moonlight settled inside the cart. A firefly seemed to
glitter on the nose of his passenger. Everything looked strange and
mysterious and wondrous to Hiraman. In front was the huge open
ground, from Champanagar to Scindia village! What if she was a
female dacoit or demon?

Hiraman's passenger turned on her side. The moonlight fell full on
her face and Hiraman all but screamed—oh God! She was an angel!

The angel's eyes opened. Hiraman turned his face back to the
road and clicked his tongue at the bullocks. Sticking his tongue to
his palate, he made a ti-ti-ti-ti sound. Hiraman's tongue seemed to
have dried up into a piece of wood!

'Bhaiya, what is your name?'

Just like a gramophone!.... Every pore of his body sang. He
couldn't speak. Even his bullocks pricked up their ears on hearing
this voice.

'My name! My name is Hiraman!'

His passenger smiled...in that smile there was a fragrance.

'Then I will call you mita, my friend, not bhaiya. My name is
also Hira.'

'Isss!' Hiraman didn't believe her. 'There is a difference between
the names of men and women.'

'Yes, my name is also Hirabai.'

Hiraman and Hirabai, what a big difference between the two!

Hiraman scolded his bullocks: 'Will you cover a distance of thirty
kos by listening to our chatter? The one on the left is full of
wickedness.' He hit the bullock on the left lightly with his whip.

'Don't beat him; let them go slowly. What is the hurry?'

Hiraman was in a quandary—how should he address Hirabai in
order to chat with her? Should he use the more informal 'tohun'
or the more formal 'ahaan' or 'aap' with which one addressed one's
seniors in his language? One could converse a little in the more
formal city dialect, but it was only in the village dialect that one
could chat freely.

Hiraman had always disliked the mist that descended in the
mornings in September-October. He had lost his way many times
in the past. But, today, he was happy even in the dense morning
mist. The breeze carried the smell of the rice plants in the fields on
the river bank. On festive days, this was the perfume that permeated
the entire village. Once again, the champa flower bloomed in his

cart. And in that flower sat an angel.... Jai Bhagwati!

Hiraman peered out of the corners of his eyes, his passenger... mita.... Hirabai's eyes were gazing at him unblinkingly. An unknown melody sprang up in his heart. His entire body was trembling. He said, 'You feel very bad when I hit the bullock?'

Hirabai understood that Hiraman was truly a hira, a diamond.

This forty-year-old, strongly-built, dark-skinned rustic youth was not particularly interested in anything in this world except for his bullock cart and his bullocks. At home, he had an older brother who tilled the land. The brother had a wife and children. More than his brother, Hiraman respected his bhabhi. He was afraid of her. Hiraman had also been married, but even before his child bride could attain puberty and come to his home, she died. Hiraman couldn't remember his bride's face.... A second marriage? There were several reasons why he hadn't married a second time—his bhabhi's stubborn insistence that she would only agree to marry him to a young virgin who hadn't crossed puberty. That meant a five or seven-year-old girl. Who believes in or follows the Sarda Act that had fixed the age of marriage for girls? And a family would give their daughter for a second marriage only if they were in dire straits. But if his bhabhi had decided, that was it. Even his brother could not disagree with her. Hiraman had made up his mind he would not get married. Why ask for trouble? Once he got married, how would he continue being a bullock-cart driver! He could give up everything but he could never give up driving his bullock cart.

Hirabai had rarely met a man as honest as Hiraman. He asked her, 'In which district is your home?' As soon as he heard the name Kanpur, he burst out laughing, startling the bullocks. Hiraman had a habit of lowering his head while laughing. When he stopped laughing, he said, 'Wah, Kanpur! Then there should also be a Nakpur?' And when Hirabai said that indeed there was a Nakpur too, he doubled up with laughter.

'What a world this is! The kind of names! Kanpur, Nakpur!' Hiraman stared at the flower-like earrings in Hirabai's ears. He shivered a little as he saw the gem of her nosepin—a drop of blood!

Hiraman had never heard of Hirabai. He didn't consider women who worked in the nautanki as disreputable…he had seen the women who worked in these companies. The owner of the circus company was a woman, and along with her young, grown-up daughters, she would come to the tiger cart, give the tiger food and water, pet him lovingly. Her elder daughter had fed Hiraman's bullocks bread and biscuits as well.

Hiraman was smart. As soon as the mist dissipated, he put together a makeshift curtain with his blanket for the opening of the cart. 'Just two hours! After that it will be difficult to go on. You won't be able to bear this season's morning sun. We'll park the cart at Tegachiya, on the banks of the Kajri River. We'll spend the afternoon there….'

He spotted a cart coming towards him when it was still quite far away and instantly became alert. He turned his concentration to his bullocks and the path in front. As the carts passed each other, the driver asked, 'Has the fair broken up?'

Hiraman answered that he didn't know anything about the fair. His passenger was a vidagi, a girl going home, either to her maternal home or her husband's home. Hiraman gave him the name of some village!

'Where is Chhattapur-Pachira?'

'It could be anywhere, how does it matter to you?' Hiraman chortled at his own cleverness. Even after putting up that curtain, his back was still tingling.

Hiraman looked inside through a hole in the parda. Hirabai was examining her teeth in a mirror the size of a matchbox. Hiraman was reminded of a necklace of tiny cowrie shells he had once bought from the Madanpur fair for his bullocks, a row of very small, very tiny cowrie shells.

The three trees of Tegachiya could be seen from far away. Pulling aside the curtain slightly, Hiraman said, 'See, this is Tegachiya. Two of the trees are banyans with hanging roots and the third...what is that flower called, just like the flower printed on your kurta; it has a strong perfume; you can get the fragrance even at a distance of two kos; people mix the flower with khamira tobacco and smoke it too.'

'And those buildings you can see beyond the mango grove, is that a village or a temple?'

Before lighting his bidi, Hiraman asked, 'Can I smoke? You won't mind the smell?... That is Namalgar estate. It belongs to a relative of the raja whose fair we're coming from. What a time that was!'

By saying 'What a time that was', Hiraman introduced a bit of spice in the conversation. Hirabai drew the curtain and fixed it on one side...she smiled broadly.

'What time was that?' Hirabai asked eagerly, resting her chin on her hand.

'The time of the Namalgar estate! What a time that was and look what it's come to today.'

Hiraman knew how to rouse curiosity with his talk. Hirabai said, 'Have you seen those times?'

'No, but I've heard.... How the estate was lost—it's a very sad story. It is said that a god was born in that home. Now tell me, a god is a god after all, isn't that so? If he leaves heaven and is born in the mortal world, who can withstand his brilliance! His forehead glowed with a lustre, like a sunflower. But no one could see this for what it was. Once an Englishman and his wife came in a car. Even he didn't recognize him as a god, but she did. Seeing the sunflower-like lustre, she said—"Raja sahib, listen, this is not the child of a human being, this is a god".'

Mimicking her speech, Hiraman made full use of damn-fat-latt sounds. Hirabai laughed heartily at this...when she laughed, her whole body shook.

Hirabai adjusted her veil. Hiraman felt as if...felt as if....

'Then? Then what happened, mita?'

'Isss...you like hearing stories? A black man may become a raja, even a maharaja, but he will remain a black man. How will he get the intelligence of a sahib! The matter was laughed off. Then the god began appearing regularly in the rani's dreams. "If you can't serve me, then let it be, I won't stay in your home." Then the god started playing his game. First both the tusked elephants died, then the horse, then pat-pataang....'

'What is pat-pataang?'

Hiraman's feelings fluctuated every second. He felt as if a warm glow was spreading inside him...a woman from the abode of gods had stepped into his cart. A god was after all a god!

'Pat-pataang! Money, riches, goods, cattle, everything vanished! The god went back to heaven.'

Hirabai looked at the temple spires as they disappeared from view and drew a long breath.

'But as he left, the god said, in this country now, only one son will ever be born, never two. I'm taking all the wealth with me, but leaving behind goodness and wisdom. All the gods and goddesses left with him, only Saraswati maiyya stayed behind. That is her temple.'

Seeing some merchants approaching, their country horses carrying jute, Hiraman dropped the curtain again. Calling out to his bullocks, he began singing the hymn of praise, usually sung during a performance of a dance-drama.

Jai maiyya Saraswati, we entreat you;
Come to our aid, come to our aid.

Hiraman asked the merchants cheerfully, 'What price does the mahajan give for the jute?'

The merchant with the lame horse replied: 'Twenty-seven-twenty-eight is the lower price, thirty is the higher price. The price depends on the quality of the goods.'

A young merchant asked, 'What's the news on the mela? Which nautanki company is performing, Rauta or Mathuramohan?'

'Only the people at the mela know what is going on in the mela!' Once again, Hiraman invoked the name Chhattapur-Pachira.

The sun had climbed a little higher in the sky. Hiraman began talking to his bullocks—'Two more kos! Just gather a little more strength and keep going. You're thirsty now, aren't you? Do you remember that time when, near Tegachiya, a fight broke out in the circus company between the clown and the sahib who made the monkeys dance? The clown started grinding his teeth and screaming just like a monkey...God knows where these people come from.'

Once again Hiraman peeped through the hole in the curtain. Hirabai was sitting up, her eyes fixed on a piece of paper. Hiraman was feeling light-hearted today. He kept remembering all kinds of songs. Twenty-twenty-five years ago, people performed dance-dramas like the bidesiya, and the boys who danced sang such beautiful songs. Hiraman remembered a song that young boys sang during their performances:

> *My love, he has turned against me! My love...!*
> *Arre, if it was a letter, anyone could read it; if it was a letter...*
> *Hai! My fate, oh my fate...*
> *No one can read my fate, my love...oh my fate...!*

Hiraman beat a rhythm on the shaft of the bullock cart with his fingers. Manuvaan Natuva, the dancer in the boys' troupe, had a face just like Hirabai's...where had that time gone? The dance troupes would come to the village every month. Whenever Hiraman went to watch the performances, he would hear no end of it from his bhabhi. His brother would tell him to get out of the house.

Today, it seemed Saraswati maiyya was with him. 'Wah, how well you sing!' said Hirabai.

Hiraman's face turned red. He lowered his head and started laughing.

Today even Tegachiya's Mahavir Swami was with Hiraman. There was not a single bullock cart below Tegachiya. Normally there would be a big crowd of carts and drivers. There was just a lone cyclist sitting and resting. Invoking Mahavir Swami's name, Hiraman stopped the bullock cart. Hirabai started drawing the curtain aside. For the first time, Hiraman spoke to Hirabai with his eyes—the cyclist was looking in their direction.

Before unfastening the bullocks, Hiraman steadied the cart by propping it up with a bamboo pole. Then, staring at the cyclist in an intimidating manner, he asked, 'Where are you going? To the mela? Where are you coming from? From Bisanpur? Bas, you're so tired after travelling such a short distance? What kind of a young man are you!'

The cyclist, a thin, young man, mumbled something, lit a beedi and stood up.

Hiraman wanted to protect Hirabai from the eyes of the world. He looked all around him to make sure there was no bullock cart or horse in sight.

The narrow waters of the Kajri River meander close to Tegachiya before turning eastward. Hirabai kept looking at the buffaloes lolling in the water with herons perched on their backs.

'You can go and wash your face and hands in the water,' said Hiraman.

Hirabai got down from the cart. Hiraman's heart started thudding...no, no! Her feet were not turned backwards, they were not the other way round. But why were the soles so red? Hirabai walked towards the ghat, head lowered modestly, slowly, like young girls of the village would. Who would say she was a woman from the nautanki company!... No, not a woman, a girl. Maybe even a virgin.

Hiraman sat down in the cart propped up by the bamboo pole. He peered inside the canopy. After looking around, he put his hand on Hirabai's pillow. Then, resting his elbow on the pillow, he leaned down. The fragrance settled inside his body. Touching the embroidered flowers on the pillow cover, he inhaled deeply, hai re hai! So fragrant! Hiraman felt as if he had just got up after smoking five ganja-filled chillums. He saw his face reflected in Hirabai's tiny little mirror. Why were his eyes so red?

When Hirabai came back he laughed and said, 'Now you guard the cart, I'll just be back.'

Hiraman took out his carefully stored vest from the cloth bag he carried on his journeys. He shook out his gamchha, threw it on his shoulder and set off, with a bucket in his hand. His bullocks went 'hoonk-hoonk,' as if saying something to him. Hiraman continued walking but turned and said, 'Yes, yes, everyone is thirsty. I'm coming back with some grass for you, don't misbehave!'

The bullocks flapped their ears.

Hirabai didn't even realize when a freshly bathed Hiraman returned. Watching the flowing water of the Kajri River, her eyes had become drowsy with the sleep that had eluded her all night. Hiraman brought refreshments, curd, rice, and sugar, from the village nearby.

'Wake up! Eat something!'

Hirabai opened her eyes, surprised. In one hand a clay pot full of curd and a banana leaf. In the other, a bucket full of water. In his eyes, a warm entreaty!

'Where did you get all these things?'

'This village is famous for its curd...you'll get tea only in Forbesganj now.'

The tingling had left Hiraman's body.

'Spread out a leaf for yourself too.... What? If you won't eat, then put it all away in your bag. I won't eat either.'

'Isss!' Hiraman said bashfully. 'All right! But first you eat.'

'Why all this before and after? Sit down.'

Hiraman felt at ease. Hirabai spread out the leaf for him with her own hands, sprinkled water on it, and took out the rice. Isss! I'm blessed! I'm blessed! Hiraman saw, Bhagwati maiyya was accepting the offering with her red lips. He was reminded of a red-beaked mountain parrot pecking at rice and milk.

ᔑ

It was twilight.

Hirabai, sleeping under the canopy, and Hiraman, sleeping on the ground on a dhurrie, woke up at the same time. Carts going to the fair had stopped near Tegachiya. Children were making a commotion.

Hiraman got up with a start. Peeping inside the canopy, he gestured to her—the day was getting over. While hitching the bullocks to the cart, he didn't reply to any of the questions from the other drivers. Calling out to his bullocks, he got the cart moving and said, 'She's a lady doctor from the hospital in Sirpur Bazaar. She's going to see a patient. Nearby, in Kudmagam.'

Hirabai had forgotten the name Chhattapur-Pachira. When the cart had gone some distance, she laughed and asked, 'Pattapur-Chhapira?'

Hiraman laughed until he got stitches in his sides. 'Pattapur-Chhapira! Ha ha! They were drivers from Chhattapur-Pachira, how could I have used that name! Hee-hee!'

Smiling, Hirabai began looking towards the village.

The road went through Tegachiya village. The village children saw the cart with the curtain and, clapping their hands, started chanting lines they had learnt by heart:

In a red doli
A red bride
Eating a paan!

Hiraman laughed...bride...a red doli! The bride eats a paan, then wipes her mouth with the bridegroom's turban. Remember the children of Tegachiya village, oh bride. When you return, bring some jaggery laddoos. May your bridegroom live a hundred thousand years! A long-standing dream of Hiraman's had come true! How many such dreams he had dreamed! He is returning with his bride. Children in every village clap their hands and sing. Women peep out from courtyards to look at them. The men ask, 'From where is this cart coming, where is it going?' His bride draws the curtain a little and looks out. There were so many other dreams too....

After leaving the village, he looked inside the canopy from the corners of his eyes; Hirabai was deep in thought. Hiraman also became lost in his thoughts. After a while he began humming:

Don't lie my dearest, we all have to go up to God.
There's no elephant, there are no horses, no cart—
We have to go on foot. My dearest....

Hirabai asked, 'Why, mita, don't you have a song in your own language?'

Now Hiraman could look Hirabai in the eyes without any shyness or hesitation. Could a woman from a dancing company be like this? The owner of the circus company was a memsahib. But Hirabai? She wanted to listen to village songs in the local language. He smiled. 'Will you understand the language of the village?'

'Yes!' Hirabai nodded. Her earrings swung to and fro.

For a while Hiraman quietly urged his bullocks to keep moving. Then he said, 'You're determined to hear a song? You won't take no for an answer? Isss! You are that keen to hear a song from the village? Then we'll have to leave this path. How can anyone sing on a busy road like this?' Hiraman pulled the rope attached to the left bullock and steering the right one off the road, said, 'Then we won't go through Haripur.'

Seeing him get off the road, the cart driver behind Hiraman shouted, 'What are you doing? Where are you going, turning away from the road?'

Swinging his whip in the air, Hiraman replied, 'What do you mean, turning away from the road? That road won't go to Nananpur.' Then he muttered to himself, 'This is a bad habit among people in this country. They'll cross-question someone going his own way a hundred times. Arre bhai, if you are going somewhere, go…. Rustic fools, all of them!'

After turning the cart onto the road to Nananpur, Hiraman loosened the reins. The bullocks slowed their pace, from a quick trot, they began ambling along.

Hirabai saw that, in truth, the road to Nananpur was very desolate. Hiraman understood the doubt in her eyes. 'There's nothing to worry about. This road will go to Forbesganj, and the people on the way are nice…. We should reach by nightfall.'

Hirabai was in no hurry to reach Forbesganj. She had developed such faith in Hiraman that there was no question of any doubt or fear in her mind. Hiraman smiled contentedly. What song should he sing! Hirabai liked both songs and stories...isss! Mahua the ghatwarin—the rivergirl? 'All right, since you are so interested, listen to this song about Mahua the ghatwarin. It is both a song and a story.'

Goddess Bhagwati had boosted his morale, after such a long time. Jai Bhagwati! He decided to empty his heart out.

'Listen! Even today, there are several ancient ghats along the Parmar River associated with Mahua ghatwarin. She was from these parts! She was just a ghatwarin, but she was so noble, one in a hundred. Her father would be insensible all day, drunk on liquor and toddy. Her stepmother was a veritable witch! She was in cahoots with all sorts of people, including those who stole and sold ganja, liquor, and opium in the stealth of the night. Mahua was a young girl. But that witch made her work so hard that her bones started showing. Even when she became of marriageable age, she made no attempt to find her a husband. Listen to what happened one night!'

Hiraman started humming softly, then cleared his throat—

Hey—a-a-a in this young age
In the rainy season, like the swelling river

My story is as turbulent,
Ae maiyya, the night is terrifying
My heart is beating hard, like the crackle of lightning....

Oh ma! A river swelling in the rainy season, a fearful night, the crack of lightning, I'm just a little girl, my heart is pounding. How can I go alone to the riverbank? That too, to oil the feet of some stranger, a traveller from afar. My stepmother has shut the door in my face. The clouds rumble in the sky and the rain comes pouring down. Mahua starts crying, thinking of her mother. If her mother were alive, she would hold her close to her heart on such terrible days. Ae maiyya, did you keep me in your womb only to show me this day? Mahua becomes angry with her mother—why did you die alone, she says, reproaching her to her heart's content.

Hiraman saw that Hirabai, her elbow resting on the pillow, was lost in the song, gazing at him…how innocent she looked, her face so rapt.

Hiraman introduced a quiver in his voice:

Hoon-oon-oon-re, now my mother the witch
Why wasn't I given salt to taste in the house of my birth and then
killed off
Was it for this day that you brought me up, for this day that you
gave me your milk, utgan

Hiraman paused for breath and asked, 'Can you understand the language or are you just listening to the song?'

Hira answered, 'I understand. Utgan means ubtan—what you rub on the body.'

Hiraman said in wonder, 'Isss! So what was to be gained by crying and weeping! The merchant had paid the full price for Mahua. He dragged her by the hair, pulled her on to the boat and told the boatman to untie the boat and hoist the sail! The boat, its sails open, flew on the water like a bird. All night Mahua wept, tormented, struggling. The merchant's servants threatened her and frightened her: "Keep quiet, otherwise we will throw you into the water." That was it, Mahua knew what she had to do. The morning star came out from behind the clouds, then hid again. And that's when Mahua jumped into the water with a splash…. One of the merchant's servants had become enamoured of Mahua as soon as he set eyes on her. He jumped in after her. It was no joke to swim against the current, that too in an August river in spate. But Mahua was the daughter of a true ghatwarin. Does a fish ever get tired in the water? Fluttering like a migrating fish, slicing through the water, she made her escape at full speed. And behind her, the merchant's servant kept crying out to her, "Mahua, wait, I'm not coming to catch you, I'm your friend. We will stay together all our lives." But….'

This song was very dear to Hiraman. When he sang of Mahua ghatwarin, he could see the swollen, roiling August river, the moonless night, the crack of lightning between the dense clouds. In the glow of the lightning, he could see glimpses of the young Mahua battling the waves. The fish swam faster and faster. He felt as if he himself was the merchant's servant. Mahua didn't listen to anyone. She didn't even turn around to look. And he was tired, swimming for so long....

This time it seemed that Mahua had got caught. As if she had allowed herself to be caught. He had touched Mahua, caught her and his tiredness had vanished. Swimming against the current in a river surging and swelling for fifteen-twenty years, he had found his shore. The tears of joy couldn't be held back....

He tried to hide his wet eyes from Hirabai. But Hirabai, who had stolen into his heart, had seen everything it seems. Controlling the quiver in his voice, Hiraman scolded his bullocks, 'God knows what there is in this song that makes them drag their feet. It's as if someone has dumped hundreds of kilos on them.'

Hirabai drew a long breath. A joyful thrill settled on every part of Hiraman's being.

'You are an ustaad, mita!'

'Isss!'

The winter sun started wilting early in the day. Hiraman tried to explain to his bullocks that they must reach Nananpur before sunset. 'Firm up your hearts and step up your pace...ae...chhi chhi! Move, bhaiyan! Le-le-le-ae hey!'

He kept calling out to his bullocks till they reached Nananpur. Before every cry, he reminded them of past events—don't you remember how many carts there were when the chowdhary's daughter got married; how we were better than all of them! Yes, that's the pace we want now. Le-le-le! It's only six miles from Nananpur to Forbesganj! Just two hours more!

Tea was being sold at the Nananpur bazaar these days. Hiraman brought his pot filled with tea...he knew that women from the nautanki company keep drinking tea all day, every hour. It's as if tea was their life!

Hira laughed uproariously at this. 'Arre, who told you that an unmarried man mustn't drink tea?'

Hiraman was overcome with shyness. What could he say…it was a matter of modesty. He had had tea before, from the hands of a mem from the circus company and seen its effect. What heat there was in tea!

'Drink it, guruji,' Hira laughed.

'Isss!'

The lamps had been lit at the Nananpur Bazaar. Hiraman lit the lantern he carried on his journeys and hung it at the back of the cart…. These days even villagers who live ten miles away from the city consider themselves to be city dwellers. They fine carts that don't have lights. What a bother!

'Don't call me guruji.'

'You are my ustaad. The scriptures say that the one who teaches even a letter of the alphabet is a guru and the one who teaches a raga is also an ustaad.'

'Isss! You know the scriptures as well? What did I teach you? Am I…?'

Hira laughed and began humming, '*Hey-a-a-a. In the rainy season…!*'

Hira was surprised into speechlessness…isss! Such a sharp mind! Just like Mahua ghatwarin!

The cart creaked and lurched down the slope of a dry streambed. Hirabai placed a hand on Hiraman's shoulder. Her fingers stayed there for a long time. Hiraman tried to shift his gaze to his shoulder a few times. When the cart reached the incline, Hira's fingers, relaxed until then, tightened again.

The lights of Forbesganj glimmered in front of them. The glow of the fair, a short distance from the city…. The lantern in the cart threw dancing shadows all around…. To eyes misty with tears, every source of light looked like a sunflower.

Forbesganj was like home for Hiraman!

God knows how many times he had come to Forbesganj, carrying loads for the fair. With a woman? Yes, once. The year his brother's wife had come as a bride from her maternal home to her husband's home. That time too, he had covered the cart from all sides with canvas, creating a room....

Hiraman began covering his cart with canvas when they reached the parking site. In the morning, Hirabai would speak to the manager of the Rauta nautanki and join the company. The fair was starting the day after tomorrow. The fair grounds were full. Just one night. She would stay in Hiraman's cart this entire night...no, not in Hiraman's cart, in a house!

'Where is this cart from...oh, Hiraman, it's you! How come you're here at the fair? What are you carrying?'

Cart drivers from different villages and communities sought each other out, parked their carts and set up camp. Hiraman was a little flustered seeing Lalmohur, Dhunniram, Palatdas, and other drivers from his village. Palatdas peered under the canopy of his cart and was startled. As if he had just spotted a tiger. Hiraman gestured to all of them to keep quiet. Then looking at the cart from the corner of his eyes, he whispered, 'Quiet! She is a company woman, she is from the nautanki dance company.'

'From the company-ee-ee-ee?'

Not one, now there were four Hiramans! They looked at each other in utter amazement...What weight there was in the very mention of the word company! Hiraman noticed that all three had fallen into a stunned silence. Lalmohur moved away a little, signalling that he wanted to talk to Hiraman. Hiraman turned towards the canopy and said, 'No hotel or restaurant will be open at this time, I'll go to the halwai and get some pukka food!'

'Hiraman, listen.... I won't eat anything now. Here, you have something to eat.'

'What is this, money? Isss!' Hiraman had never eaten any kind of food, kachha or pakka, in Forbesganj, by paying money. After all, what were the cart drivers from his village for? He couldn't take the money. He said to Hirabai, 'Now don't argue needlessly. Keep the money.' Seizing the opportunity, Lalmohur too moved closer to the canopy. Making his salutations he said, 'Two extra people can easily eat the rice that's being cooked for four. It's being cooked in the camp. Heh-heh-heh! We are all from the same village. With all of us here, why should Hiraman eat from the hotel or halwai?'

Hiraman pressed Lalmohur's hand and said, 'Don't talk nonsense.'

Moving some distance away from the cart, Dhunniram gave vent to his suppressed emotions—'Isss! You are too much Hiraman! That year, a tiger from the company, this year a woman from the company!'

Hiraman said sotto voce, 'Bhai re, she is not a woman from our parts who will keep quiet despite hearing loose talk. For one, she is from the west and on top of that, she is from the company!'

Dhunniram expressed his doubts—'But we have heard that company women are prostitutes.'

'Dhat!' Everyone dismissed his words scornfully, 'What kind of a man are you! Will a prostitute stay in the company! What a stupid thing to say! You've just heard, you've never seen, have you? How do you know?'

Dhunniram admitted his mistake. Palatdas thought of something— 'Hiraman bhai, she's a woman, how will she stay alone all night in the cart? Say what you want, a woman is after all a woman. She might need something.'

Everyone thought this made sense. Hiraman said, 'That's true. Palat, you stay close to the cart. And, remember, be careful when you talk to her, all right?'

...Hiraman's body exuded the fragrance of roses. That time, the tiger's smell hadn't left his body for months. Lalmohur sniffed at his cloth—'Ehh!'

Hiraman stopped in his tracks—'What should I do, Lalmohur bhai, tell me! She's insisting that we see the nautanki.'

'For free?'

'Won't word of this reach the village?'

Hiraman said, 'See the nautanki one night and then bear with a lifetime of criticism? It's like a village hen trying to strut about in a city style!'

Dhunniram said, 'Will your sister-in-law get annoyed even if you watch for free?'

Next to Lalmohur's camp was the camp of cart drivers who ferried wood. Their chief cart driver, old Miyaanjaan, puffed on his hookah and asked, 'Why, brother, who is carrying something from the women's bazaar?

The women's bazaar! That's what they call the area where prostitutes live.... What is this old man saying? Lalmohur whispered in Hiraman's ears, 'Your body smells of perfume. Really.'

Lahsanva was Lalmohur's cart attendant. He was the youngest of them. He had come here for the first time but so what? He had been working for the gentry since childhood. Every now and then, he scrunched up his nose, as if he could smell something in the air. Hiraman noticed that Lahsanva's face was flushed... Who was coming, making such a racket?—'Is that you, Palatdas? What is it?'

Palatdas came and stood silently. His face had also turned red. Hiraman asked, 'What happened? Why don't you say something?'

What could Palatdas say? Hiraman had warned him to be careful while talking. He had gone and quietly sat in Hiraman's place in the cart. Hirabai asked, 'Are you also with Hiraman?' Palatdas nodded his head to indicate a yes. Hirabai lay down again.... Looking at her face and listening to her voice, Palatdas's heart started beating fast; God knows why. Yes! The young Sita, tired, had lain down just like this in the Ramleela. Jai! Siyavar Ramchandra ki jai! A kind of devotional chant swelled inside Palatdas's heart. He was a servant of Vishnu, a singer of devotional songs. He expressed a desire to press the tired Sita maharani's feet by signalling with his fingers; as if they were dancing on a harmonium's keys. Hirabai sat up angrily, 'Arre, are you mad? Go away, go...!'

Palatdas felt as if sparks were coming out of the angry company woman's eyes—chatak-chatak! He fled....

What answer could Palatdas give! He was thinking of how he could run away from the fair. He said, 'Nothing. I've met a merchant. I have to go to the station right away and load the goods. The rice will take time to cook. I'll come back by then.'

While eating, Dhunniram and Lahsanva grumbled about Palatdas to their heart's content. He was a petty man. A low, base person. He kept track of every penny, he was obsessed with money. After eating, Lalmohur's group broke camp. Dhunni and Lahsanva yoked their carts and began walking over to Hiraman's camping site. Hiraman stopped in his tracks and said to Lalmohur, 'Just smell this shoulder of mine. Smell it and see....'

Lalmohur sniffed the shoulder and closed his eyes. An indistinct sound came from his lips—'Eh!'

Hiraman said, 'So much fragrance just from the touch of her hand! Understood?'

Lalmohur caught Hiraman's hand—'Did she place her hand on your shoulder? Really? Listen, Hiraman, there will never be another opportunity like this to see the nautanki. Yes!'

'You'll come to see it?'

All of Lalmohur's thirty-two teeth shone in the light of the crossing.

When he reached the camp, Hiraman saw that someone was standing next to his cart and chattering away to Hirabai. Dhunni and Lahsanva spoke in unison, 'Where were you? The company has been looking for you!'

Hiraman went over to the canopy and saw—arre, this was the same servant who had carried the box, made Hirabai sit in the cart in Champanagar before melting away in the darkness.

'You've come, Hiraman! Good, come here.... Here's your fare and here's your tip! Twenty-five-twenty-five, fifty.'

Hiraman felt as if someone had flung him from the sky to the earth. Why someone, it was this man, the man who had carried the box. Where had he come from? The words that sprang to the tip of his tongue remained at the tip of his tongue...isss! A tip! He stood silently.

Hirabai said, 'Here, take it. And, listen, come to the Rauta company tomorrow morning and meet me. I'll get a pass made for you.... Why don't you say something?'

Lalmohur said, 'The lady is giving you a tip as a reward, take it

Hiraman!' Cut to the quick, Hiraman looked at Lalmohur.... This Lalmohur had no idea how to talk properly.

Everyone heard Dhunniram muttering to himself, even Hirabai— How can a driver leave his cart and bullocks to go and see a nautanki in the fair?

Taking the money, Hiraman said, 'What can I say?' He tried to laugh...the woman from the company is going to the company. What of Hiraman! The man who had carried the box moved ahead, showing the way and said, 'This way.' Walking behind him, Hirabai paused. Addressing the bullocks, she said, 'All right, I'm going, bhaiyyan!'

The bullocks twitched their ears at the word 'bhaiya.'

ঽ

'Brothers, tonight! On the stage of the Rauta Music (Sangeet) Nautanki company! See Gulbadan, come and see Gulbadan! You will be delighted to hear that the famous actress from Mathuramohan company, Miss Hiradevi, who sets thousands of hearts aflutter with her every move, has come to our company. Remember. Tonight. Miss Hiradevi Gulbadan...!'

This announcement created a great deal of enthusiasm and excitement in every part of the fair ground...Hirabai? Laila, Gulbadan...? She can cast any film actress in the shade.

I am crazy about your flirtations style,
How can I express my desire for you, beloved
My only desire is that you glance my way
And I look back at you with my body and soul.

...Kirrrrr....karrrrrr...ghan-ghan-dhadaam!

Every man's heart had turned into a big drum!

Lalmohur came panting and running to the camp—'Ai, ai Hiraman, what are you doing sitting here, come and see all the cheering. They're cheering Hirabai with bands and music and printed pamphlets.'

Hiraman got up in some agitation. Lahsanva said, 'Dhunni kaka, stay at the camp, I also want to go and see.'

Who was going to wait for Dhunni's reply! All three began following the nautanki company group, which stopped at every corner, turned off the music and made the announcements. Hiraman listened ecstatically to every word. Hearing Hirabai's name being called out, and along with the name, all the words extolling her beauty and how everyone was crazy about her, Hiraman patted Lalmohur's back and said—'What a blessing! What a blessing! Isn't it?'

Lalmohur said, 'Now tell me! Will you still not see the nautanki?' Dhunniram and Lalmohur had been trying to persuade him since the morning—'Go and meet her. She invited you to come as she left.' But Hiraman kept saying the same thing—'Dhat, why should I go to meet her? She's a company woman who has gone back to the company. What does one have to do with her now! She won't even recognize me.'

But deep inside, Hiraman had been sulking. After listening to the announcement, he said to Lalmohur, 'We should really go and see the nautanki, isn't it, Lalmohur? What do you say?'

They conferred with each other and set off for the company. When they reached the tent, Hiraman gestured to Lalmohur, indicating that the burden of starting the conversation was his. Lalmohur knew how to speak the formal city language. Lalmohur said to a man in a black coat, 'Babu sahib, just a moment.'

The man in the black coat said haughtily, 'What is it? Why are you here?'

At this show of hauteur, Lalmohur's polite city language began slipping, 'Gulgul...no-no...bul-bul...no....'

Quickly Hiraman salvaged the situation, 'Can you tell us where Hiradevi is staying?'

The man's eyes turned red in an instant. He called out to the Nepali guard standing in front, 'How did you allow these people to come inside?'

'Hiraman!'

Where did that familiar gramophone voice come from? Pulling back the curtain of the tent, Hirabai called out, 'Come here, inside!

Now look here, Bahadur. Get to know this man. He is my Hiraman. Understood?'

The Nepali watchman looked at Hiraman, smiled and went away. He went to the man in the black coat and said, 'He is Hirabai's man. She has said not to stop him.'

Lalmohur brought a paan for the Nepali guard. 'Take this!'

'Isss! Not one but five passes! And all eight-anna ones! She said that as long as you are at the fair, come and watch the performance every night. She is so considerate; she thinks of everyone. She said take passes for yourself and all your friends. Company women have a special way about them! Isn't it?'

Lalmohur touched the pieces of red paper and said, 'Pass! Wah re Hiraman bhai!... But what will we do with five passes? Palatdas hasn't come back as yet.'

'Let that unlucky fellow be. It's not written in his fate...but yes, first everyone will have to swear on god that no one in our village, not even a bird, should come to know about this.'

Getting excited, Lalmohur said, 'Who the hell will say anything in the village? If Palta creates trouble, I won't bring him with me next time.'

Hiraman had left his pouch of money with Hirabai. Who knew about the fair! Every year there were all kinds of pickpockets. You couldn't even depend on your companions! Hirabai had agreed. She had taken the little black cloth bag and put it away in her leather case. There was a cloth covering the case and a shiny silk lining inside. Now his mind was at rest.

Together Lalmohur and Dhunniram praised Hiraman's intelligence; complimented him on his destiny. They ran down his brother and sister-in-law under their breath. They were lucky they had a jewel of a brother like Hiraman! If they had had someone else for a brother....

Lahsanva was going around with a long face. God knows where he'd disappeared to after listening to the announcements, he had come back only now after dark. Lalmohur rebuked him as if scolding a servant, cursing him roundly in the bargain, 'You're a good for nothing!'

Putting the khichdi on the stove, Dhunniram said, 'First let's decide who will stay with the carts.'

'What do you mean who will stay? Where is Lahsanva going?'

Lahsanva burst into tears, 'Ae-ae malik, I beg of you. One glimpse! That's all, just one glimpse.'

Magnanimously, Hiraman said, 'All right all right, why just one glimpse, watch for an hour. I'll come away.'

The drums began two hours before the nautanki was to start. And the moment the drumming began, people descended like so many moths. Seeing the crowd in front of the ticket window, Hiraman was very amused, 'Lalmohur, look at the people pushing and jostling!'

'Hiraman bhai!'

'Who, Palatdas? Where did you carry your load to?' asked Lalmohur, as if he was talking to a stranger.

Wringing his hands Palatdas asked for forgiveness, 'Yes, I am guilty; I'll accept whatever punishment all of you want to give me. But the truth is that delicate Siya Sukumari....'

Hiraman's heart swelled with the beat of the drums. He said, 'Look, Palat, don't think she's like one of our village women. See, she's given a pass for you too; take your pass, watch the show.'

Lalmohur said, 'But you'll get the pass on one condition. Every now and then Lahsanva also....'

There was no need to tell Palatdas anything. He had already had a word with Lahsanva.

Lalmohur placed the second condition before him: 'And if anyone in the village somehow comes to know of this....'

'Ram-Ram!' said Palatdas, biting his tongue with his teeth.

'The gate for the eight anna seats is there,' Palatdas informed them. The guard at the gate took the passes and examined each of their faces carefully, one by one. He said, 'These are passes. Where did you get them from?'

Now if someone could listen to Lalmohur's city language! Seeing his high-and-mighty attitude, the guard got nervous. 'Where did we get them from? Go and ask your company. And not just four passes, there is a fifth one too.' Lalmohur took out the fifth pass from his pocket and showed it to him.

The Nepali guard was standing at the gate for the one-rupee seats. Hiraman called out to him, 'Hey policeman! Brother! You were introduced to me this morning, and now you've forgotten us?'

The Nepali guard said, 'These are all Hirabai's people. Let them go. Why are you stopping them when they have passes?'

The eight-anna section!

This was the first time the three of them had seen this 'cloth house' from the inside. In front was the section with chairs and benches. The curtain had a picture of Ram going to the forest. Palatdas recognized the scene. Folding his hands he paid his respects to the pictures of Ram, Sita, and Lakhan drawn on the curtain. 'Jai ho, jai ho!' Palatdas's eyes filled with tears.

Hiraman asked, 'Lalmohur, are these pictures standing still or moving?'

Lalmohur had already become acquainted with the members of the audience sitting next to him. He said, 'The performance will be behind the curtain. This is just the introduction to allow people to gather.'

Palatdas knew how to play the drum, that's why he was shaking his head to its beat and keeping time with a matchstick. By exchanging bidis, Hiraman had also got to know one or two people sitting near him. Covering his body with a blanket, one of Lalmohur's acquaintances said, 'There's time before the dance begins, I'm going to take a nap till then...the eight anna section is the best of all sections. It's high up and right at the back. Nice warm straw on the floor! Hey-hey, all those sitting on chairs and benches in this cold weather will have to keep getting up to drink tea.'

He told his companion, 'Wake me up when the show begins. No-no, wake me up not when the show starts, but when Hiriya arrives on stage.'

A little spark blazed in Hiraman's chest.... What a rogue! He signalled to Lalmohur with his eyes, 'There's no need to talk to this man.'

...Dhan-dhan-dhan-dhadaam! The curtain rose. Hey-hey, Hirabai arrived on the stage right away! The 'cloth house' was packed to the rafters. Hiraman's mouth fell open in wonder, God knows why Lalmohur was laughing so much, what was so funny? He laughed, without any reason, every time Hirabai sang a new stanza.

Gulbadan was holding court. She was proclaiming: whoever will make a grand throne will get any reward he asks for! Is there any such artiste, if so he should present himself, and make the throne!

Kirrkirr-kirri! She could certainly dance! And what a voice!

Do you know, said someone, Hirabai doesn't take paan-bidi, cigarettes or tobacco, nothing!

He's right. She's a very principled whore!

Who said she was a whore! There's no stain on her teeth.

She must be washing her teeth with powder.

Never...who is this man, talking nonsense! Calling a company woman a prostitute!

Why are you getting so upset? Who are you, the whore's pimp?

Beat the bastard! Beat him!

In the middle of all the commotion, Hiraman's voice tore through the cloth house, 'I'll break everyone's neck, one by one.'

Lalmohur was busy whacking the people in front of him with his whip. Palatdas was sitting astride someone's chest.

'Bastard, you're abusing Siya Sukumari, and that too being a Muslim?'

Dhunniram, who'd been quiet from the beginning, slipped out the moment the fighting started.

The man in the black coat, the nautanki manager, came running to the scene with the Nepali guard. The police inspector began lashing out with his whip, hitting everyone. Slashed by the whip, Lalmohur flared up; he started giving a lecture in his formal city language,

'Daroga sahib, you want to hit us, go ahead, hit us. Doesn't matter. But do look at this pass, there's another pass in my pocket too. You can have a look, huzoor. Not tickets, but passes! Now if someone abuses a company woman in front of us how can we spare such people?'

The company manager understood what had happened. He tried to pacify the police inspector, 'Huzoor, I know what happened. All this mischief is by the Mathuramohan company people. They want to create a scene during the show and ruin the company's reputation. No, huzoor, let these men go, they are Hirabai's people. The poor thing's life is in danger. Remember what I told you!'

The moment he heard Hirabai's name, the police inspector let the three go. But their whips were taken away from them. The manager sat them in the one-rupee section. 'Sit here. I'm sending paan for you right away.' The audience calmed down and Hirabai returned to the stage.

The drumming started again.

After a while, all three of them suddenly remembered Dhunniram—arre, where did he go?

'Malik, o malik!' Lahsanva was shouting from outside, 'O Lalmohur malik!'

Lalmohur yelled back in a high-pitched voice, 'Come in from here, from here! The one-rupee gate.' All the spectators turned to look at Lalmohur. The Nepali guard brought Lahsanva to Lalmohur. Lalmohur took the pass out of his pocket and showed it to him. As soon as he arrived, Lahsanva said, 'Malik, who said what? Just tell me. Show me his face, I need but one glimpse!'

Everyone saw Lahsanva's broad, flat chest. Even in this cold weather, he was bare-bodied! These people had come with their henchmen! Lalmohur calmed Lahsanva down.

No one ask them what they saw in the nautanki. How could they remember the story! Hiraman felt that from the very beginning, Hirabai had eyes only for him as she sang and danced. Lalmohur felt Hirabai was only looking at him. She understood that Lalmohur was more powerful than Hiraman! Palatdas understood the story...

what else could it be but the Ramayana. The same Rama, the same Sita, the same Lakhanlalla and the same Ravana! Ravana disguises himself in myriad ways when he tries to snatch Sita away from Rama. Rama and Sita also change their appearance. Rama is the son of the gardener who will make the grand throne. Gulbadan is Siya Sukumari. The gardener's son's friend is Lakhanlalla and Sultan is Ravana. Dhunniram had developed high fever! Lahsanva liked the clown's part the best, especially when he sang, 'Little bird, I will take you to the Narhat Bazaar!' He wanted to make friends with the clown…. 'Won't you be my friend, clown sahib?'

Hiraman remembered part of a song, 'I am slain, Gulfam!' Who was this Gulfam? Hirabai wept as she sang, 'Oh, yes, I am slain, Gulfam!' Tidididi…poor Gulfam!

Handing their whips back to the three of them, the policeman said, 'Who goes to see a dance performance carrying whips and sticks?'

The next day the news spread all over the fair—Hirabai had run away from the Mathuramohan company, that's why the Mathuramohan company hadn't come this time…though its goondas had…but Hirabai was no less. She was quite a player herself. She'd got thirteen village musclemen of her own, all armed with lathis… who dared say, 'Wah, my sweetheart'. No one had the nerve!

⌣

Ten days, ten nights!

All day Hiraman would ferry loads for a fee. As evening came, the drums would start. With the sound of the drums Hirabai's call would resound in his ears: Bhaiya…mita…Hiraman…ustaad…guruji! All day, some musical instrument would play in a corner of his heart. Sometimes the harmonium, sometimes the dholak or the nagada, sometimes Hirabai's anklets. Hiraman would sit, stand, walk around, all to the rhythm of the music. Everyone recognized him, from the company manager to the man responsible for drawing the curtain… he was Hirabai's man.

Every night before the nautanki began, Palatdas would fold his hands and do a namaste with great devotion. One day Lalmohur had gone to make Hirabai listen to his formal city-style of talking. Hirabai didn't even recognize him. He was hurt. His servant Lahsanva had given him the slip and joined the nautanki company. He had become friends with the clown. He filled water and washed clothes all day. What was there in the village for him to go back to! Lalmohur was sad. Dhunniram fell ill and went home.

That morning Hiraman had carried three loads to the station. For some reason he found himself remembering his sister-in-law. He hoped Dhunniram had not said anything in his feverish state! Even before he left, he was talking such nonsense—Bulbadan, takhthajaara! Lahsanva was having a whale of a time. He must be looking at Hirabai all day long. He said, 'Thanks to you, Hiraman malik, I am so happy. After I wash Hirabai's sari, the water in the wooden tub fills with the perfume of roses. I leave my shoulder cloth to soak in that water. Here, do you want to sniff it?'

Every night he heard this from someone or the other—Hirabai was a whore. How many people could he fight! How could people talk so loosely without knowing anything? But people curse even a king behind his back. Today he would meet Hirabai and tell her, because you work in a nautanki company, people tarnish your reputation. Why don't you work in the circus company? When she danced in front of everyone, Hiraman's pounding heart burned with jealousy. A circus company has a tiger...who would dare go near her! She would be safe and secure there! Where is this cart coming from?

'Hiraman, ae Hiraman!' Hearing Lalmohur's voice, Hiraman turned around...what load was Lalmohur carrying?

'Hirabai is looking for you at the station. She is leaving.' He said all this in one breath. She had gone in Lalmohur's cart to the station.

'She is going? Where? Hirabai is going by train?'

Hiraman unhitched his cart. He said to the watchman at the goods godown, 'Bhaiya, take care of my cart and bullocks. I'll be back right away.'

'Ustaad!' Hirabai, hands and face covered with an odhni, was standing at the door of the women's waiting room. Holding out the money bag, she said, 'Here! Oh God! You're finally here, I'd given up hope of seeing you. I won't be able to meet you again.... I am going, guruji!'

The man who had carried her box was wearing coat and trousers today and looking like a proper sahib. He was giving orders to the coolies as if he was a master ordering his servants, 'Load this in the women's compartment. Understood?'

Hiraman stood silently holding the bag in his hands. Hirabai had taken the bag out of the folds of her kurta...it was warm, like the body of a little bird.

'The train is coming.' The box-carrying man said, making a face and looking at Hirabai. The expression on his face was clear: why so much...?

Hirabai became playful. She said, 'Hiraman, come here, inside. I am going back to the Mathuramohan company. It is the company of my home...You'll come to the Banaili fair, won't you?'

Hirabai placed her hand on Hiraman's shoulder...this time the right shoulder. Then, taking some money from her own bag, she said, 'Buy a warm shawl for yourself....'

Finally, after a long time, Hiraman found his voice, 'Isss! All the time, money! You keep this money...what will I do with a shawl?'

Hirabai's hand paused in mid-air. She looked carefully at Hiraman's face. Then she said, 'You're feeling very sad. Why, mita? Mahua the ghatwarin has been bought by the merchant, guruji!'

Hirabai's throat choked with tears. The man who had lifted the box called out from outside, 'The train has arrived.' Hiraman came out of the room. The man glowered and said, 'Get off the platform. If you're caught without a ticket, you'll have to spend three months in jail....'

Quietly, Hiraman went out through the gate.... It was the rule of the railways! Otherwise Hiraman would have set this box-carrying man's face right....

Hirabai got into the train compartment right in front of him.

Isss! Even after sitting in the train, she continued gazing at Hiraman, without blinking. His heart burnt as he looked at Lalmohur, always following him, always trying to get his share.

The train gave a whistle. Hiraman felt as if a voice had erupted from within him and along with the whistle, risen in the air— koooooisss! Chhhii-chhakk! The train moved. Hiraman crushed the toe of his right foot with the heel of his left foot. His heartbeat stabilized. Hirabai was wiping her face with a purple handkerchief. She waved the handkerchief and signalled to him...now go.... The last compartment passed by; the platform was empty...everything was empty...hollow...only some goods train bogeys! It was as if the world had emptied out! Hiraman went back to his cart.

Hiraman asked Lalmohur, 'When are you returning to the village?'

Lalmohur said, "Why will I go back to the village now? This is the time to earn some money! Hirabai has left, now the fair will break up.'

'All right. Do you want any message to be delivered home?'

Lalmohur tried to convince Hiraman. But Hiraman turned his cart onto the road towards his village. Now what was left in the fair! A hollow fair!

Right next to the railway line, the rough path for bullock carts stretched far into the horizon. Hiraman had never been on a train. An old yearning arose in his heart, the yearning to travel in a train, go to Jagannath temple, singing all the way. He didn't have the courage to turn back and look at the empty canopy of his cart. Even now, he felt a tingling in his back. Even today, a champa flower blossomed every now and then in his cart. The beat of the drum splintered on the broken thread of a song, again and again!

He turned and looked—no sacks, no bamboo, not even the tiger.... angel...goddess...mita...Hiradevi...Mahua the ghatwarin—no one. The mute voices of moments gone by wanted to be heard. Hiraman's lips were trembling. Perhaps he was taking his third vow—about carrying a company woman as a passenger...

Suddenly Hiraman chastised his bullocks and, hitting them with his whip, said, 'Why are you constantly looking back at the railway line?' The bullocks sped up. Hiraman started singing softly, '*Oh, yes, I am slain, Gulfam....*'

THE SOUL OF BHOLARAM

HARISHANKAR PARSAI

Such a thing had never happened before.

For tens of thousands of years, Dharmaraj had been allotting living quarters in heaven or hell to countless people based on their actions and recommendations made on their behalf. But this had never happened before.

Chitragupt was sitting in front of him, wiping his spectacles over and over, wetting his fingers with his tongue to turn the pages, consulting register after register. But he could not find the mistake. Finally, very irritated, he slammed the register shut with such force that a fly got caught between the pages. Plucking it out, he said, 'Maharaj, the records are fine. Five days ago, Bholaram's soul renounced his body and set off with Yamdoot for this world but it hasn't arrived yet.'

'And where is the yamdoot?' asked Dharmaraj.

'Maharaj, he is missing too.'

At that moment, the door opened and a yamdoot came in, looking very flustered. Toil, worry, and fear had made his already ill-favoured face even more hideous. As soon as he saw him, Chitragupt yelled, 'Arre, where were you for so many days? Where is Bholaram's soul?'

Yamdoot folded his hands and said, 'Oh most compassionate one, how can I tell you what happened? I've never been deceived before but Bholaram's soul has tricked me. Five days ago, when the soul left Bholaram's body, I caught it and began my journey to this world. As soon as I stepped out of the city, I hopped on to a swift air current with it. That's when it escaped my clutches and vanished God knows where. In these five days, I have scoured the entire universe, but can't find any sign of it.'

Enraged, Dharmaraj said, 'You fool! You've grown old bringing in souls year after year, but an ordinary old man's soul gave you the slip.'

The messenger bowed his head and said, 'Maharaj, I have not been remiss at all. Even the best lawyers have never escaped my seasoned hands. But this time, there's been some sorcery at work.'

Chitragupt said, 'Maharaj, this kind of trade has become very common on earth these days. People send things to their friends and the railway people pinch them en route. Railway officers wear socks taken from hosiery parcels. Bogies after bogies of goods trains are cut off on the way. And another thing, leaders of political parties are whisking away Opposition leaders and locking them up. Could it be that Bholaram's soul has been carried off by an adversary of his to subject it to further suffering after death?'

Dharmaraj looked at Chitragupt with scorn and said, 'You too have reached retirement age. Who could have had any problem with someone as insignificant and pathetic as Bholaram?'

At that moment Narad muni stopped by on his wanderings. Seeing Dharmaraj sitting silently, he asked, 'What is it, Dharmaraj, why are you looking so worried? Has the problem of hell's living quarters not been solved as yet?'

Dharmaraj said, 'That problem has been solved long ago. In the last few years, several skilled and talented craftsmen have entered hell. Many were building contractors who constructed poor quality buildings after taking all the money. High-level engineers have also arrived; they had joined hands with the contractors and siphoned off money from five-year plans. There are overseers who had embezzled money by marking attendance for workers who never showed up to work. They've erected many buildings in hell very quickly. So that problem has been sorted out but another, very grave complication has arisen. A man called Bholaram died five days ago. The messenger was bringing his soul here when it gave him the slip and ran away. He has combed the entire universe, but can't find the soul. If this kind of thing starts happening, it will mean the end of the difference between sin and virtue.'

Narad asked, 'Did he owe any income tax? Maybe they stopped him.'

'There can be tax only if there's an income. He was penniless,' Chitragupt said.

'It's an intriguing matter. All right, give me his name and address. I'll go to earth,' said Narad.

Chitragupt looked up his register and told him, 'His name was Bholaram. He lived with his family in a one-and-a-half-room ramshackle house next to the drain in Jabalpur City's Ghamapur mohalla. He had a wife, two sons, and a daughter. He was around sixty years old. A government servant. He retired five years ago. He hadn't paid the rent for one year; that's why the landlord wanted to throw him out. But then Bholaram left the world itself. Today is the fifth day. If the landlord is like landlords everywhere, he would have thrown out the family as soon as Bholaram died. So you will have to wander around quite a bit in search of them.'

Narad recognized Bholaram's house from the sound of the combined weeping of mother and daughter.

He went up to the door and called out, 'Narayan! Narayan!' The girl saw him and said, 'Move on, maharaj!'

Narad said, 'I don't want alms; I want to make some enquiries about Bholaram. Send your mother out, beti!'

Bholaram's wife came out. Narad asked, 'Mother, what illness did Bholaram have?'

'What can I say? His illness was poverty. It's been five years since his pension was due but he never got a penny. He would put in an appeal every ten–fifteen days, but either there would be no reply or, if there was a reply, it would be that we are considering the matter. In these five years, we sold all the jewellery we had in order to eat. Then we sold all the pots, pans, and dishes. There was nothing left. There was nothing to eat. Eaten up with worry, starving, he died.'

Narad asked, 'What can you do, mother? That was how long he was destined to live.'

'Don't say that, maharaj! He could have lived many more years. If he had got his pension of fifty–sixty rupees, he could have supplemented it with some other work and got by. But what can we do? He left his job five years ago and we haven't got a penny till now.'

Narad didn't have the time to listen to this sad saga. He came to the point. 'Mother, tell me, did he have any extra special love for anyone here, someone he couldn't bear to be parted from?'

The wife said, 'One is naturally attached to one's children, maharaj.'

'It could be outside the family too. I mean, some woman—'

The wife looked at Narad and growled, 'Don't just say any nonsense, maharaj! You are a holy man, not a loafer. He never raised his eyes to look at another woman ever in his life.'

Narad laughed and said, 'Yes, you are right to think this way. This is the foundation of every good household. All right, mother, I'll take your leave.'

The woman said, 'Maharaj, you are a holy man, a superior being. Can't you do something so that we get his pension that's been stopped all this while? At least these children will have a full stomach for a few days.'

Narad was moved. He said, 'Who listens to holy men? I don't have a religious establishment here. Even so, I'll go to the government office and try to do something.'

Narad left and made his way to the government office. He spoke to the babu sitting in the very first room about Bholaram's case. The babu checked the files carefully and said, 'Bholaram did send petitions but didn't put the necessary weight on them, that's why they must have flown away somewhere.'

Narad said, 'Bhai, there are so many paperweights here. Why didn't you put one of these?'

The babu laughed, 'You are a holy man, you don't understand worldly matters. Paperweights are not the kind of weights you need to put on petitions. Anyway, meet the babu sitting in that room.'

Narad went to that babu. He sent him to a third babu, the third sent him to a fourth and the fourth to a fifth. After Narad had wandered around, meeting twenty-five to thirty babus and officers, a peon said to him, 'Maharaj, why are you getting involved in this problem? Even if you keep coming here for one year, nothing will happen. Go straight to the big man. Make him happy, and your work will get done right away.'

Narad reached the bade sahib's room. The peon stationed outside was dozing, so nobody stopped him from going in. Seeing him enter without a visiting card, the sahib got very annoyed. 'Do you think this is a temple that you've come charging in? Why didn't you send a chit?'

Narad said, 'How could I? Your peon is sleeping.'

'What do you want?' the sahib asked haughtily.

Narad explained Bholaram's pension case.

The sahib said, 'You are an ascetic. You don't know the customs and procedures of offices. Actually, Bholaram made a mistake. Bhai, this is also like a temple. You have to make offerings and do good deeds here too. You seem to have been close to Bholaram. His petitions are in the air, you should put some weight on them.'

Narad thought: this weight issue again. The sahib said, 'Bhai, we are talking about government money. A pension case goes to dozens of offices. It is bound to take time. You have to write the same thing dozens of times in dozens of different places, only then does it become pukka. You end up expending as much stationery as your pension. Yes, it can be speeded up but....' the sahib paused.

Narad said, 'But what?'

With a crafty smile, the sahib said, 'But you need weight. You haven't understood. The weight of your beautiful veena can also be placed on Bholaram's petition. My daughter learns music. I'll give it to her. The musical notes will come out even better from a holy man's veena.'

Narad panicked a little at the thought of his veena being snatched from him. But he recovered, placed his veena on the table and said, 'Here, now put out the pension order quickly.'

The delighted sahib offered him a seat, put the veena in a corner and rang the bell. The peon presented himself.

The sahib ordered, 'Get Bholaram's case file from the senior clerk.'

In a short while, the peon returned with the file packed with a hundred to hundred and fifty applications by Bholaram. The file also contained the pension papers. The sahib looked at the name on the file and, just to make sure, asked, 'What name did you say, sadhuji?'

Narad thought the sahib was hard of hearing. So he said loudly, 'Bholaram!'

A voice came out of the file, 'Who is calling out to me? Is it the postman? Has the pension order arrived?'

Narad was startled. But in the next instant, he understood what had happened. He said, 'Bholaram! Are you Bholaram's soul?'

'Yes,' said the voice.

Narad said, 'I am Narad. I have come to take you away. Come, heaven is waiting for you.'

The voice said, 'I'm not going. I'm stuck in the pension petitions. I like it here now. I can't leave my petitions and go anywhere.'

CITY OF DEATH
AMARKANT

R am stepped out of the house. He peered around him nervously, looking in all directions, like a crow. Above, the sky was stretched tight like a clean blue tent. The park in front, the other houses, and the treetops were all bathed in mellow sunshine. Usually by this time, the entire mohalla would echo with a pleasant commotion but there were no women or children to be seen today. A frightening coiled-up silence had settled all around. Groups of two or four people stood huddled in front of some houses, their faces close to each other, whispering conspiratorially. He was a short, thin, middle-aged individual whose shirt was torn at the shoulder, and whose trousers were so creased they looked like pyjamas. His eyes were red and swollen. He lifted his head and looked at the sky and a deep sigh escaped him.

After walking a few steps, he suddenly stopped. He was anxious, his ears pricked up as he looked around him. He thought he heard a commotion coming from the neighbouring mohalla, with people shouting, 'Kill, kill,' as they ran in his direction. A knife gleamed in front of his eyes. Should he run into his house? He stepped back two paces. But the groups of people standing in front of the houses continued talking. A little reassured, he began listening to the sounds carefully, and that's when he understood what was happening. A pack of dogs was fighting in the neighbouring mohalla. 'These days even the dogs are fighting so much,' he thought to himself and tried to smile, but the smile disappeared like a little water bubble.

It was around eight o'clock. After many days, the curfew had been lifted for four hours in the morning and four hours in the evening. Before he left the house, his wife had whimpered, 'Be careful.' He himself was so afraid, so vigilant that another person's advice seemed ill-omened. He thundered, 'Do you *want* something to happen?' His wife started crying and he felt remorse at his behaviour as he left the house, but in that atmosphere of fear and terror, every tender emotion drowned like a tiny pebble in a flood.

Two other people from the mohalla joined him as they had decided. The three of them moved ahead, their faces haggard. They looked at each other as if they had committed some crime!

'Any news?' asked one of the three, mumbling, barely moving his lips.

'A man was knifed near the station,' the second man informed the others.

'Was he Hindu?'

'No, he was a Mohammedan.'

'Was a girl's body found in Himmatganj?'

'Yes.'

'Mohammedan?'

'No, Hindu.'

Ram was listening quietly. He felt as if someone was twisting his heart and squeezing out the blood. Suddenly, they fell silent. There was a long brick wall enclosing the mohalla. But attempts to separate people have never worked, and the wall had been broken in the middle to create little paths. The mohalla on the other side was of Muslims. After Independence, both mohallas had lived together peacefully. They had dealings with each other. The Hindus bought milk from the Muslim milkmen and the Muslims bought, and took on credit, provisions from the Hindu traders. They visited each other during weddings and helped each other out. Often there were cricket and football matches between the boys of the two mohallas. About two or three years ago, a boy called Jameel had become very popular in Ram's locality. He was fond of singing and acting in plays. He had played the role of Subhadra in the play *Vir Abhimanyu*. He had performed the role of a historical Hindu woman with great sincerity. His enthusiasm was so extreme that while enacting the mourning at Abhimanyu's death, he disregarded the director's instructions and fell down six times, banging his head hard on the floor. Because of this, he became famous among the Hindus as a true artiste, but all this ended suddenly and now people didn't believe in anything except murder, fear, and rumours.

The three of them went beyond the wall. Each tried to walk in the middle, but none of them managed to stay there for very long. At that moment, somebody lunged at them from behind. Ram was on the extreme left, so he was the first to be startled, but the man turned out to be a young priest. He was wearing a dhoti and vest and his feet were bare. His pigtail fluttered and he had a sandal tika on his forehead. Since the curfew had been lifted, he had come to organize prayers in someone's house and he had been waiting to go back with with his fellow priests.

'I'll also come along....' he mumbled, and attempted to smile. He too tried to stay in the middle of the group. Trying to match their pace, he skittered around like a little wooden peg but soon enough, he would push his way to the middle again, like a little mouse. At first, the three of them got very annoyed with him, but later they understood his compulsion; he was, because of his attire, the most Hindu of them all.

The narrow street was as desolate as the parting in a widow's hair. Ramu remembered, as if it were a blurred dream, that he would always see at least a couple of burqa-clad women on this street. Small children would be playing in the dust. The old woman at the wood store, Kariman, would be seen crossing the road or shouting, 'Ai Shabbir!' Young men, after expending their energy in the wrestling ground, would be bathing under the tap in their loincloths. How their eyes shone and mirrored their self-confidence! But now there were just twenty, twenty-five people standing in front of the tea shop, which was a little to the left. Their heads were lowered, but their eyes were raised, as if they were glaring at everyone from beneath their brows. Their lips were curved in poisonous smiles.

The group started walking faster. Their legs felt weak. Their bodies trembled like the tinsel tomb replicas carried in Muharram processions. After they crossed the hotel, they met five PAC jawans patrolling the area. There was a Hindu locality a little ahead. Huts and straw houses. Heaps of rubbish were piled here and there. The water in the drains had congealed and turned black. An old invalid was sitting in front of his house, coughing painfully. The pandit lived in this locality, so once they reached, he left the group and began walking with his chest puffed up.

'I go out alone on dark nights too,' he laughed, showing his teeth.

When they arrived at the main road, the two friends turned into another road and Ram was left by himself. This road was usually busy and full of activity. But now there were no rickshawallahs, nor could you see the small cycle repair shops on the sidewalks surrounded by throngs of school and college boys. Many shops were shut. There was no sign of the handcart sellers with their wares of chickpeas, flat rice, and ice. Sometimes groups of workers would dart across. Just then, a band of Muslim labourers hurried across the street. They bumped into each other like sheep. Sometimes they looked around them, alert, the way dogs do.

Ram kept moving forward. He looked behind repeatedly, like a jackal does when it enters a city. He could think of nothing but his fear. He was not a coward and he had always opposed this kind of strife, but sheer terror of the unknown had leached every drop of blood from his body. A poison had entered his being and was spreading fear in him. How small he felt! What terrifying silence all around! In that silence, even a little sound felt like a mob was about to attack. If only he hadn't come out today! But how would his work go on if he didn't! He worked in a small shop in Civil Lines and if he kept missing work, his salary would be cut.

He reached a small Muslim neighbourhood. Groups of people were standing around in front of houses and shops. They stared at him with ferocious eyes. A few other people were coming and going on the street. Ram had no strength in his body but fear for his life kept him moving quickly. He kept looking around him, behind him. At that moment, a young man came running from the left. He couldn't have been older than twenty. He was wearing a vest and underpants, and had a knife in his hand. Ram had spotted him from far away. His entire body went numb. PAC jawans were sitting some distance away, and though he wanted to, he was unable to shout out to them. When the young man came running towards him, he stepped back nimbly and escaped the attack he feared might happen. The young man stared at him, then laughing, he ran, like an arrow that had been fired, into a narrow alley on the other side.

His breath had all but stopped. He wasn't even aware if he was walking or not. He saw himself dead. Was he moving his lips and mumbling to himself or was that his teeth chattering? For a second, the faces of his wife and sad children appeared in front of his eyes.

Someone else was coming towards him. He was in a lungi and shirt. He said, 'Babuji, just go straight ahead, don't worry. These bloody people come from outside and want to give the neighbourhood a bad name. I had to go somewhere and that's why this happened, otherwise I'm always here, making sure no one creates trouble. Uff, times are so bad. You buy milk from Majid the milkman, don't you?'

Ram looked at him carefully, but he couldn't assess him. Suppose he was trying to deceive him? Without pausing, he replied, 'Yes....'

'Majid is my uncle. Carry on, don't worry. Babuji, I want to say something to you. Don't go out for two-three days. Times are not good.... Okay, go ahead...I'm standing right here....'

Ram walked as if he were in a catatonic state. He felt as if the young man in underpants was still following him. Why had he laughed? He remembered that when he was studying in high school, he had once worn the same kind of underpants and vest and run a one-mile race and won.

He felt life return to his bones when he reached the chowk. A few scared-looking people were walking about. They were avoiding each other because no one was sure about anyone. Ram himself was trying to hide from everyone. A few rickshaws were parked while others were circling around. One rickshawallah went past him, shouting, 'Civil Lines, one passenger!' The rickshaw roof was stretched tight towards the front, so he couldn't see the passenger

sitting inside. He fixed the fare and clambered inside. The moment
he sat down, his body went numb again. A bearded Muslim was
sitting inside, wearing thin pyjamas and a shirt. His cheeks were
hollow and his eyes were deep-set. He was looking at Ram with an
expression of terror, but also an expression that seemed to ask—how
could he overcome this terror?

The rickshaw began moving. Their eyes kept meeting by accident.
They sat stuck to either ends of the rickshaw, so that there was no
physical contact between them. Their faces and bodies were angled
away from each other, but they looked at each other from the
corners of their eyes. Ram noticed the bearded man's gaze going
to his waist or the pockets of his trousers now and again. He knew
the reason, because he himself was stealing glances at the man's
waist. Whenever the rickshaw swung or bounced on the road, they
would be thrown against each other, but they would swiftly move
aside and go back to their respective corners.

Now the rickshaw was passing by a hotel, with eight to ten
people standing on the footpath in front. Two or three of them
looked like wrestlers and were wearing vests and red scarfs. One of
them gestured towards the rickshaw. Then all of them began glaring
at the rickshaw with bloodthirsty eyes. A cry escaped the Muslim, 'Ya
Khuda!' Ram looked at him, startled. The bearded man was resting
his head on the back of the rickshaw. He was staring upwards and his
legs were trembling violently. It didn't take Ram long to understand
why; seeing the person he himself was scared of looking so terrified
gave him some relief, but was he going to die right here! Ram had
been in the exact same condition a little while back.

'Please pull yourself together,' Ram said, shaking him.

The bearded man looked at him wretchedly, but no sound escaped
his lips.

'Are you feeling ill?'

'No.' An indistinct sound emerged from him.

'Never mind, it's all right,' Ram tried to reassure him.

These words came from him of their own accord and he was a

little surprised by this. He remembered that till a few days back, he too had been a human being. Yes, a human being! Had these words come out of his mouth because of long practice?

The rickshaw moved ahead. The bearded man sat up straight. He had collected himself now.

'These are such terrible times,' he said.

'Yes, this is such a terrible time,' Ram repeated his words.

'Human beings are dying like rats in a plague.'

'Yes, Hindus, Muslims, both are dying.'

'Poor people are dying. I am a daily wage earner, I eat when I earn. It's been three days, no food has been cooked at home.'

'Where do you work?' asked Ram.

'National Tailoring House. A man can go hungry, but he can't see his children go hungry. I had to step out today, what else could I do?'

'Yes, that's it....'

'You know, women have had to run away and so many of them are crammed into homes here, like hens stuffed into pens. What can I tell you about their condition! People are dying of hunger. Someone is selling their cycle, someone is selling their watch. People are pawning their jewellery....'

'There have been mistakes on both sides.'

'No one is innocent. I have two or three Hindu friends but they don't meet my eyes any more. Why should I lie, I do the same too.'

'This is the problem. That's why we can't progress.'

'Yes, if we live together peacefully, no one would dare target us.'

Suddenly, they went quiet. Their enthusiasm dissipated. Ram didn't feel like talking, the way a sick person doesn't feel like eating. The rickshaw was moving fast. They gazed in front of them. Every good thing seemed so unnatural. For a moment, the thought even crossed Ram's mind that the Muslim man may have said what he did to protect himself.

The rickshaw reached Civil Lines. The bearded man asked the rickshaw to stop before the main crossing. He got off, paid his fare and, without looking at Ram, began walking away. He had barely taken a few steps when he turned back, as though he'd remembered something. He came near Ram and said with a smile, as if he was imparting some good news, 'Let's see if I manage to reach home this evening or not...all right, aadab arz. Perhaps we'll meet again.'

Saying this, he turned around and started walking away quickly. He was shaking like a leaf.... The rickshaw moved forward. Ram got off at the crossing. God knows why, his eyes were full of tears. He didn't know whether these tears were a sign of gratitude towards that man or because of his own helplessness, but he was happy at this expression of sorrow. Fear hadn't allowed him to feel either happiness or sorrow, but this man had softened his heart and caused his sorrow to well up. A little while ago, he had thought of him as a killer, but he was tender, like a lamb. Majid's relative was also like this....

Ram walked to the other side of the crossing and took the road ahead. He looked around him happily. Beautiful roads and shops. Green trees. Then he remembered he had to go home in the evening. A heavy weight settled over his heart. He felt his heart sinking again. There was a strong breeze. Its rustling sounded like a woman weeping. Or was it like the sound of children moaning in pain? At that moment, a koel sitting on a tree started singing. The koel's cooing! Ever since the trouble started, the koel must have cooed so many times and he'd never noticed, but now its musical cry kept ringing in his ears.

THE TIMES HAVE CHANGED
KRISHNA SOBTI

Dawn was breaking by the time Shahni, wrapped in a thick cotton shawl, rosary clasped in her hands, reached the banks of the river. A rosy hue was spreading far above on the curtain of the sky. Shahni took off her clothes, placed them to one side and, saying 'Shri Ram, Shri Ram', stepped into the water. She filled her cupped hands with water, saluted the sun god, splashing a little water on her sleepy eyes.

The waters of the Chenab were as cold as before, and the waves were kissing each other. Far away, in the mountains of Kashmir, the ice was melting. Bouncing, rolling waves smashed against the overhanging banks, but somehow that day, the sand that stretched far into the distance seemed silent and still! Shahni put on her clothes, looked around, there wasn't even a shadow to be seen. But below, on the sand, were countless footprints. She shivered a little with fear!

She had a sense of danger and fear in the sweet silence of dawn. She had bathed here for the last fifty years. What a long time! This was the same riverbank where she had first stepped foot as a bride. And today, there was no Shahji, nor her educated son. She was alone, alone in Shahji's enormous haveli. But no! What was she thinking so early in the morning? Why was she unable to turn away from worldly matters! Shahni took a deep breath and, chanting 'Shri Ram, Shri Ram', made her way home through the bajra fields. Smoke rose from some of the whitewashed courtyards. Tann-tann rang the bells of the bullocks. Even so...even so, there was a feeling of suffocation. Even the Jammiwala well wasn't working that day. All the people here were Shahji's tenants. Shahni looked up. These fields, stretching for miles, are ours. Looking at the full, abundant fresh harvest, Shahni was swamped with a love born out of a sense of belonging. This was all because of Shahji's blessings. Lands extending right up to far-off villages, dotted with wells—they owned all of it. Three harvests in a year, the land bequeathed gold. Shahni moved towards the well and called out, 'Shere, Shere! Hussaina, Hussaina….'

Shera recognized Shahni's voice. He would, wouldn't he! After the death of his mother, Jaina, Shera had grown up in Shahni's care. He picked up the chopper and pushed it under the pile of grass lying nearby. Holding the hookah in his hand, he said, 'Ai Hussaina, Hussaina….' How Shahni's voice affected him! He had been thinking about taking the trunks full of silver and gold lying in that dark, little room in Shahni's grand haveli…. And that's when he heard, 'Shere, Shere….' Shera was enraged. Who should he vent his anger on? On Shahni? He screamed, 'Ai, are you dead!... May God give you death….'

Hussaina put aside the platter she was using for kneading dough and hurried outside, 'Coming, coming, why are you so irritated early in the morning?'

By now Shahni had come closer. She had heard Shere's angry outburst. Lovingly she said, 'Hussaina, is this any time to quarrel? He is mad. But you should be more strong of heart.'

'Strong-hearted!' Hussaina said, her voice full of pride, 'Shahni, boys will be boys, after all. Have you asked Shere why he only curses so early in the morning?'

Shahni patted Hussaina's back fondly and said with a laugh, 'Silly girl, I like the bride more than the boy! Shere….'

'Yes, Shahni?'

'I believe those people from Kulluvaal came here at night?' Shahni asked in a grave voice.

A little rattled, Shere said hesitantly, 'No, Shahni….' Without listening to Shere's answer, Shahni continued in a worried voice, 'Whatever is happening is not good. Shere, if Shahji were here today, he might have done something. But—' Shahni stopped mid-sentence. What is happening today! Shahni felt choked with emotion. Shahji had been gone many years, but—but something was melting inside her that day—perhaps memories of the past…. In an attempt to control her tears, she looked towards Hussaina and laughed gently. And Shera wondered, what was Shahni saying! No one could do anything today, not even Shahji. What had to happen would happen and why shouldn't it? Shahji could weigh his sacks of gold only because he made money from the interest he took from our brothers and friends. Shera's eyes burned with the flames of vengeance. He thought of the long-handled chopper. He looked at Shahni. No-no, in the last few days Shera had already committed thirty-forty murders. But...but he wasn't such a degenerate.... Shahni's hands floated in front of his eyes. Those winter nights.... Sometimes, after being scolded by Shahji, he would be lying in some corner of the haveli. Then, in the light of the lantern, he would see Shahni's tender hands holding a bowl of milk, 'Shere, Shere, get up, drink this.' Shere looked at Shahni's wrinkled face and found that she was smiling gently. He felt unsettled and moved. After all, what wrong had Shahni ever done to him? Whatever Shahji had done had gone with his death. He would definitely protect Shahni. But what about last night's conference! How had he agreed with what Feroz had suggested? Everything would be all right...they would distribute all the belongings!

'Come, Shahni, let me see you home.'

Shahni got up. Shera followed Shahni with firm steps as she walked ahead, deep in thought. He kept looking around uneasily. The words of his companions echoed in his ears. But what would they get from killing Shahni?

'Shahni.'

'Yes, Shere.'

He wanted to warn Shahni of the impending danger, but how? 'Shahni....'

Shahni lifted her head. The sky was full of smoke. 'Shere....'

Shera knew this fire. A fire was to be lit in Jalalpur that day, and it had been lit! Shahni was unable to say anything. All her relatives lived there.

They reached the haveli. Shahni stepped across the threshold, her mind empty. She had no idea when Shera left. Her body was frail, she was alone, without any support! She had no idea how long she lay there. Afternoon came and went. The haveli stood, its doors open. Shahni couldn't get up. As if her authority was, of its own volition, slipping away from her! The mistress of Shahji's house…but no, today, she felt no attachment. As if she had turned to stone. It was twilight but she still lay there, unable to get up. She was startled by the sound of Rasooli's voice.

'Shahni, Shahni, we've heard the trucks are coming to pick up people.'

'Trucks…?' Shahni couldn't say anything else. She clasped her hands together. In no time, the news spread all over the village. Lah bibi said in a choked voice, 'Shahni, this has never happened before, it's never been heard of before. It's a disaster, there's darkness and violence all around.'

Shahni stood still as a statue. Said Nawab bibi, her sorrowful voice full of love, 'Shahni, we never thought it would come to this.'

What could Shahni say. She herself had thought of this! She heard Patwari Begu and Jailldar talking below. Shahni understood that the time had come. She walked down like an automaton but couldn't cross the threshold. In a hollow, barely-there voice, she asked, 'Who? Who all are there?'

Who wasn't there that day? The whole village was there, the village that had once done her bidding unquestioningly. They included her tenants whom she had never considered any less than her close relatives. But, no, that day no one was hers, that day she was alone! The Jats of Kulluval were there in the huge crowd. She'd understood this in the morning itself!

Who knew what Patwari Begu and the mosque's Mulla Ismail thought. They came and stood next to Shahni. Begu couldn't bring himself to look at her. Clearing his throat softly, he said, 'Shahni, this is what God has willed.'

Shahni's feet faltered. She felt dizzy and held on to the wall. Had Shahji left her alone to see this day? Looking at the lifeless, inert

Shahni, Begu thought, 'See what Shahni is going through! But what can be done! The times have changed.'

Shahni's leaving the house was not an insignificant event. The entire village was there, standing at the door of the haveli, all the way up to the gate built by Shahji when his son got married. All the consultations and decisions in the village were taken here. Discussions about looting the haveli had also taken place here. It's not as if Shahni didn't know anything. She knew but pretended she didn't. She had never known enmity, never wronged anyone. But she didn't know that the times had changed....

It was getting late. Thanedar Dawood Khan stepped forward arrogantly but seeing the motionless, lifeless shadow standing at the door, he hesitated. This was the same Shahni whose Shahji had had tents set up near the river for him. This was the same Shahni who had given his fiancée flower-shaped gold earrings when she saw his bride-to-be for the first time. When he had come to see her in connection with the 'League' the other day, he had said in a high-handed manner, 'Shahni, a mosque has to be built at Bhaagovaal, you'll have to give three hundred rupees.' With her usual simplicity, Shahni had placed three hundred rupees in front of him. And today?

'Shahni!' Dawood Khan called out. He was a policeman, otherwise he might have teared up.

Shahni was lost, silent, unable to say anything.

'Shahni!' he came near the door and spoke softly, 'it's getting late, Shahni! Take something with you if you want to. Have you put away something or not? Any gold, silver....'

In a muffled voice, Shahni said, 'Gold, silver!' She paused for a moment and then said simply, 'Gold, silver! All that is for you people, child. My gold is spread out on every inch of this land.'

A shamefaced Dawood Khan said, 'Shahni, you are alone, you should keep something with you. At least keep some cash with you. Who knows what could happen at any time....'

'Time?' Shahni laughed, her eyes wet with tears. 'Dawood Khan, will I be alive to see a better time than this!' she said, her voice a a mix of anguish and censure.

Dawood Khan had no answer. Gathering his courage, he said, 'Shahni...a little cash is necessary.'

'No child, this house.... Shahni's throat choked with tears, 'is more beloved to me than any money. The money that is here will stay here.'

At that moment Shera came and stood nearby. From a distance he had seen Dawood Khan next to Shahni and suspected that Dawood was probably extracting something or the other from her. 'Khan sahib, it's getting late....'

Shahni started. Getting late....I'm getting late in my own house! Rebellion emerged from her whirlpool of tears. I am the queen of this house made by my ancestors and these people have grown up under my care. No, this is too much. All right, it's getting late. It's getting late. That was the only thing echoing in her ears: it's getting late, but, no, Shahni would not leave her ancestral home in tears, she would leave with pride, she would cross the threshold with her head held high, the same threshold where she had once arrived and stood like a queen. Steadying her wobbling legs, Shahni wiped her eyes with her dupatta and crossed the threshold. The old women in the crowd broke down. The one who had been their friend and companion in both happy and sad times was leaving. Who could be compared to her! God had given everything, but, fortunes changed, times changed....

Shahni covered her head with her dupatta and looked at the haveli one last time, her eyes blurred with tears. Even after Shahji's death, she had looked after the legacy entrusted to her so carefully, now that legacy itself had betrayed her. Shahni folded her hands. This was the last sight, the last salutation. Shahni's eyes would never again see this great haveli. Her love made her think: why don't I walk through the entire house one more time? She was feeling disheartened, but she wouldn't let it show in front of the people before whom she had always stood tall. This was enough. Everything was done. She lowered her head. After crossing the threshold, a few tears trickled out of the eyes of the daughter-in-law of this noble house. Shahni set off, the grand mansion was left behind. Dawood Khan, Shera, Patwari, Jailldaar, children, the very old, women, men, all followed in her wake.

The trucks were full by now. Shahni dragged herself forward. The assembled villagers were moved. Shere, the bloodthirsty Shere's heart was breaking. Dawood Khan stepped forward and opened the door of the truck. Shahni moved ahead. Ismail stepped forward and said in a heavy voice, 'Shahni, say something before leaving. Any blessing from you will come true!' And he wiped the tears from his eyes with his turban. Suppressing her sobs, her throat full of unshed tears, Shahni said, 'May God keep you well, my child, may you have joy and happiness....'

That small mass of people wept. There was not a grain of bitterness in Shahni's heart. But we—we couldn't keep Shahni with us. Shere stepped forward and touched Shahni's feet. 'Shahni, nobody could do anything, the ruling power changed....' Shahni placed a trembling hand on Shera's head and said falteringly, 'Live long, my dearest one.' Dawood Khan gestured with his hand. Some of the old women embraced Shahni and the truck set off.

It was time to move on. The haveli, the new sitting room, the high chamber, the big veranda—one by one, all of them spun in front of Shahni's eyes! She knew nothing—whether the truck was moving or whether she herself was moving. Her eyes rained tears. A shaken, unsettled Dawood Khan looked at the old Shahni. Where would she go now?

'Shahni, don't keep any bitterness in your heart. If we could have done something, wouldn't we have kept you with us? The times are what they are. The government has changed, the times have changed....'

Shahni reached the camp at night and, lying on the ground, she thought in her wounded heart, 'The government has changed... but how can money change, I've left it behind anyway, what does it matter to me....'

And Shahni's eyes filled with tears.

It rained blood that night on the villages around the green fields.

Perhaps the government was changing, the times were changing.

(July, 1948)

ESCAPE

KRISHNA BALDEV VAID

And one day, they left their work and set off from home. There was no fixed plan, no relative had fallen ill, no one's son had passed an exam, no old woman had died, no one's daughter had got engaged, no saint had arrived anywhere, there was no festival that day—there was no excuse.

In reality, it so happened that while washing the dishes, a sudden, strange whim rose in Sheela's heart and, throwing down the utensil she was holding, without even washing her hands, she ran out of the room and called out, 'Rani, o Rani!' Rani's room was on the second floor. As she was calling Rani, Sheela's gaze pierced through the emptiness and collided against the clouds in the sky and a drop of rain fell on her right eye. Instantly, she blinked and then began calling loudly again, 'Rani o Rani!'

Rani peered down from the latticed grille, asking, 'Why are you calling me so early in the morning?' Instead of replying, Sheela broke into peals of laughter. Rani didn't repeat her question but came stomping down the stairs to the courtyard, caught Sheela's braid and tugged at it. Sheela issued a laughing threat, 'Let go or I'll blacken your face.' Rani laughed and answered, 'Whose…your own?' And then they both started laughing and in the midst of all this laughter, Sheela whispered something in Rani's ear, and Rani began clapping her hands and yelling, 'Vanti…O Veeran…O Vanti….'

Vanti and Veeran lived in two rooms on a lower floor of the house and had already heard the din. Vanti was bathing in a corner of her room and Veeran was kneading some flour for the next meal. Hearing Rani's voice, Vanti threw some water on herself, wrapped her body in a dirty dupatta and came out of the room. Veeran had left the flour half-kneaded and was already standing with Sheela and Rani, laughing at who knows what. The moment they saw Vanti, all three began screaming like little children. 'Vanti is naked oye…Vanti naked….' Mortified, Vanti went back to her room, quickly put on a petticoat and kurti, and ran out buttoning the kurti. Rani moved forward and said, 'Don't run, you'll get your share.' Vanti asked in some surprise, 'Share of what?' All three replied in one voice, 'That,' and the four of them burst into giggles.

But the stifling atmosphere of the courtyard took irritated offence at this laughter and the proof of that irritability was the tight, set face of the landlady. Standing in front of her portion of the house, she all but ground her teeth watching these uncouth women and their boorish behaviour. After whispering to each other, the four women finally ended their little conference with another loud burst of laughter, and the atmosphere of the courtyard lightened. But the landlady's temper went up by a few notches.

Laughing, shouting, their bodies swaying, all four went back to their rooms. Sheela quickly washed her ash-covered hands. The pile of utensils was still there, but she began adjusting her floral-patterned salwar. Rani picked up the broom and threw it in a corner, tipped the pail full of water on the floor, wiped her hands on her petticoat, and began applying kohl to her eyes. Vanti had already finished her housework, only the fire remained to be put out. She hastily threw two or three glasses of water on the kitchen stove, realized that the entire stove had become wet but then began pleating her new dupatta. Veeran pushed the circular metal dish meant for kneading flour into a corner. Her room was littered with dirty dishes because her children had just eaten and gone out. She put away a couple of glasses and then washed up.

In a short while, the four friends locked their rooms, and came out of the courtyard, while the landlady looked on in surprise. They didn't so much as lift their eyes and look at her. Wretched women, the landlady muttered to herself and, at that moment, her husband called out from inside, 'Where have you gone, you wretched woman, what have you done?' And she went inside and began quarrelling with her husband.

The four women were out on the street, running, one behind the other, as if they were primary school students. Rani was out of control. She tied her dupatta around her waist, wrapped her braid around her head like a turban and walked as if she were the younger sister-in-law of Rani Khan. She had crossed the alley and reached the street when Sheela called out to her to stop.... 'Where are you going...there's nothing on that side...do you want to go to the jungle...!' She was yelling so loudly that some students on Nawabganj Road turned to look. Only after Sheela shouted repeatedly did Rani stop. They conferred with each other and decided they should take a tram from Subzi Mandi. And when Vanti asked—'Where will you go?' all three laughed and replied, 'Wherever you take us.' Vanti laughed at this and set off towards Subzi Mandi.

A tram was waiting. They ran inside and sat down and when the conductor asked Sheela, 'Where do you want to go?' Sheela laughed and answered, 'Ask her.' The conductor, irritated by the unprovoked laughter, flared up and said, 'Ask whom?' Sheela laughed again and said, 'Why are you getting angry, I meant her...ask Rani.'

'Am I going to find out in a dream who Rani is?' said the conductor, losing his temper.

'I am Rani!' Rani got up and began walking in the moving tram and the next instant she stumbled and fell into the lap of an old man.

Sheela, Vanti, and Veeran burst out laughing. Getting up from the old man's lap, Rani said, 'Why are you laughing, he's like your father,' whereupon everyone sitting in the tram started laughing and the old man could only look on foolishly. Lurching and staggering, Rani made her way back to her seat.

When they got off the tram at the Qutub Road station, the conductor, addressing no one knows whom, said, 'What strange, vulgar women.' And one of the men sitting in the tram said to his wife, 'There's no modesty left these days,' and the old man was telling the youth seated next to him, 'How that saali fell so hard on my lap' and the youth tried to figure out whether the old man was disapproving of the woman's misdemeanour or whether he was mentally smacking his lips.

After getting off the tram, they discussed where they should go. When Rani, finger on her face, said, 'Hai, where have we come?' Sheela answered with great innocence, 'To our father-in-law's place.' At this, all of them laughed so loudly that everyone standing nearby stared at them. They were doubling over with laughter, oblivious to the cars coming from both sides, honking at them. When a car lightly brushed Rani's legs, her laughter turned into a scream and she turned around and sent the car driver packing with a few familiar, homely abuses.

They moved to the side of the road, and suddenly Sheela (whose whim had brought them out of the house in the first place) said, 'Will you go to Connaught Place?' Everyone had heard the name. Vanti's husband brought her a string of flowers from Connaught Place on the first of every month, on his way back from the office. Veeran's Ramdayal also visited Connaught Place, where he had regular buyers for his inexpensive biscuits. Rani herself had been there twice—once when her husband had taken her to see an Independence Day procession at her request and another time when she had wandered there on her own while out in the city. Sheela's suggestion was instantly accepted and they got onto a tonga.

The horse was going quite fast, but Rani, nose in the air, said to the tongawallah, 'Will he keep going like this, dhinchku-dhinchku?' The affronted tongawallah prodded the hind legs of his horse with a stick, so that the horse sped along, talking to the wind. Clippety-clop went the horse's feet on the hard road and the tongawallah kept looking from Rani to Sheela who was sitting next to him as if he were asking for some sort of reward, but Rani and Sheela were running even faster than the horse. Rani's dupatta had slipped from her head, it couldn't be seen anywhere on her body. It had fallen down—near her feet. Sheela's hair had escaped from her braid and was rippling all over the place. Vanti and Veeran sat like little children, their knees resting on the seat, looking ahead.

Rani was saying, 'Valle o balle!'

Sheela was saying, 'Hai Ram, so fast!'

The tongawallah was saying, 'If you want, I can make him go faster!'

Vanti and Veeran, sitting behind, piped up, 'Yes, bhai, faster, faster!'

The tongawallah, standing on the footboard, shouted, 'Aaa hahaha....'

Passers-by couldn't see the tonga clearly because it was going so fast, but everyone had a comment to offer. If they had been able to gather in one place, they would have unanimously declared that the women in the tonga were prostitutes, no wonder it was going so fast.

But the women in the tonga were not prostitutes, and the tongawallah was disappointed once they reached Connaught Place. Instead of giving him a reward, Rani said to him, 'Bhai, we only have eleven-and-a-half annas, now will you kill us for two paisa?'

Rani's words probably came as a bit of a shock to the tongawallah. Immediately he said, 'Rani, you keep this too!'

No sooner had he said this than Vanti, Veeran and Sheela burst into laughter, as if three fountains had been set off. At first Rani was taken aback, but when she understood what had been said, she laughed so much that she could barely stand and she sat down right there, saying 'Ui ui!' The tongawallah said to himself, 'She must be mad,' and began walking away slowly with his horse.

When she recovered, Rani said, wiping her eyes, 'But how did this wretched creature find out my name?' Vanti replied, 'Bhai, who doesn't know you?' At this, a second wave of laughter was about to erupt when the tongawallah said, 'If you want, I can take you to the Qutub.'

After going a little further, the tongawallah turned around again.

'Take your mother or your sister to the Qutub,' Rani said in the unique tone that only housewives have and then told her friends, 'Come, let's go, this wretched creature is following us like a dog.' And they set off towards Odeon Cinema.

Rani said, 'This is Cannad Plates.'

Veeran said, 'Not Cannad Plates, Karnaat Place.'

Vanti said, 'What nonsense, the name is—Kanaas Plate.'

Sheela said, 'Whatever the name, this is the place, isn't it?'

Rani said, 'Why don't you ask somebody?'

'Go on, go to your tongawallah....'

At the mention of the tongawallah, Rani suppressed a smile and said, 'The wretched creature even found out my name.'

They stopped outside Odeon and looked at the posters, then went closer, hesitantly and timidly, and slowly entered the porch of the cinema. Wandering around, they ended up outside the men's toilet. For a few seconds they wondered what was inside, then Rani pushed the door open and crying, 'Ui ma' ran out. Running, skidding, they came out and asked Rani, 'What happened?' But Rani kept laughing and laughing and when the others pressed her, she said, 'A man....' and began laughing again. 'Are you thinking of the tongawallah?' asked Veeran and Vanti. Changing the subject, Sheela said, 'Isn't there a Hanuman ji temple somewhere here...'

'Forget the Hanuman ji temple. Have we come for an outing or to pray in a temple? No doubt some fat priest will be sitting there scratching himself.'

'Are you speaking from experience?' said Sheela and she started laughing again.

And just like this, laughing, loafing, they spent the whole day till evening. Their throats were sore from laughing, and they had eaten all sorts of nonsensical things—gol gappe, aloo tikiya, chaat ke patte, chana jor garam, they'd sampled everything you could find outside of Connaught Place's big hotels. They walked around Connaught Place's verandas many times, stood in rapt wonder in front of shops—so many shops. They had confused plenty of people with their laughter and now their legs began to ache a little. And something was pulling them homewards. It was like a chain dragging them away.

'Come, let's rest for a while, the grass is so green.'

But instead of saying 'Yes' or 'No' in reply, Veeran said in a low voice, 'Shouldn't we go home?' The word home was like the sound of a brick or a stone hitting a clay pot.

Their faces fell.

'What will you do at home?' asked Rani bravely. But this feeble rejoinder had no effect on the bitter clouds of reality that had dispersed in the sky to perchance settle on their minds.

'What is there at home?' said Rani again, as if she was trying to explain something to herself.

'Nothing!' replied Sheela, as if to say why are you asking something to which you know the answer!

And the four friends, instead of sitting down on the green grass, set off home.

'Let's take a tonga,' said Rani, but no one laughed.

'Why have Vanti and Veeran suddenly fallen so silent...?' said Sheela.

'I was thinking about what vegetables I should cook tonight,' answered Vanti.

Instead of making fun of this, Rani said, 'You can take some of my dal left over from the morning.'

So, asking the way, trying to sort out niggling domestic problems, arguing over household issues, gossiping about their neighbours, a bit envious of each other, mentally doing the accounts of paise and annas, they began walking home with quick steps.

WHERE LAKSHMI IS HELD CAPTIVE

RAJENDRA YADAV

Wait, this story is not about Lord Vishnu's wife, Lakshmi, but about a girl called Lakshmi, who wants to escape from her prison. It's natural to be confused between the two, which is what happened to Govind for a brief moment.

When Govind woke up in a panic, he was drenched in sweat and his heart was beating so fast he felt it might stop altogether. He blinked five or six times in the dark. At first he couldn't figure out where he was, how he'd got there—it was as if he had lost all sense of direction and place. When the clock in the hall outside struck one, he couldn't tell where the clock was, or where *he* was for that matter. Slowly, he became aware of himself and his surroundings, wiped the sweat from his neck vigorously. The khat-khat sound he had heard was still resounding in his head.

Govind wondered—had it been a dream or was it real—that someone had knocked on his door three or four times, begging tearfully, 'Take me away, take me away.' That voice had pierced his consciousness in such a mysterious way that he got up, overwrought and agitated—was it really someone's voice or was it all in his head?

Then slowly he remembered that he had fallen asleep so overwhelmed with thoughts about Lakshmi that she had pervaded his dreams as well. But, really, that voice was so unusual and so clear! He had often heard that if a particular woman or man appeared in one's dreams and said, 'Take me away, take me away,' they would also point you to a location and if you dug there you would find pots full of gold and silver and within no time you would be rolling in money. Sometimes, it was also said, if someone unworthy tried to unearth the wealth, he would only find coal and a few useless coins, or he would get leprosy, or there would be a death in his family. Could it be a Lakshmi of this kind who was calling out to him from deep below the earth? He kept thinking and the story of Lakshmi once again took shape in his mind. He lay there as if in a trance.

From somewhere far away, another clock struck the hour.

Govind couldn't contain himself any longer. Making sure that the quilt was firmly tucked in from all corners, he carefully took out an arm—only till the elbow—and picked up the half-burnt candle lying next to the books and notebooks in the almirah. He found some matches and then, making sure he wouldn't have to fully expose his other arm to the cold, lit the candle and stuck it on the lid of the inkpot by dripping some wax on it. In the quivering light, he saw that the door was firmly shut and the faint light that came from the second floor through the the skylight had also gone out. Everything was so quiet. Though the light switch was just above his bed, he was reluctant to stand up in the cold, with or without the quilt and, moreover, he was afraid of what Lala Ruparam would say in the morning: 'You're studying very late these days.' The implied meaning was, of course, that he was consuming too much electricity.

Then, stealthily, as if someone were watching him, still keeping his hand firmly inside the quilt, he withdrew the magazine lying under his pillow, opened it to page 47 and stared at it for the twentieth time. Only when the 1 a.m. Pathankot Express roared by did he come out of his trance. On pages 47 and 48, which were open in front of him, certain sentences had been underlined in blue ink. The page had also been dog-eared to draw special attention to the underlined sentences. Till now Govind had read those lines more than twenty times. He looked around with fearful eyes and then read them again.

No matter how many times he read the words, his heart would start beating hard, and his head would buzz in the same way as it had when he had first got the magazine. In the interim, his mind had gone through many dire phases; he kept staring at the letters printed in black ink. Gradually he felt as if the rows of letters were like the net on a window from behind which peered the passive face of a young girl, her hair spread out all around her. He remembered a story he had heard in his childhood. A prince out on a hunt got separated from his companions. Wandering around, astride his exhausted horse, he came upon a grand, deserted fort in the middle of a desolate wilderness near the seashore. He could see an extremely beautiful princess sitting at a window high up; she had been imprisoned there by an evil demon. Even the briefest of descriptions was enough for the picture of the princess to become clear in Govind's mind. He felt as if that princess was peeping out from behind the underlined printed lines—her cheeks streaked with dried tears, her lips like parched paper...her face withered and her silken hair akin to a spider's web—and saying: 'Release me, release me!'

Govind felt as if someone was nudging his mind, urging him to free this unknown princess. Once or twice he had a strong desire to banish this excitement by pacing up and down in the two-foot-wide passage between his bed and the wall of his small room.

Had Lakshmi really written all this for him? But he hadn't even seen Lakshmi! Even if he wanted to conjure up a young girl's face in his imagination, what would it be like? There were other reasons, too, that made him afraid to imagine Lakshmi as a beautiful girl—he didn't know her age or what she looked like....

Govind knew very well that these lines had been drawn to attract his attention. Even so, he didn't want to believe in this rather unexpected event. He didn't think of himself as worthy of a girl's interest or intent. He had heard a lot about cities, but he'd never thought that within a week of passing his Intermediate in his village and coming to the city, such a 'fortunate' event would happen.

Whenever he read those lines, his head swam as if he were looking down from a ten-storey building. When he'd first set eyes on the pages, he'd jumped as if a hot coal had suddenly appeared in his hand.

He'd been in the hall that had the mill in it, doing the day's accounts on a large, slender register lying open on an old wooden box, which in turn stood on a brick platform, when Lala Ruparam's youngest son, Ramswarup, who was around nine or ten years old, came and stood next to him. Hands stuffed inside the pockets of a tattered chesterfield, which had clearly been cut from an older brother's overcoat, he stood there, looking fixedly at him.

On his very first day when Govind was doing the accounts, then too this boy had come and stood next to him. That day, Lala Ruparam was also present, so just to show that he was taking an interest in his landlord's son, Govind asked the boy his name, age, the school he attended, the class he was in, and so on. Ramswarup was his name, he was nine, and he was studying in Class IV in Chungi Primary School. After that, morning or evening, Govind only had to see the shadow of his chester to know that he was around. He wore shorts under the coat, so his legs were always bare, and on his feet were very old canvas shoes, whose open, torn shoelaces reminded him of a dog's shorn tail.

After staring at him for a while, the boy took out a magazine from his coat, placed it before him and said, 'Munshiji, Lakshmi jiji has said that she wants something else to read.'

'All right...I'll give something tomorrow,' he said, a little irritated.

He was upset at the title of 'munshiji' that he'd been bestowed with. The image that came to mind was of a bent man with a pen stuck behind his ear, wearing a round, soiled topi and an old coat—this was an image Govind, a young man in his early twenties, couldn't stomach.

Lala Ruparam was from his village—he may even have been in school with his father in some classes. When Govind came to the city, keen to be self-reliant while continuing with his studies, he looked around for a part-time job, or tuitions, and met Lala Ruparam in that connection. The latter responded with great enthusiasm, invoking Govind's late father, 'Bhaiyya, you are like my child, just look at the accounts of our flour mill for an hour or so every day, stay comfortably in the little room next to the mill and finish your studies. You'll never be short of flour here.' Immensely grateful, Govind had accepted happily and come to stay in the little room. On the first night, Lala Ruparam explained how the accounts had to be written, his eyes big and round like the eye of a peacock feather behind the thick spectacles he wore for his cataract-afflicted eyes, his fat lips smiling. He sought to elevate his status by calling him 'munshiji', and Govind had been startled. He decided that after settling down, he would politely object to the use of this word. Hearing the epithet 'munshiji' from Ramswarup, he frowned. That's why he replied so curtly.

'Definitely give them tomorrow,' Ramswarup repeated the request.

'Haan bhai, I will,' he muttered through gritted teeth. He'd heard the name Lakshmi very often. Though his room was separate from the rest of the house and close to the street, the skylight opened out into the inner courtyard of the lower storey. Lala Ruparam's family lived on the floor above. Below, there was a flour mill and a storeroom stocked with all kinds of things. He developed an acute interest in 'Lakshmi', because whether he was in his room or outside in the hall, every five minutes he would hear her name in so many different ways—'Lakshmi bibi has said this', 'The money is with Lakshmi bibi', 'Give the keys to Lakshmi bibi'. And Govind had begun recognizing the thin, sharp, authoritative voice that rang out in reply. He guessed that the voice belonged to Lakshmi. But what was she like? Sometimes his heart would beat hard at the thought of getting a glimpse of her. But he decided he had to first settle in and establish himself, so he didn't even try to raise his eyes and look inside. He realized that the voice he heard must be Lakshmi's and that she was important…the problem was he couldn't see anything inside the house. There was the hall with the mill that opened out to the street. After the hall was a long passage, about eight or ten feet long, and above the courtyard was an iron grille, which jangled whenever people walked on it, distracting him every time. The children sometimes jumped up and down on it. But you couldn't see anything unless you crossed the entire passage on some pretext or the other. However, the tap and bathroom were in the courtyard, because of which it was forever musty, and every morning when he went there, though he kept his head lowered like a good boy, he tried to gauge what was happening upstairs. He didn't dare raise his head and look openly. After closing the one and only door to his room, he would stand on the bed and peer through the dusty, spiderweb-covered skylight, but all he could see was the roof and about a foot-and-a-half of the iron grille. Many times he felt as if two tiny feet had walked by. After much effort he spotted the ankles too—yes, they belonged to a girl for sure because he also caught a glimpse of a sari border...he took a deep breath, climbed down from the bed and in a very theatrical manner, beat his fist on his chest and murmured, 'Oh cruel Lakshmi, at least show me a glimpse of yourself....'

'Munshiji, you are just looking, why don't you write?' When Ramswarup saw Govind tapping his teeth slowly with the back of the pen and staring unblinkingly at the accounts book, somehow he figured out that whatever he was thinking about, it had nothing to do with the accounts in front of him....

Startled, he looked at the boy...smiled embarrassedly at being caught, and then suddenly it hit him like a flash of lightning— Lakshmi must be Ramswarup's sister. She must surely resemble him. He looked at Ramswarup's face carefully to see if he was good-looking or not. Then he smiled at his own foolishness and stretched a little. Gathering the blanket tightly about himself, he spoke with uncharacteristic affection, 'All right, munna, I'll give it tomorrow morning.' He wanted to talk to him about Lakshmi, but the watchman and Salim, the mechanic, were right in front of him, working....

The truth was that he was tired. Pretending to be busy all of a sudden, he went back to the accounts. After countless recommendations his name had finally appeared on the college notice board in the list of students who had been admitted. He had bought some books and notebooks on his way here, and wanted nothing more than to get to his room as soon as he could, lie down...and fall asleep thinking of all kinds of things: Who is Lakshmi? What is she like? Who can he ask about her? In any case, there was no one of his own age or trustworthy enough. Suppose he asked someone and

Ruparam found out? But today was just his third day here. Mentally, he went through the magazines and storybooks that he had and wondered which one he should send this time. After a while, after a respectable interval had passed, he could quietly slip in a short letter addressed to a friend. The language of the letter should be such that he wouldn't be caught.... It was in the book by mistake, he could say easily if it was intercepted—he hadn't remembered that the letter was there. There could be twenty different explanations. He smiled at the clever foolishness of his imagination.

This magazine had come from the Lakshmi he thought about so much—she would have touched it with her soft hands, put it under her pillow, placed it next to her...perhaps she had read it while lying down, she may have slept with it on her breast. A thrill ran through him. Did Lakshmi think of him at all? Though he was busy doing the accounts, he began turning the pages of the magazine furtively and abruptly stopped when he saw the dog-eared page—who had folded the edge of the page? A thousand thoughts whirled around his head. He picked up the magazine and placed it on his accounts ledger. The folded page was open. Seeing the markings in blue ink on the page, he almost jumped. Who had made these markings? There were no such markings before....

'I love you more than my own life....' He read the words above the blue line.

'Oh! What is this now....?' He became so agitated, he quickly looked at the mechanic, Salim, and Dilawar Singh, but they were busy with their own work. His eyes automatically slid to the next line.

'Take me away from here....'

'Oh!'

The third line—'I will hang myself....'

Govind was so panic-stricken, he immediately shut the magazine. He looked around him uneasily, had anyone else caught on? Perspiration broke out on his forehead and his heart started beating like the motor of the mill. He hid the magazine below his knees. What if the wretched watchman saw the colourful picture on the

cover and decided to ask for it? He was desperate to see those lines
again; but he didn't have the courage to do so. Was it really Lakshmi
who had made these markings? What if someone was playing a
prank on him? But why would someone play a prank, and why
him? Who would have the courage to do this? He'd just been here
for three days.

He took out the magazine again and began turning the pages.
No, those were the only markings. He read those three lines again
and felt as if an airplane had started shrieking in his head. Govind's
head was whirling, his heart was beating hard, and he had all but
forgotten the accounts he was writing. He scratched his ear with
the back of his pen, tried to look fixedly at the columns showing
deposits and expenses. But he felt as if his heart would burst and
his mind would explode the way a fountain-firecracker erupts...who
could he ask? Who had made these markings? Was it really Lakshmi?

He couldn't believe this sweet truth. I may not have managed to
get a glimpse of her, but she must have surely seen me. Arre, these
girls are very smart. Govind had a sudden desire to get a mirror right
away and look at himself through Lakshmi's eyes—how did he look?

But who was Lakshmi? Widow, virgin, married, abandoned? How
old was she? What was she like? He had a strong desire to get up
that instant, run inside and go pelting up the courtyard stairs—and
wherever Lakshmi was, in whichever room, to shake her hard by
the shoulders and ask, 'Lakshmi, Lakshmi, did you write all this?
You don't know how unfortunate I am, Lakshmi. I'm not worthy
of this good fortune.' And really, the thought of this unexpected
good fortune made his heart contract so hard that tears sprang to
his eyes. Looking unblinkingly at a bulb hanging from a string, he
sank into a deep reverie about his past and his future; then gently
flicked away the tears brimming at the corner of his eyes, as if he
was offering sandalwood to a god. His limp hand was still holding
the pages of the magazine.

Once again he looked at those lines—suppose Lakshmi ran away
with him? Where could they go? How would they live? What would

happen to his studies? If they got caught later, what would happen? But in any case, who was this Lakshmi?

A multitude of questions about Lakshmi crowded his mind, as if a pack of hunting dogs had been let loose or as if someone was cruelly and mercilessly pounding on his head with a hammer. Just as a man falling off a roof feels the entire world spinning around him for that instant, Govind too saw hundreds and thousands of little things shimmering in front of his eyes, before vanishing in an instant. Sitting in front of the old, small box placed on the high, square brick platform, Govind was writing the accounts but was unable to match the figures, and the resultant scraps of paper that lay scattered here and there continued to lie in disarray. Placing both his elbows on the open ledger, he covered his eyes with the palms of his hands...the nerves near his temples felt like they were snapping. He had never seen or heard of such a thing...not even in the cinema or in novels. Truly, what was the meaning of these markings? Had Lakshmi drawn these lines? Maybe some child had drawn them. A startled Govind once again opened the page—no, would a child mark only these particular lines? And the lines were so straight and steady, they couldn't be the handiwork of a child. Could someone have made those markings to upset him for no reason at all? It's possible that this Lakshmi was very naughty and had done this just to confound him.

Though Govind was thinking all these thoughts with his eyes closed, he was afraid that the mechanic and watchman might understand what was going on in his head merely by looking at him. But the person he was most afraid of was Lala Ruparam. Any time now, wearing an old, dirty, full-sleeved, cotton wool-filled jacket, wrapped in a decrepit, greasy shawl, he would come down the stairs slowly, with great difficulty, panting, steadying himself with a walking stick....

Suddenly, hearing the thak-thak of the stick, Govind removed his hands from eyes with a start and found that Lala Ruparam was actually coming down the stairs. The wretch materialized as soon as he thought of him—had he noticed him just sitting around? Quickly, Govind shoved the magazine further below his knees and got busy staring at the papers spread out in front of him. The mechanic and the watchman also stopped whispering to each other. Lala Ruparam crossed the passage and came in.

His eyes, magnified by his thick glasses, looked scary. There was a cap filled with cotton wool on his head, and its mudguard-like flaps meant to cover the ears were folded up, giving him the look of a Puranic demon with horns. His face was full of wrinkles and his spectacle frames were broken just above his nose; he had tied them with string to make them stay in place. His teeth were false and perhaps loose as well; because he was forever moving his jaws to push them back, it seemed like he was always chewing gum. Seeing his jaws moving and hearing the strange noises that emanated from his mouth made Govind want to throw up. Every time he spoke, Govind tried not to look in that direction. Lala Ruparam's head also wobbled, like the bobblehead of an old man with a loose spring. Soiled knee-length dhoti; socks that had been bought in a military scrap market wrapped with bandages that perhaps eased arthritic aches and pains; old, torn boots without laces that gaped open—whenever he looked at him, Govind thought this man's end was near.

When Lala Ruparam came close, he smiled an oily smile to welcome him. 'Lalaji, sit here…' he said, smoothing out a thick crease in the rug that covered the brick platform, a rug filled with holes and hundreds of ink stains. The crease had formed on account of Ramswarup standing very close to the platform.

Panting, Lalaji indicated that he was all right without saying anything. Facing Govind, he sat down in the tin chair, still panting. He had a respiratory illness and was forever panting like a thirsty dog.

As he sat down, for a moment, Govind trembled with apprehension: had the wretch found out? Could he have come to make some enquiries? Though Lala Ruparam, after he'd eaten his meal, did usually come by at this time, he was sure that somehow the old man had caught on. His heart sank. Ruparam was still panting. Head bent, Govind continued working on his accounts. Eventually, he said, 'Lalaji, my name appeared in the college list today.'

'I see!' said Lalaji in the middle of a cough. One hand pressed down on the stick that rested on the ground, the other hand was in a pouch that held a rosary, and as his fingers turned the beads round and round, he gave the impression that one of his arms was without a hand.

The atmosphere was growing heavier by the minute when something happened.

Ruparam had just gathered his breath and opened his mouth to speak when the iron grille over the courtyard vibrated violently and noisily, as if a very heavy object had been flung on it. And then something, probably a ladle, fell on it with a loud clang; after that tongs, pincers…and then it seemed as if someone was hurling a bucket, a pan, griddle etc. on the grille. Water and some small objects began falling through the grille. There was such an uproar, so much loud wailing, it was as if a fire had broken out.

Govind sat up with a jerk—had a fire actually broken out? He darted a questioning look at Lala and was so astonished, he was rendered speechless. Lala certainly looked worried but not as if something terrible had happened and he should rush to find out what it was. The mechanic and watchman kept looking and smiling at each other with sly looks and shooting glances at Lala. No one looked particularly bothered. The noise and clamour grew louder, things were still being thrown about and the noisy rattling of the iron grille echoed everywhere. What was going on? The excitement almost caused his ribs to snap. He was about to ask Lala what was going on when, pressing down hard on his stick, Lala hauled himself up with great difficulty and dragged himself back to the narrow passage from where he had come. As he left, he shut the door softly behind him. Freed of his presence, the mechanic and watchman relaxed, smiled at each other, cleared their throats and then smiled once again, this time without any inhibition. Govind, who had been staring at Lala, now turned to look at them. And when he couldn't bear it any longer, he got up. He shook the blanket around him, which flapped like the feathers of a rooster, wrapped himself in it and, keeping an eye on the magazine, stepped down from the platform. For a while he stood uncertainly, then went to the door of the passage, trying to figure out if he could see or hear anything. In that din, three or four voices could be heard faintly through the crack in the door and among them, the loudest was the voice he had come to recognize as Lakshmi's. Good God, what had happened? Had someone fallen down, had a fire broken out, had someone got bitten by a snake or scorpion? But the way these people were just sitting around, it seemed as if nothing untoward had happened. Why had that wretch shut the door behind him? Now the iron grille was vibrating so noisily, it was like someone was doing the tandav on it. That thin, high-pitched, screaming female voice that he had decided was Lakshmi's was talking so fast and so loudly that—despite many attempts—he couldn't understand a word.

'Why are you so troubled, babuji?' Hearing the watchman's voice he stood up straight. He was saying smilingly, 'Chandi has woken up.' The mechanic laughed.

Govind felt very irritated. Something serious was going on and these rogues were having fun! Even so, he turned around, both anxious and eager.

Everything in this big room and in the small hall was covered with a fine powdery layer of flour. At one end, bathed in flour, the mill stood silently like an elephant made of black stone, with the sheath meant for collecting the ground grain looking like its trunk. Straight ahead, was a motor, from where a wide wooden plank worked the mill. A railing had been placed here for safety. On the wall in front was a big, square, red piece of wood with a skull and crossbones on it and the word 'Danger' written below in both English and Hindi. Next to this platform was a long chain that hung down from the roof, part of a big iron weighing scale. One side dangled up in the air, like the hand of a Kathakali dancer in action, because the other scale was piled with a variety of weights, from the lightest to the heaviest. Lala Ruparam often scolded the watchman, reminding him to remove the weighing scale and put it away at night. But sometimes the flour mill would run till midnight and the workers would start coming in as early as five in the morning—and Dilawar Singh didn't particularly like touching the ice-cold weighing scale at that time. He said that during the war, he'd picked up enough cold guns before going for early morning parades, so was he destined to touch cold steel all his life? And so he would leave it hanging from the ceiling. But because it was right in the middle of the room, he bumped into it whenever he went to open the door and in the quiet of the night he would let fly a volley of Army curses. An old calendar, sacks of grain and flour were dumped at one end; there were also canisters, bundles of cloth, and a sturdy stool on which to climb and pour the grain into the mill. At the moment, the watchman, wrapped in his old greatcoat—a relic from his soldiering days during the First World War—sat hunched on the edge of the cot. His legs, encased in high boots, were stretched out on the floor. He was smoking a bidi and chatting softly with the mechanic, Salim.

There was a burning brazier between him and the mechanic; every now and then, he picked up a bit of the wood or coal lying nearby and threw it in, and occasionally, with a show of indifference, extended his hands or feet to soak in the warmth. Salim, head bent, was busy immersing tyre tubes in a bucket of hot water and inspecting punctures. Around him were ten or twelve red-black tubes, rubber trimmings, scissors, screws, pliers, solution, a leather box, and in one corner, hanging tyres and a pile of ten or twelve cycle wheels. More than half the room was covered with all these things.

When Govind walked over to him, he was bent over the tube puncture, making marks with a pencil he had wet with his saliva (though the tube was already wet and there was a water-filled bucket in front of him). He was laughing and saying, 'This is what the jamadar sahib said?' Then, raising a brow, he said, 'If Lala allows… his daughter has the shadow of a djinn on her, I can get her treated by our Maulvi Badruddin sahib, he'll cure her in minutes.'

The penny dropped for Govind: was Lala's daughter possessed? Suddenly he remembered a Brahmin widow, Tara, from his village. Whenever she was possessed, she would pick up the pots and pans in the house and throw them about, her body would turn rigid, froth would emerge from her mouth, her neck would twist this way and that, and her eyes and tongue would pop out. Who was Lala's daughter? Was it Lakshmi? Oh God, let it not be Lakshmi; his heart sank with dread. Now that the din had died down, all he could hear was the occasional, far-off sound of someone crying. Maybe someone had just had a fit of some kind, that's why these people were so unconcerned.

The watchman said for Govind's benefit, 'Mistri, one day you will really give that poor old man a heart attack. And, listen, your maulvi doesn't have a cure for this particular djinn, do you understand? This is a different thing altogether. Come, babuji, sit.'

The watchman indicated the stool while remaining seated. Though he called Govind 'babuji', he didn't have any special regard for him. For one, Govind was from a small town and he had been a watchman in the city for twenty years; for another, he had been in the army and travelled all the way to Cairo—he considered himself superior to Govind in age, experience, refinement. But Govind wasn't thinking of all this. Leaning on the stool, he asked worriedly, 'What was the commotion about? What was happening?'

The mechanic raised his head and looked at him, then his eyes met the watchman's smiling ones. Stroking his salt-and-pepper moustache, the watchman said, 'Nothing, babuji, a child must have dropped something upstairs.'

The mechanic said, 'Jamadar sahib, why are you lying? What don't you tell the truth? How long can it remain hidden from him?'

'Why don't you tell him?' said the watchman, taking out a bundle of bidis from his pocket, loosening the paper packet by rolling it in his hands as if it were a ball of dough, extracting a bidi and tossing it to the mechanic. He took one out for himself, blew on both the ends, then, looking for a burning coal in the brazier with which to light it, continued in a preoccupied manner, 'You know everything, don't you?'

Govind's irritation grew at the suggestive manner of both men. There was definitely something amiss, something they were avoiding telling him. Tongue sticking out, the mechanic was rubbing the punctures with sandpaper. Whenever he did something with full concentration, he stuck his tongue out, curling it up towards his lips. Looking at the bald spot on top of his head, Govind thought that baldness was usually associated with wealthy people; but this wretch fixed punctures in the middle of the night. Head still bent, the mechanic said, 'Now should I tell babuji the story or break my head over these tubes? The bloody things have rotted and melted, but he won't change them. I feel like picking up the whole lot and throwing them into the stove, we'll see what happens tomorrow morning....'

'What are all these tubes for?' asked Govind, trying to establish some fellow feeling between them. 'They really are in bad shape.'

'You don't know?' This time the mechanic abandoned his work and looked at Govind carefully. 'This is the trash from the two dozen rickshaws that your Lala runs. There are so many rickshaws, they need repairs and maintenance on a daily basis, so employ a full-time mechanic and be done with it. But, no, I'm stuck with the tube-tyres and the rest of the repairs are done by the mechanic Ali Ahmed.' Then he asked, 'You're new here, babuji?'

'Yes, it's just been two or three days. I've come here to study,' said Govind. His stomach was churning in agitation, but he was trying to restart the thread of his questions from a new angle.

'That's why,' said the mechanic. 'That's why you're asking all this. You keep his accounts for him at night, don't you? In a few days he'll get you to teach his son too.' He smiled and lit the bidi the watchman had given him.

'Abey, why are you telling him all this? He's from the same village, he knows everything,' said the watchman.

'No, I don't know anything,' Govind assured them. 'Lala's father had moved to the city, you see, so we don't know anything. Please tell me, what is it?' Govind asked in a respectful, slightly ingratiating manner.

Swayed by his eager curiosity, the mechanic said, 'It's nothing, the Lala's elder daughter, she gets fits. Some say it's hysteria, but, babuji, my conjecture is that these aren't fits, she's in the grip of some evil spirit. The poor thing has no idea what's happening to her.'

'Is she a widow?' Govind interrupted him quickly with a beating heart—hai, let it not be Lakshmi.

This time he didn't miss the way they smiled as their glances met. Taking a long drag from his bidi, the watchman became grave and said, 'Aji, he hasn't even got her married.'

'What is her name?' Govind couldn't contain himself.

'Lakshmi.'

'Lakshmi!' The cry escaped his lips and it was as if someone had abruptly drained out all his strength. His body, that had been taut with curiosity and excitement, went slack.

At this, the watchman laughed in a very knowing way, as if to say—right, you also know?

A very natural question arose in Govind's mind, how old was Lakshmi?

But the watchman asked, 'So, babuji, do you really know nothing about his household?'

'No, bhai, I told you, didn't I, I know absolutely nothing,' said Govind in a tone of surrender.

'But Lakshmi's story is well known all over the city,' said the watchman.

'Perhaps you don't know because you're new,' he said, looking at the mechanic again. 'What do you say, mechanic sahib, I may as well tell babuji the story.'

'Arre lo, what is there to ask? What is there to hide? If he stays here he'll find out sooner or later.'

'All right then, listen yaar....' The watchman began, getting into the mood, 'You probably know, this Lala of ours is one of the city's most well-known misers as well as one of its richest people....'

'Obviously, the one who is a miser is certain to be rich,' said the mechanic.

'No, mechanic sahib, if you want to listen to the whole story, don't interrupt,' the watchman was annoyed by the interjection.

'All right, all right, go on,' the mechanic smiled like an old man.

'During the wedding season, thousands of kilos of flour gets ground here in this mill, even at other times, at least a few hundred kilos gets ground every day. During the war, he bribed some officers and clerks and managed to get a few contracts. You know that whoever gets a military contract has it made. You should have seen how famous 'Lakshmi Flour Mill' was those days. So many sacks piled up, just like sand-filled sacks on the war front. He also made a lot of money at that time, selling grain meant for the military at whatever price he could get and completing the quota by buying cheap, poor quality stuff and mixing chalk in it. He made money from black marketing, cheating, thieving—there was no limit to the things he did. Apart from this, he has a big soap factory and a fairly large shoe workshop. His sons look after those. There is a fleet of twenty-five to thirty rickshaws and five trucks. He has more than ten-twelve houses, from where he gets rent. He lends money on interest. He's probably got quite a lot of land in the village. The saala doesn't have just one thing! No one knows what his other sources of income are, he keeps doing something or the other. God only knows! Day and night, he's fixated on some scheme or the other. He's got crores. And the most surprising thing is he's accumulated all this wealth only in the last twenty-five, twenty-six years.' Because he'd been in the military, Dilawar Singh was fond of talking and had recounted stories of his officers at the front, accounts of his own bravery—all duly embellished with spice—so often that he had become an accomplished raconteur. With every shift in tone, his eyes and face displayed different emotions.

Listening to him with interest, a thought popped into Govind's head: Lakshmi gets fits, so could it be that she had underlined those sentences when she was in that state and they had no special significance? He felt deep disappointment at the thought, but he asked, sounding astonished, 'Only twenty-five, twenty-six years?'

Lighting a fresh bidi, the watchman nodded his head vigorously. Govind wondered, and how old would Lakshmi be?

'And you've seen how his miserliness has no limits! He's old, has a breathing ailment, his body trembles; but if there is even a one paisa profit to be made he will walk ten miles in the sun, panting all the way, catch him taking any means of transport. Come summer and he is bare bodied, a dhoti around his waist—half of which is tied and the other half just wrapped around him. In the winter too it's the same attire. I've seen him like this for the past ten years. Never gets the house repaired, never gets it painted or cleaned, but is always alert as to who is using how much electricity, is there a tap or fan on for no reason. He admitted his son in a tax-free school; he keeps the girl at home. He'll argue and fight with rickshawwallahs and truck drivers for hours over every paisa, night and day he tells the chakkiwallahs how they can save on flour, till they're absolutely fed up of him. Flour worth a lot of money is sold to hotels every day, that's separate. Since the day the mill opened, not once has this household had to buy flour from the bazaar. Believe me, his income must be at least twelve-fifteen thousand, but if you look at him, would you believe it? There isn't even a chair for visitors, forget about offering them paan. Who will say that he's a rich man? He's getting on in years, even then, he's obsessed with money! He is not interested in anything else in the world. There may be meetings, societies, strikes, holidays, anything—but Lala Ruparam is busy in his own world. In order to pay his servants as little as possible, he supervises their work himself. He doesn't say anything to me because he has a little confidence in me; also he needs me the most. But every other servant is sick of him. The best part is everyone knows he's crazy. Nobody really listens to him. Behind his back everyone tries to cheat him, they laugh at him, curse him....'

'How many children does he have?' asked Govind, seeing the

watchman getting carried away by irrelevant talk.

'I'm coming to that point,' said the watchman in a leisurely manner. 'Truthfully speaking, babuji, I'm astonished by how much wealth he's created, but what will the wretch do with the wealth now? People accumulate wealth to enjoy its benefits, but this wicked man is only fixated on collecting wealth. He is so obsessed with it he has completely forgotten the purpose of being rich.' Then, in a philosophical mood, staring at the ashes in the fire, Dilawar Singh said, 'At this advanced age he still has such a lust for hoarding money, when will he spend it? Honestly, babuji, sometimes when I think of him, I feel very sorry for the old man. He still runs around chasing money, come rain or shine. He can't spend a single paisa, as if it belongs to someone else. Believe me, if he dies tomorrow, who will he have collected all this money for? Alive or dead, all this wretched man can do is accumulate money like a servant, he doesn't spend any of it, nor can he see anyone else touch it—just like a snake sits on top of a treasure, unable to consume it, and never allowing anyone else to either. Just guarding it and continuing to hoard it....' And overwhelmed with pity for Lala Ruparam, the watchman took a deep breath. Then, in the next second, he clicked his teeth and said, 'And sometimes I feel like taking a knife, clambering on to the bloody man's chest and jabbing it into him as if he were a piece of jelly. I feel like making him vomit out every paisa he's collected in his stomach. He doesn't want to spend anything on himself, fine, but he doesn't even want to indulge his own children, what will become of all this money?'

'How many children does he have?' Once again, Govind became impatient. Actually he wanted the watchman to abandon these philosophical utterances and quickly come to the main point: Lakshmi.

The watchman smiled at his own propensity to wander off on a tangent, and said, 'He has four children. His wife is dead, he doesn't let any relative even peep inside his house, there's not a single servant upstairs. He's just kept a decrepit old woman there, that's all, people say she's his older brother's wife. She's the one who looks after everything. At least I have seen no one else. He himself has three boys and a girl....'

'The two older sons don't stay with him....' this time the mechanic spoke.

'Yes, they stay separately. One looks after the shoe workshop, the other takes care of the soap factory. This saala doesn't trust them either. He keeps all the documents and account books with him; he goes there every evening religiously to collect the money. But the sons are also very smart, and they are a little fond of the good life. Mark my words, mistri, after he dies, they will make up for all his parsimony.' Then he said, 'And what else did you say? The question of all of them staying together.... Well, brother, as long as they were unmarried, it was all right; but now their wives have arrived on the scene, a child has also arrived, so he goes around carrying him in his lap all day. He has a virago in his house, doesn't he, no one can get along with her.'

Instantly Govind thought of Lakshmi. A shiver ran down the length of his body. 'Who? Lakshmi.' The words came out of his mouth of their own accord.

'Yes, this whole story is because of her, she is the key to this whole treasure chest. If she hadn't been there, where would all this have come from? She's the one who changed his fortunes, otherwise what did he have?' This time the watchman spoke as if he were actually sharing a big secret.

'How, bhai, how?' Govind asked. His head swam. What was this paradox? For a second, the thought flashed in his mind—was he using Lakshmi to earn money? Demon! Wretch!

The watchman smiled once again at his agitation and said, 'His own father was hardly well off, he left behind a relatively poor household when he died. At the most, the two brothers would have inherited a thousand rupees each. Both were already married. With the idea of starting a business, he speculated in the market and lost everything. His older brother Rochuram opened a flour mill. In the beginning, things didn't go well; but after his daughter Gauri was born, his fortunes kept improving. Our Lala used to work there, both husband-wife lived there very simply. Once his daughter arrived, Lala Rochuram really became a lala. Old-timers in their family believed that girls born in the family were the harbingers of good fortune. Our Lala began going to witch doctors, Sufi mystics, making a vow here, a pledge there—day and night it was just one thing, dear god, let me have a girl. And somehow, god heard his plea and a girl was born to him. You won't believe this but Ruparam's fortunes began changing. Who knows whether it was some secret buried treasure or whether it was a miracle, but Lala Ruparam's stars turned. He became convinced that all this was because of his daughter's grace, that she really was a goddess. He named her Lakshmi and, sahib, it has to be said, she really did come like a Lakshmi to his house. In a few days, a 'Lakshmi Flour Mill' opened. He just had to touch dirt and it would turn to gold, he had to but pick up a piece of gravel for it to become a diamond. Then came the war and he prospered even more. He started getting large contracts. He bought houses one after the other—then the trucks arrived. Meanwhile, Rochuram too was flourishing, and both brothers would say with pride, 'In our homes, our daughters come as Lakshmis.' Then something happened, something that changed the whole picture...' Dilawar Singh knew this was the climax of his story. In order to prime the eagerness of his audience, he took a few unnecessary drags of his bidi, finished it and then said, 'Gauri had reached marriageable age. Maybe Lala Rochuram heard a few rumours about her and some boy in the neighbourhood. People started pointing fingers, so he got Gauri married. And that was it, she got married and it was as if everything went to pieces. As soon as she left the house, Lala Rochuram lost a big case, and look at god's ways, his flour mill caught fire. Some people said it was the work of an insider, an enemy within. Whatever it was, once a big elephant collapses, getting up is very, very difficult. People fleeced him and he lost everything. Meaning, he was totally wiped out. Everything collapsed and he had to sell the last item in the house, down to the smallest ring of hardly any value. One day they found Lalaji's bloated corpse in a pond. Our Lala Ruparam was stunned, his ears pricked up, and he mounted guard on Lakshmi. He pulled her out of school. And from that day, till today, the poor thing has never even come downstairs. No one can go inside the house nor leave it. In the beginning, there was some talk of getting a master to teach her; but when he heard that masters who come home sweet talk their charges into running away with them, he abandoned the idea. Lakshmi wept, screamed, but this monster refused to send her out of the house. I believe the girl is nice-looking....'

Butting in, the mechanic said, 'Not just nice-looking.... I have seen her myself. It's like lightning crackles every time she passes by. She's one in a hundred....'

The watchman didn't disagree, indeed, accepted it, and said, 'We heard that she was much praised at school too, but this man ruined everything. He was convinced that the girl was Lakshmi incarnate and that if she went away, everything would be finished. Because of this fear, he doesn't allow anyone inside the house and nor does he get her married. He keeps an eye on every small thing she does, like a policeman. He gives in to everything she says. He honours her every demand, but he won't allow her to leave the house. Lakshmi turned 16, 17, 18, 19...year after year went by. At first she would fight with everyone. She became short-tempered, stubborn. Sometimes she would abuse everyone, even hit them, then who knows what happened, she began crying loudly for hours every night, then slowly, she started getting fits....'

'And how old is she now?' Govind asked in the middle of the sentence.

'Nobody knows her exact age; but at a guess, she must be at least twenty-five, twenty-six?' Lips twisting with disgust, the watchman continued, 'What will a young girl do if not get fits? In the last five-six years, things have come to such a pass that during her fits, she goes completely mad for those one or two hours. She jumps around, shouts filthy abuses, cries or laughs for no reason, picks up things and flings them to the ground. Smashes whatever is in front of her. Starts beating up whoever comes in front of her, takes off all her clothes and throws them away. Naked, she slaps her thighs and tells her father, 'Here, you've kept me for yourself haven't you, come, eat me, chew me, enjoy me....' He gets beaten, abused; he does everything for her, but he won't relax the guard around her for an instant. He sits quietly, head in hands, and listens to everything. What life does the poor girl have? He's her father, so he can't enjoy her and he certainly can't let go of her. I'm too old now, otherwise sometimes I think I would run away with her, and to hell with what happens....'

Govind felt his heart grow heavy. He saw the reflection of the brazier's dull fire flickering in the old watchman's wet eyes.

Late at night, lying in his candle-lit room, thinking about Lakshmi, Govind visualized every little thing he had heard. As the candle wept hot tears of wax, once again he read those underlined sentences in its dim, murky light, hemmed in on all sides by the darkness:

'I love you more than my life.'

'Take me away from here....'

'I'll hang myself and die....'

A question cropped up in Govind's mind: am I the first person to get so upset by this call for help or were there others before me who heard this voice but pretended they hadn't? But can you really hear a young girl's voice and pretend you never heard it?

LORD OF THE RUBBLE

MOHAN RAKESH

They had come to Amritsar from Lahore after seven-and-a-half years. Attending the hockey match was an excuse, they were more interested in seeing those houses and bazaars that had become foreign to them seven-and-a-half years ago. You could see groups of Muslims wandering around the different streets. They gazed at every little thing with such enthusiasm, it was as though the city was not just an ordinary city but a full-fledged attraction centre.

Going through narrow bazaars, they reminded each other of all the old, familiar things—Look, Fatehdina, there are fewer sugar shops in the bazaar! Sukkhi bhatiyarin used to have a furnace in that corner, right there where a paanwallah is sitting now...look at the salt market, Khan sahib! Every lalain here has so much salt in her that...!

Ornate plumed turbans and red Turki caps were seen in the bazaars after a long time. Many of the Muslims who had come from Lahore had been forced to leave Amritsar during Partition. Seeing the inevitable changes that seven-and-a-half years had wrought, their eyes either filled with astonishment or clouded with regret. Vallah! How did Katra Jaimalsingh become so wide? Did all the houses on this side burn down? Wasn't Hakim Asif Ali's shop here? Now a cobbler has usurped it?

Snatches of such conversations could also be heard—Wali, the masjid is still there, as it was! They haven't turned it into a gurdwara!

Wherever the Pakistanis went in the city, people looked at them with eager curiosity. Some fearful folk still stepped aside when they saw the Muslims walking towards them, but others went forward to embrace them. Mostly they asked the visitors questions such as: What is Lahore like these days? Is Anarkali as lively as it used to be? We've heard that the Shah Almi Gate Bazaar has been built anew? Has there been any special change in Krishan Nagar? Has the

Rishwatpura there really been built from money got from bribes? They say that the burqa has completely vanished from Pakistan, is this true? There was such affection in these questions, it was as if Lahore was not a city, but a close relative of thousands of people, and they longed to hear about the well-being of that dear relation. The visitors from Lahore were the guests of the entire city for that day and people were thrilled to meet them and chat with them.

Bazaar Baansa was a derelict bazaar in Amritsar that had largely been inhabited by lower-class Muslims before Partition. It mostly had shops selling bamboo and wooden roof beams, all had been destroyed in a fire. The Bazaar Baansa fire was Amritsar's most terrifying fire and for a while there was the fear that the entire city might burn down. The fire had consumed many of Bazaar Baansa's neighbourhoods. It had eventually been brought under control, but for every Muslim home that was burnt, four to six Hindu homes had also been reduced to ashes. Now seven-and-a-half years later, many new buildings had come up in their place, but there were still piles of rubble here and there. These little hills of debris sitting next to new buildings created a strange ambience.

But even on such a day, Bazaar Baansa saw no hustle and bustle, no excited throngs, because most of the people who lived there had perished along with their houses, and as for those who'd survived and left, perhaps none of them had the courage to return. There was only a thin old Muslim man who ventured into the deserted bazaar that day. Looking at the new buildings and burnt houses, he felt he had strayed into a maze. When he reached the lane that turned left, he made as if to enter, but then hesitated and remained standing. As if he couldn't believe that this was the lane where he wanted to go. On one side of the lane, a few children were playing and a little further, two women were screaming abuses at each other at the tops of their voices.

'Everything has changed but the way people talk hasn't changed!' said the old Muslim softly to himself. He stood where he was, leaning on his walking stick. His knees stuck out of his pyjamas.

There were three or four patches sewn on his sherwani, just above his knees. A small child came crying out of the lane. He called out to him cajolingly, 'Come here, bete! Come, I'll give you something, come.' And he put his hand inside his pocket, looking for something he could give to the child. For an instant, the child stopped crying, but then he pursed his lips again and began wailing. A young girl, around sixteen or seventeen, came running out of the lane, caught the child's arm and took him back into the lane. Now the child squirmed, trying to free his arm even as he continued crying. The girl picked him up, gathered him tightly to her, kissed him and said, 'Keep quiet, khasam-khane! If you keep crying, that Muslim man will grab you and take you away! Keep quiet, I tell you!'

The old Muslim had taken out a coin to give the child, now he put it back in his pocket. He removed his cap, scratched his head a little, then tucked the cap under his arm. His throat was dry and his knees were trembling a little. Taking the support of a wooden platform of a closed shop just outside the lane, he put his cap back on his head. In front of the lane was a three-storeyed house. Once that space had been used for storing tall piles of wooden beams. On an electric wire in front sat two plump eagles, inert and unmoving. There was a patch of sun near the electric pole. For a while, he gazed at the tiny specks of dust floating in the sunshine. Then the words 'Ya malik!' escaped from his mouth.

A young man swinging a bunch of keys came towards the lane. Seeing the old man, he said, 'Why are you standing here, miyanji?'

The old man felt a faint quiver in his chest and arms. He moistened his lips with his tongue, looked at the young man carefully and said, 'Bete, your name is Manori, isn't it?'

The young man stopped twirling the bunch of keys, closed his fist around them and asked in some astonishment, 'How do you know my name?'

'Seven-and-a-half years ago you were this high,' said the old man, trying to smile.

'You've come from Pakistan today?'

'Yes! We used to stay in this very lane,' said the old man. 'My son Chiragdin was your tailor. We had built a new house here six months before Partition.'

'Oh, Ghani miyan!' Manori said, recognizing him.

'Yes, bete, I am your Ghani miyan! I can't meet Chirag, his wife and children, but let me at least see the house once!' The old man removed his cap, rubbed his head, and controlled his tears.

'You left much before, didn't you?' said Manori, his voice full of sympathy.

'Yes, bete, it was my cursed bad luck that I left alone, much earlier. If I had stayed here, then along with him, I too....' As he spoke, he felt he should not have said this. He stopped the words from coming out of his mouth but let the tears that had gathered in his eyes flow.

'Let it be, Ghani miyan, what is the point of remembering all that?' Manori took Ghani's arm. 'Come, let me show you your house.'

The news travelled all over the lane that a Muslim standing outside had been about to grab Ramdasi's little boy. His sister reached in the nick of time, otherwise that Muslim would have taken him away. As soon as they heard this, all the women who had been sitting on their little stools in the lane, picked them up and went inside their homes. They called out to the children playing outside and brought them indoors. When Manori entered the lane with Ghani, it was empty save for a hawker and Rakkha pehelwan, the wrestler, who was sprawled out in the shade of the peepal tree at the well, fast asleep. Yes, there were many faces peeping out from the windows and from behind doors. A soft whispering began when they saw Manori and Ghani together. Even though his beard had turned white, no one had any difficulty in recognizing Chiragdin's father, Abdul Ghani.

'That was your house,' Manori gestured towards a pile of rubble, some distance away. Ghani stumbled for a moment and looked at it with anguished eyes. He had accepted the death of Chirag and Chirag's wife and children long ago. But he was not prepared for the tremors that shook his body when he looked at the condition of his new house. His tongue dried up and his knees trembled even more violently.

'This rubble?' he asked in disbelief.

Manori saw the changed expression on his face. Holding Ghani's arm more firmly to give better support, he replied in a flat tone, 'Your house burnt down then itself.'

Leaning heavily on his walking stick, Ghani walked towards the rubble. It was mostly just mud, with bits of broken and burnt bricks peeping out here and there. Anything that had been made of iron or wood had been taken away long ago. Only a charred door frame had somehow been left behind. At the far end were two burnt almirahs, a faint white coating covering their blackened surface. Coming close to the rubble, Ghani said, 'This is what's left? This?' And it was as if his knees gave way; clutching the burnt door frame, he sat down right there. A few seconds later he rested his head on the door and a sob escaped him, 'Haye, oye, Chiragdina!'

The charred door frame had stood, head held high, for seven-and-a-half years, but its wood had completely rotted. As Ghani's head touched it, fragments fell off all around him. Some fell on Ghani's cap and hair. Along with the shards of wood, an earthworm too fell down and started crawling on the bricks that lined the side of the open drain, just six or eight inches away from Ghani's feet. It was searching for a hole where it could hide, but finding nothing, it thumped its head on the ground a couple of times, then veered the other way.

More and more people peeped out of their windows. They whispered that something was going to happen today.... Chiragdin's father, Ghani, has come, and so the truth will come out as to what happened seven-and-a-half years ago, everything will come out in the open. People felt that the rubble itself would narrate the whole story to Ghani:

Chirag was eating his dinner upstairs in the evening when Rakkha pehelwan called him—he asked Chirag to come down for a minute as he had something to say to him. Those days the pehelwan was the king of the lane. He had a great deal of influence among the Hindus. And Chirag was Muslim. Chirag got up in the middle of his meal, and went downstairs. His wife, Zubeida, and daughters, Kishwar and Sultana, peered down from the windows. Chirag had barely crossed the threshold when the pehelwan grabbed him by his shirt collar, pulled him close, threw him down and clambered on to his chest. Chirag caught his hand, the one that held a knife, and shouted, 'Rakhe pehelwan, don't kill me! Hai, help me someone!' Upstairs, Zubeida, Kishwar, and Sultana screamed in terror and, still screaming, ran downstairs to the door. One of Rakhe's disciples seized Chirag's flailing arms and Rakha, pinioning Chirag's thighs with his knees, said, 'Why are you screaming, you sister... I'm giving you Pakistan, here is Pakistan, take it!' And by the time Zubeida, Kishwar, and Sultana reached the spot, Chirag had got Pakistan.

The windows of the nearby houses had shut by then. Those who had witnessed the scene closed their doors, to absolve themselves of any responsibility for what had happened. Even through closed doors they could hear Zubeida, Kishwar, and Sultana screaming for a long time. That night Rakhe pehelwan and his companions sent them to Pakistan too, but through another route. Their dead bodies were not found at Chirag's house, but recovered later from the canal.

For two days, Chirag's house was ransacked. After everything had been looted, someone—no one knows who—set the house on fire. Rakhe pehelwan vowed that he would bury the arsonist alive since he had decided to kill Chirag only because he wanted the house. He had even bought the necessary ingredients to purify the house. But till today, no one had discovered who lit the fire. For seven-and-a-half years Rakkha regarded the rubble as his property and wouldn't allow anyone to tie their cows or buffaloes there or set up a stall of any kind. No one could remove a single brick from that rubble without his permission.

People hoped that Ghani would come to know what had happened just by looking at the rubble. And Ghani was scrabbling at the mud of the rubble with his nails, throwing it on himself, cradling the door frame in his arms and weeping, 'Say something, Chiragdina, say something! Where have you gone, oye? Oh Kishwar! Oh Sultana! Haye, my children, oye! Why did you leave Ghani behind, oye!'

And fragments of wood from the door frame kept falling.

Rakkhe pehelwan who was sleeping under the peepul tree, woke up, either at someone's prodding or of his own accord. As soon as he came to know that Abdul Ghani was here from Pakistan and was sitting on the rubble of his house, a little phlegm bubbled up in his throat and he had to cough and spit it out on the ground near the well. He looked towards the rubble, as wheezing, laboured breaths emerged from his chest, and his lower lip stuck out.

'Ghani is sitting on his rubble,' his disciple Lachche pehelwan said, sitting down next to him.

'How is it his rubble? It is our rubble!' said the pehelwan, in a voice hoarse with phlegm.

'But he is sitting there,' said Lachche said, a furtive, significant look in his eyes.

'If he is sitting, let him sit. You make the chillum!' Rakkhe spread his legs out a little and patted his bare thighs with his hands.

'Suppose Manori has told him something?' Lachche said in the same significant manner as he got up to fill the chillum.

'Will Manori invite trouble upon himself?'

Lachcha went away.

Old peepul leaves were scattered on the base of the well. Rakkha kept picking them up and crushing them in his hands. When Lachche handed him the chillum with a cloth wrapped around its base, he took a drag and asked, 'Did Ghani talk to anyone else?'

'No.'

'Here, take this.' Coughing, he handed the chillum to Lachcha. Holding Ghani's arm, Manori was coming towards them from the rubble site. Squatting on the ground, Lachcha began taking deep drags of the chillum. His gaze flitted from Rakkha's face to Ghani's.

Holding Ghani's arm, Manori was walking a step ahead of him—

as if trying to ensure that Ghani would walk past the well without seeing Rakkhe. But given the way Rakkha was sitting sprawled out, Ghani had spotted him from far away. As he reached the well, he spread out his arms and said, 'Rakkhe pehelwan!'

Rakkhe lifted his head and looked at him with narrowed eyes. An indistinct wheezing sound came from his throat, but he didn't say anything.

'Rakkhe pehelwan, don't you recognize me?' Ghani said, lowering his arms. 'I'm Ghani, Abdul Ghani, Chiragdin's father!'

The pehelwan examined him from top to bottom. Abdul Ghani's eyes had acquired a sort of shine on seeing him. His wrinkles smoothened out a little beneath the white beard. Rakkhe's lower lip quivered. Then a heavy voice emerged from his chest, 'How are you, Ghaniya!'

Ghani again made as if to raise his arms but seeing no reaction from the pehelwan, he stopped. Taking the support of the peepul tree, he sat down on the base of the well.

The whispers from the windows above grew even more urgent now that the two of them were face to face. Surely the story will come out…then maybe there will be some sort of abusive exchange between the two…. Now Rakkha can't do anything to Ghani. Times have changed now…look at him, fancying himself the owner of that rubble! Actually, that rubble is neither his, nor Ghani's. That rubble is the property of the government! That wretched man doesn't even let anyone tie their cow there! Manori is also a coward. Why didn't he tell Ghani that Rakkhe was the one who killed Chirag and Chirag's wife and children? Rakkha is not a man, he's a bull! All day he wanders about the lane like a bull! Poor Ghani has become so thin! The hair on his beard has turned completely white!

Ghani sat on the stone base of the well and said, 'See Rakkhe pehelwan, see how the world changed overnight! I had left behind a complete, happy family and today I have come here, to see this mud! This is the only memory left of a once flourishing household! But to tell you the truth, I don't feel like leaving this mud and going away!' And his eyes glistened with tears again.

The pehelwan drew his legs together, picked up his towel from the parapet of the well and threw it over his shoulder. Lachche passed the chillum to him. He began taking drags.

'You tell me, Rakkhe, how did it all happen?' asked Ghani, somehow arresting the flow of his tears. 'You people were close to him. There was a brotherly love between all of you. If he wanted, couldn't he have taken refuge in any of your homes? Why didn't he have that much sense?'

'That's how it was,' Rakkhe himself felt that his voice had an unnatural kind of echo. Dribbles of thick saliva stuck to his lips. Sweat was trickling down from his moustache into his mouth. He felt as if his forehead were being pressed down by an unknown weight and his spine craved some support.

'How is it with all of you in Pakistan?' he asked. There was tension in the nerves of his neck. He wiped the sides of his body with his towel and spat out the phlegm clogging his throat.

'What can I tell you, Rakkhe?' said Ghani, stooped over his walking stick which he held with both his hands for support. 'Only my God knows how I'm going on. If Chirag had been with me, things would have been different.... I had told him so many times to leave with me. But he was stubborn, he kept saying he wouldn't leave the new house and go—this is our lane, there is no danger here. The innocent little dove didn't think that there may be no danger from the lane, but there could be danger from outside! All four lost their lives trying to guard the house! Rakkhe, he set great store by you. He used to say that as long as Rakkhe is there, no one can do anything to me. But when there was a threat to his life, not even Rakkhe could stop it.'

Rakkhe tried to straighten himself because his spine was hurting badly. He felt a severe pressure on the joints of his waist and thighs. It was as if something deep inside his intestines was preventing him from breathing. His entire body was soaked in sweat and the soles of his feet were smarting. Blue lights, like the lights of sparklers, swam in front of his eyes and floated away. He felt a gulf between his tongue and his lips. He wiped the edges of his lips with his towel. And prayed, 'Dear God, you are the only one, you are the only one, you are the only one.'

Ghani saw that the pehelwan's lips were drying up and the circles around his eyes had deepened. He put his hand on his shoulder and said, 'What had to happen, happened, Rakhiya! No one can undo it. May God protect the wisdom of a wise man and pardon the foolishness of a fool. I came and saw all of you, and it is as if I have seen Chirag. May Allah keep you well!' And, pressing down on his stick for support, he hauled himself up. As he made to leave, he said, 'All right, Rakkhe pehelwan!'

A low sound came from Rakkhe's throat. He folded his hands together, still clutching the towel. Looking around him with grief and a sense of longing, Ghani slowly made his way out of the lane.

In the windows above, the whispers continued for a while—after leaving the lane Manori must have definitely told Ghani everything.... See how Rakkhe's mouth dried up in front of Ghani! How will Rakkha face people now? He'll stop a cow from being tied to the rubble, will he? Poor Zubeida! She was so good! A forsaken fellow like Rakkhe with no home to call his own, what respect would he have for anyone's mother or sister?

After some time, the women came down from their houses into the lane. The children began playing gilli danda. Two girls of about twelve or thirteen started quarrelling over something.

Rakkha kept sitting at the well till late in the evening, puffing at his chillum, clearing his throat and spitting out phlegm all the while. Many passers-by asked him, 'Rakkhe shah, we heard that Ghani had come from Pakistan today?'

'Yes, he had come,' was the reply Rakkhe gave every time.

'Then?'

'Then nothing. He went away.'

At night, like every night, Rakkha went and sat down on the wooden bench in front of the shop outside, to the left of the lane.

Every day, he would call out to people he knew who happened to be walking by, ask them to sit next to him and give them advice on market speculation and tips on matters of health. But that day he sat there and gave Lachche an account of the journey he had made to Vaishno Devi fifteen years ago. Sending Lachche away, he entered the lane and found that Loku Pandit had tethered his bull near the pile of rubble and, as was his habit, he started pushing it and shooing it away, 'Tat-tat-tat…tat-tat!'

After having chased the bull away, he slumped down lethargically in front of the rubble. The lane was deserted. The municipality hadn't put up any lights, so it got dark when evening fell. Water flowed in the open drain below the rubble, making a faint sound. Cutting through the silence of the night were indistinct noises from the rubble…chiu-chiu-chiu…chik-chik-chik…kirrrr-rrrr-riririri-chirrrr…. A lone crow flew in from somewhere and perched on the door frame, causing fragments of wood to scatter. The crow's activities made a dog, lying in the corner, growl and get up and start barking loudly—bow-wow-wow! The crow sat timidly on the door frame for a while, then, flapping its wings, flew off to the peepul tree. The crow having flown away, the dog came down to where the pehelwan was sleeping and started barking at him. Trying to make him go away, the pehelwan said loudly, 'Durr, durr, durr… durre!' But the dog came closer and continued barking—bow-wow-bow-wow-bow-wow….

The pehelwan picked up a clod of mud and threw it at the dog. The dog stepped back a little but didn't stop barking. The pehelwan shouted abuses at him, then got up, slowly made his way to the well and lay down there, on the base of the well. As soon as he moved away, the dog went down the lane, turned towards the well, and continued barking. When, after barking for a long time, he couldn't spot anyone moving around in the lane, he shook his ears once, went back to the rubble, sat down in a corner, and began growling.

A DEATH IN DELHI

KAMLESHWAR

The fog is everywhere. It is nine in the morning, but all of Delhi is enveloped in mist. The streets are damp. The trees are wet. Nothing is clearly visible. You can make out the bustle of life only by the sounds. These sounds are lodged in our ears now. There are sounds coming from every section of the house. Vasvani's servant has lit the stove, like he does every day, and the hissing sound can be heard through the wall. In the room next door, Atul Mavani is polishing his shoes. Upstairs Sardarji is putting Fixo on his moustaches. The bulb outside his curtained window is glowing like an enormous pearl. All the doors are closed, all the windows have curtains, but every part of the house resonates with the clink and clatter of life. On the third floor, Vasvani has shut the bathroom door and opened the tap....

Buses are speeding through the fog. The joon-joon sound of heavy tyres comes closer and then fades away. Motor-rickshaws are speeding recklessly. Someone has just pushed down the taxi meter. The phone is ringing in the house of the doctor next door and some girls are walking to their morning shift in the lane behind.

It is bitterly cold. The streets shiver and honking cars and buses slice through the fog and hurtle away. The streets and footpaths are crowded, but each person, wrapped in the mist, looks like a restless, lost spirit.

These spirits are quietly growing in the sea of mist...the buses are crowded. People are huddled on the cold seats, some are hanging in the middle of the bus, as if they have been crucified, Christ-like, arms upraised, no nails in their hands, just the shiny, frigid metal bars of the bus.

And amidst all this, from far away, comes a funeral procession.

The newspaper has a report of this funeral. I just read it. It must be news of this particular death. It's printed in the newspaper—Seth Diwanchand, a renowned and well-liked businessman from Karol Bagh, died in Irwin Hospital tonight. His body has been brought to his kothi. Tomorrow morning, his funeral procession will pass through Arya Samaj Road on its way to the Panchkuian cremation ground where it will be ritually consigned to the flames....

This must be the funeral procession coming down the street right now. Some people, wearing caps and mufflers, are quietly walking behind the bier. They are walking very slowly. I can see a little, I can't see everything, but it seems to me that there are some people behind the bier.

There is a knock on my door. I put aside the newspaper and open the door. Atul Mavani is standing outside.

'What a hassle, yaar, no ironwallah has turned up today, just give me your iron,' he says and I feel relieved. For a moment, I was scared that he might suggest joining the funeral procession. I immediately give him the iron, secure in the knowledge that Atul will now iron his pants and depart for his embassy rounds.

∽

Ever since I had read the news of Seth Diwanchand's death, I was on tenterhooks every second: suppose someone comes and says we should join the funeral procession despite the bitter cold. Everyone in the building knew him and they're all decent, worldly people.

At that moment, Sardarji's servant comes racing down the stairs noisily and opens the door to go out. To reassure myself some more, I call out to him, 'Dharma! Where are you going?'

'To get butter for Sardarji,' he answers from the door and, taking advantage of the situation, I hand him some money to get me cigarettes.

Sardarji is getting butter for his breakfast, this means he isn't going to join the funeral procession either. I feel a little relieved. If Atul Mavani and Sardarji have no intention of going, there's no reason for me to go. Both of them and the Vasvani family were better acquainted with Seth Diwanchand than I was. I had just met him four or five times. If these people are not going to participate, there's no question of my having to go.

I spot Mrs Vasvani on the balcony. There is a strange pallor on her beautiful face, and on her lips, a faint redness from last evening's lipstick. She has come out wearing her gown and is now tying her bun. She is saying, 'Darling, just give me the paste please....'

I feel even more relieved. This means that Mr Vasvani is not going for the funeral either.

Far away, on Arya Samaj Road, the funeral procession is moving forward, ever so slowly....

∽

Atul Mavani comes to return the iron. I take it and want to close the door, but he walks in and says, 'Did you hear, Diwanchandji died yesterday?'

'I read it in the newspaper.' I give a direct reply, to prevent any further talk of this death. Atul Mavani's face has a white tinge, he has already shaved. He goes on, 'Diwanchand was a good man.'

Listening to him, I get the feeling that if the conversation proceeds further, there will be a moral responsibility to join the funeral procession, so I say, 'What happened to that work of yours?'

'Just waiting for the machinery, that's all. As soon as that happens, I'll get my commission. This commission work is so crass. But what can be done? If I can get eight or ten machines passed, I will start my own business,' says Atul Mavani. 'Bhai, when I first came here, Diwanchandji helped me a lot. I got some work only because of him. People really respected him.'

My ears prick up on hearing Diwanchand's name again. At that moment, Sardarji pokes his head out of the window and asks, 'Mr Mavani! What time should we leave?'

'The time was nine o'clock, but perhaps because of the cold and fog, it might get a bit delayed,' Atul says and I guess that they're talking about the funeral procession.

Sardarji's servant, Dharma, has given me the cigarettes and is upstairs, setting the tea on the table. Just then Mrs Vasvani's voice can be heard, 'I think Premila will definitely be there, isn't it, darling?'

'She should be there...you should get ready quickly,' says Mr Vasvani, crossing the balcony.

Atul is asking me, 'Coming to the coffee house this evening?'

'I might,' I say, wrapping my blanket around me, and he goes back to his room. In just half a minute, his voice can be heard again, 'Bhai, is there electricity in your place?'

I answer, 'Yes.' I know he is heating water with an electric rod, that's why he asked.

'Polish!' The boot polish boy calls out in his usual polite manner, as he does every day, and Sardarji beckons him upstairs. The boy sits outside and begins polishing while Sardarji gives instructions to his servant: Bring the lunch at one o'clock sharp, roast the papads, make the salad....

I know that Sardarji's servant is a scoundrel. He never reaches on time with the food, nor does he cook what Sardarji likes.

ᘓ

Outside, on the street, the fog is still dense. There is no sign of the sun. Vaishnav, the kulcha-chholawala, has put up his stall on the street. He is arranging the plates like he does every day, and their clink and clatter is audible.

Bus number 7 is leaving. Many Christs, hanging on crosses, are in the bus and the conductor is distributing tickets in advance to the people in the queue. Every time he returns change to the passengers, the tinkle of small coins can be heard till here. The black-uniformed conductor looks like the devil in the midst of the fog-enveloped ghostly forms.

And the bier has reached a little closer by now.

ᘓ

'Should I wear the blue sari?' asks Mrs Vasvani.

Vasvani's reply is muffled, it sounds as if he's adjusting the knot of his tie.

Sardarji's servant has cleaned his suit with a brush and draped it on a hanger. And Sardarji is standing in front of the mirror tying his turban.

Atul Mavani appears again, portfolio in hand. He's wearing the suit he got made last month. His face looks fresh and his shoes gleam. As soon as he arrives, he asks me, 'Aren't you coming?' And before I can ask him where he calls out to Sardarji, 'Come, Sardarji! It's getting late. It's already ten.'

Sardarji comes down the stairs. Vasvani looks at Mavani from upstairs and asks, 'Where did you get this suit stitched?'

'From Khan Market.'

'It's very well stitched. Give me the address of your tailor.' Then he calls out to his missus, 'Now come along, dear…. All right, I'll wait downstairs.' He walks down to where Mavani and Sardarji are standing, feels the fabric and asks, 'The lining is Indian?'

'English!'

'Excellent fitting!' he says and notes down the address of the tailor in his diary. Mrs Vasvani appears on the balcony—the damp, chilly morning is making her look even more beautiful than usual. Sardarji sends a discreet message to Mavani with his eyes and lets out a soft whistle.

○

The bier is right below my room now. It is accompanied by a few men and a couple of slow-moving cars. People are busy talking to each other.

Mrs Vasvani comes down, fixing the flower in her bun and Sardarji starts adjusting the handkerchief in his pocket. Before they leave, Vasvani asks me, 'Aren't you coming?'

'You go ahead, I'm coming,' I say, but in the next second I wonder—where is he asking me to go? I am still standing there, thinking about this when the four of them leave the house.

The bier has moved a little further by now. A car comes up from behind and slows down as it reaches the procession. The driver has a brief conversation with one of the people walking in the funeral procession, then the car speeds ahead with a whoosh. The two cars behind the bier also streak forward.

Mrs Vasvani and the other three go towards the taxi stand. I keep watching them. Mrs Vasvani is wearing a fur collar and the Sardarji is either showing her his leather gloves or giving them to her. A taxi driver comes forward, opens the door and all four get inside. Now the taxi is heading this way and I can hear the sound of laughter from inside. Vasvani is saying something to the driver, while pointing to the procession....

I'm watching everything silently and I don't know why, but now I think that the least I could have done is participated in Diwanchand's funeral procession. I know his son quite well and at such a time, one shows sympathy even to an enemy. I couldn't bring myself to go because of the cold...but the thought that I should go keeps bothering me.

The taxi with the four of them slows down near the bier. Mavani pokes his head out and says something; then the taxi cuts across to the right and moves ahead.

I get a bit of a jolt and, putting on my overcoat and chappals, go downstairs. My feet automatically take me towards the bier and I start walking behind it silently. Four men are carrying the bier on their shoulders and seven men are walking alongside—I am the seventh. And I think, everything changes when a man dies! Last year Diwanchand got his daughter married and there were thousands of guests. There was a line of cars outside his kothi....

Walking alongside the bier, I reach Link Road. The Panchkuian cremation ground is at the next turn.

As the bier turns the corner, I see a throng of people and a line of cars. There are a few scooters too. A group of women is standing to one side. I can hear their loud voices. Their posture, their bodies have the same suppleness you see in Connaught Place. Everyone's hair has been styled differently. Cigarette smoke is rising from the crowd of men and dissolving in the mist. The red lips and white teeth of the women talking to each other are shining and their eyes have a certain arrogance....

The bier has been placed on a raised platform outside. A hush descends on the gathering. The scattered groups of people move closer and stand around the body and the chauffeurs holding floral bouquets and garlands wait for a signal from their employers.

I happen to glance at Vasvani. He is trying to signal his missus with his eyes to go and stand closer to the body, but she is busy chatting to another woman. Sardarji and Atul Mavani are also standing there.

The face of the body has now been uncovered and the women are placing flowers and garlands around the body. The chauffeurs, their duty done, are standing near the cars smoking cigarettes.

One of the women, after placing a garland, takes out a handkerchief from her coat pocket, dabs her eyes with it, starts sniffing, and then steps back.

Now all the women take out their handkerchiefs and make sniffling sounds.

Some men have lit incense sticks and placed them near the head of the body. They stand quite still and motionless.

From the sounds it seems as if the women have suffered a more severe shock.

Atul Mavani has taken a paper from his portfolio and is showing it to Vasvani. I think it's a passport form.

Now the body is being taken into the cremation ground. The crowd is standing outside the gate, watching. The chauffeurs have either finished their cigarettes or stubbed them out and are standing, alert, next to their cars.

The body has gone inside.

The men and women who came to mourn are leaving. There is the sound of car doors opening and slamming shut. Scooters are starting and some people are moving towards the bus stop on Ring Road.

∽

The fog is still thick. The buses are going by and Mrs Vasvani is saying, 'Premila has called us this evening, we'll go, won't we, dear? The car will come. That's all right, isn't it?'

Vasvani nods, indicating his acceptance.

The women leaving in their cars smile at each other in farewell. Some 'bye-byes' can be heard. The cars are starting and leaving.

Atul Mavani and Sardarji have moved towards the Ring Road bus stop and I stand and think, if only I'd got ready and come, I could've gone straight to work from here. But it's half past eleven now.

The pyre has been lit and four or five men have sat down on a bench under a tree. Like me, they too seem to have just come along. They must have taken leave from office, otherwise they would have got ready and come.

I can't decide whether to go home, get ready and go to work or to make this death an excuse and take the day off—after all, there has been a death and I did join the funeral procession.

THE HOMECOMING

USHA PRIYAMVADA

Gajadhar babu looked at the pieces of luggage piled up in the room—two suitcases, basket, bucket. 'Whose box is this, Ganeshi?' he asked. Ganeshi, fastening the bedding, said with a mixture of pride, sorrow, and shyness, 'My wife has packed some besan laddoos. She said Babuji is fond of them, but now we won't have the chance to look after you.' Though happy at the prospect of going home, Gajadhar babu also felt melanchonic, as if he were severing ties with a world that was familiar, loving, simple.

'Once in a while, do remember us and ask after us,' said Ganeshi, tying the rope around the bedding.

'If you need anything, write to me, Ganeshi. And get your daughter married by November.'

Ganeshi wiped his eyes with the corner of his shoulder cloth. 'If you won't support us, who will? If you had stayed on here, we would've been more confident about getting her married.'

Gajadhar babu was ready to leave. This room, his railway quarter, where he had spent so many years, looked ugly and naked now that his belongings had been cleared away. Friends and acquaintances had taken away the plants, leaving behind bits of mud scattered here and there. But the thought of staying with his wife and children was enough to banish the slight pang of grief he was experiencing at leaving.

Gajadhar babu was happy, very happy. After thirty-five years of service he was retiring and leaving. He had spent most of these years alone, by himself. In his solitary moments, he dreamt of the time he would be able to go and live with his family. This is what had kept him going all these years. In the eyes of the world, his life could be viewed as successful. He had built a house in the city, married off his older son, Amar; his daughter, Basanti, and the two other children were studying in senior classes. Because of his job, Gajadhar babu had lived in small-town stations all his life, and his wife and children had stayed in the city, so that his children's education could continue uninterrupted. By nature, Gajadhar babu was an affectionate person, desirous of receiving affection in return. When the family was together, he chatted and laughed with the children after returning from work, indulged in a bit of loving banter with his wife—their departure always filled him with intense loneliness. The thought of spending time in his empty house would be unbearable. Despite not having a romantic disposition, he would remember little things about his wife with a great deal of love. How, even in the summer afternoons, despite the heat, she would keep the cooking fire alight till two and make hot rotis for him when he came back from the station. Even after he'd finished eating, she would heap a little more food on his plate and insist, very lovingly, that he eat it. When, tired and exhausted, he would come home, she had to just hear the sound of his footsteps and she would hasten out of the kitchen, and he would smile shyly. When Gajadhar babu remembered all this, he became quite melancholy. Now, after so many years, he was finally going to live amidst that love and warm regard again.

Gajadhar babu removed his cap and put it on the charpoy, took off his shoes and pushed them to the side. From inside the house came the sound of laughter—it was Sunday and all his children were together, having breakfast. A fond smile appeared on Gajadhar babu's dried, slightly wizened face; still smiling, he went in without signalling his arrival with a cough. He saw Narendra, hand on waist, probably imitating some dance move he had seen in a film the previous night, while Basanti was doubled over with laughter. His daughter-in-law, Amar's wife, completely oblivious to where the end of her sari was, whether it was covering her body properly or not, was chortling uninhibitedly. Seeing Gajadhar babu, Narendra sat down with a thump and, picking up his cup of tea, stuck it to his lips. His daughter-in-law sobered up and quickly covered her head, but Basanti's body kept shaking as she tried to suppress her giggles.

Gajadhar babu looked at them smiling. Then he said, 'Well, Narendra, what mimicry were you up to?' 'Nothing babuji,' said an embarrassed Narendra. Gajadhar babu wanted to participate in the revelry but the moment he arrived, everyone became quiet and he felt a growing sense of despondency. Sitting down, he said, 'Basanti, give me some tea too. Is your amma still doing her prayers?'

Basanti looked towards her mother's room and said, 'She'll be done any minute now' and began straining the tea for him. His daughter-in-law had already left quietly, now Narendra too took the last sip of his tea and got up. Only Basanti, out of consideration for her father, waited for her mother to emerge from the kitchen. Gajadhar babu took a sip of his tea, then said, 'Bitti, the tea is insipid.'

'Let me put some more sugar,' said Basanti.

'Let it be, I'll have some when your amma comes.'

A little later his wife came out with a prayer pot filled with water and, reciting a hymn incorrectly, poured the water into the tulsi plant. As soon as she saw her, Basanti stood up. His wife looked at Gajadhar babu and said, 'Arre, you're sitting all by yourself, where is everyone?' A sharp pain flared in him, as if from a little splinter in his heart, 'They've all got busy with their own work—they're still children, aren't they?'

His wife went into the kitchen. She looked disapprovingly at the unwashed dishes lying around. Then she said, 'Dirty dishes everywhere. No one bothers doing things the right way in this house. Finish your prayers and go straight into the kitchen!' She called out for the servant, getting no response, she raised her voice and called out again, then looked at her husband and said, 'Bahu must have sent him to the bazaar.' She took a deep breath and lapsed into silence.

Gajadhar babu continued sitting, waiting for his tea and breakfast. Suddenly he remembered Ganeshi. Every morning, before the passenger train arrived, Ganeshi would make hot puris and jalebis. By the time Gajadhar babu woke up and got ready, Ganeshi would have prepared the tea and jalebis and kept them ready for him. And what excellent tea, filled to the brim in a glass tumbler, with a full two-and-a-half spoons of sugar and a thick layer of cream. The passenger train might arrive late at Ranipur but Ganeshi was never late with the tea. He'd never had to tick him off.

The complaining voice of his wife struck his thoughts like a blow. The whole day goes in these household irritants, she was grumbling. A lifetime has passed running this household. No one gives a helping hand.

'What does bahu do all the time?'

'She just lies around. Basanti at least goes to college.'

In a moment of enthusiasm, Gajadhar babu called out to Basanti. When Basanti came out of her sister-in-law's room, Gajadhar babu said, 'Basanti, from today you are responsible for the evening meal. Your bhabhi will cook the morning meal.'

Making a long face, Basanti said, 'Babuji, I have to study too.'

Gajadhar said tenderly, 'You can study in the morning. Your mother is old now, her body no longer has the strength it once did. You and your bhabhi should help in the housework.'

Basanti was silent. After she went away, her mother said softly, 'Studying is just an excuse. She is not interested, and why should she be? She has no time, she's always holed up in Sheela's house. There are grown-up boys there, I don't like it one bit. If I forbid her, she doesn't listen.'

After finishing his tea, Gajadhar babu went into the sitting room. The house was small and arranged in such a way that there was no proper place for Gajadhar babu to stay. The chairs in the sitting room had been pushed against the wall and a narrow charpoy had been placed in the middle of the room for Gajadhar babu. It was a makeshift arrangement, like you would make for a guest. Lying in the room, sometimes he would become aware of the impermanence of his situation. He was reminded of the trains that would arrive and then, after stopping for a while, set off for some other destination.

Because the house was small, the arrangements had to be made in the sitting room itself. His wife did have a small room inside, but one side was crowded with jars of pickles, tins of rice, and boxes of ghee. On the other side were old quilts wrapped in rugs and tied with twine and a big tin trunk full of everyone's winter clothes. In the middle of the room ran a clothesline on which Basanti would carelessly throw her clothes. He tried his best not to go to that room. Amar and his daughter-in-law had the second room in the house and the third, in the front, was the sitting room. Before Gajadhar babu arrived, the sitting room had had a set of three cane chairs that Amit had got from his wife's family. The chairs were padded and upholstered in blue and had cushions embroidered by his daughter-in-law.

Whenever his wife had some particularly lengthy grievance to air, she would spread out her mat in the sitting room. One day she turned up with her mat. Gajadhar babu initiated a conversation about the household, he could see the way things were in the house. Very gingerly, he said that now that there was less money coming in, expenses would have to be curtailed.

'All the expenditure is necessary, where can I cut? I've grown old watching where every paisa is going, I've never been able to indulge myself by buying nice clothes or anything I wanted.'

Gajadhar babu looked at his wife, wounded. He was aware of his condition, his means. It was natural that his wife, feeling the pinch of their circumstances, would talk about it, but he was jolted by the complete absence of any sympathy. If she had asked for advice about the household, he wouldn't have minded. But it was as if he was the one responsible for all the problems of the family.

'What do you lack, Amar's mother? You have a daughter-in-law in the house, there are children; money is not the only thing that makes someone rich,' Gajadhar babu said and, indeed, he believed it. But his wife didn't understand. 'Yes, there's so much happiness having a daughter-in-law in the house isn't it? She's gone to the kitchen to cook today, let's see what happens.' Saying this, his wife closed her eyes and went to sleep. Gajadhar babu was left staring at her. Was this his wife, the memory of whose soft tender touch and smile had kept him going all his life? He felt as if that charming

young girl had got lost in the journey of life and he was utterly
unfamiliar with this woman who had taken her place. His wife's
heavy body, in deep slumber, seemed unsightly to him, her face
rough and lustreless. Gajadhar babu looked at her for a long time,
then lay down and began staring at the ceiling.

There was the sound of something falling down and his wife
got up with a start, 'Looks like the cat knocked something over,'
she said and went inside. When she returned, she looked sulky. 'See,
bahu left the kitchen open and the cat overturned the bowl of dal.
Everyone is ready to eat, now what will I feed them?' She paused
for breath and said, 'She used up an entire tin of ghee just to make
one vegetable dish and four parathas. No concern for the person
earning money with such difficulty, here she is wasting things. I
knew all this housework was beyond everyone.'

Gajadhar babu felt that if his wife said one more word, his ears
would start to ring. Pressing his lips tightly together, he turned away,
his back to his wife.

∽

Basanti had deliberately cooked the dinner so indifferently that it
was inedible. Gajadhar babu finished his meal silently but Narendra
stood up and said, 'I can't eat this food.'

Basanti snapped back, 'So don't eat, no one is begging you to.'

'Who asked you to cook?' shouted Narendra.

'Babuji asked me.'

'This is what Babuji thinks up while sitting around.'

Ma asked Basanti to get up and cajoled Narendra into a better
mood by cooking something for him and feeding him herself.
Gajadhar babu said to his wife, 'She's a grown-up girl and she
doesn't know how to cook.'

'Arre, she knows everything, she just doesn't want to do anything,'
answered his wife.

The next evening, Basanti peeped into the kitchen, then changed
her clothes and came out.

Gajadhar babu asked her, 'Where are you going?'

'Next door, to Sheela's house,' said Basanti.

'No need, go inside and study,' said Gajadhar babu in a stern voice. After hovering indecisively for a bit, Basanti went inside. Gajadhar babu went for a walk every evening. When he returned, his wife said, 'What did you say to Basanti? She's been sitting with a long face since evening. She hasn't eaten anything either.'

Gajadhar babu got irritated. He gave no reply. He decided he would get Basanti married off soon. After that day, Basanti avoided her father. If she had to go out anywhere, she would use the back door. When Gajadhar babu questioned his wife about this a few times, he was told, 'She's sulking.' This made Gajadhar babu even angrier. Look at the attitude of the girl, just because he stopped her from going out, now she won't speak to her father. Then his wife informed him that Amar was thinking of moving out.

'Why?' asked Gajadhar babu, astonished and confused.

His wife didn't give him any clear answer. Amar and his wife had a long list of complaints. According to them, Gajadhar babu was always lying around in the sitting room, and when they had visitors, there was nowhere for them to sit; he still thought of Amar as a little boy and with no thought of the occasion, would tick Amar off; Amar's wife had to work and listen to her mother-in-law's taunts about her slovenliness. 'Was there any such talk before I arrived?' asked Gajadhar babu. His wife shook her head. Before, Amar had lived here as master of the house—there were no constraints on his wife, there were regular convivial gatherings of Amar's friends and many rounds of tea and snacks would be ferried back and forth from the kitchen. Basanti too liked it this way.

Gajadhar babu said quietly, 'Tell Amar there's no need to make any hasty decisions.'

The next day when he returned from his walk, he found that his charpoy was no longer in the sitting room. He was about to ask what happened when his eye fell on his wife who was in the kitchen. He opened his mouth to ask 'Where is Bahu?', then, as if remembering something, kept quiet. When he peeped into his wife's little room, he found that his charpoy had been placed in the middle of all the pickle jars, quilts, and assorted tins. Gajadhar babu took off his coat and looked around for somewhere to hang it. Then he folded it and, moving some clothes aside, hung it on the rope strung across the room. Though he hadn't eaten anything as he normally did in the evening, he went and lay down on his charpoy. All said and done, his body was old and ageing. He did walk a little every morning and evening, but by the time he returned, he was tired. Gajadhar babu remembered his large, airy quarter. His carefree life, the hustle and bustle of the station every morning when the passenger train came, the familiar faces of old friends and acquaintances, the khat-khat of the wheels on the tracks, which was nothing less than sweet music to his ears. The screeching sound of the engines of both the fast and slow trains was the companion of his solitary nights. Some people from Seth Ramjimal's mill would drop in occasionally—that was his group, those were his companions. That life now seemed like a lost treasure. He felt as if he had been cheated by life. He hadn't got even a tiny drop of what he had wanted from his life.

Lying down, he listened to the various sounds of the house. The inconsequential sparring between the daughter-in-law and mother-in-law, the sound of water from an open tap falling into a bucket, the clatter of pots and pans in the kitchen and, in the middle of it all, the twittering of two little birds—and suddenly he decided that henceforth he would not interfere with anything that happened in the house. If there was no other place for the man of the house except this charpoy, then he would lie here. If it was shifted somewhere else, he would go there. If there was no place for him in his children's lives, he would live like a stranger in his own house…. After that day, truly, Gajadhar babu didn't say a word. When Narendra came asking for money, he gave it without asking why. Basanti stayed in the neighbouring house till after dark, he didn't say anything—but what hurt him the most was that his wife didn't seem to care about this change. She was oblivious to what he was going through. In fact, she was pleased that her husband was no longer interfering in household matters. Sometimes she said, 'It's the right thing to do, you shouldn't intervene, the children have grown up, we are just doing our duty. We are educating them, we'll get them married.'

Gajadhar babu, cut to the quick, gave his wife a hurt look. He felt he was nothing but a source of money for his wife and children. His wife wore sindoor in her hair and had some prestige in society because of him, but she felt she had to put a plate of food before him twice a day and that was it, she was done with her duty. She was so engrossed in her sugar and ghee tins that they had become her entire world. Forget becoming the centre of her life, Gajadhar babu no longer had any enthusiasm for his marriage. But even after deciding not to interfere in any household matter, he couldn't become part of the home environment. He was out of tune with the rest of the household, like his charpoy in the well appointed sitting room. All his joy sank into profound apathy.

ᔆ

Despite all his promises, one day Gajadhar babu did end up interfering. His wife, as was her habit, was grumbling about the servant, 'He's such a shirker, he filches money every time you send him to the bazaar to buy something, and when he sits down to eat, he can't stop eating.' Gajadhar babu had always felt that the lifestyle of the house far exceeded what they could afford. Listening to his wife, he thought keeping a servant was unnecessary. There were three men in the house, surely one or the other could do these little errands. That day itself, he paid off the servant and sacked him. When Amar came back from the office, he called out to the servant. His wife told him, 'Babuji has told the servant to go.'

'Why?'

'He says it's too much expense.'

This was a very simple, straightforward conversation, but Gajadhar babu was stung by his daughter-in-law's tone. He didn't go for his customary walk that day, his heart felt so heavy. In his listlessness, he didn't even get up to switch on the light. Unaware of this, Narendra was telling his mother, 'Amma, why don't you talk to Babuji? Sitting around all day, now he's got rid of the servant too. If Babuji thinks that I'm going to pile my bicycle with grain and take it to the flour mill to get it ground, I'm not.'

'Yes, Amma,' that was Basanti, 'I'm supposed to go to college, then come back and sweep the house, I can't do it.'

'He's old,' Amar muttered. 'He should just sit quietly. Why must he interfere in everything?' Then Gajadhar's wife said sarcastically, 'He even sent your wife to the kitchen to cook. She finished off fifteen days' ration in five days.' Before the daughter-in-law could respond, she disappeared into the kitchen. After a while, when she came into her room and switched on the light, she saw Gajadhar babu lying there and was taken aback. She couldn't make out his feelings from the expression on his face. He was lying down, silent, his eyes closed.

∽

Letter in hand, Gajadhar babu went inside and called his wife. She came out, wiping her wet hands on her sari-end, and stood next to him. Without any preamble, Gajadhar babu said, 'I've got a job in Ramjimal's sugar mill. Instead of sitting around doing nothing, it's better if I earn some money for the house. He had asked me earlier as well, but I'd refused.' He paused, as if a tiny ember still glimmered in a fire that had been put out, and said, his voice low, 'I had thought that after being away from all of you for so many years, I would stay with my family when I finally got the time. Anyway, I have to leave the day after. Will you come with me?'

'Me?' said his wife, disconcerted. 'If I go, what will happen here? This big household, and then there's an adolescent girl who hasn't yet reached maturity....'

Gajadhar babu cut her short and said in a tired, defeated voice, 'All right, stay here. I said it just like that.' And sank into a deep silence.

∽

Narendra tied up his bedding with great speed and called a rickshaw. Gajadhar babu's tin trunk and thin bedding was loaded on it. Holding a basket of laddoos and mathri for his snack time, Gajadhar babu sat down in the rickshaw. He cast a glance at his family, then looked away and the rickshaw set off. After he left, everyone went back inside, and bahu said to Amar, 'Take us to the cinema please?' Basanti jumped up and said, 'Bhaiya, me too!'

Gajadhar babu's wife went straight into the kitchen. She put the leftover mathris into a container, took it to her room and placed it next to the various other tins, then came out and said, 'Arre, Narendra, take Babuji's charpoy out of the room. There's no place to even walk.'

TRISHANKU

MANNU BHANDARI

'The four walls of a house provide security to a person but also confine him. School-college develop a person's mind but, at the same time, in the name of rules, regulations, and discipline, his or her personality also gets blunted. The thing is, brother, everything has its opposite within itself!'

I'm not giving these examples from some book. I don't have the ability to read such weighty tomes. These are snatches of the conversations and arguments that take place in our home day and night. Our house, the wrestling ground of intellectuals. Here, in the midst of cigarette smoke and coffee cups, there is big talk, and major rhetorical revolutions come to pass. In this house there is more talk, less action. I haven't read this anywhere but, looking at my home, it certainly seemed to me that working was perhaps forbidden for intellectuals. Mother dear, after amusing herself with a light three-hour job, was free for the day. The time left after reading and writing was spent in talking and arguing or lying down. She was of the view that the mind becomes active only when the body is inactive, and so for twelve hours out of the twenty-four hours in a day, she wanted to keep her mind active. Father dear was two steps ahead! If he had his way, he would bathe at his table.

The topic that is discussed the most in our home is modernity! But, wait, don't interpret modernity in the wrong way. This modernity is not about cutting your hair or eating with a knife and fork. This modernity is the modernity of real, genuine intellectuals! What that is exactly, even I don't know for sure, but, yes, there's always a great deal of talk about abandoning established practices and customs. You should kick such customs aside, if you embrace them, you are the one who will get a kick.

Every subject in the world is the focus of discussions and arguments but there's one topic that is especially dear to everyone: marriage. Marriage, that is, ruin and destruction. Conversations that begin on a light note all of a sudden reach an intellectual plane—the institution of marriage has become utterly hollow...the husband–wife relationship has become so artificial and forced...and then marriage is made fun of with much vigour and spirit. Often, in these arguments, the women are ranged on one side and the men on the other and things sometimes became so heated I thought some of the couples would end up divorcing. But that never happened. All the friends continued in their neat and securely organized marriages. But, yes, the tone and manner of the arguments continue to be the same even today!

Now think about it, if they curse marriage, then it is necessary to support free-love and free-sex. In this, the men were the most enthusiastic and at the forefront—as if they could experience half its pleasure by just talking about it. Papa himself was a big supporter! But it so happened that when a young, quiet, and retiring distant female relative who stayed in the house and never participated in such discussions acted on these principles, all that modernity went dhummmm! It was Mummy who took care of everything in an easy, natural way, and by tying her down in a meaningless marriage, gave meaning to her life. Though this is a very old story and I heard it mentioned only in hushed tones and muted whispers.

Actually Papa–Mummy also had a love marriage. It's another matter that from the time I was old enough to understand things, I never saw them being affectionate with each other, instead I only saw them arguing constantly. Mummy had had to fight with Nana, and for a long time. Despite this, theirs was not a marriage of argument but a marriage of love and Mummy used to mention this with great pride. Pride not because of the marriage itself but because of the way she had battled Nana for it. She'd repeated the conversations between Nana and herself so often, I knew them by heart. Even today when she talks about it, there's a flash of contentment on her face, that she did something outside of established norms.

So, this is the kind of house I'm being brought up in—in a very free, independent way. And one day, suddenly, I grew up. I didn't feel the fact of my growing up as much from the inside as from the outside. There's an entertaining incident connected with this. It so happened that right opposite our house was a barsati—a single room with a sprawling terrace. Every year, a few students would come and stay there. They would walk up and down the terrace as they studied, but I never noticed them, perhaps because I was not of the age to have any interest in them. This time, I saw that two boys had moved in. They were just two, but in the evening a big crowd of their friends would gather, and not just their terrace, the entire neighbourhood would come alive! Fun, laughter, music, song, and the passing of sharp comments and jokes on the girls who lived nearby and happened to come into their sights. But their real focus was our house...to be clear, me. If I came out on the veranda to do anything, some remark or the other would fly and land there and I would quiver to my core. For the first time I became aware of myself...and that I was the centre of someone's attention. If I were to be honest, I found this first awareness very thrilling and I felt new in my own eyes...new and grown-up!

It was a strange situation. When they would pass those remarks, I would burn with anger, though there was nothing rude or uncouth about the remarks. They were more in the nature of light-hearted fun. But when they became busy with each other or if they were absent, I would keep waiting...and wrestling with an unknown restlessness. My attention was forever fixed in that direction and I was always hanging around outside my room, in the veranda.

But the neighbours were fed up of the boisterous, loud behaviour of these boys. Our neighbourhood was inhabited by the lalas of Hathras-Khurja. Those who had adolescent girls at home would threaten to break teeth and legs, because for them, the future of their daughters was in danger. The neighbourhood was all aflame but my parents had no idea what was going on. The fact is, they lived as though they were on an island. Away from everyone, despite living in the midst of everyone.

One day I told my mother, 'Mummy, these boys who live opposite us, they keep passing remarks at me. I'm not going to stay quiet; I'll answer back.'

'Which boys?' asked Mummy in surprise!

Amazing! Mummy didn't know anything. My tone a mixture of irritation and delight, I told her everything. But there was no reaction from her.

'Tell me who these boys are...' she said calmly and went back to her reading. I didn't like her indifference to what, for me, was a scandalous matter. If it had been any other mother, she would have taken them to task with the utmost severity. But not my mother.

As the afternoon waned and the boys gathered on the terrace, I told Mummy, 'Look, these are the boys who keep looking and passing comments.' I don't know if there was something in the way I said this, but Ma kept looking at me unblinkingly, then smiled gently. After sizing up the boys on the terrace, she said, 'They look like college boys but they're like little kids.'

I felt like saying: if kids won't tease me, then who will, old people? But at that moment, Mummy said, 'We'll call them for tea tomorrow evening so you can make friends with them.'

I was speechless!

'You'll call them for tea?' I couldn't believe what Mummy was saying.

'Yes, why, what happened? Arre, all this happened in our time that boys and girls couldn't meet each other, and you had to be content with passing comments from far away. Times have changed now.'

I was ecstatic at the thought. I felt my mother really was someone very exalted. These people will come to our house and make friends with me. All at once I began feeling I was very alone and that I desperately needed to make friends. I didn't really know anyone in the neighbourhood and the only people who came home were Mummy–Papa's friends.

I went through the next day with great anxiety. Who knows if

Mummy will keep her word or whether she said it impulsively. And if that were the case, then that was the end of the matter! In the evening, just to remind her, I said,

'Mummy, will you really call those boys?' These were my words, but the emotion was actually Mummy, please go and call them!

And, indeed, Mummy did go. I don't remember Mummy going to anyone's house in our neighbourhood more than three or four times. I waited for her to return with bated breath. I experienced an unfamiliar thrill in every part of my body. What if Mummy brings them with her? Suppose they behave rudely with Mummy? But, no, they didn't seem like that. Mummy returned after about an hour! Very happy!

'They were struck dumb when they saw me. They thought that till now people were sitting in their homes and threatening to come and break their arms and legs, and I had actually turned up to give them a good hiding. But the poor things looked after me so well! They are very sweet kids. They've come from outside—they couldn't get space in the hostel, so they've taken up this room. We'll call them over when Papa comes home in the evening!'

I learnt for the first time how ponderously time passes when you're waiting for something. When Papa came, Mummy elatedly explained the whole story to him. Pride and gratification that she was doing something quite out of the ordinary overflowed from every word. Papa was scarcely going to hold back either. He too was delighted.

'Call the boys! Arre, let them come and have fun, let the kids enjoy themselves.' Mummy-Papa were pleased that they had got such an excellent opportunity to display their modernity.

The servant was sent to bring them over and the whole lot of them appeared in the very next instant! Mummy introduced them properly and there was an exchange of hi-hellos.

'Tanu bete, make tea for your friends!'

Oh crap! When Mummy's friends come, it is 'Tanu bete, go and make tea,' and when it's Tanu's friends, then too Tanu should make the tea! Glumly I got up.

Everyone had tea. There was much laughter and bonhomie. They kept defending their reputation by saying that everyone in the neighbourhood was after them for no reason. They hadn't done anything to annoy anyone. Whatever they may have done was just for fun.

Papa said encouragingly, 'Arre, this is the age for all this. If we got a chance even at this age, we wouldn't hesitate.'

A wave of laughter surged from one end of the room to the other. After about two hours, they got up to leave and Mummy said, 'You should think of this as your home. Come over whenever you feel like it. Our daughter, Tanu, will have pleasant company. Sometimes she can study with you. Also, if you feel like eating anything in particular, let me know, I'll have it cooked for you.' Bowled over by Papa's openness and Mummy's warmth and affection, they went away. But they had actually been called to become friends with someone and that poor someone ended up becoming a mere spectator to the whole show.

There was a great deal of discussion about them long after they had left. Calling those very boys who had been teasing your adolescent daughter to your house for tea so that they could become friends with her, why, the whole thing was so thrilling. From the very next day, Mummy began recounting what had happened to everyone who dropped in. Mummy was an expert at making even the dullest thing seem interesting, but here, this story itself was riveting. Whoever heard it said, 'Wah, this is wonderful. You have such a healthy outlook on such matters. Otherwise, people talk big but suffocate their children and don't hesitate to spy on them if they have the slightest suspicions about them.' And Mummy would bask in the praise, and say, 'But of course. Be free and keep your children free. When we were young, there were so many restrictions on us. We were told: don't do this, don't go there. At least our children shouldn't be suffocated in this manner.'

But at that moment, Mummy's child was becoming the victim of another kind of suffocation because though she was supposed to be the heroine of the play, it was Mummy who had become the heroine.

Anyway, the outcome of the entire affair was that the behaviour of those boys changed completely. They had no choice but to live up to the mantle of decency that Mummy had thrown on them. Now when they saw Mummy-Papa on the roof, they would greet them with a namaste and when they saw me, they would throw a 'Hi' and a smile in my direction. Instead of those mocking remarks, now we actually had conversations…very open and free conversations, and there was just enough distance between our veranda and their roof that we could talk to each other if we spoke a little loudly. It was another matter that the entire neighbourhood heard our conversations and heard them with a great deal of interest. As soon as we'd start talking, four or five pairs of ears and bodies would attach themselves to each window. It wasn't as if girls had never had romantic liaisons in the neighbourhood. There had even been incidents of girls running away from home. But all that had happened furtively and in utmost secrecy. And when the people of the neighbourhood discovered such a secret, they felt intense gratification. The men, twirling their moustaches with smug satisfaction, and the women, gesticulating dramatically with their hands, would broadcast the news, adding generous amounts of salt and spice to it. Their attitude was: We have seen the world, no one can make a fool of us. But here the situation was the opposite. Our conversations were so open that people listened by hiding behind windows but even then they couldn't find anything that would give them any inner gratification.

But things had to get out of hand and they did. What happened was that the gathering on the roof slowly started moving to my room. Every day, sometimes two, sometimes three or four boys would instal themselves in my room and there would be long hours of chatting, joking, laughing about everything in the world. There would be music and singing and rounds of tea and other refreshments. When Mummy and Papa's friends would come in the evening, one or the other of the boys would still be hanging around. When all those people who had initially praised the idea of 'be free and let others be free' saw this type of freedom, you could see the doubt in their eyes. A couple of Mummy's friends even said to her, sotto voce: 'Tanu is moving very fast'. Mummy's enthusiasm began waning and then, the thrill of doing something against established norms completely dissipated. Now she had to face the naked truth that her very naïve, inexperienced daughter of tender years was always surrounded by three or four boys. Mummy's situation was such that neither could she fully accept the situation, nor was she able to reject what she herself had started so eagerly.

Eventually one day she called me, made me sit next to her and said, 'Tanu bete, these people come here every day and stay for so long. After all, you have to study too. I've been noticing that your studies are getting affected. This can't go on.'

'I study at night,' I said carelessly.

'I don't think you study anything at night, how much time do you get anyway? In any case, I don't like these noisy gatherings on an everyday basis. They can drop in once in a while after every five or six days for some chit-chat, but right now, someone or the other is parked here every single day.' The tinge of displeasure in her voice became more pronounced.

I didn't like Mummy's tone, but I stayed quiet.

'You've become very friendly and frank with them, tell them they should go and study, and let you study too. And if you can't say it, I will.'

But it didn't come to that. Because of the pressure of studies and because of the lure of Delhi's other attractions, the hostel boys started coming over less and less often. But Shekhar, who lived in the room in front, would turn up every day, sometimes during the afternoon, sometimes in the evening! I hadn't noticed many things about him when he was part of the group, but those aspects of his personality came out clearly when he was alone. He spoke little, but tried to say a great deal without words and all of a sudden, I began understanding his language of silence...not just understanding it, but replying as well. Soon I realized that something like love was growing between Shekhar and me. I would probably not have realized this in the normal course but after watching Hindi films, I found no difficulty in understanding it.

As long as there was nothing to hide, everything was very open, but the moment that 'something' happened, so did the desire to hide it from everyone's eyes. When the other boys came, they would make a racket from the stairs itself, talking in loud voices. But whenever Shekhar arrived, he would slink in and we would talk in whispers. They were ordinary conversations—about school, college. But they became special because they were conducted in whispers. When love is clandestine and hush-hush, it becomes very thrilling, otherwise it's plain vanilla! But Mummy had a sixth sense that could ferret out every secret of the people in the house. Even Papa was afraid of it. She lost no time in figuring out what was going on. No matter how noiselessly Shekhar walked in and no matter which corner of the house she was in, she would instantly appear or call out from wherever she was: 'Tanu, who is in your room?'

I noticed a strange look of worry on Mummy's face at Shekhar's behaviour. That Mummy would be worried by it had never crossed my mind. In a household where there were discussions about all kinds of romantic liaisons—between unmarried youngsters, married people, love affairs of people with two or three lovers—for such a household, this should've been a very ordinary matter. When you're friendly with boys, it's possible that love can happen. Perhaps Mummy thought this whole situation would unfold like the present-day art films—of which she was an admirer and supporter—where, from beginning to end, nothing sensational ever happened.

Whatever it was, I was definitely perturbed that Mummy was worried. Mummy was not just my mother but also my friend and companion. We talked about everything under the sun, laughed and joked with each other like two close friends. I wanted her to talk to me about this business but she didn't say anything. But whenever Shekhar came, she would abandon her customary indifference and hover around my room in a vigilant manner.

One day I came downstairs, ready to go out with Mummy when I bumped into a gracious-looking woman from the neighbourhood. After the namaskars and enquiries about each other's well-being, she came to the real purpose of her visit.

'Are these boys who stay on the roof opposite your house related to you?'

'Not at all.'

'Really? They are always at your place in the evenings, so we thought they must certainly be related to you.'

'They are Tanu's friends.' Mummy threw this at her with such indifference and lack of hesitation that the woman's attempts to fire an arrow at her target failed and she had to leave, crestfallen.

She left and I felt that now Mummy would pick up the topic and scold me a little. The neighbour hadn't achieved what she set out to do but she did place a weapon in Mummy's hands which could make things difficult for me. Mummy had been grappling with some internal conflict for quite a few days now, but all she said was:

'It seems as if…always busy poking their nose into someone else's house.'

Not only was I reassured, I took this as a green signal from Mummy and speeded things up in my life. But I made sure that of the three hours I spent with Shekhar, at least one was devoted to studying. He taught me with great earnestness and I studied very diligently too. Yes, in between, he would pass me little notes where he'd write the kind of lines that would thrill me to the core. Even after he left, those lines, the emotion behind those words would make every vein in my body sing and I would be lost in them.

Another world, a big, full, colourful world was taking shape inside me. I didn't feel the need for anybody else. It was as if I was complete in myself. Even Mummy, always with me, was fading away and maybe that's why I'd stopped paying attention to her. Everyday conversations did happen, but just that—nothing else.

The days were passing and I was lost in myself, sinking deeper and deeper into my own world—quite oblivious to the outside world!

One day I came back from school and changed my clothes. I clamoured for my food, ate it, cribbing all the while and when I went to my room, Mummy, who was lying down, called me:

'Tanu, come here.'

It was only when I went closer that I noticed for the first time that Mummy's face was flushed with anger. The penny dropped. She picked up a book from the side table, pulled out five or six pieces of paper from it and showed them to me. Tauba! I wanted Mummy's help with studying so I had given her this book when I left. Shekhar's notes had got left behind in the book by mistake.

'So this is how your friendship with Shekhar is going? This is the studying that happens sitting here...this is why he comes here?'

I was silent! I knew it was the height of foolishness to answer back when Mummy was angry.

'I let you be...gave you freedom, but this doesn't mean you misuse it!'

I remained silent!

'A slip of a girl but look at her exploits! The more leeway you give, the more she keeps grabbing! One slap and all this romance will vanish in two minutes....'

I suddenly flared up at this remark. I looked up at Mummy angrily—but wait, this was not my Mummy. This was not Mummy's manner, nor was the language hers. But the sentences sounded very familiar. I felt as if I'd heard all this before and it suddenly struck me like a flash of lightning—Nana! But Nana had died so many years ago, how had he suddenly come to life? And that too, inside Mummy...who had fought him ceaselessly ever since she'd begun making sense of the world...she had opposed every single thing he'd said.

Mummy's 'Nana-type' lecture continued for quite a while, but I remained completely unmoved. If there was one thing bothering me, it was this: how come Nana had installed himself inside Mummy?

And then a strange, tension-filled silence settled on the house, especially between Mummy and me. No, Mummy wasn't even in the house, it was between Nana and me. I can explain myself to Mummy, I can understand her views, but Nana? I couldn't understand this language, this attitude, so there was no question of talking or discussing anything. Yes, Papa is also my friend, but of a different kind. Playing chess, arm-wrestling, extracting favours that Mummy hadn't agreed to…. As a child, I always clambered onto his back and even today, I do the same unhesitatingly and get him to agree to whatever I want. But despite being 'my dear friend' I always confided my personal feelings only to Mummy. And there was utter silence on that front—having knocked Mummy down, Nana was fully in command of her.

I had discreetly shown Shekhar the red flag so he'd stopped coming over and the evenings stretched interminably.

Many times I thought of going to Mummy and asking her in a forthright way why she was so angry. You know about my friendship with Shekhar. I never hid anything from you. And if there is friendship, then all this is inevitable. Did you think that we'd be like brother-sister? But then the thought came…Mummy isn't even around, so I can't go and tell her all this.

It's been four days, I haven't seen Shekhar. Just a slight indication was enough for him to stop coming to the house, indeed, stop coming to the roof altogether. Even his friends who stayed in the hostel couldn't be seen on the roof, nor did they come to the house. If one of them had come I could have at least asked after him. I knew he was emotional to the point of foolishness. He didn't even know what exactly had happened here. It seems as if the mere possibility of Mummy's anger had crushed all of them.

But since yesterday, the tension on Mummy's face had definitely relaxed a little. It was as if the sternness that had frozen over her face had melted. But I decided that Mummy should be the one to break the ice.

In the morning, bathed and fresh, I was ironing my uniform behind the door. Outside Mummy was making tea and Papa was buried behind the newspaper. Mummy didn't realize that I had finished my bath and come out. She said to Papa:

'Do you know what happened last night? I don't know, I've been feeling bad since then—I couldn't even sleep.'

Hearing the softness of Mummy's tone, my hand froze and my ears pricked up.

'I woke up to go to the bathroom in the middle of the night. In front, the roof was in pitch darkness. Suddenly, a reddish star-like light shone. I was startled. I looked carefully and slowly made out a silhouette. Shekhar was standing on the roof smoking a cigarette. I came back quietly. I went again after two hours and saw he was still pacing the roof in the same way. Poor thing, I don't know what to think. Tanu is also so subdued these days....' Then, as if reproaching herself, she said, 'First give them liberty, then when they move forward, pull them down. Is this fair?'

A deep sigh of relief came from within me. An indescribable sensation surged in my heart and I felt like running to Mummy and flinging my arms around her. It felt as if Mummy had returned after a long absence. But I didn't do anything. Yes, now I would speak freely. In the last four days, so many questions had been swirling about in my head. But now...now Mummy is here, and with her at least everything can be discussed.

But when I came home I was taken aback by what I saw! Shekhar was sitting in a chair, his head in his hands, and Mummy was sitting on the arm of the chair, gently stroking his forehead and his back. Seeing me she said in a very natural, normal way:

'Look at this crazy boy. He hasn't gone to college for four days. Nor has he had anything to eat or drink. Set a place for him also to eat along with you.'

And then Mummy sat next to him and very lovingly entreated him to eat. But despite pressing him to, Shekhar didn't stay on after he finished the meal. Full of gratitude towards Mummy, he went away and such a tide overflowed inside me that all the questions I'd thought of vanished inside it.

The entire situation took time to return to normal, but it did. Shekhar began coming after every couple of days and when he did, we mostly spoke about study-related things. Expressing remorse at his behaviour, he promised Mummy that he would never do anything that would give her cause to complain. On the days he didn't come I would talk to him two or three times a day, for a short while, from the veranda itself. This love story, conducted in the open, with the permission and cooperation of everyone in the house, lost its novelty for the neighbours and after cursing these dangerous times, they abandoned their interest in the matter, till such time as some scandal might emerge.

But there was one thing I did notice. Whenever Shekhar stayed a little later than usual in the evening or if he came in the afternoon as well, Nana would start stirring within Mummy and you could see that reflected on Mummy's face. Mummy would attempt with all her might not to let Nana speak, but she didn't have the power to banish him totally.

Yes, this entire business did end up becoming the subject of everyday conversations between Mummy and me. Sometimes she would joke, 'This Shekhar of yours, he's a very limp sort of fellow. Arre, at his age boys should want to loaf about, have fun. What is this constant hanging around on the roof like some lovelorn Majnu, staring in this direction?'

I would just laugh.

Sometimes she would get very emotional and say, 'Why don't you understand, bete, I have so many ambitions for you! I have so many dreams for your future.'

I would laugh and say, 'Mummy, you are too much. You dream dreams about your life and you have dreams about my life as well... leave some dreams for me!'

Sometimes she would say, as if trying to explain something to me: 'Look, Tanu, you are still very young. All your focus should be on your studies and you should banish all these unnecessary obsessions from your mind. When you're older, fall in love and get married by all means. In any case I'm not going to find a boy for you—find someone yourself, but you should have enough sense and maturity to make a proper choice.'

I understood she didn't approve of my choice right now, so I asked, 'All right, tell me, Mummy, when you chose Papa, did Nana approve of him?'

'My choice! I made a choice at the age of twenty-five, after having completed my education—intelligently, after thinking over everything, understand?'

Mummy would say this, hiding her agitation under her anger. Age and education—these are the two points on which Mummy always pins me down. I was good at studies and, as for age, I felt like saying, 'Mummy, what your generation used to do at twenty-five, my generation will do at fifteen, why can't you get this?' But I would remain quiet. Nana's name has already cropped up, what if he awakens?

The mid-term exams were coming up and I was completely focused on my studies. No more comings and goings, and all the music and singing was at a standstill. I studied so hard that Mummy was delighted. Maybe a bit reassured too. After the last exam, I felt as if a burden had lifted. Light of mind, I wanted to have some fun. I asked Mummy:

'Mummy, Shekhar and Deepak are going for a movie tomorrow, can I go with them?' I had never gone out with them but after studying so hard, I deserved at least this much of freedom.

Mummy looked at my face for a few seconds, then said: 'Come here, sit! I want to talk to you.'

I went and sat down but couldn't understand what there was to talk about—either say yes or say no. But Mummy had an incurable habit of talking. Her yes-no wouldn't emerge until it had been wrapped in 50-60 sentences.

'Your exams are over, I myself was making a plan to go see a movie. Tell me, what movie do you want to see?'

'Why, what's the matter if I go with them?' My voice was so

full of irritation that Mummy stared at me.

'Tanu, I have given you full liberty, bete, but walk only so fast that I can keep up with you.'

'Tell me plainly, will you let me go or not? This is all useless talk…I can also walk with you—where did this business of walking with you come from?'

Stroking my back, Mummy said, 'I will have to walk with you. If you fall face down, there has to be someone to pick you up, isn't it?'

I understood that Mummy was not going to let me go, but by refusing so lovingly, I couldn't even fight with her. Arguing with her meant listening to an elaborate philosophical lecture—that is, a fifty-minute class. But I couldn't understand what, after all, was the objection to going with them. Everything was a 'No'. She always said that when they were growing up, they were scolded and told 'Don't do this, don't go there', and now she herself is doing it. I'd had enough of all this big talk. I got up and stormed off to my room. Yes, I did toss this line out before flouncing off: 'Mummy, the one who walks will fall, and the one who falls will get up and get up by themselves, they don't need anyone else.'

I don't know if my words had an effect on her or whether something nagged her from within but that evening she called Shekhar and three or four other boys who were visiting him to our place and set up a proper party in my room with plenty of hot food. The mood of the evening was such that all my resentment of the afternoon washed away.

The exams were over and the weather was pleasant. Mummy's behaviour was in accordance with it and so the whole friendship saga, which had come to a standstill, picked up again. It was as if there was no space for anything else these days. But then again, a shock.

That day when I returned from a friend's place I heard Mummy's stern voice:

'Tanu, come here!'

Her voice was enough to indicate danger. For a second, I was unnerved. When I went in, her face was hard, like before.

'Do you go to Shekhar's room?' Mummy fired a salvo at me. I understood that someone from the back alley had tattled on me.

'Since when have you been going?'

I felt like saying that the person who gave you this news would no doubt have told you everything else as well...and would've probably embellished the story too. But the way Mummy was boiling with anger, it was prudent to remain quiet. Though I couldn't understand why Mummy was angry. What was the big deal if I'd gone to Shekhar's room a few times for a short while? What sin had I committed? But everything Mummy does doesn't necessarily have a reason... bas, it all depends on her mood.

It was a peculiar problem—there was no point talking when Mummy was angry but my silence fanned her rage even more.

'Remember I had told you in the beginning itself that you should never go to their rooms. He sits here for hours at a stretch, that's not enough for you?'

The lines of distress, rage and panic on her face kept getting deeper and I didn't know how to explain everything to her.

'It's a good thing those people who stay in front came and told me—do you know, this head hasn't bent before anyone till today, but today I couldn't raise my eyes in front of them. I won't be able to show my face to anyone because of you. Everyone in the lane is doing thoo...thoo...to us. You've disgraced us.'

Disaster!

This time the entire neighbourhood was talking from within Mummy! It was astonishing that Mummy, who till today, had kept herself aloof from the neighbourhood, in fact, used to make fun of them—today, she was singing their tune.

Mummy's lecture was in full flow but I had switched off. When her anger cools down, when Mummy is back to being herself again, then I will explain to her—Mummy, you're unnecessarily making such a big deal of a small thing.

But I don't know what kind of dose she'd taken this time that her anger showed no signs of cooling down, and her anger started making *me* angry.

Then a strange kind of tension grew in the house and this time perhaps Mummy told Papa everything. He didn't say anything. From the beginning he had stayed out of the whole affair but now there was an unspoken tension on his face.

When a similar incident had occurred around two months ago, I'd been cowed down but this time I vowed that if Mummy was going to behave like Nana, I too would have to open a front against him just like Mummy had...and I'll do it. Let me show her that I am your daughter and I'm following your lead. You broke away from established norms, all my life you fed me this tonic, but no sooner did I take my very first steps in this direction, you began making strenuous efforts to drag me back to the line you had drawn.

I thought up a whole lot of logical points with which I would one day have a proper argument with Mummy. I'd tell her clearly: Mummy, if you had to impose all these restrictions on me, you should have raised me accordingly right from the start. Why did you talk of giving freedom, why did you teach me about freedom if it was all going to be lies? But this time I was so upset, it was as if my heart had burnt and turned to ashes, I just stayed listlessly in my room, silent, lost in myself. If I felt too overwhelmed, I would cry! I'm usually all over the house, chattering and laughing, but now I turned absolutely silent and withdrawn. Yes, there was one sentence I kept repeating: 'Mummy, you should understand that I too will do what I please.' Though I had no clear idea of what it was I wanted to do.

I don't know what happened in these three or four days. Cut off from the world outside, shrunk inside myself, I was thinking of ways I could open a front against Mummy.

But this afternoon I couldn't believe my ears when I heard Mummy yelling from the veranda:

'Shekhar, tomorrow all of you will leave for home for your holidays, come over this evening with your friends for dinner.'

I don't know what internal struggles Mummy had to go through to arrive at this moment.

And that night, Shekhar, along with Deepak and Ravi, was busy tucking into the food at the dining table. Mummy was feeding them as lovingly as before. Papa was joking with them as openly as he always had, it was as if nothing had happened in the interim. A few heads poked out from the windows of nearby houses. Everything was as easy and natural as it had been before....

I was the only one looking at the whole situation with an objective eye and thinking that Nana was in every way Nana—a hundred per cent—and that's why it was easy for Mummy to fight him. But how can one fight with this Mummy who is Nana one second and Mummy the next?

ALL NIGHT LONG

KAMTANATH

'So tell me.'

'What should I tell you?'

'Did you never have a relationship with anyone?'

'No.'

'Nothing, not even a little bit?

'No.'

'I can't believe that.'

'I swear on you.'

'Why take a false oath?'

'You don't believe me?'

'How can I believe you! Should I believe everything, whether it's true or false?'

She was quiet for a while. Then she said, 'Is it necessary that every girl should have had a relationship with someone or the other before getting married?'

'In today's world, it's not possible that such a thing never happened.'

'And what about boys?'

'For boys, too.'

'So you too must have had relationships?'

'Yes.'

'With how many girls?'

He began to think. 'One...two...three.' He counted on his fingers. 'Yes, with three. That's it,' he said.

'So, tell me.'

'What should I tell you?'

'Don't tell me.' She fell silent.

They were newly married. The previous night, they hadn't slept a wink. And tonight, too, it was getting to be 2 a.m. The room was lit by a zero-watt bulb that bathed the room in a blue light.

It was winter. They were lying almost fused together under a silk quilt, indulging in silly banter. And somehow the conversation had turned to this subject.

After keeping quiet for some time, the girl touched him with her soft, gentle fingers.

'Tell me, please,' she said.

'All right, I'll tell you,' he said, and began fondling her.

'Go on...you are really like that,' the girl said, pushing him away.

'What do you mean "like that"?'

'I don't know.'

'Then why did you say "like that"?'

'Because I felt like it.'

'You'll do whatever you wish?'

'Yes.'

'All right. Then I will also do whatever I wish.' And once again, he began pulling her close to him.

'Let me be. Go on.'

'Where shall I go?'

'Go to those three.'

'All right.' He pulled her towards him with some force and again began fondling her.

This went on for a while. Then the girl asked again, 'Tell me, please.'

'What should I tell you?'

'Tell me about those girls.'

'All right. But on one condition.'

'What?'

'You will also have to tell me.'

'All right.'

'What do you mean all right?'

'I will also tell you.'

'This means you too have something to tell?'

'Hisht...!'

'What is hisht? Am I a dog or a cat that you're saying hisht to me?'

'It just slipped out. Sorry.'

'All right, but you will also have to tell me.'

'What should I tell you? I never had anything.'

'Then why did you say you'll tell me?'

'All right, I'll tell you. But first, you.'

'Should I tell you everything truthfully?'

'So, were you going to lie?'

He pulled her close to him. The girl turned on her side and placed her hand on his chest.

'The first girl used to stay here itself, in the house opposite ours,' he began.

'What was her name?'

'Bitti.'

'Bitti? What was her real name?'

'I didn't name her Bitti.'

'Bitti must be her pet name. Her real name must have been something else.'

'Yes, her real name was something else.'

'What was it?'

'Lakshmi.'

'Then?'

'Then what?'

'Tell me the whole story, no.'

'The whole story? All right. It so happened that everyone at home had gone out of town. For some wedding. My exams were going on. So I was left alone at home. That was when Lakshmi really looked after me. She would bring bread and tea for me every morning. Then breakfast. And then lunch and dinner. She would wash my clothes too. She even cleaned my room. She would do everything. You tell me, if someone does so much for you, won't you feel a little something for them?'

'People do all this out of their own interest too.'

'What was her own interest here?'

'Didn't her family object?'

'Her family wasn't here. I told you, she had come here to be with her relatives.'

'Her relatives should have stopped her.'

'Why should they have stopped her? She used to study from me too. She was very good at her studies.'

'Did she stay in your room at night as well?'

'Yes, till about 11, 12.'

'In that case you must have done everything with her.'

'Yes, almost everything.'

'For how many days was she here?'

'About two months.'

'Where is she these days?'

'In her own home.'

'Where?'

'Badayun.'

'Is she married?'

'She wasn't until some time ago. I don't know about now.'

'Does she write letters to you?'

'Now she doesn't. She used to.'

'You must have also written to her?'

'Yes, I wrote a few.'

She was silent for a while.

'Why have you gone quiet?' he asked.

'Just like that.'

'Don't you want to hear about the other two girls?'

'Tell me.'

'Okay, let it be.'

'No, no, tell me.'

'I'll tell you. The second was Shikha.'

'Where was she from?'

'She used to study with me in the university. She was very beautiful. All the boys in the university, why just boys, even the professors were crazy about her.'

'Were you also crazy about her?'

'Yes. You could say that.'

'How does one go crazy over someone?'

'Don't you know?' Again, he started to make love to her.

'Are you explaining to me how one becomes mad for someone?'

'Yes!' He gave her a gentle slap.

'Let it be. I've understood. That's enough. Now don't hit me.'

There was silence for a while. Then she said, 'Tell me what happened after that, please.'

'What should I tell you? She sat next to me in class. Slowly we fell in love with each other. She used to stay in the hostel. Her father was posted somewhere outside. In the beginning, we would meet in class. Later we started meeting outside as well. We often went to the cinema together.'

'You must have done all sorts of things in the cinema?'

'Why, did someone do similar things to you?'

'Hisht...sorry!'

'If you say "hisht" again I'll slap you.'

'All right, I won't say it again. Now, tell me what happened after that.'

'After that,' he was quiet for a bit and then said, 'I really did love that girl. She used to write very beautiful letters.'

'Do you have them?'

'Yes! Want to see them?'

'Yes, please. I want to see them.'

'I won't show them to you.'

'Don't show them. She must have made you swear you wouldn't.'

'You know how everything is done.'

'Hish...sorry!'

But he had slapped her even before she said sorry. His hand hit her with some force.

'Did it hurt?' He began stroking her head gently.

'No...why didn't you marry her?'

'Who?'

'Her.'

'The marriage couldn't have happened. Though if I had been persistent, maybe she would have agreed.'

'Why didn't you insist?'

'If I had, then how would you have been here today?'

'So what if I hadn't been here! She would have. It would have been good for you.'

'Why?'

'Because you loved her, na.'

'But I love you too.' He began fondling her again.

'I'll show you her letters one day.' He moved away and said, 'She was a very decent girl.'

'Why?'

'What do you mean why, she just was! She got a first class in her MA.'

'Getting a first class makes her a decent girl?'

'Does it make her wicked then?'

'Fine, where is she now?'

'She got married.'

'Where?'

'In Delhi. Her husband is a lieutenant. In the army.'

'You don't get any letters now?'

'No.'

'Did you do everything with her?'

He was silent for a moment.

Then he said, 'No.'

'You couldn't do everything you wanted?'

He was quiet. Finally he said, 'I'd marry her today if she agreed.'

'And me?'

'You could stay too. Don't people have two wives?'

'They can have more than two also.'

He made no reply.

'And who was the third?'

'She was someone from Sitapur. I worked there in a college for a while.'

'Who was she?'

'She was my landlord's daughter.'

'What was her name?'

'Do I have to tell you her name?'

'Don't tell me.'

'Her name was Shakun.'

'What did you do with her?'

'What did I do? I used to stay at her place. I used to eat at her place. In a way, I was a paying guest. I used to chat with her. There was no purdah. Slowly an attachment developed. It's all a question of coming into contact with someone. A man and a woman who keep meeting each other will naturally form an attachment.'

'You must have definitely done everything with her. She used to stay with you.'

'Let me tell you something. She was married.'

'Where was her husband? Wasn't he staying with her?'

'There had been some fight with her in-laws. That's why she was staying in her parents' home. Once, while I was there, her husband came to fetch her. But she didn't go.'

'You must have stopped her.'

'Why would I have stopped her?'

'Then, why didn't she go?'

'Who knows? Maybe she wasn't satisfied with her husband.'

'Did she have children?'

'No.'

'Who else was there in the house?'

'Her mother, father, and a younger sister.'

'You must have had something going on with the younger sister too?'

'She was very young. Seven, eight years old.'

'Then you must have had a free run. How old was she?'

'She was a little older than me. Must have been twenty-six, twenty-seven.'

'Then she was quite mature.'

'Why, is twenty-six, twenty-seven a very advanced age?'

'Isn't it?'

'How old are you?'

'Twenty, twenty-one.'

'You're a little girl.'

'Hish…okay, okay, I won't say it.'

His hand stopped midway. Again, he started fooling around with her.

'All right, now, you tell me,' he said after a pause.

'What should I tell you? I never had anything with anyone.'

'Now, look here, don't tell lies.'

'I swear.'

'I don't believe in all this "I swear" business.'

'So how can I convince you?'

'I won't believe you in any case.'

'But you must believe me.'

'Arre, what is the big deal? I'm not blaming you or anything. Haven't I told you everything? As I said, in these matters it's nobody's fault. It's just a matter of meeting someone and forming a relationship.'

'I'm not saying it's not. But I never had a relationship with anyone.'

'Didn't any boys stay near your house?'

'There were many. But no one came to my place. My papa was very strict in these matters.'

'All right, where did you study?'

'Dayanand Anglo-Girls College.'

'Wasn't it a co-educational college?'

'No.'

'No one came home to teach you?'

'A master sahib used to come when I was in high school.'

'How old was he?'

'Must have been sixty, sixty-five.'

'No one among your relatives tried to form a connection with you?'

'No.'

'You must have visited your girlfriends?'

'Of course I did.'

'Didn't they have any brothers?'

'Of course they did.'

'Didn't they talk to you?'

'Why would they talk to me?'

'What do you mean why? These days everything goes. In fact, these days girls themselves find girlfriends for their brothers so that they can enjoy their own freedom.'

'My friends were not like that.'

'So you never had a relationship with anyone?'

'No.'

'That's very unfortunate for you.'

'Why?'

'Only someone who has loved someone knows the joy of love. Or someone who has been loved.'

He was quiet for a second and then said, 'All right, but what about a situation where you liked someone but never had an opportunity to take it forward. Did that happen?'

'No.'

'Or someone who liked you but never made a move?'

'Now, how would I know about that?'

'One can make out everything.'

She was quiet.

'Tell me. Didn't I tell you everything? After all, I'm not going to divorce you now. In any case, if someone liked you, it wasn't your fault that he did.'

She remained quiet.

'If you don't want to tell me then don't.'

'I don't really know,' she said after a while. 'Yes, when I used to go to college, I'd see one particular boy quite often. He followed me to college a few times. I also spotted him a couple of times when I was returning from college.'

'He never spoke to you?'

'No.'

'Maybe he threw some line at you while passing by.'

'No. He would just look and sometimes follow me, then cross the road and walk on the footpath on the other side. He seemed like a simple, guileless sort.'

'This means there was a place for him in your heart.'

'Why should there have been a place in my heart for him?'

'You're calling him simple, good.'

'So should I call him wicked? He never did anything untoward.'

'Is following girls around something that good, decent men do?'

'Then I suppose he was wicked.'

He was quiet for a bit. Then he said, 'He never gave you a letter?'

'No.'

'You swear you're telling the truth?'

'Yes.'

'All right, put your hand on my head and swear.'

'You said you don't believe in all this "I swear" business.'

'But you believe in it?'

'Neither do I.'

'Then why did you say "I swear" earlier?'

'Sometimes these things just slip out.'

'Anyway, place your hand on my head and swear that you never spoke to that boy. And that you didn't exchange any letters or notes with him.'

'Which boy?' she said, placing her hand on his head.

'The same boy you were talking about just now.'

'I swear on you I didn't.'

'Say it properly, the full thing.'

'I swear on you I never spoke to that boy, nor did I exchange any letters or notes with him,' she said, biting off each word clearly.

The boy didn't say anything. He still didn't believe her.

A few moments of silence passed. Then the girl said, 'Are you angry?'

'Not at all.'

'Then why are you quiet?'

'So should I spend the whole night yakking with you?'

His tone was very different. The girl suddenly shrank into herself, anxious, timid. She didn't know what to say.

FORGIVE ME

SHIVANI

Trapped in Hiravati's unusual cave, sheltering from the snowstorm, Sridhar had turned into a primitive man, the bonds of his control broken by a surging tide of emotion; he wanted to give his tired body and mind complete rest.

He always worked hard on every speech of his and for this particular one—given the upcoming election—he had to make sure he knocked down his political rival. He picked up his milky-white cap from the table and placed it on his head. Until he put this magical contraption on his head and ran his hand along its knife-edge, Devi Saraswati, with the veena and boon-giving staff, remained angry with him. After wearing his cap, he stood in front of the mirror and smiled. The impressive reflection was even more attractive than the reality.

Broad forehead, sharp nose, voluptuous Cupid lips, and smooth skin. Sridhar wasn't satisfied with his smile. He smiled even more engagingly. The attraction of that disciplined smile with its tightly closed lips was quite unique.

Who could tell he was fifty-five years old? What was the life-giving nectar-like herb he fed his black hair? Last year, during an overseas trip, this very question had been addressed to him in a roundabout way by many foreigners who had left their youthful years behind them.

The gentle, sweet-voiced Indian had given a concise explanation for this illusion of youth, 'The secret of my eternal youth—a healthy mind and a healthy body.' Then he would reveal his personality, as if he were opening a velvet box, and enchant the crowd by showing them the two dazzling rows of his small pomegranate seed-like teeth.

Pretty, young foreign women, holding on to their youth as if it was something they had tied up in a knot that would go with them to their graves, would surround him and ask, 'Excuse me, but where did you get these dentures made? We'd like to get them made too.'

'You will have to go very far,' he would say with a laugh, pointing to the sky with his finger. 'Fortunately, most Indians have only one dentist, the Almighty.'

And the pretty, young foreign women would stare at him in disbelief.

Today, once again, he looked at the same immaculate, much discussed set of teeth as he stood in front of the mirror, hands linked, practising the speech he was to deliver the next day. This was his daily routine. Whether it was the Vidhan Sabha or a public gathering, he never jumped into the arena without a full rehearsal in front of the mirror. That's why there was a permanent varnish-like glow of self-assurance on his round face.

He was not like some of his colleagues who didn't bother to do any homework for their speeches and therefore blanked out in the middle, wandered off topic and ended up looking very foolish. Sometimes their silly antics made him hang his head in shame. Their secretaries wrote disconnected speeches in flowery language; and they would put on a crisp sherwani and cap, and then give the speech as if they were reciting a dirge or lament. Flowery language wasn't everything. The topic in question had its own importance, but his foolish fraternity didn't seem to know that. Who could explain this to them? As long as they heard the sound of people clapping and were gifted flower garlands, they were happy. But Sridhar had begun to understand people. You could no longer deceive today's intelligent public. That's why he always kept his mind ready, and overflowing with knowledge. His choice of words and the vitality, energy and modulation of his voice had within it the rhythm of dhrupad-dhamaar. Just like a clever magician traps his audience in a web of artful utterances as he releases a fluttering pigeon from his hands, makes it disappear and, to further confuse his viewers, moves the big toe of his foot (covered with a sheet) to make it seem as if that was the same pigeon moving its head.

'There it is, there it is. He's hidden it there,' the audience would say. 'What, this? This is the big toe of my foot, bhai.'

By removing the sheet and moving the big toe of his foot, a clever magician manages to make the audience that thinks it's smarter than him feel abashed. With numerous such juicy little turns, that lively speaker catches even the severest critic in the illusory net he creates with his melodious voice. The attractiveness of Sridhar's personality may well have been a gift of the Almighty, but his abilities were not God-given. There was a long history of tireless hard work behind that prowess.

Sridhar was born into an ordinary home. His father was the priest of a Shiv temple, his mother died the day of his birth; he was born under an unlucky constellation. Subsisting on a diet of fat red mountain rice and salt, he would cross miles of hilly terrain to go to school. He was just eight when his father too passed away. Afraid of what people would say, his tau, his father's elder brother, took him in. The ill-treatment meted out to him by his tai and his daily negotiation of the narrow mountain paths that climbed and dipped, made him adept, early on, at tackling the ups and downs of life. That's why, the moment he reached high office, he sought, with all the energy at his command, to rectify the educational facilities in his backward birthplace. It was the result of his unswerving intent and dedication that today, those silent inaccessible peaks where you couldn't even hear the chirping of birds once, now resounded with expositions in subjects like history, geography, and arithmetic. In some places he had even opened mobile schools. The moment it began snowing, mules carrying the headmaster, teachers, students, indeed the entire school, would descend into the valley. That's why he could afford to sit back, content and unconcerned, and get victory banners stitched, not just for one but for the next many elections. The public didn't have the courage to even utter a squeak in the middle of a speech by this gentle saint in his warm leggings and sherwani, and white, crisply folded cap. Each and every well-chosen sentence of his speech would effortlessly segue into the next, like a string of pearls. So much so that he knew beforehand which utterance of his would evoke thunderous applause and would pause at the appropriate moments in his speech. This devious political player understood very well when to thrill his listeners by talking in their local language, and when to mention the international renown he had acquired without making it sound as if he were boasting. Suddenly he stood in front of the mirror in an arrogant Napoleon-like pose, a man who didn't think much of anyone else. His arrogance wasn't based on lies. Villages that had never even seen kerosene lamps were now bathed in electricity harnessed from the swift-flowing Alaknanda, all thanks to him. But had the crown that was his cap made him a badshah just like that? Hadn't his ribs been pounded into dust by merciless police lathis? Hadn't the terrible white soldiers with their batons given him a long wound between his thick, bow-shaped eyebrows, leaving him with a permanent mark that was like a decoration, a victory sign of the fight for freedom? And his youth, imprisoned—voluntarily—within the four walls of Almora jail, then scorched by the intense heat and burning summer winds in Naini jail, could that be forgotten so easily? But was it just love for the country that had made him sacrifice everything? All of a sudden, his elation faded. Why had he run away from the village? Why had he deliberately gone on an unnecessary dharna in front of the English commissioner's bungalow, eagerly holding out his wrists to accept handcuffs as if they were rakhis?

Sridhar's white cap became drenched in sweat.

Yesterday, flying over his village, he had seen from the window of his plane his Taj Mahal, his long-forgotten monument of love, and he had been unable to sleep the whole night.

His lips quivered as he let out a deep breath. He took off his cap and, fanning himself with it, sank down into an armchair.

That bitter taste hadn't left his mouth even after twenty-five years. Half-lying on the armchair, eyes closed, Sridhar himself began to pick at the old wounds of his memories.

In his early manhood, his moustache had appeared on his face like a new guest. Fed up of his tai's ill-treatment, he had started living with a missionary mem who lived at the boundary of the village. People said that the old woman had taken him to the church with her and made a pukka Christian out of him. He didn't become a Christian, but the love and discipline the foreign mem gave him definitely made a man of him. Before she died, the selfless old woman ensured that he passed the university exam. It is true that the poor thing had spent her meagre savings on Sridhar's education, but she left behind an everlasting legacy in the form of a Kuber-like treasury for her good-looking adopted son—her gentleness, sweetness in speech, and sincere, honest behaviour. This was the legacy that enabled Sridhar to occupy a place of high importance in the hearts of the villagers. Not just in his own village—the unique combination of imagination and wisdom in this justice-loving young man had left its stamp on far-flung villages too. Whereas once villagers would go to the court in Almora, for insignificant matters or for issues of land or jewellery, now Sridhar would slice through the most difficult, festering matters with his surgically sharp legal knife. He had been unanimously chosen as the leader of the village. There was just one problem. Their popular leader was a number one runaway. The villagers had requested him many times to permanently take on the post of the village judge, but Sridhar was an inveterate wanderer! Today he'd be at the ashram of an aghori baba, tomorrow at Sabarmati. Whenever he would come to the village, all sorts of cases would be presented in his court. One night someone had cut three or four steps in another's field and stealthily incorporated them into his own, someone else had run off with his brother's beautiful wife while the brother was away in the army.

In each and every case, he would find out who was guilty and who was innocent. People said he had done Parthiv pooja in a Shiv temple and received this unique boon from Shivji. His decisions were always acceptable to both sides.

It was during a strange case in his village that he first set eyes on that Sadie Thomson whose legendary tales of beauty and depravity he had been hearing about for quite some time. It was as if the Maugham heroine, the insolent Sadie herself was sitting there, wearing a lehenga-odhni. The case had been slapped against her by her twin sister Pirbhavti; behind the two women stood a big crowd consisting of the entire village.

'Do justice, Lal sahib!' That's how everyone addressed the adopted son of the elderly foreign woman. 'I braved the animosity of her in-laws and clasped this snake to my bosom and in just one month she bit me.' Grabbing her by the hair, Piru threw her to the ground at Sridhar's feet, and landed a kick for good measure.

A hesitant Sridhar stood up hastily. But that tall, slim Kshatrani with manly wide shoulders flicked the dust from her clothes and stood up, as if she'd fallen only because her foot had slipped. There was not a hint of shame or mortification on her face, nor did she respond to the way her sister had insulted her in a public gathering. But her bright, lovely face reddened for an instant. The next moment, the insolent young woman sat down on a nearby mound, chewing at a blade of grass as if she were some sort of queen. The young judge was flummoxed by this Bhuwal Sanyasi kind of case. Dhansingh's wife, Piru, had brought home her beautiful twin sister, Hiru, a month ago. Her sister's husband had been a gang coolie. Some months ago, the dynamite that had blown apart cliffs had also blown Hiru's good fortune to smithereens. Since then, Pirbhavti grew more and more distraught as she heard the stories of her eighteen-year-old sister's misfortunes: her mother-in-law burnt her with a hot coal, her brother-in-law hit her on her forehead and so on. One day she brought Hiru home. But a month had barely gone by when Hiravati—while Pirbhavti was absent—attacked her sister's marital sanctity. Pirbhavti caught her red-handed.

Meanwhile the guilty Dhansingh was trying to paint himself as completely blameless in his wife's eyes. 'God created two similar faces at one moment, you do justice, Sarkar, is it my fault or the Almighty's fault? I admit I caught this girl by the hand and clasped her to my chest, but she also came willy-nilly into my embrace, laughing all the while. The same face, same dhoti, same laughter. Now was bloody Dhansingh wearing pumpkin spectacles!'

Dhansingh's cheap joke about pumpkin spectacles was much appreciated by the crowd and Sridhar had to stand up to stop a particularly loud wave of laughter. 'Brothers, you know I don't like this kind of laughing and joking in the panchayat. Dhansingh Thakur should say whatever he has to say clearly.'

'Now how much clearer can I be, my provider?' Dhansingh Thakur was enjoying the situation. 'Shall I remove my dhoti and become naked? What else can I say to the panchayat? I swear on the Ganga, this girl kept looking at me and laughing. If she'd said just once "I'm your sister-in-law," would I have touched her?'

Sitting on the mound, that girl continued looking at him and laughing. Sridhar glanced at both the sisters. It was true, they looked like they'd been created from the same mould. The only difference was the difference between two kinds of dhotis—one still crisp, yet to see its first wash and the other washed umpteen times by the dhobhi.

'This shameless man is lying!' Pirbhavti said, looking at her husband with loathing, standing straight, chest out, in the midst of the members of the panchayat.

'Look at my condition, Lal sahib!' Her voice trembled in agitation. 'Isn't my skirt tied at the neck? I am so obviously pregnant and this girl has such a flat stomach.'

This argument, as if made by some clever criminal lawyer, at once complicated the case. After adequately displaying the bulge of the final days of her pregnancy, she sat down, panting like a dog.

What she said was right. The two sisters' faces might be the same, but there was no possibility of confusion regarding the state of their bodies.

The slender, beautiful girl sitting on the mound chewing a blade of grass continued to look enigmatic. The panchayat members retired to the back of a smelly cowshed to discuss the matter with Sridhar. This was the usual custom of this unique court before it gave its final verdict.

Who knows what Lal sahib will decide! His decisions have always been matchless.

Sridhar's grave voice echoed as it struck the mountain temple with the force of a kettledrum, 'Brothers, the jury says Dhansingh Thakur is innocent.'

'Bless you, Lal sahib,' Dhansingh's five brothers, like the five Pandavas, began throwing their caps in the air.

'Maybe,' Sridhar continued, 'maybe Thakur could only see his sister-in-law's face in the dark and not her body. And both the sisters' faces are exactly the same. You will agree to this….' Several pairs of eyes swung in unison towards the face of the leading lady of this drama. 'It is definitely Hiravati devi's fault. Could you not scream out of fear and panic?'

By asking this question, Sridhar was being kind, trying to loosen the reins on an intractable filly, perhaps hoping that she would take the opportunity this question offered her and say yes, I panicked. But she remained silent, head bowed, smiling in that enigmatic way of hers. The justice-loving Sridhar's blood boiled looking at this perverse young woman and her blatant indifference to any wrongdoing on her part. Even before, he had received anonymous letters from this village asking for the removal of the whore Hiravati who had landed in the village from somewhere else.

'Hiravati devi, you will be given ten more minutes. If you still can't say anything in your defence, the members of the panchayat will have to give their verdict,' said Sridhar in a firm voice.

Hiravati looked at Sridhar indifferently, then fixed her gaze on the red sun sinking behind the Dronagiri mountains like a ball of fire, as if she would drown the panchayat's meaningless query with the sun. Forget ten minutes, even if she were given ten years, Hiravati would have perhaps continued smiling in that philosophical way.

Defeated, the members of the panchayat gave their verdict: because both sisters had the same features, and the difference in their bodies was not permanent, after she was free of her pregnancy, Pirbhavti would once again become the exact image of her twin sister and the possibility of Thakur Dhansingh repeating his deadly mistake would increase manifold. And so Shrimati Hiravati was ordered to leave the boundary of the village within twelve hours.

As soon as she heard the verdict, Hiravati stood up and turned to look at Sridhar, smiling. She opened her mouth for the first time, 'All right, panchon! From today I will live in the leper sahib's cave. That is outside the border of your village, isn't it?'

Once again, she smiled her coquettish smile, slaying the flirtatious young men of the village. But the crowd was struck dumb. What was this girl saying? She was going to stay in the kodhi sahib's cave? Long ago, a foreign painter had started living in the rail tunnel-like, naturally formed dark cave that was surrounded by sweet apple, pear, walnut, and wild fig trees. According to the villagers' stories, the cave was now the permanent home of that same sahib's spirit. When the foreigner had come to live in the cave, he had hidden the evidence of his ghastly disease on his Greek god-like handsome body so that there was no outward sign of it. The villagers used to call him 'Padri sahib'. But slowly, like a ruthless enemy hiding in a ditch, his disease attacked him and, defenceless, he could not battle it. First the fingers of his hands went, then his eyelids. And within a year, he started limping badly. For a while, using his stump-like hands, he decorated the cave walls with his extraordinary art. But one day, the paintbrush fell from his hands. However, sahib was still not willing to accept defeat. The artistic hands that had blessed a paintbrush now picked up a spade. He brought saplings of golden apple and pear trees and with his deformed hands, the kodhi sahib created what was to become a heavenly garden of fruit and flowers. It was true that he would not live long enough to taste the fruit, but don't people who drink the sweet water from a well remember the person who had dug the well?

Meanwhile, the disease had spread everywhere. Eventually perhaps his mental agony became even more unbearable than his physical agony. He had once taught the son of a milkman, so every day the boy would pour a little milk into a mug left out on the ledge.

One day when the boy came, the mug wasn't there. He peeped in through the window, let out a scream and ran away. Sahib's lifeless body was swaying as it hung from an unseen peg on the cave wall.

After that, no one had the courage to go there. A couple of missionaries came from Almora, buried him in his garden and went away. Every year, kodhi sahib's garden, with its gloriously ripening apples and pears, would blossom in vain, only to shrivel and wither away like a flower whose perfume no one had bothered to inhale. People said that every evening, kodhi sahib, swinging from the roof of the cave, would jump down and go to his garden, which he would guard with great vigilance. Listening to Hiravati's superhuman vow to live in that very same cave, her sister said, 'Huh, we've heard many such people pledging to live in that cave!'

But when, on the third day, someone saw that this audacious girl had actually had the gall to go to the bazaar to sell the golden apples from sahib's garden, the entire village was stunned. In a few hours, after she had sold all the apples in her basket and was on her way to her new home, smiling, carrying bundles of household goods, the village women started whispering to each other, 'Did you see the size of those apples and peaches, like big round bombs! That's because the manure is from the kodhi sahib's bones!'

After that, every third day, Hiravati would place baskets full of fruit on her head and, body swaying, walk to the bazaar. Sometimes she would sell pears, sometimes walnuts and occasionally bhindi, which were like the monstrous fingers of some massive demon. 'Seems like this wanton girl has ensnared the kodhi sahib's spirit, otherwise where did this unseasonal bhindi come from?' the women would say.

But whether the bhindi was from this world or another, it would sell in a jiffy and the basket would fill with make-up, beauty products and toiletries. Sometimes a square mirror lying in the basket would dazzle the eyes of village girls who were of the same age as Hiravati. Sometimes the sight of shiny red and green silken bangles on those fair hands that looked like dainty lotus stems would make everyone jealous. Hiravati too deliberately kept tossing the fuel of her growing prosperity into the fire of envy that the married women of the village burned in. Kodhi sahib's apples that were as big and round as bombs gave a rosy hue to her cheeks. Because of her daily fruit diet, this wood nymph's lovely face had a flawless glow, like a newborn baby's, as if someone had smoothened it with butter. Groups of flirtatious young village boys began, on purpose, to haunt the path she took to sell her fruits. For one, ever since she had started living in that spooky cave, her stock had shot up among the younger lot in the village. That mountain peak was the notorious haunt of lions and bears. On top of that, climbing and descending the steep three-mile incline every day was not a joke. And then the presence of kodhi sahib's spirit after coming home at the end of day. 'The witch is doing some black magic in the cremation ground,' her own sister went around saying. But that enticing, mysterious cave-dwelling Kapalkundala didn't care. From the window of the Shiv temple, Sridhar could clearly see Hiravati's long cave on the upturned nose of the mountain top. Sometimes a lamp would flicker there, like a firefly, and sometimes a plume of smoke would hover above the cave's chimney. 'Is Hiravati really doing black magic in the cremation ground?' Sridhar would wonder.

He had seen village boys, middle-aged men, even toothless old men watch with greedy eyes as that rare beauty made her way down narrow mountain paths. The seductive swing of her hips as she balanced bundles of grass on her head was not deliberate. That alluring suppleness was a God-given gift to every young Kumaoni woman who cut and sold grass. That perfect swinging walk with the straight back of a trained dancer, for which air hostesses who fly high in the skies undergo months of disciplined training, balancing a book on their heads, comes naturally to young girls from remote hills as soon as they start carrying those inhumanly big loads of grass on their heads.

There would be whistling noises when Hiravati, balancing a big bundle of grass on her head, would walk down with her dancer's gait. The large dupatta would be tied tightly at the waist, and as the buttons of the well-fitting waistcoat popped open, they would reveal the gentle rise-and-fall of a web of blue-and-yellow necklaces, even as her feet moved on the ground with regular footsteps, as if to a musical, poetic rhythm. 'I have to remove Hiravati's inauspicious shadow from my pure village,' Sridhar would reiterate this resolve to himself every day. But Hiravati could not be given any punishment now. She was outside the boundary of the village. Recently, the immoral Hiravati had started giving him an even bigger headache. The Shiv temple was at the gate to the village and every day when she passed by, she would, for no reason at all, cough, clear her throat, and loudly ring the temple bells.

Saying 'Shambhu, harhar!' she would sometimes rattle the chain of his door, and add, 'Get up, judge sahib! It's time for your court.'

The sound of her frivolous laughter was like poison to Sridhar. He would swallow his anger and say nothing. First of all, she was a woman, and on top of that, such a woman, without any self-respect! Why talk to her at all. He would pull his quilt up over his head and go back to sleep. One day Hiravati landed up earlier than usual. She didn't—perhaps deliberately—ring the temple bells. The night was almost over when Sridhar awoke to the sound of someone whispering. It was the month of Kartik. Maybe it was one of the women who came for Parthiv-puja and bathed the Shivling with milk and curd. Or maybe a dog had wandered in to lick the Shivling. Sridhar picked up a lathi and tip toed to the window. Just yesterday, a black bitch had entered and desecrated the milky Shivling.

'I couldn't catch her yesterday, I'll make sure I break her back today,' thought Sridhar as he peered through the window. But it was another shadow that was desecrating the Shiv temple with her impure presence. Kneeling before the Shivling, eyes closed, Hiravati was singing, her voice sweet, tender and full of emotion—

Narayana Narayana
What I said, what was unsaid
What I did, what I didn't do,
Forgive me

Forgive, my lord!
Narayan, he Narayan,
What I did, what I didn't do,
Said, unsaid
Forgive everything,
Forgive me, my lord

Tears streamed down her face, it was as if she was anointing the Shivling with them. What sorrow was making the ebullient Hiravati, who laughed and teased with her eyes every day, cry in this fashion? A confused, bewildered Sridhar longed to know the secrets that lay in the heart of this young woman. On padded feet he walked closer to the window and flattened himself against it. Oh, Hiravati was leaving the village! Next to her was a basket with her clothes, toiletries, utensils etc. Maybe she was crying because of her sister, maybe because of the villagers' heartless behaviour. That he could have made Hiravati cry would never have struck the spartan, dispassionate young man even in his dreams. All he could do was try and find some explanation for her actions in his head, put the chain back on his door and go to sleep. Till then, no hint of corruption had singed his innocent mind. For him, Hiravati was like a beautiful wild rose; seeing it sway in the breeze was something an aesthete could appreciate, but it never crossed his mind that you could pluck the rose and inhale its fragrance too.

No one saw Hiravati the next day, or the day after that, in fact, no one saw her for a few days. 'Kodhi sahib's spirit must have dragged her away to his grave,' said the village women, making Sridhar laugh inwardly. He had seen Hiravati leave with her things. Well, it was good that she'd gone. The boil had burst. It hadn't needed to be lanced.

But exactly one month later, Hiravati was seen climbing the narrow mountain path with lazy footsteps, the fake shine of her white metal jewellery amplifying the genuine lustre of her youth, causing the women of the village much heartburn and provoking her sister-turned-rival wife who was standing in her courtyard to utter fury.

'Where is this wretched girl coming from after blackening her reputation? Why didn't she die there itself...?' she screamed, causing many women to peer out of their windows. Sridhar was sitting outside, spinning his sacred thread. Hiravati, glowing in her new jewellery, whirled around. 'I had gone to drown myself, Didi!' she laughed and Sridhar noticed the two captivating dimples in her cheeks for the first time as she gave a big smile. 'But those foreigners wouldn't let me drown. They said: "Hiravati, who would drown such a diamond of a body! Such a body should be adorned." Look, Didi, multi-layered necklaces of gold and silver, all of them given by the foreigners.'

Pirbhavati spat with disgust and shut the door, and Hiravati, with the tinkling sound of her brazen laugh echoing around her, climbed the mountain path.

After that, Hiravati didn't come down for many days. It seemed like the sympathetic foreigners had given her enough provisions. 'Maybe she's fallen ill, who knows,' thought Sridhar. Then he got irritated with himself. What was it to him? Let that wretched Hiravati die. What was the point of getting irritated? But at night, Menaka, glittering in her fake ornaments, would descend on the stage of Vishwamitra's dreams and create such turmoil that Sridhar would prostrate himself before the Shivling and say, between muffled sobs, 'What kind of punishment are you giving me, Bholenath? Why am I holding out my arms to attain such a degenerate woman in my empty dreams?'

A snake of perversion had found its way into the fortress of his austerity and restraint through a weak, unprotected gap. Now there was only one way to crush it. Early next morning he would get up and leave for Sabarmati where he would first bind and then place the devious enemy hiding in his heart at Bapu's sacred feet. Only then would he find peace. But would the wily enemy hiding in his heart be caught so easily? It was near impossible to contain this simian, constantly leaping between the branches of immoral thoughts and deceitful arguments, with human logic. Sridhar left the village at night itself. But he didn't take the usual path to the bus station and instead struck out on another path, but that turned out to be never-ending and led into a deep forest. Irritated that he couldn't find his way, an exhausted Sridhar sat down to rest next to a waterfall, only to be startled by a groan, as if someone nearby was in pain. Was it someone else like him who had lost his way? It was the month of Magh. It was teeth-chatteringly cold. A light drizzle had turned into a thunderous rain of hail stones that crashed on the cliffs with a rhythmic beat that sounded as though it had been created by a skilled tabla player. He leapt towards a cluster of trees for shelter, only to collide against the source of that pain-filled moaning.

'Who's there?' The darkness was like a black blanket and his voice came out muffled.

'Oh Lal sahib, it's you! You have saved me, Shambho.... I'm Hiravati.'

His feet were caught by the same iron fetters whose grip he was trying to break free from and flee the village. Hiravati was sobbing as if she was going to die.

'I was going back after cutting grass. I sprained my leg. Just drag me to my cave and dump me there, Lal sahib! I won't forget your kindness.'

Sridhar was in a peculiar quandary. He understood Hiravati very well. Was this not an excuse for this demonic lioness to drag him to her cave and satisfy her notorious hunger?

'Don't delay, Lal sahib! The killer will be here soon...can't you tell, the smell is already here,' she said impatiently, and Sridhar was startled. Sridhar, who had lived in forests since he was a child, recognized the unbearable stench of the king of the jungle, and the stench was coming closer.

Still conflicted, he bent and picked up Hiravati, who was lying helplessly on the wet grass, in his strong arms.

'Ah, gently, Lal sahib! You're hurting my foot. Hai! Pick up my sickle at least,' Hiravati whimpered.

'Your sickle can go to hell. Tell me, where is your cave?' snapped Sridhar, panting a little. Hiravati's strong, sturdy body seemed extra heavy.

Shrinking a little, Hiravati gave him instructions and, after following many narrow, precarious little mountain paths, they reached the cave.

'Bas, just leave me here. May God make you a Lat-Commissioner, Lal sahib! If I hadn't met you, that wretch would have surely eaten me today.'

As soon as he entered the cave, Sridhar felt as if he was standing next to a blazing hot furnace—the difference between the temperature outside and inside was the difference between the sky and the earth. After placing Hiravati on the ground, he was wiping his sweat with a handkerchief when Hiravati, who was limping till now, leapt towards a boulder lying nearby and, pushing it forward, shut the mouth of the cave with it.

'Baap re baap!' Limping, she stood back, leaning on the rock. 'Sometimes the bastard comes on silent, padded feet, like a cat. Look,' she dragged Sridhar to the chink in the opening to the cave. 'Look,' she whispered, laughing.

Just then, every corner of the forest echoed with the sound of a frightful roar. Even the normally brave Sridhar broke into a sweat. Resting its bloody paws on the rock that blocked the entrance to the cave, its golden yellow mane spread out on its shoulders like the flowing matted hair of sages and hermits, Kumaon's cruel man-eater let out another mighty roar.

'Every day this bastard comes and sits like this, waiting for the chance to just pop me into his mouth and eat me up. Have you seen his paws? How broad they are—broader than yours.'

Lovingly, Hiravati bent to hold the palm of Sridhar's hand, but he jerked it away and stepped back. 'Leave me, let me go.'

'Where?' Hiravati smiled impudently. 'Your Dadaji is sitting outside, resting on his paws and your broad shoulders won't fit through this narrow window. Sit down, I'll light a fire, have some tea and rest for a while. You can go after that, do you think I'll tie you up and keep you here?'

Defeated, Sridhar sat down. It looked like it had started snowing outside. Enveloped in a strange silence and stillness, the mountain peaks stood motionless. Outside the rock, sitting with a kind of unrelenting grandeur, the jungle lion sometimes roared impatiently, sometimes, like a cotton carder, shook his bow-like shoulders, sending scraps of cotton wool-like snow flying in the air.

Hiravati lit a piece of wood that burned bright as a torch and stuck it near the stove. Sridhar stood up, stunned at the artwork in the cave that was lit up by the flashing plume of light. Was this the miracle of kodhi sahib's divine paintbrush? Here, in the Kangra-Garhwali style, was Krishna's bride running through the rain-soaked, impenetrably dark night on the way to her rendezvous; somewhere else a beloved stood at a doorway, heels dug in, waiting for her lover. Here, putting to shame the sculpture tradition of Gujarat Solankis, an apsara, her naked chest covered by her champak-like fingers, and there, the exact replicas of Shaiva doorkeepers, weaving a sombre web, just like the wall paintings of Ajanta. Ensnared in this web of Khajuraho and Konark-style lions, tigers, apsaras, yakshis, and matchlessly beautiful snake nymphs, Sridhar circled the entire cave and then bumped into Hiravati standing at the rock that blocked the entrance, holding a cup of hot tea.

Only when the hot tea spilled on his cold feet did he jump.

'It looks like my queen's palace has enchanted Lal sahib! See this wolf in sheep's clothing? How he used to roam around like a big padre. If he didn't have this knowledge in him, would he have been able to create these pictures of naked women? Did he make any picture of his Jesus? Here, have some tea. Let me see, has that chowkidar gone or not?' Giving Sridhar the glass, she peeped out of the little gap.

'The killer has gone. Look how it's snowing! It's become like Badrinath-Kedarnath. Once it starts snowing in these parts, it doesn't melt for seven-eight days. Chalo, two are better than one.' Sipping her tea, she inched a little closer to Sridhar's feet.

Foolish Hiravati! Did she think Sridhar had never walked on narrow, snowy mountain paths? Now she will see, how, arms spread out, he will skate away, like a puff of air. He had just moved forward to shift the rock when a sharp gust of frigid wind struck the burning torch and put out the flame. The cave was engulfed in pitch darkness. He moved his hands and feet futilely. Wherever he turned, two soft, tender hands caught him. Were there many versions of the laughing-giggling Hiravati? Or had kodhi sahib's unseen spirit brought to life the beauties, apsaras and celestial enchantresses on the walls of the cave! But that sweet voice came from only one throat, and it was a voice Sridhar recognized only too well. She was definitely of this world.

'Don't be foolish,' Hiravati said. 'Where are you running away? On such icy cold nights, even birds freeze to death on the branches of trees. And then, do you think my chowkidar would have left? He'll be lying in wait for you in some ditch. Let that bastard eat such a golden body? Hiravati isn't such a fool.'

Grazing her soft cheek against his shoulder, in the manner of a pet cat, she inched closer to him. Forget touching any woman, he had never even touched the shadow of a woman. He flared up, her touch felt malignant to him. If there was a man-eater outside, there was a second man-eater inside. Suddenly, his control snapped, and flames leapt out from latent embers, hissing to life.

'Move away, what do you think I am?' Panting hard with excitement, helplessness and fury, he went forward to shift the rock, but Hiravati, arms crossed, stood blocking the way, 'I'll see who will remove me from here.'

Sridhar tried but couldn't get past Hiravati's golden body that stood in front of him like an impregnable boundary wall, jolting him with the shock of hundreds of charged wires. Who knows how long they stood there in the darkness of the night, confronting each other like a mongoose and snake. In the end, the mongoose won.

'Come,' said Hiravati in a quiet voice, holding both of the vanquished warrior's hands, 'Did you think me so shallow? Hiravati may have many bad qualities, but she never lies. I have two straw mattresses. You can sleep on one without any problem. If I touch you, may I be accused of eating the meat of a cow.' Hiravati took out the mattress from a shelf, placed it on the floor and then, holding his hand, led him to it, as if taking a bashful newly-wed bride to a bed of flowers.

Hiravati wasn't lying. Sridhar, lying down, holding his breath, heard the sound of the second mattress being dragged out and dumped on the ground, and he realized that the 'enemy camp' had placed it some distance away and that Hiravati was not playing any devious trick on him.

In a little while, Hiravati fell into a deep sleep, like an innocent baby. But Sridhar, still agitated, kept tossing and turning. Now that she had herself moved away, another worry robbed him of his sleep. Why did Hiravati keep a second straw mattress? Did she have to often make arrangements for visitors who walked in to spend the night here?

But why was his head aching? Who didn't know Hiravati in the village? She wasn't some irreproachable, forever-faithful-to-her-husband kind of woman, was she?

Grappling with this dilemma, he didn't realize when he eventually fell asleep. When he woke up in the morning, Hiravati had shifted the stone at the entrance. The fleeting, scattered sunlight spreading through the cave showed the unique wall art in a new light. He was looking at the art exhibition, captivated, when, involuntarily, his eyes moved to Hiravati. Watching her bending, blowing into the fire, he felt as if he were seeing the beautiful Hiravati for the first time.

Hiravati too perhaps felt a tingle at his captivated gaze. Smiling, she raised her head and an embarrassed Sridhar turned away as if he'd been caught stealing.

'Here, have some hot tea,' Hiravati handed him the glass and began folding her solitary straw mattress.

Had she given him all her warm blankets and shivered all night herself?

'So much snow has fallen. The sun won't come out for three or four days now,' said Hiravati, peering out of the gap.

Was Hiravati in collusion with the sun god? The snow fell

ceaselessly for four days. The cliffs, covered with thick, frozen layers of snow, became invisible. Under the weight of the heavy snow, the enormous wild fig, rubber, and deodar trees snapped and broke as if they were twigs used for cleaning teeth. Sridhar paced around like a caged lion in that snow-covered igloo-like cave, similar to the picture in the geography book that he'd studied as a child.

'You can hit your head against the wall thousands of times, judge sahib,' Hiravati said with a laugh, 'you won't be able to take one step outside.'

Hiravati left no stone unturned in looking after her curt, brusque guest. She kept taking out little bundles from all sorts of invisible recesses and niches in the walls. Grapes, walnuts, apricots, roasted cashews, milk sweets, sohan halwa, local yam roasted in the oven, and tangy green salt. Sridhar well knew that his hostess couldn't have acquired all these difficult-to-procure provisions by telling the beads of her rosary. How could he even touch this ill-begotten wealth? For two days he survived by gulping down glass after glass of black tea. Her face drawn, Hiravati also went to bed hungry. But on the third day, she attacked while the enemy slept. Even before Sridhar woke up, she'd cooked and seasoned vegetables with such aromatic spices that Sridhar forgot all his refinement, his fussing and pickiness. She placed the vegetables on fresh, fragrant rotis cooked with grain that had been ground in a special pot and slathered with butter, saying, while clutching his feet, 'Why are you sitting hungry and thirsty, Lal sahib? Am I untouchable? You are Gandhi baba's bhakt. He doesn't even consider Mehtars untouchables.'

This argument vanquished Sridhar. After that he demolished roti after roti. Maybe there was nothing left for Hiravati. After eating he went to sleep and slept as if he were Kumbhkaran.

There was no way of differentiating between day and night inside the cave. But that particular day, God knows why, Hiravati didn't light the torch like she did every day. A sharp gust of icy wind woke Sridhar with a start. He was overcome with anguish at his own selfishness, seeing Hiravati's plight, sitting huddled on her mattress, without any covering, shivering in the bone-chilling wind.

'Hiravati, do you have nothing to cover yourself with?' he asked. Hiravati was startled by this chameleon-like transformation, this expression of sympathy from a person who had spent the last three days without saying a word to her, who had burned her with the intimidating flame-like fury in his eyes. But just like the first drop of water on a scalding, blazing desert dries and vanishes the instant it touches the sand, similarly no sooner had that tender query left Sridhar's throat than it dried up.

Hiravati made no reply. But the distress of this self-respecting young woman trembling in the dark touched the one who was laden with four blankets. This beauty had, in his dreams, singed his sleep-drowned eyes, now, in this endless winter night, that dream began taking shape, pulsing, almost dancing in his wide-awake eyes.

'Hiravati!' he called out in a hoarse voice. Hiravati understood very well this husky call when it emanated from a man's throat. Her dilated, infatuated gaze tore through the darkness, and the tender young wanton didn't hesitate for a second.

The next day, the sun, which had been sulking for five days, pushed its way through a thin crack in the cave's ventilation system, and Sridhar woke up with a start. Her forehead resting on his shoulder, Hiravati was sleeping as if she'd been sleeping like this with him for ages.

'All the needs and desires within Sridhar Sharma, born in the gotra of Rishi Bharadwaj.' Sridhar remembered the vow he had made just a few days before during the Parthiv-puja at the Shiv temple. He started getting up almost in a panic.

Hiravati woke up. 'What are you doing? Lie down. I'm feeling cold.' Holding him tightly with both hands, she pulled him down to her side and made him go back to sleep.

The sun that had come out for a moment once again hid behind some clouds and yet again the stinging rain of hailstones drove Sridhar's conscience away.

Hiravati now spun him around as if he was a wooden spinning

wheel tied to a thread, bouncing him in whatever direction she wanted and then pulling him towards herself. He was no longer the cultured, well-educated Sridhar Sharma of the Bhardwaj gotra, he was now a primordial caveman arisen from the rubble of the centuries, who had no gotra, no culture. He had learnt to light a fire by rubbing two stones together, and grown so adept at devouring the dry-roasted meat like a glutton that he would make the cave resound with his wild laughter as he leapt to grab one more greasy, meat-covered bone from his beloved cave companion. Sometimes he would crush her so hard in his arms, it was as though he wanted to make mincemeat of her. And Hiravati? Had the padre sahib used her as a model when he had beautified the walls of the cave? Those curved sidelong amorous looks, the suppleness of Mandodari, those shapely limbs, she would have fit perfectly in the mould of the incomparable beauties imprinted on the walls.

'Hiravati!' One day, deliberately, he asked her an asinine question. He knew she never lied. 'Is it true, what the villagers say about you, Hiravati?'

Her face drained of all colour. In the middle of all the fun and pleasure, it was as if someone had caught her by the hair and thrown her to the ground.

She didn't say a word. The tears trickling down her bloodless cheeks gave Sridhar the answer he sought.

If it wasn't true, would the loquacious Hiravati sit silently, shedding tears?

Taking a deep breath, he got up without eating that day. Chhee chhee, Hiravati was such a contemptible woman! If it hadn't snowed, if the weather had been clear, he might even have bumped into a couple of her lovers.

That day too Hiravati sat next to the stove for a long time, trembling, without having eaten anything. Sridhar kept tossing and turning, sometimes coughing, sighing loudly, sometimes moaning for no reason at all. But in the end, the hungry beggar, seeing the leftovers of the feast, a feast as grand as a wedding banquet, once again forgot his culture, upbringing, conscience, intent—and moved towards the plates with leftover food.

'Hiravati!' he called out in a hoarse voice.

Why would Hiravati miss her chance?

On the sixth day, strong sunshine melted the snow. Hiravati went out to gather the twigs that had fallen from the broken trees. Sridhar was standing at the window when his body thrilled to the sound of bells ringing in a Shiv temple in a faraway valley. 'You have punished me enough for my earlier sins, prabhu.'

He folded his hands to the invisible Shivling, 'Forgive me, and give me strength.' So saying, without glancing at the cave, he left with the swiftness of an arrow being released from a bow.

After that, till today, he had never crossed the threshold of his village. Sridhar had dismissed Hiravati who had entered his life like an ill-omen with a glance, and killed its malign aura. For years, he wandered around as a patriot, someone who loved his country with the extraordinary and reckless love of a madman. He was unafraid of the red-faced goras, nor was he scared of the policeman's lathi.

Once he heard news of Hiravati when he was in jail. One of his comrades had come to visit him. 'Hiravati, from our village, she was in this jail too. They've taken her to Bareilly today.'

Hiravati! Suddenly, countless beauties and snake nymphs were etched on the black walls of Almora Jail. 'Hiravati! What had she been sent here for?' And then, hearing the detailed account of her heinous crime, Sridhar was struck dumb.

The village postman had seen Hiravati drowning her baby boy in the Alaknanda, and by the time he ran and got the village accountant, the tiny corpse had already disappeared in the fast currents of the river.

'Such a shameless, naked woman,' his comrade was saying. 'She ruined the reputation of our village. The official asked her, "Hiravati devi, is it true that you were just sitting there after drowning your child?"

'Head bent, the sinner kept smiling the way she had smiled in your court.

'"Whose child was it?" the official asked, so she said, "Sarkar, you keep touring these mountains night and day. You must be drinking water from many waterfalls. Sometimes you may have caught a cold. Can you tell which waterfall caused the cold?"

'We were shocked! Now she's paying for her crime, the murderess!'

Today, after so many years, the memory of that murderess had upset Sridhar to the point of agony. Was she still living in the same cave? Had those tender hands really flushed that tiny body in the swift snow-chilled currents of the Alaknanda so mercilessly?

Sridhar looked at the watch on his hand. He hadn't practised his speech fully even once. He had given himself a headache digging out forgotten corpses from the funeral pyre. Didn't he have enough worries of his own? Fed up of his invalid wife's petulant, luxury-loving nature, he wandered through jungles on unnecessary tours, like a forest creature. He had married off his four daughters but his attempts to take on his crafty, corrupt sons-in-law in the manner of William Bentinck eradicating thugee had earned him their animosity. Meanwhile, his only son had grown his hair out like a girl and wrecked the reputation of his family name. During a student strike, this family heir had himself carried black flags and burnt an effigy of his father, making a special place for himself in the student community. The father had had to sacrifice everything to become a leader, but his son achieved this feat in three days, by burning seven buses, breaking countless benches in government buildings, and overturning a train coach. To save himself from this turmoil, Sridhar sought refuge elsewhere, only to be confronted with even more turmoil. He set off to do an aerial survey of the drought-stricken land of his birth, but the memories of his ruined Taj Mahal, his own monument of love in that forgotten valley, awakened the pain of a dormant ulcer in him.

'Sorry, sir!' his PA said in an annoyed, irritated voice. 'There's a crazy woman who's come to meet you, she looks a little mentally unstable. She says she's from your village. She wants to meet you once and will go away after that. She's refusing to take no for an answer.'

The PA hadn't even fished his sentence when the woman of unsound mind, with a lump of jaggery tied in a grimy bundle on her head, entered the well-appointed room and shrank into the silk curtain like a patch of cloth stitched to hide a hole.

'How has she come, here? Did the fact that I was thinking of her draw her here?' thought Sridhar to himself. The warrior so used to fighting the double-edged swords of his political opponents found himself shaken at her appearance. His PA was a wily fellow. If he'd heard even a partial account of Hiravati's tarnished past, he would have stored it away with the alertness of a press reporter. Had Sridhar not seen the character assassination of many of his colleagues being done openly all the time?

'Come, come Hiravati, my sister,' he said with a laugh.

Hiravati gave a start. Till now she had been looking at the paintings on the walls of his luxurious room with the same captivated expression with which he had gazed, twenty-five years earlier, at the walls of her cave.

'Sit, Hiravati!' There was no trace of a husky lover's call in that weary voice. This was a tired traveller affectionately inviting another traveller to come sit with him and rest awhile. But a hesitant Hiravati didn't sit on the sofa. Without removing the bundle from her head, she sat down near Sridhar's feet, like a dog driven away by naughty street urchins who threw stones and clods of mud at her every day, but who had now been summoned lovingly by a long-separated master, and was moving towards him, still scared and unsure.

'Hiravati, why are you silent?' Sridhar's throat clogged up.

Even after so many years, this luminous woman's presence had the power to make him feel like a hypnotized snake, swaying, dancing to her tune.

How exhausted Hiravati looked. Her thin hair had turned white, the sweet redness of her lips had turned blue. The dark circles below her pensive eyes revealed the pain she had gone through. Several necklaces hung down over her torn waistcoat, but there were just two or three beads left on the grimy black threads, like the scattered beads of her one-time youth.

'Where are you living now?' Sridhar asked his second question.

'In the same sahib's cave.'

Hiravati's voice had turned strange and heavy. It was the kind of hoarse voice that was called a 'whisky voice' abroad, had the unfortunate woman started drinking as well?

'Why did you do that, Hiravati?' The moment the question left his mouth, Sridhar broke into a sweat. Why had he committed this foolishness? Didn't he know Hiravati never lied?

'He opened his eyes as soon as he was born.' Hiravati wiped her eyes with a soiled odhni. 'I recognized them. I told a lie for the first time in the court. He had your light eyes. The same nose. He had the same lopsided smile, the dusmaniya. I thought, my reputation is anyway mud, why should I drag your name through it? The entire village worshipped you. As he grew up, everyone would have known whose son he was.'

Sridhar sat as if he had turned to stone.

'I'll be going, sahib. It's time to leave. I'd told the sahib outside that I would just see you and leave.'

And, having done that, Hiravati left. Had she ever lied? Not one word of complaint for having wronged her, not one accusation, no pleading, no assertion of any right.

Carrying a piece of jaggery wrapped in a dirty odhni on her head, she walked away.

Someone—perhaps Emerson or maybe someone else—had said that a courtroom in this world may forgive a culprit and set him free, but the court in his heart never would.

Today, the culprit who had run away decades ago stood, head bowed, bound in chains in the courtroom of his heart.

Suddenly he got up. He took off his cap and threw it away. He took out a thick, rough woollen shawl gifted to him by a villager and wrapped it around himself. Now no one would be able to recognize him. He jumped out on to the road from a window at the back. Looking around, he arrived at the chilly road that would take him to the temple. A long row of tall willow trees bent down to almost touch the side of the lake. There were a couple of coolies shivering in the cold on the deserted road. And Sridhar himself, wrapped in his shawl like a village rustic. Every now and then, the snow-chilled wind from the lake would slap against his ears and he would tuck his neck in, like a turtle. After climbing the temple steps, he paused to rest.

Touching the row of bells in front of the solitary temple set off the musical tinkle of a jal tarang, and the entire temple echoed with the sound. Those sweet tinkling bells took Sridhar to the forgotten valley of his past, dragging him there by his finger.

This was the same statue of the vermilion-red stone goddess before whom he had bowed his head and asked for so much. Husbands for his daughters, release from his shrewish wife, wisdom for his wayward son, victory in elections. But no desire for salvation, or for glory. Wrapped in his shawl, this abject, helpless supplicant stood motionless, like a statue, his eyes closed. For a second he felt as if—even though she was not present there physically—the scared, shy woman of his dreams, his cave lover, her black, torn lehenga flapping, a dirty bundle with a lump of jaggery on her head, was sitting close to him and singing in a tender voice:

> *What I said, what was unsaid*
> *Forgive me*
> *Forgive, my lord*

THE HUMAN MEASURE

DOODHNATH SINGH

As soon as the car started, Pitaji asked his son to switch off the transistor. 'Why are you listening to this rubbish? Is this news! Who's doing what, who's talking the usual nonsense, how are we concerned? Useless!' he muttered crossly.

Seeing his angry scowl, the boy switched off the transistor. 'I was going to listen to songs,' he said defensively.

'Will songs provide food?' Pitaji snarled. He turned around and looked back at his wife, daughter, and elder son's two children. Seeing their baba glaring at them, the children got scared.

'And where's Napni?' asked Pitaji.

The son explained that Napni and Adhikariji and the peon were in the car behind them.

'How many miles to Bhagalpur?' asked Pitaji.

He was told how far Bhagalpur was.

Pitaji took out a soiled, dirty purse from his pocket, opened it, and counted ten-rupee notes.

'At how many places will we have to pay goonda tax?' Pitaji asked the driver.

'Wherever there is a pile of bricks and stones, bamboo rods, and poles,' said the driver, keeping his eye on the road.

'And how much?' asked Pitaji.

'The bigger the goonda the higher the tax,' said the driver.

There was no fixed rate or receipt, they discovered.

'But we'll have to keep track of the amount. We have to get the money back from the girl's father. Why should we pay?' said Pitaji.

'That is true, sahib,' said the driver.

'And you remember how everything else has to be done, don't you?' Pitaji asked his son.

And the boy said yes, like a meek, obedient son.

'You are now an officer. You have position. Now you have value. When you were doing nothing and were at the mercy of those bastard examiners and members, it was another matter. Now it's different. This is the time to take revenge on society. Don't lose your head over the girl the moment you see her and start drooling in anticipation. Your behaviour was anyway never up to the mark but now you're an officer. These people are big cheaters. Tread carefully and don't start doing hee-hee. And no political arguments. I understand the game of politics very well. Everyone looks after their own interests but gives sermons on Ram Rajya to others. And tries to portray themselves as being very good and pure. You're ignorant of all this now. When you mature, you'll understand. Right now, your skin is thin, it will smart. I'm worried you won't be able to manage the situation. You'll be diffident and modest. The girl's father is a small-time politician, an MLA of the Communist Party. He's sure to talk big. He'll make a show of simplicity. He'll be very humble. He'll trick us with his words. It's a way to deceive us. All the big talk in this world is for trickery and deception. By involving us in such talk, he'll try and take our attention away from the girl. She'll be all dressed up and painted. Don't get caught in his attempt to mislead you—understood?' Pitaji turned and stared at his officer son. The son looked at him from the corners of his eyes and agreed with him.

'When we were tricked, did anyone feel any pity or sorrow for us? That blasted father-in-law of Premlata! Asked for the horoscope. After getting it, he gave us the runaround for three months. Kept trying to assess how much money we would give. When he felt it won't work, he said, 'The girl's horoscope says she can't have children.' But when I threw crisp notes at his face, when I stuffed five lakhs up his arse then santaan-yog happened? How has Premlata become the mother of four children? I'd literally killed myself earning that money. I never let even two rupees slip out of my hands. But I had to give up all my savings. I was left with nothing! I will have my revenge. Crooked people deserve to be treated the same way.' Pitaji looked at the driver.

'The goondas haven't turned up yet?' he asked the driver.

'They will, sahib!' said the driver.

'And one more thing....' Pitaji looked at his son.

The son was quiet! 'If she has light eyes, then reject,' said Pitaji.

'Why?' the son summoned his courage.

'A girl with such eyes is hard to control,' said Pitaji.

'Meaning?'

'Meaning nothing.' Pitaji was irritated.

'Now keep quiet, won't you?' said his wife from the back seat.

'And we'll have to look at the colour of her skin very closely,' said Pitaji.

'You're there for that, aren't you?' said the wife.

'Arre bhai, there's a lot of trickery, cunning, and illusion out there. I've heard that there are hairdressers and beauticians who can apply such paints, you'll never be able to make out the real colour,' said Pitaji.

At this, his adolescent daughter laughed.

'Ae buchiya, you'll be able to make out, won't you?' Pitaji asked.

'Yes, Pitaji,' said the girl.

'And what is the height of the bride in the biodata?' Pitaji asked.

'Five feet six inches,' said his daughter.

'And how tall is Napni?' Pitaji asked again.

'Five feet three inches,' said his daughter.

'So when the bride stands next to Napni, we'll have to see if she's about three inches taller,' said Pitaji.

'And if she's shorter by a bit, then, sahib?' the driver asked, having some fun.

'How will she be shorter?' Pitaji said in some surprise.

'Yes, sahib, one should make sure everything is all right in the beginning itself,' the driver butted in again.

'And no useless jabbering. How are we concerned with what

is happening in Uttar Pradesh? We are family people. Somehow we've kept body and soul together. We steer clear of politics.' Then Pitaji fell silent.

ℭ

A long green branch had been placed across the road and four people were signalling the car to stop. Pitaji took out his purse in a trice. He took out a ten-rupee note. He put a few more ten-rupee notes in a second pocket. Then put the purse in the inner, secret pocket. If money has to be given at other places, it wouldn't be a good idea to keep taking the purse out. Suppose they snatch the purse itself, Pitaji thought. Both the cars came to a standstill, one behind the other. Pitaji opened the door and stepped out.

'Well?' Pitaji asked, clutching the ten-rupee note in his fist.

'Tax,' one of them said.

'Tax?' Pitaji expressed surprise.

'Donation,' said another.

'Donation for a party?' asked Pitaji.

'Congress, Communist, BJP...think whatever you like,' said someone.

'Oh...so you people play politics,' Pitaji said, smiling.

'Is he an asshole?' a boy said.

Pitaji placed the ten-rupee note in his hand. The boy stared at it. Rolled the note into a cylinder, spat on it and made to hand it back to Pitaji.

'What is this?' Pitaji shrank a little.

'Returned your money after marking it... Bloody bribe-taker, how much have you swallowed?'

The boy took the note that was wet with his spit and threw it at Pitaji's face.

Pitaji saved himself by twisting away.

'Where are you from?' asked a second boy.

'Dumraon,' Pitaji answered at once.

'Saala, one of raja's useless fellows.' Two of the boys laughed.

"It's an ill-omened day today,' said Pitaji.

'What did you say?'

'Nothing to you,' Pitaji swiftly changed the subject.

'You're corrupt! The saala is a looter.... He loots the government and the people! He hoards money. Travels in two cars and then spouts philosophy.'

Pitaji smiled, signifying neither yes nor no.

'You see this green branch? We'll shove it from behind you and push it out into the universe,' said one boy.

'No, bhaiya, I am happy to see all of you.'

'You're happy?'

Once again Pitaji smiled both yes and no.

'Abe, you'll regret it, take out the money,' the boy pounced on him.

'How much, sahib?' the driver asked, coming out of the car.

'Seventy for two cars.'

The driver took the money out of his pocket and handed it over.

'Pick up that note, Panditji, and stick it on the tilak on your forehead.' The boy moved away to the cars parked behind.

℅

And so, after paying tax in a few other places also, Pitaji and party reached Bhagalpur. 'Keep track of the accounts,' Pitaji said to the driver and got out of the car. The hotel was oily-sleek and the street was lively. It turned out that their son's to-be father-in-law had sent his apologies. He was in a demonstration and therefore unable to receive them. But he would be there soon. Dumping his luggage and offspring in the rooms, Pitaji grumbled, 'I understand everything—everything. Do whatever you want. You'll pay for it. He knew we were coming, didn't he? Going to the demonstration was more important than us? If this is the beginning of the performance, what will the full drama be like? Will you change the destiny of the country? An old delusion of the Communists.

'There are so few of them, but they think they make up the whole country. Arre, you've grown bald, your face has dried up, you've spent your whole life trying to be a leader, how many revolutions have you been part of? There's an unmarried girl in the house and you've gone to salute a red flag somewhere. We've reached here after risking our lives, saving ourselves from a whole lot of bloody criminals and the red leader is missing. So we'll go missing too. We'll also vanish....' Pitaji made a gesture with his hands to signify disappearing.

'Ay Napni, come here,' he called out loudly.

Napni came and stood in front of him—a dusky, thin, almost emaciated girl.

'Bhaiya measured you properly with the tape, didn't he?' Pitaji asked.

Napni nodded in assent.

'You weren't wearing high heels when he measured you?'

'No,' Napni said, looking down.

'You're wearing them now.' Pitaji looked at Napni's feet.

Napni said nothing.

'Doesn't Upadhiyaji feed you?' Pitaji looked at her thin body.

The girl remained silent.

'Look up.' Pitaji suddenly became alert.

Napni raised her eyes.

'Look straight at me,' said Pitaji.

Napni looked at him.

'Ay bhai, she has light eyes.' Pitaji got up and started pacing the room.

'Why are you troubling her?' Pitaji's wife said finally.

'Troubling?' Pitaji glared at her.

'What else! You've been going on and on, Napni-Napni! Go, beti!' Pitaji's wife said to the girl.

Napni rushed to the other room and began crying on Pitaji's daughter's shoulders.

'That's why I say, that's why,' Pitaji said irritably, 'women have no brains in their skulls. Brahma hasn't given them any. A small spoon's worth, that's all. First she's cat-eyed, on top of that she cries. That's why we got looted all the way.' Pitaji slumped on the sofa.

'First of all, Upadhiyaji did you a favour by sending his daughter, but throughout the journey all you've been doing is going 'ay Napni, ay Napni' to everyone.' His wife got up and went towards the washbasin.

∫

After a while, Dikshitji arrived with his entourage, his 'amle faile'. The words, 'amle faile', were Pitaji's, who was peering down from the balcony. Dikshitji bade farewell to his companions downstairs and came up in the lift. He folded his hands in front of Pitaji. In response, Pitaji moved his head slightly.

'My apologies, Panditji, I was in a demonstration,' said Dikshitji.

'Was it necessary to go today?' said Pitaji.

'It was today's issue so the protest had to be today itself, isn't it?' said Dikshitji.

'Protest...hunh.' Pitaji shook his head.

'Your journey was comfortable?' asked Dikshitji.

'Comfortable? Arre, you could say we barely managed to escape with our lives.'

'Oh...but the drivers know about that,' said Dikshitji.

'You mean you know? And you're a political leader?' Pitaji's brows knitted tightly in anger.

'Poverty...unemployment...an uncertain future, friend.... There are many reasons,' said Dikshitji apologetically.

'Friend?' said Pitaji.

'That came out of habit. I should have said "panditji". Nothing can be done now, I've been in the party since the age of fifteen. It's become a habit,' said Dikshitji.

'What will happen by staying in such a party?' asked Pitaji.

'What will happen? Meaning?' Dikshitji was startled.

'What will happen means what will happen,' Pitaji laughed.

'I think our views don't match,' said Dikshitji.

'Some people, on the pretext of their ideas, lose their way all their life, Dikshitji.' Pitaji delivered what he thought was a brilliant remark to which there could be no comeback.

'And some do this without any ideas at all,' said Dikshitji.

'Both are thieves,' said Pitaji.

Dikshitji laughed, because that was all he could do. But Pitaji also laughed.

'I believe bridegrooms get stolen in your parts?' Pitaji asked suddenly.

'Stolen?' Dikshitji didn't quite understand.

'If a boy becomes an officer, his life is immediately in danger. I believe they have lists. They're always looking out. And these Ranvir Sena members help them. The rate depends on the post. If it's a Collector it's five lakhs—and this is just for the kidnapping. If the mother and father protest, kill him. They can also get him married to some maimed, crippled girl. Once the wedding takes places, there goes the wedding night....' After this exposition, Pitaji fell silent.

'You are a very simple man, Panditji,' said Dikshitji with a laugh.

'That I am. I brought this up to check whether we are a target,' said Pitaji.

'If you had such silly doubts you should have called me,' Dikshitji said, a little distressed.

'My son is also an officer,' Pitaji said, looking at his son.

'You are our guest, Panditji.' Dikshitji glanced at the boy.

'Arre, we have stepped inside Lanka, that's why the doubts. Where can we run?' said Pitaji.

Dikshitji wanted to say 'Ufff!' but said, 'All right, I'll take your leave. And I'll send my daughter and wife. Actually it would have been better at home, but since you wanted a hotel.... I have a meeting. Now it's all up to you.' Dikshitji folded his hands.

'There's no need for you to stay. If you are here, the girl will feel shy,' said Pitaji.

Dikshitji took his leave.

~

After about an hour, Dikshitji's wife arrived with her daughter and daughter's friend. Pitaji's wife greeted her hesitantly, giving her a look of suspicion. When the bride did her pranaam, Pitaji said, 'All right, it's all right' almost as if he were looking at something dirty and unclean. The girl was asked to sit on a chair. Her friend stood behind her, holding on to the chair. Both the women sat on a sofa. The officer bridegroom and his sister, and the two small children were on a long sofa in front of the bride. Both the children stared at the bride unblinkingly. Pitaji's attention was first drawn to the bride's feet, that is, to her sandals. Sniffing a conspiracy, he shook his head and signalled his son and wife in turn.

'How much did you settle on this time?' Adhikariji whispered in Pitaji's ears.

'Six lakh rupees, a car, and all the expenses for the wedding,' Pitaji whispered back.

'He's a comrade, how will he give all this?' Adhikariji.

'If he's a comrade, he can go to hell.' Pitaji.

'You should have thought of that before.' Adhikariji.

'That was for him to do. What about the donations he collects for the trade union?' Pitaji.

'Communist people are not like that.' Adhikariji.

'You are a bloody donkey.' Pitaji

'A donkey can only be friends with a mule,' said Adhikariji.

Tickled by this, Pitaji caught hold of Adhikariji's hand. It was not the occasion to laugh out loud. The son was interviewing the bride and she was responding shyly. Whenever she bent her head, lapsing into silence, the officer would ask something flirtatiously, enjoying the situation, 'Arre, look me in the face, won't you.' At this, the girl would become even more shy. Then, her friend standing behind her would offer comfort by patting her on the shoulder.... Pitaji, sitting with Adhikariji, was keeping one eye and one ear on his son, to figure out if he was getting attracted to the girl or not.

'Where is Napni?' Pitaji asked suddenly, looking at his wife. 'What is her name?' For the first time it struck Pitaji that she might have another name.

'Parmita,' said Pitaji's wife.

'Upadhiya sasur,' Pitaji snorted. 'Nothing to eat in the house but they've named her Parmita! Where is she?' Pitaji looked at his wife.

'In the other room.'

'Parmita bitiya, come here,' Pitaji called out loudly.

Parmita came into the room, head bowed, as if she was the one who had come to be 'seen'. The bride's mother was glaring at Pitaji—what derogatory terms he had used for Napni's father once he got to know her real name. Pitaji caught the disapproving look of his to-be daughter-in-law's mother.

'Let me tell you how we got into the habit of calling her Napni,' said Pitaji, addressing the girl's mother. 'Her father eats one ser of polished rice every morning. When this girl was little, she used to take little handfuls of the rice from the pot in her hands. Her mother would gauge the amount by the handfuls she'd take out. Eight handfuls would be just right. So Upadhiyaji used to say, she's my napni (measuring tool). She's the one who measures my rice properly, if someone else does it, it's either too much or too little.... That's how we got into the habit of calling her Napni-Napni.' Pitaji showed his white teeth.

Boiling with rage, Napni looked at Pitaji.

His wife too was shocked by this narrative, the way it was told and by her husband's power of imagination, that is, his effortless ability to tell lies. Adhikariji felt his friend could embarrass anyone.

'Now stop it, bete, you've heard her voice. What is left to interview? Move away from there,' said Pitaji.

The officer son got up and sat on the other end of the sofa.

'Beti, just remove your sandals,' Pitaji said to the bride.

The girl looked at him as if she didn't quite understand.

'Sandal,' the officer son or the young man eager to become a husband gestured to the girl to take off her footwear.

The girl's dusky face flamed copper. Almost shaking, she took off her sandals.

'And, you, you move away from behind the chair.' Pitaji signalled to the bride's friend severely.

'Why?' Adhikariji whispered into Pitaji's ears.

'Can't you see, they've made this dark girl stand behind so that Netaji's daughter looks less dark. I smell a conspiracy,' Pitaji whispered back.

The bride's friend moved away from behind the chair and sat down next to Dikshitji's wife.

'Now stand up, bitiya!' Pitaji said to the bride. The girl stood up.

'Napni, go stand next to her,' said Pitaji. Napni went and stood next to the bride.

'Stand level with her,' Pitaji said, as if he was a carpenter taking measurements.

Everyone looked. Pitaji looked at his wife, son, and Adhikariji.

Adhikariji also kept staring with appraising eyes.

'Liar,' Pitaji said in Adhikariji's ears. 'She's the same height as Napni.'

'Parmita beta, take bitiya to the washbasin and wash her face,' said Pitaji.

'What will you do now?' Adhikariji in Pitaji's ear.

'Deceit,' said Pitaji.

'Yes, they've deceived you but how will you say no?'

'We'll say it,' Pitaji whispered.

'How?'

'The way we've said it many times before.'

A little irritated, Adhikariji looked at his friend.

'We'll say your daughter's horoscope shows she can't have children,' Pitaji whispered.

Adhikariji looked afraid.

Pitaji gave Adhikariji's shoulders a hefty slap.

✧

Parmita (or Napni) held the bride's hand and took her to the washbasin in the bathroom.

'I'll wash up myself,' said the girl, splashing her face with water. She was washing off both her anger and her tears at the same time. Even after wiping her face with a towel, her tears wouldn't stop. Her eyes had turned red. She looked at Parmita who was standing close by.

'You are looking more beautiful than you did earlier,' said Parmita.

The girl smiled through her tears. Then once again, she became agitated. She saw that Parmita was also crying.

'Why are you crying?' asked the bride.

'Can't you slap that man on his face?' said Parmita.

'Really!' The bride moved a little closer to her. Parmita shook her head, as if she was the bride.

The girl went and stood in front of the mirror. She took the pins out of her bun and shook her hair free. Throwing the dupatta carelessly around her shoulders, she went out of the bathroom. Everyone stared at her in amazement and some horror. Parmita slunk into a corner. The girl's mother stood up.

'You are an idiot,' the girl slapped Pitaji's face hard and then went clattering down the stairs.

ᶴ

'She had light eyes,' said Pitaji to Adhikariji on the way back in the car.

'Perhaps,' Adhikariji laughed.

FEAR

OMPRAKASH VALMIKI

Afternoon had turned to evening and they were still wandering about, lost. They had scoured many of the city's shabby settlements without any success. Eventually, exhausted, they reached the settlement on Sahasradhara Road. It was an isolated place near the river, with about eight or ten families. It must have been a river once, but now it was merely a rain-fed stream. Bricks and stones had been joined to erect walls. Grimy old tin sheets placed on these rough, uneven walls gave the structures the appearance of houses.

Kalu's house was to the right, just after entering the neighbourhood. Compared to the others, Kalu had taken over a much larger space. He had also made a pig pen in the courtyard. There was a water tank at ground level. Eight or ten pigs, pushing each other, were literally falling on their food, making chhap-chhap noises. A tiny piglet was trying to reach the water tank from underneath a fat, strong one. The fat pig pushed it away with its snout. The piglet began running circles around Kalu, making cheen-cheen noises. Kalu was furious at the fat pig. With an obscene oath, he hit it hard on its back with a bamboo stick.

The two of them arrived at Kalu's courtyard and stopped. They had parked the scooter outside. Seeing the small, round little piglets milling about the bigger ones, their eyes lit up. As soon as they entered the courtyard, Dinesh told Kalu, 'We need a piglet.'

Kalu looked them up and down and said, 'Take whichever one you like.'

'How much?' Dinesh asked.

'Is it an offering for a puja?' Kalu wanted to know.

'We need it as an offering for Mai Madaran,' said Kishore, who had come with Dinesh.

'All right...four hundred rupees, fixed price,' said Kalu in a flat,

235

matter-of-fact tone.

The price took Dinesh's breath away, 'That's too much....'
Pretending that he hadn't heard Dinesh, Kalu began pushing the
pigs away from the water tank; the piglets pounced on the leftovers.
Both Dinesh and Kishore's faces fell. They looked at each other.

After having wandered about unsuccessfully the whole day, they
had reached the conclusion that it was their manner and way of
speaking that led to the inflated prices wherever they went. They had
already wasted a lot of petrol going from one squalid neighbourhood
to another on the scooter. Despite that, they hadn't had any success.
Someone on DL Road had told them that Kalu had four or five
piglets.

'Quote a proper price...this one won't even give five kilos of
meat.' Dinesh tried to haggle.

'If you want five kilos of meat, there are many shops in the bazaar.
Go and buy it from there. It will be cheaper.' Kalu glared at them.

Seeing them bargaining, Kalu's wife also came out. Kishore was
irritated with Kalu's manner, 'If we wanted to buy it from a shop,
why would we have come here?'

'Bhaiji, tell us properly, how much will you take?' Dinesh tried
once again.

'I will take nothing less than four hundred rupees. You can ask
me once, you can ask me ten times....' Kalu asserted.

Dinesh looked at Kishore. The question 'What should we do now'
was clearly pasted on his face. Kishore also thought four hundred
rupees was too much.

But he whispered, 'I think we should just buy it.' Dinesh tried
one last time, 'At least reduce the price a little...we've come from
so far. You should reduce it on account of caste and community.'

Ignoring them, Kalu told his wife, 'Go, get my cycle, these people
aren't going to buy anything. I knew it as soon as I saw them. You're
wasting your time as well as mine. These are pant-shirt wearing
babus. They are just roaming around on their scooter. Otherwise
they wouldn't come to even piss in these parts. They're desperate

to become Baamans (Brahmins) after getting educated. But these wretches can't even become Baamans. Let's talk if you're prepared to pay four hundred...otherwise go and look elsewhere.'

Every word of his stuck in Dinesh's throat like a bitter pill. At any other time, he might have answered back. Controlling himself, he said, 'All right...here's four hundred rupees...catch one of the piglets....'

Dinesh put the money in Kalu's hand. Kalu counted the four hundred-rupee notes many times. He held each note up against the sun and examined it. Turned it over and looked at it. Putting the money in his pocket, he said, 'Catch one...that one roaming around with its tail in the air.'

Faltering a little, Dinesh said quite humbly, 'Bhaiji, we need to make an offering of this piglet in our puja to Mai Madaran.... We stay in a colony...we can't kill it, roast it, cut it, and do all that there.... Can you do that here itself?'

Kalu's eyes became round and almost popped out of his rough, harsh face. 'The price was for a live pig. Not to kill it and give it to you. Even so, well, never mind, since you don't have an option, I'll take fifty rupees to kill it.'

Dinesh asked in some amazement. 'Fifty more?'

'Then take the piglet and do it in your home.... I don't have that much time and taking a life is not an easy thing to do. Fifty is actually very little. You are from my own community...if a Baniya or Baaman had come my rate would have been different,' Kalu said in a hard voice.

Kishore had been standing silently for quite some time. He found Kalu's manner very offensive. He couldn't help asking, 'So do Baniyas and Baamans also come to buy....' Kalu didn't reply. He gave Kishore a sidelong glance.

'All right, we'll give you fifty more. Catch this one and get him ready....' Dinesh said helplessly.

'You people sit for a while...I'll be back in ten minutes. I have to go up to the Rinspna Bridge.... I have some important work. I've set up a time with someone.' Kalu picked up his cycle and went out of the courtyard. They were left staring after him. He left without giving them a chance to say anything.

∽

Kalu had left about thirty minutes ago. There was still no sign of him. The two of them were fed up waiting. Dinesh called out to Kalu's wife and asked, 'Where has he gone? We're getting late.'

'Now what can I say...wait for a little longer,' she replied from inside. She came out a couple of times. Without saying anything, she went in again.

Every second seemed endless to them. They had a lot of work to do after they got home. They had to make preparations for the puja. In any case, it would be evening by then.

Seeing them sitting there, many children and elderly people from the neighbourhood gathered in the courtyard. Everyone stared at the two of them. There was a peculiar atmosphere of suspicion. More than Kishore, Dinesh was getting testy. He was feeling uneasy in this place.

They had been waiting for more than an hour. Dinesh began to get cranky. He berated Kalu's wife angrily, 'Where has he gone? How long can we keep sitting here? We've given him the money too.'

'How do I know where he has gone! He's like this. I don't know when he will be back.... Take the piglet and go....' Kalu's wife replied in her plain, simple manner.

Dinesh and Kishore looked at each other. They couldn't decide what they should do. They couldn't take the piglet to their colony and kill it there. They also had to roast it, which was out of the question in the colony flat. If people got wind of all that, there would be a real scene. Even those who knew nothing would come to know the truth. Dinesh had seen the kind of hatred that existed when it came to matters of caste. Just imagining people behaving like that with him gave Dinesh the shivers.

He asked Kalu's wife, 'Isn't there anyone else who can prepare the animal?'

'No, there's no one here. Only he does this…. No one else knows how to,' Kalu's wife said bluntly.

Dinesh's temples were getting warm. Every now and then, he felt angry with his mother. She had got them into this mess. How much he had tried to make her understand. Ma, if you have to do your puja, do it with fruits and flowers, halwa-puri…but she wouldn't agree. She was fixated on just one thing. 'While he was alive your father never let me worship Mai Madaran. When we got married, my father had said clearly that in our family we conduct the Mai Madaran puja. And in your home too you will have to do it. At that time, your father didn't say anything. But later he changed his mind. Dinu, son, can anyone leave their gods and goddesses! What is a tree without its roots? We have to worship in our own way. What is there to be ashamed of?'

Ever since his Mama, his maternal uncle, started filling Ma's ears, she'd started talking like this. Dinesh had never participated in such a puja before. Yes, he'd certainly seen it once or twice in his mother's home. In any case, Pitaji was always more friendly with the people in his factory. As far as family and relatives went, there was just his mother's place. Dinesh had the same kind of values that his father had.

He had even told his uncle in an undertone, 'Mama, these things can't happen in this colony. We have to live with everyone here. If somebody sees what we're doing, what will they say? Things are different in a basti, in more traditional, crowded areas. There, everyone belongs to the same community.'

Mama's anger boiled over and he said, 'Even after studying so much, you people have remained stupid and ignorant. How can you say that we should change the way we worship just because others don't like it!' Mama had narrated stories of Mai Madaran's rage and created such terror that Ma became very frightened. Suppose something bad happened.

Before they left the house, Mama had given Dinesh and Kishore special instructions. Examine the piglet properly before buying. It should not be castrated; its ears and tail shouldn't be cut or torn.

Seeing Dinesh lost in thought, Kishore interrupted his reverie, 'Where are you lost? Let's go. We'll catch the piglet ourselves and kill it. We'll roast and cut it here itself.'

'I've never done all this,' Dinesh expressed his inability to do the task at hand.

'What is there to killing it? My father used to kill it with one blow. You just have to stick a knife into its heart.' Kishore said simply.

'But I have never done all this,' said Dinesh falteringly.

'I haven't done anything like this either.... Though, I've seen my father do it. But you will have to do it. Because you are the one who has to do the puja,' Kishore offered by way of argument.

After a great deal of effort Dinesh agreed but in his heart of hearts, he wasn't prepared for it. He felt as if he were going to commit a crime.

With the help of Kalu's wife they tried to separate the piglet from the horde. But they couldn't get their hands on it. Again and again, it would break free and join the group. Its mother growled at Dinesh and Kishore. The growling frightened both of them. This became a source of entertainment for the assembled crowd. The children and elderly people laughed at their attempts.

Dinesh tried to catch the piglet a couple of times. But it freed itself and ran away. Its mother charged at Dinesh. He just about saved himself from a fall. Even Kalu's wife felt like giggling. Hiding her laughter, she said, 'Aji, this is not for you. You only know how to sit in an office and write with your pen all the time, you can't even catch a tiny little piglet....'

Her words irritated Dinesh. Both he and Kishore were drenched in sweat. Kalu's wife suggested, 'Don't catch the animal from its waist, grab it from the feet. Pick it up and go inside through the door. I'll shut it after you and latch it.'

Somehow, Dinesh managed to separate the baby from the other pigs. Then Kishore caught hold of its hind legs and, lifting it, pushed his way into the house. Dinesh ran behind him. Kalu's wife quickly latched the door, the whole operation was done in the blink of an eye. Hearing the little pig's mewling, the mother pig, fearsome in her rage, jumped up and began battering the door. All the other pigs moaned and whimpered in unison. It was a scene to strike terror in everyone's hearts. Dinesh's very soul trembled with fear.

Beating at them with a stick, Kalu's wife managed to herd the pigs into their pen. They were still whining. The stifled cries of the piglet could be heard from within the house. Kishore was holding it still by pressing it down with his knee. Kalu's wife had opened the latch and come inside. As soon as he saw her, Kishore asked for a knife. She brought a long knife generally used to cut fruit. The moment he took the knife in his hands, Dinesh's heart began sinking. He was in agony.

'Before killing it, put some turmeric on its ears, take the name of Mai Madaran and sprinkle water on it,' said Kishore, pressing the piglet down firmly.

Kalu's wife brought the turmeric. Dinesh put some on the piglet's ears and meditated momentarily on Mai Madaran.

Closing his eyes, he thrust the knife into the pig's chest with all his might. A kind of savagery took hold of him, visible in his eyes and face. His eyes became bloodshot. As soon as the knife pierced the piglet, the entire house, the courtyard echoed with the sound of its screams. Even the soot-covered walls trembled. Dinesh had pushed the knife in with so much force that it came out on the other side. A jet of hot blood gushed out. The blood was collected in a vessel.

After writhing in agony for a bit, the piglet lay still. Dinesh had not yet managed to get back to his normal self. He gaze was fixed on the lifeless body of the pig lying on the floor.

Kishore put the blood-filled vessel to one side. Now the problem was the roasting. Without roasting it over fire, the chopping couldn't be done. They looked at Kalu's wife questioningly. She answered simply, 'There's a litchi garden at the front of the house. Go and collect some dry leaves.'

Kishore told the grubby children who were standing around, 'Go and get some dry leaves. We'll give you five rupees.' They just had to hear the words 'five rupees' and in no time, the little vanar sena had collected a pile of leaves.

They lit a fire with the dry leaves and began roasting the piglet. The smell of burning flesh spread all over and they turned the pig around in the tall, leaping flames of the fire. After roasting it properly, they washed it at the tap outside, scrubbed it thoroughly and then sat in the courtyard to dissect it. This was a new experience for Dinesh. Kishore was doing the dismembering in a crude, awkward fashion. Kalu's wife helped him with alacrity.

After quickly finishing the chopping, they put everything into a sack. Placing the sack on the scooter, they set off for their colony. They were completely exhausted. Apart from the dirt and ash, their hands and feet were stained with blood.

It wasn't long before the hazy gloom of the evening set in. The horizon was turning red.

Before parking the scooter, Dinesh had been mindful of his surroundings. He was extremely alert. The minute the scooter came to a stop, Kishore hastily picked up the sack and went inside. There was no one outside the flat at that time. A few children were playing on the street, absorbed in their game. Even so, Dinesh was anxious. As if he'd stolen something and brought it home.

Dinesh shut the door as soon as he went inside. He was scared that someone may turn up just at that moment. If someone did come, it would be a problem. It would be difficult to hide everything.

Ma had begun the preparations for the puja. Kishore and Mama were busy cutting the meat into little pieces.

Dinesh's attention was fixed on the door. He would start at the slightest noise. He had instructed everyone that the door should not be opened for anyone. His biggest worry was Ramprasad Tiwari. He was a regular visitor. Sometimes he had a meal with them. The days he ate with them, Ma would not even put garlic in the food. They cooked meat only occasionally. And that too only when they were sure that Tiwari wouldn't turn up. In all these years, Ramprasad

Tiwari had not come to know that they were SC. Many times, when Ramprasad Tiwari had held forth against reservations, he had become abusive. He used derogatory terms for Babasaheb and Bapu, and spoke about them in the vilest language. At such times Dinesh remained silent or tried to change the subject. In any case, Dinesh did his best to avoid such conversations.

Despite all this, they were close friends. But Dinesh was well aware that the day caste came between them, this friendship would dissipate like a bubble of water.

Dinesh was worried most about Ramprasad Tiwari. If he showed up, how would they turn him away? He never even waited for them to open the door. He'd just walk in. He wouldn't be content until he'd gone to every corner of the house. Dinesh was getting more and more anxious. He felt as if he had got caught in a web of his own making.

If any neighbours' kids came, he could send them away with some excuse or the other. But it wouldn't be so easy to turn Ramprasad Tiwari away.

Every second was torture for Dinesh. His mental uneasiness was turning into acute distress.

As the preparations for the prayers were going on, his heart began beating faster and faster. Ma lit the prayer lamp and placed it on the floor, next to the wall. She arranged all the things needed for the prayers right there. Hot embers from dry cow dung cakes were placed in front of the lamp. Following Mama's directions, Dinesh poured an offering of ghee into the embers. A flame leapt up. Ma covered her head with her pallu and bowed. They took Mai's blessings. Little sugar cakes, cooked meat, roasted liver and tiny pieces of roti were held over the flame and offered to the deity. The smoke emanating from the ghee caused a strange aroma to spread throughout the house.

The puja ceremony was about to end when the bell rang. The sound was enough to get Dinesh's heart racing. He felt as if there had been an earthquake. He looked at his mother with fear and alarm.

Ma said, 'Go and see who's there.'

'Who…it'll be Tiwari, who else,' Dinesh said, his voice fading. 'Send him away from the door itself…tell him I'm not at home. If he comes in, it will be a big problem,' he said, articulating each word forcefully. He felt his heart sinking.

Ma opened the door just a little bit. Ramprasad Tiwari was standing there. Paan juice trickled down from the right side of his mouth. From the half-open door, Ma said mechanically, 'Dinesh has gone out. He'll be back late.'

'Where has he gone?' asked Tiwari.

'He didn't tell me….' Ma tried to evade the question.

'But where has he been since morning? I saw him during the day, coming out of that dirty settlement on Sahasradhara Road. There was a sack on his scooter. I called out to him. But he didn't stop,' Tiwari said with some surprise.

Ma was silent. She was trying to avoid any further conversation. Seeing that Ma wasn't saying anything, he said, 'All right, give me a glass of water and I'll be off….'

'Wait…I'll get it,' Ma turned towards the kitchen hastily.

Dinesh was listening closely to their conversation from the puja room. Every word of Tiwari's pierced him like an arrow.

Tiwari drank the water, handed the glass back to Ma and said, 'There's a strange smell….'

Ma didn't say anything. 'All right, I'll leave then….' And he walked away quickly. Ma shut the door and took a deep breath. Tiwari had gone but he'd left a dead silence behind him.

Dinesh felt as if someone had drained all the blood from his body. He felt jittery. Tiwari had seen him coming out of that Sahasradhara neighbourhood. He was shaken at the thought.

Everyone finished eating and went to sleep. But he stayed awake, preoccupied and distracted. After Tiwari's departure, he was filled with a deep, profound sadness. He grew more and more anxious. It was as if, every second, someone was pricking him with sharp thorns.

Drowsiness and exhaustion made his eyelids heavy. But sleep eluded him. He was in turmoil. What would happen tomorrow when he met Tiwari?

He tried to sleep. He had barely dozed off when he woke up with a start. He felt as if the mother pig was standing in front of him, eyes red and bloodshot, baring her long teeth. Behind her stood Tiwari, brandishing a long knife and advancing towards him. His eyes were full of hatred, a hatred steeped in contempt. Frightened, Dinesh switched on the light. He could hear the piglet whimpering.

Mama and Kishore were sound asleep. He tried to exercise some control over himself.

He was soaked in sweat. His throat was dry. He went to the kitchen to drink some water. He felt as if the entire kitchen was smelling of the piglet's burning flesh. He returned without drinking the water. He lay down on the bed and tried to sleep.

The moment he closed his eyes, Tiwari and the mother pig appeared in front of his eyes once more. Again, he sat up. Ma was sleeping in the other room. When the light was switched on, she too woke up. She called out, 'Dinu, you're still awake, you have to go to work in the morning.'

Dinesh heard his mother's voice as if it was coming from far, far away.

A fuzzy blur descended in front of his eyes. He felt as if the mother pig was ready to pounce on him and Tiwari, knife in hand, was coming towards him, cruelly. Terrified, he called out to his mother.

The cry turned into a scream, and everyone woke up. Ma got up, alarmed and scared. She ran to him, 'What happened, Dinu?'

Dinesh's eyes blazed like red-hot coals. His body was burning as if with a fever. There was a fearsome shadow of utter terror on his face. Ma tried to place her hand on his forehead. He jerked her hand away.

He shouted, 'Look…she's standing in front of me…look…Tiwari is also standing there…he has found out…he will tell everyone… everyone….' He was screaming.

Seeing his condition, Ma also started screaming. Dinesh got up and ran to the door. Kishore and Mama tried to restrain him. But he ran out so fast, they couldn't stop him.

He opened the door and was on the street. He started running down the road. Mama and Kishore ran after him. The lights in the neighbouring flats came on.

Dinesh was running as if he'd taken leave of his senses. The ghrrr-ghrrr sound of the mother pig and Tiwari's loud, cruel laughter pursued him. He felt an unknown fear in every vein of his body. He kept running. His scream rose and got lost in the silent hush and stillness of the night.

Mama and Kishore were left far behind. The faint yellow lights of the street tried, sadly and sorrowfully, to fight the darkness.

WAR

SHAANI

It was when we were at war with Pakistan. The air was heavy. People were scared, the fear was deep. The sky had sunk and shrunk—colourless, dusty and frightening. Moments in time had lengthened manifold. Weighed down by terror, insecurity and uneasiness, the day would dawn before it was supposed to and die well before the evening, before it was supposed to. Then, as soon as evening set in, the night would deepen and people would huddle close together in their homes and not talk for hours.

'Did you hear! Rizvi has been stripped of his charge.' Shankardutt heard this as soon as he reached the office one day and was taken aback by the news.

'Meaning? Has he…his job….'

'No, he still has his job. But the work he's been doing for years has been taken away from him. The director said that given the circumstances, it's not appropriate to leave such important work to Rizvi. It's a matter of the nation, after all….'

'The whole thing is so insignificant!' Shankardutt felt like laughing. First of all, it really was a pointless and rotten department and on top of that, the work Rizvi had been doing all this while was utterly trivial! But even if he wanted to, the director wouldn't be able to do anything in the matter, though he was the head of department, and as for Rizvi, he was merely an ordinary employee.

There were just four Muslims in the department, and only three were of any consequence. The fear and terror that had gripped the city's Muslims since the war started could be felt most palpably in the city's offices. Every other day, it seemed that a riot or brawl would break out any second. Actually, ordinary Muslims skulked about, the way rabbits do in bushes, in a strange, helpless state of fear and wariness. People would close their doors and windows and

247

listen to the news on Pakistan Radio at low volume and when they met, they would talk to each other timidly, in the manner of rabbits.

Then something happened in the middle of these fearful times. One night, the city's respected Muslims organized a public meeting and the next day a big board was found hanging on a monument in the heart of the city with 'Rashtriya Muslim Sangh' written on it.

Hamid Ali, a well-known, reputed personage, who had twice done the Haj, was elected president of this organization. Many strong appeals to take nationalistic oaths, signed by Hamid Ali, were made to Muslims, and Qureshi took up the job of sending these appeals to newspapers and presses.

'Well, friends? How far is Lahore?'

For two consecutive days in the middle of the war, this was the question with which the office opened. Whether it was the destruction of tanks or of people, there were some extremely strange and electrifying rumours in the air. The biggest rumour of all was that the Indian army, slicing through the Pakistani army as if it were a bed of carrots and radishes, was advancing inexorably and would seize Lahore any day now.

'Well, sahib, how long does it take for an army of brave soldiers to cover a distance of ten or twelve miles?'

That day, Qureshi was the first to ask this question. The office had just opened. Rizvi had also arrived and like every day, was quietly turning the pages of a newspaper. Although Qureshi had asked this question of the whole office, he first cast a fleeting, meaningful glance at Rizvi.

'It can take ten hours, ten days too, and even ten years....'

'Ama, say ten minutes, ten minutes!' said an office clerk known for his cowardice, with such fervour, as if he was not a clerk but a captain in the army.

'Yaar, let Lahore come to us,' a voice piped up from the table close by. I'm thinking of settling down there. I've heard that the bloody city is really beautiful.'

'Yes, it is, but what will you do there?'

'Why, anything—it has newspapers, it has presses. What do you think, yaar, suppose I establish a Hindi press there, how would that be?'

'I'm going to open a hotel,' said another gentleman ecstatically. 'There's plenty of money in bloody hotels. If nothing else, at least one will be free from this slavery....'

'Tomorrow I'm going to make a money order for 13 rupees 15 annas,' someone suddenly announced loudly from the centre of the office, standing in front of Rizvi. 'Do you know in whose name? In President Ayub's name! He is so poor. As soon as Partition happened, he took 13 rupees 15 annas from us and ran away. If you don't believe me, check the old accounts of the Chhindwara military canteen...'

At that moment, Rizvi, who had been sitting at the table, head bent, as if he hadn't heard anything, got up all of a sudden and, without looking at anyone, strode out of the room. For a second everyone was silent, but the next moment Qureshi looked at everyone with a wink and people nudged each other.

'Did you see, Duttji?' someone launched a direct attack at Shankardutt. 'Why did this happen suddenly, right now? Did he get angry?'

Shankardutt could do nothing but stare at his attacker's face when Qureshi jumped in, saying, 'Aji, what will poor Duttji say? Why, just the day before yesterday when I took the Rashtriya Muslim Sangh appeal to him, the dear sir began saying what appeal and why? He flatly refused to sign. He said, am I a treacherous person that I have to go around furnishing proof of my integrity...?'

ᔨ

'Switch off the lights... switch off the lights...!'

The volunteers' voices could be heard from far away—mocking voices that seemed like they had returned after dashing against a lonely mountain. Outside there was a murky, awful hush, as if the entire city had been dropped into a dark and cold cave. Every now and then, the sound of fighter jets would emerge from a corner of the sky, and then, like a demon's flickering tongue, that sound would lick the roof and parapet of every house before receding. And then, the same dreadful hush and the same boundless throbbing darkness in which one felt the sound hadn't gone but had paused on the roof.

'Now bombs are being dropped on cities—on civilians!' said Shankardutt, sighing, as if he was talking to himself. Then he looked at Rizvi who was sitting with both knees folded up. The room was dimly lit by the light of a dull, feeble candle and to prevent this light from leaking out, the doors and windows had been shut and the curtains tightly drawn. The glass panes of the skylights had also been covered with paper.

'Did you see today's newspaper?' Shankardutt felt as if his voice was coming from far away. 'The civilian hospital was bombed and bits of flesh from the bodies of innocent patients were thrown up in the air…. Hare Ram, will God ever forgive us for this cruelty? I feel….'

At that moment the flame of the candle flickered and wavered. It was as if a wave of darkness came and ricocheted off the partially lit floor of the room. Rizvi lifted his head from his knees. His lips parted but he didn't say anything. He merely shook his head. Shankardutt got up and went close to him and, in a cajoling tone, with deep affection, said, 'Ama, just forget it!'

'What?'

'All that….'

'What should I forget, Duttji?'

'Should I repeat everything and once again make you feel bad?' said Shankardutt, placing a hand on Rizvi's shoulder lovingly. 'Wasim, I will keep saying this—lamenting injustice today is like dashing one's head impotently at someone's death. Do you think you'll win over this world, a world which is even more cruel than war, with your childish stubbornness?'

'Switch off the lights!' The voice rang out from another block. This time, it came from quite far away, but it seemed as if they were once again in front of the quarter. Shankardutt stood up and adjusted the curtains even more carefully.

A big scene had erupted over a little thing.

There had been a blackout in the city for the past many days. It was not in the cantonment area, yet there was danger. As soon as it was evening, the entire city would descend into the same cold, dark cave. Whether it was out of a sense of civilian duty or out of fear for their lives, people were extremely alert and responsible. There were bands of volunteers to enforce the blackout in every neighbourhood.

Today, too, like every other day, bands of volunteers had arrived, calling out to everyone, but one of the groups, after arriving in this block, stayed put and didn't go ahead—it stopped in front of Rizvi's quarter. Perhaps the curtain in one of the windows had moved slightly and a beam of light had leapt out of the quarter on to the road.

'Switch off the light!' someone called out sharply. Rizvi was at home. He peeped out but paid no attention, and continued reading.

'Why, sahib, are you deaf?' two young men came forward and rattled the latch with all their might.

'What is it?' Rizvi came out, his manner a mix of enquiry and anger and perhaps the situation started to go downhill from here. 'I fully understand my duty, the light is off,' Rizvi said finally.

'If it's switched off, then where is this light coming from?' someone said angrily. 'From my in-laws' house?'

'That's a candle. I lit it to read.'

'Doesn't a candle give out light?'

'That makes no difference. I'll adjust the curtain.'

'Whether it makes a difference or not, put out the light!' a zealous young man shot out like an arrow towards the door but Rizvi stopped him midway.

'That light will not be put out!'

'It will be put out!'

'No, it won't!'

'It will!'

'There's no point insisting,' said Rizvi. 'First go and get the candles put out in the quarters in front!'

'Leave that to them! We are talking to you!'

'Why should I leave it? Are they covered with diamonds and pearls?'

For a second the young man could only stare at him, dumbfounded, then all of a sudden he roared like a lion so that the entire colony echoed with his words, 'That light *will* be put out!'

There was a numb silence, and then a voice broke through the darkness, 'Beat up the bloody traitor!'

'Traitor! Traitor!'

For a few moments Rizvi stood trembling in the dark, then all at once he leapt to where the voice was coming from.

By the time Shankardutt arrived and salvaged the situation, it was far too late.

✓

'Bhaijaan!' About ten minutes after both of them had come in and composed themselves somewhat, Shankardutt was startled by a tearful voice. It was Begum Rizvi from behind a door, sounding choked, as if her voice had caught in her throat.

'Bhaijaan, do us a favour. Tell him to give me and the children some poison first and put us to sleep, then he can tackle the world... and leave us to God.'

After that, her voice suddenly choked as the tears welled up and Shankardutt felt as if his own throat was full of thorns. He looked towards the door and got a glimpse of Begum Rizvi's dupatta, but he didn't say anything. Both of Rizvi's children, Appu and Saba, were standing close to the curtain, looking scared. Especially Appu, who was gazing at Shankardutt with such still, frightened eyes that Shankardutt himself shrank in fear. All of a sudden it struck him that he too was a Hindu. After so many years, for the first time in this house...and then as if for the first time he noticed that Rizvi was still sitting in the same condition—torn shirt, dishevelled hair, and dried blood on his bruised lower lip....

'Appu bete!' Shankardutt called out to him softly, in a subdued voice, 'Beta, come to your uncle!'

Appu didn't come. He stared hard with those same frightened eyes and then moved closer to the curtain.

'Get some clothes for papa, bete!' he said calmly.

The clothes came after a while. Appu was the one who brought them, but after putting them down he left without a word. Shankardutt held out his hand to try and catch him but the boy slipped out of his grasp like a fish. Shankardutt was a little stung but he just laughed wanly and said, 'Appu is angry with me.'

Did Rizvi hear this or not? Shankardutt himself was looking at him, yet not really seeing him.

Is Appu genuinely not angry? Is it true when people say that children have a unique ability to differentiate between good and bad? But now, after so many years, how had he suddenly become bad? Could it be that in the recent past there was some talk about him in the house and the children were affected by it? All these questions were coming up now. There had been nothing till yesterday.

It was the eleventh day of the war. The same blackout and darkness. He had dropped in yesterday again, he sought them out the way water seeks a slope.... If someone were to ask the childless Shankardutt who was really responsible for him spending so many evenings in this house—Rizvi or Appu, would he be able to give an answer? And who was it in truth? The years-long friendship with Rizvi or Appu's high-pitched squeal as he flung himself into his arms at the door, 'Our uncle has come...our uncle has come...!'

The room was shrouded in darkness except for a little light, like the flickering embers of a fire. The same speeding planes seeming to pause on the roof every now and then...outside the entire city was cold and silent like a grave.

'Our uncle!' Appu came like he did every day, but unlike his usual habit, he didn't put his small little arms around his neck, and neither did he....

'Uncle, do you know when this war will end?'

Shankardutt was taken aback, 'Why, bete?'

'Tell me, when will it end?'

'But why?'

'Ammi was asking. She said, go and ask uncle.'

Shankardutt looked at the curtain inside. Was Begum Rizvi standing there? No, she wasn't there. But why was this question for uncle, why not for papa? For a second he felt as if he was being pushed into a witness box. Gathering Appu's little body in his arms, he said softly, 'I don't know, bete!'

Before Appu could say anything, they heard that same sound from far away. In a few seconds it came tearing through the sky and the silence, so harsh, so terrifying that Appu clung to him. After a while, Appu raised his fear-filled eyes to the roof and said, 'Uncle, don't you feel scared?'

'I do, bete!'

'You too?'

'Yes, me too.'

'These were fighter planes, weren't they, uncle?'

Shankardutt nodded.

'Are they going to drop bombs?'

'Appu, go inside!' Rizvi interrupted him.

'Who fights in a war, Uncle?'

'Soldiers fight, bete!'

'What are soldiers like?'

'The men who are in the army, they are called soldiers.'

'Okay, understood. Like our uncle from Pakistan is a soldier. Isn't that so?'

'Yes, bete, he must be fighting too.'

'With a gun?'

'Yes, with guns, with grenades, with tanks.'

'Who sends them to the army, Uncle?'

'The nation sends them, bete!'

'Nation? Who is a nation?'

'Bete...nation....' Shankardutt had to think for a moment. 'A nation is where people live, like you and me—we are the nation, bete!'

'But, Uncle, you were saying you are afraid of fighting. Then why were these people sent?'

'Appu!'

This time Rizvi's tone was stern. Appu looked at his papa for a moment, then turned back to him and said, 'Okay, Uncle, one more thing—aren't soldiers frightened?'

'Of whom?'

'Of fighting, of bullets. Don't they get hit by them?'

'They do.'

'Truly?'

'Yes.'

'Then they die?'

'They die.'

'Truly?'

'Yes, bete. Truly.'

Appu's small brow was furrowed and his tiny lips parted with astonishment and worry. After staring at him for a second with a strange look, he suddenly asked, 'So, Uncle, why doesn't the police catch them?'

Could Shankardutt answer this question? If Rizvi hadn't scolded and silenced Appu even more severely this time, what would he have said?

'He really bothers everyone!' Rizvi said softly after Appu had gone.

'Yes, he really does!' Shankardutt said, taking a deep breath. 'Wasim, do you remember that day when Appu asked you a question to which you had absolutely no answer. That question troubles me even today....'

Rizvi looked at him with questioning eyes, then as he remembered, his eyelids lowered of their own accord.

It was a holiday. The same sitting room. The same two people. The same silence, stretching on and on. Begum Rizvi was inside.

Appu was outside, playing with his friends. Suddenly he left his game, came straight to his papa and his next question was like a bullet.

'Papa, are we Hindu or Muslim?'

'Why?' Taken aback, Rizvi tried to evade the question, 'Go out and play, bete! Let us talk.'

'No, first tell me,' Appu insisted, 'Are we Hindu or Muslim?'

'But why?'

'Tell me!'

'All right, Muslim.'

'Where does Allah miyan stay, Papa? Up in the sky, isn't it?'

'Yes.'

'And Bhagwan?'

'He also stays there.'

'In the same place?' A deep question swam in Appu's eyes as he said this. Afraid that he would have more queries, Rizvi said, 'Go and play outside....' But Appu was impatient to ask yet another question and both of them wanted to get away from him.... Rizvi looked towards the veranda to avoid meeting his eyes.

As always, a small bird was sitting on the mirror that hung in the veranda, pecking away at its reflection.

DAJYU

SHEKHAR JOSHI

The first time Jagdish babu saw him was at the small café with the big signboard in the marketplace. He was fair-complexioned, with clear blue eyes, golden hair, and a joyful spring in his step. He had the suppleness of a drop of water sliding down a lotus leaf. From the playfulness in his eyes, he looked to be about nine or ten years old and perhaps that is indeed how old he was.

When Jagdish babu, taking a long drag from his half-smoked cigarette, entered the café, the boy was clearing plates from a table. By the time Jagdish babu sat down at a corner table, he was directly in his line of vision. As if the boy had been waiting for him, for someone to arrive at that very spot, for hours. He didn't say anything. Yes, to show humility, he bent a little and just about smiled. After taking the order of a single chai he smiled again as he went away and returned with the tea in the blink of an eye.

Human emotions are strange. Even in an uninhabited place, without the company of other people, a person may not feel alone. But one can feel lonely in a crowd of hundreds of men and women, amidst a clamour of voices. Everything can appear unfamiliar and so very alien!

Jagdish babu had come from a faraway place, he was alone. In the hustle-bustle of the chowk, in the din of the café, everything felt unfamiliar to him. Maybe after a few days, after he'd got accustomed to it, he would feel a sense of intimacy in the same environment. But, today, it didn't seem intimate at all, it seemed distant, far removed even from the edge of intimacy! And then quite spontaneously, he began remembering the people of his village, the school and college lads, the cafés and hotels in the city close by.

'Chai, shaab!'

Jagdish babu flicked the ash of his cigarette into the ashtray. He felt as if these words had a music that embodied everything he was missing. He decided to check whether his conjecture was accurate.

'What's your name?'

'Madan.'

'All right, Madan! Where are you from?'

'I'm from the hills, babuji!'

'There are hundreds of hills—Abu, Darjeeling, Mussoorie, Shimla, Almora! Where is your village, in which hill?'

Smiling, he said, 'Almora, shaab, Almora.'

'Which village in Almora?' asked Jagdish babu, interested in the exact location.

This question made Madan somewhat diffident. Perhaps embarrassed by the unusual name of his village, he said evasively, 'It's very far shaab, must be around 15–20 miles from Almora.'

'Even so, it must have a name,' Jagdish babu insisted.

'Dotyalagon,' he replied hesitantly.

The dark shadow of loneliness on Jagdish babu's face cleared and when he smiled and told Madan that he was from a nearby village, the boy almost dropped his tray out of sheer delight. Madan tried to speak but the words wouldn't come out of his mouth. He seemed lost, as if he were trying to look back into his past.

The past—village…high mountains…river…Eeja (mother)…Baba…Didi…Bhuli (younger sister)…Dajyu (older brother)!

Madan felt as if someone close to him was reflected in Jagdish babu's face! Eeja? No, Baba? No, Dadi…. Bhuli? Yes, Dajyu!

In a few days, the gulf between Madan and Jagdish babu, of being strangers to each other, was bridged. Now, as soon as he sat down at a table, Madan would call out—

'Dajyu, Jai Hinnn….'

'Dajyu, it is so cold today.'

'Dajyu, will it snow here too?'

'Dajyu, you ate very little yesterday.'

Just then a voice from some other corner would call out 'Boy' and Madan would reach even before the echo of the voice could

be heard! After taking the order, he would ask Jagdish babu as he
went by, 'Dajyu, do you want anything?'

'Get some water.'

'Getting it, Dajyu,' Madan's voice would be heard as he waited
on another table. He would repeat the word 'dajyu' with the same
eagerness and affection with which a mother kisses her son after a
long separation.

After a few days, Jagdish babu's loneliness receded. Not just the
chowk or the café, the whole city seemed like home to him. But
now the constant repetition of the word 'dajyu' grated on his nerves.
As for Madan, he was forever saying 'dajyu' even if he was serving
at another table....

'Madan! Come here.'

'Coming, Dajyu.'

Jagdish babu's dormant middle-class sensibilities were stirred to
life by this latest reiteration of the word 'dajyu'—the slender thread
of affection and familiarity couldn't withstand the sharp blade of
self-conceit and ego.

'Dajyu, shall I get you some tea?'

'No, I don't want tea, but what is this dajyu-dajyu you keep
shouting day and night? Don't you have any concern for someone's
prestige?'

Jagdish babu's face was flushed with anger, he no longer had any
control over his words. He didn't even pause to think whether the
boy would understand the meaning of the word 'prestige' or not,
but Madan, without being told, understood everything.

Madan was deeply hurt by Jagdish babu's behaviour. Giving the
manager the excuse of a headache, he went to his tiny room and
wept, his head buried in his knees, his breath coming in sobs. Away
from his village and home, it was natural for Madan to display his
affection for Jagdish babu. For the first time in his life as a migrant,
he felt as if someone had forcibly pulled him away from his eeja's
lap, from the arms of his baba, from his didi's bosom.

But sentimentality is fleeting. Once the anguish is released in the form of tears, a person makes a better decision than when he's in the midst of those emotional moments.

Madan went back to work as before.

The next day, while going to the café, Jagdish babu ran into Hemant, a classmate from his childhood days. After reaching the cafe, Jagdish babu signalled to Madan but got the feeling that Madan was trying to avoid him. Only when he called out to him a second time did Madan turn up. Today, there was no smile on his face, nor did he say, 'What shall I get you, Dajyu?' Jagdish babu himself had to say, 'Two chais, two omelettes,' but even then, instead of saying, 'Coming right up, Dajyu,' Madan said, 'I'll just get it, shaab,' and went away. As if the two of them were strangers to each other.

'He seems to be from the hills,' Hemant made a guess.

'Yes,' Jagdish babu answered brusquely, before changing the subject. Madan brought the tea.

'What is your name, boy?' Hemant asked, a note of condescension in his voice.

For a few seconds, a heavy silence descended on the table. Jagdish babu's eyes were fixed on the cup of tea before him. Memories of previous occasions swam in front of Madan's eyes…. Jagdish babu asking him his name just like this one day…then…. 'Dajyu, you ate so little yesterday'…and another day, 'Don't you have any concern for someone's prestige?'

Jagdish babu raised his eyes to look at Madan and felt as if any moment the boy would explode like a volcano.

Hemant repeated his question, his tone insistent, 'What is your name?'

'Everybody calls me "boy", shaab.' With this brief answer, Madan turned away. His face, flushed with emotion, looked even more beautiful.

THE SPIRITS OF SHAH ALAM CAMP

ASGHAR WAJAHAT

[1]

The days somehow pass in Shah Alam camp but the nights are the worst. There is such anguish all around that only Allah can help. There are so many voices in the camp that even a whisper in the ear can't be heard. Such yelling-shouting, noise-clamour, weeping-screaming, sighs-sobs....

At night, the spirits come to meet their children. The spirits stroke the heads of their orphaned children, look into their empty, silent eyes with their own vacant eyes and speak to them. They clasp the children to their breasts. Their heartrending screams before they were burnt alive keep reverberating in the background.

When the entire camp goes to sleep, the children wake up. They wait to see their mothers...to eat a meal with their fathers.

'How are you, Siraj?' Amma's spirit asks, gently caressing his head.

'How are you, Amma?'

His mother looks happy. She says, 'Siraj...now...I am a spirit... now no one can set me on fire.'

'Amma...can I too become like you?'

[2]

After midnight the flustered, agitated spirit of a woman came to Shah Alam camp searching for her child. The child was not in that other world, nor was he in the camp. The child's mother felt her chest would burst. The spirits of the other women started helping the woman look for her child. Together they searched every corner of the camp. They went to her old neighbourhood. The houses are still burning there…ghoon-ghoon. Because they were spirits, they could enter the burning houses…they looked in every nook and cranny but couldn't find the child.

Eventually the spirits of the women went to the rioters—they were preparing petrol bombs for the next day, cleaning their guns, polishing their weapons.

When the mother of the child asked them about her son, they laughed and said, 'Oh, you crazy woman, when ten-twenty people are burnt all at once, who keeps track of one child? He is sure to be lying in a heap of ash somewhere.'

The mother said, 'No, no, I have looked everywhere…I couldn't find him anywhere.'

Then one of the rioters said, 'Arre, is she the mother of the boy we hoisted on our trishul?'

[3]

The spirits come to Shah Alam camp after midnight. They bring food from heaven, they bring water, they bring medicines, and they give them to their children. This is why no child in Shah Alam camp is without clothes, or hungry, or sick. This is also why the Shah Alam camp has become so famous. It is well known in far-off countries.

When an important politician from Delhi came on a tour of Shah Alam camp, he was delighted and said: 'This is an excellent place…all the Muslim children in the country should be sent here.'

[4]

The spirits come to Shah Alam camp after midnight. They stay with the children all night, watch over them intently…think about their future.

'Siraj, now you should go home,' his mother's spirit said to him.

'Home?' Siraj shrank with fear. Shadows of death started dancing on his face.

'Yes, how long will you stay here? I'll come to see you every night.'

'No, I won't go home...never...never....' Smoke, fire, screams, clamour.

'Amma, I will stay with you and Abbu.'

'How can we stay with you, Sikku?'

'Bhaijan and Aapa also stay with you, don't they?'

'They burnt them also along with us, didn't they?'

'Then...then I will...go home, Amma.'

[5]

The spirit of a little boy comes to Shah Alam camp after midnight... the child looks like a shining firefly at night...he flits around here and there...runs all over the camp...leaps and jumps about...does a bit of mischief...doesn't lisp...speaks clearly...clings to his mother's clothes...holds on to his father's finger.

Unlike the other children in the Shah Alam camp, this child always looks very happy.

'Why are you so happy, child?'

'You don't know...everybody knows.'

'What?'

'That I am proof.'

'Proof? Proof of what?'

'Proof of bravery.'

'Whose bravery are you proof of?'

'Of those who ripped open my mother's stomach and took me out and cut me into two pieces.'

[6]

The spirits come to Shah Alam camp after midnight. The spirit of a young boy's mother came to see him. The boy was surprised to see her.

'Ma, why are you so happy today?'

'Siraj, today I met your grandfather in heaven. He introduced me to his father...and he in turn introduced me to his grandfather and great-grandfather. I met your great-great-great-grandfather.' His mother's voice was bursting with happiness.

'Siraj, your great-great-great-grandfather was a Hindu...Hindu... understand? Siraj, tell everyone this. Understand?'

[7]

The spirits come to Shah Alam camp after midnight. A sister's spirit came one night. The spirit was looking for her brother. While searching, the spirit saw her brother sitting on the steps. The sister's spirit became happy. She leapt towards her brother and said, 'Bhaiya...' The boy pretended he had not heard. He kept sitting like a statue.

The sister again said, 'Listen, Bhaiya.'

The brother still didn't respond. Nor did he look at his sister.

'Why aren't you listening to me, Bhaiya?' asked the sister loudly and the brother's face flushed red like fire. His eyes boiled over with emotion...he jumped up and began beating his sister savagely. People collected around them. Someone asked the girl what she had said that her brother had begun thrashing her. The sister said, 'I just called him Bhaiya.' An elderly person said, 'No, Salima, no; why did you make such a big mistake.' The old man started weeping bitterly and the brother began hitting his head against the wall.

[8]

The spirits come to Shah Alam camp after midnight. One day, an old man's spirit came with all the other spirits to Shah Alam camp. The old man was bare-chested, his dhoti tied high, chappals on his feet and he had a bamboo staff in his hand. He had a watch tucked inside his dhoti somewhere.

The spirits asked the old man, 'Do you have a relative in the camp too?'

The old man said, 'Yes and no.'

The spirits thought he was crazy and left him and he began circling the camp.

Someone asked the old man, 'Baba, who are you searching for?'

The old man said, 'I am looking for people who can murder me.'

'Why?'

'Fifty years ago I was killed by a bullet. Now I want the rioters to burn me alive and murder me.'

'Why do you want this, Baba?'

'Only to tell the world that I didn't die when they killed me with a bullet, nor will I die if they burn me alive.'

[9]

A political leader asked a spirit in the Shah Alam camp, 'Do you have a mother and father?'

'They were killed.'

'Brothers and sisters?'

'None.'

'Anyone?'

'No.'

'Are you comfortable here?'

'Yes, I am.'

'You get food etc.'

'Yes, I do.'

'Do you have clothes etc.?'

'Yes, I do.'

'Do you need anything?'

'Nothing.'

'Nothing?'

'Nothing.'

The political leader was happy. He thought: this boy is sensible. He's not like other Muslims.

[10]

The spirits come to Shah Alam camp after midnight. One day the Devil's spirit came with the other spirits. Looking around him, the Devil was ashamed and embarrassed. He couldn't meet people's eyes. He tried his best to avoid them. Keeping his head down, he tried to find a place where he wouldn't see anyone. Eventually the people cornered him. In truth he was ashamed and said, 'I had no hand in what happened. I swear by Allah, I had no hand in it.'

The people said, 'Yes...yes. We know. You couldn't do something like this. You have a standard to maintain, after all.'

Sighing with relief, the Devil said, 'A burden has been lifted from my heart...all of you know the truth.'

The people said, 'A few days ago Allah mian had come and He said the same thing.'

TIRICH

UDAY PRAKASH

This incident is connected with Pitaji. And with my dream and also with the city. And with that inborn fear of the city.

Pitaji had turned fifty-five. He was thin, his hair was absolutely white like the down on an ear of corn. It was as if his head was covered with cotton wool. He used to think a lot—far more than he spoke. When he did speak, we would be relieved, as if breath that had been held for long finally escaped. At the same time we would also be afraid. It was a big mystery for us children. We knew that the vault containing all the knowledge of the world was with Pitaji. We knew that he could speak all the languages of the world. The world knew him and, like us, gave him respect even as it feared him.

We were proud to be his offspring.

Sometimes, though this would happen only a couple of times in many years, he would take us with him when he went for an evening walk. Before setting off, he would fill his mouth with tobacco. Because of the tobacco, he would be unable to say anything. We would find this silence very grave, splendid, wondrous and solemn. If, along the way, my younger sister tried to ask him something, I would immediately try and reply, so that Pitaji wouldn't have to speak.

Actually, this task was difficult and fraught with risk. Because I knew that if my answer was wrong then Pitaji would have to speak. That would be difficult for him. For one, he would have to get rid of the tobacco juice, and then, because he lived in another world, it would be hard for him to come out of that world and travel from there to here. Though there was nothing special about my sister's questions. For instance, what do you call that bird sitting on the dry branch of the tree in front of us? And since I knew all the birds I could tell her that that was a blue jay and it was important to see it on Dusshera day. I tried to ensure that Pitaji would not be disturbed

267

and left free to continue with his contemplations.

My mother's and my own wholehearted effort was to see that my father lived in his own world happily and peacefully. He should not be forced out of there. It was a very mysterious world for us, but Pitaji solved many problems about our home and our lives while remaining there. Like the time the question of my fees arose—at that time all the glasses had vanished from our house and everyone was drinking water from a lota. For two days Pitaji was completely quiet. Ma too wondered if he had forgotten about the fees or whether the solution to this problem was beyond him. But early morning on the third day, Pitaji gave me a letter in an envelope and sent me to Dr Pant in the city. I was very astonished when the doctor gave me sherbet to drink, took me inside the house, introduced me to his son and gave me three hundred-rupee notes.

We were proud of our father, we loved him, we feared him and having him with us, being with him, made us feel as if we lived in a fortress. A fortress that had deep moats dug around it, with high turrets, whose walls were made of hard red rock, a fortress that was impregnable from any outside attack.

Pitaji was an extremely strong fortress. Inside, in that enclosed space, we forgot everything and would run around and play. And I would sleep soundly at night.

But that day, in the evening, when Pitaji came back from his stroll, there was a bandage tied around his ankle. After a while, quite a few people from the village arrived. It turned out that Pitaji had been bitten by a tirich, a poisonous lizard, in the jungle.

All of us knew that no man could survive the bite of the tirich. At night, in the hazy and dusty light of the lantern, many people from the village gathered in our courtyard. Pitaji sat in the middle, on the ground. Then Chuttua the barber from the neighbouring village also turned up. He was known for drawing out poison with leaves from the castor oil tree and ash from dried dung.

I had seen a tirich once.

There was a crack in one of the rocks among the pile of enormous rocks near the pond. These rocks became very hot in the afternoon. I saw the tirich come out of that crack and go to the pond to drink water.

Thanu was with me. He told me that this was a tirich, it had a hundred times more venom than a black cobra. He was the one who told me that a snake bites you only if you step on it accidentally or tease it deliberately. But a tirich charges the moment you look into its eyes. It comes after you. You should never run straight if you want to escape from it. You should run in a zigzag fashion, or in circles, round and round.

Actually, when a man runs, he doesn't merely leave the imprints of his feet on the ground, he also leaves his own scent in the dust. The tirich chases this scent. Thanu told me that to trick the tirich, a person should first run fast for a short distance, taking small steps, feet close together, and then leap forward in four or five long jumps. Sniffing all the while, the tirich will come running, it will speed up when it comes to the marks of the feet that are close together, but it will get confused when it comes to the point where the person took long jumps. It will keep wandering, lost, till it locates the next set of footprints with the scent trapped in them.

We knew two other things about the tirich. One, the moment it bites someone, it runs away and urinates somewhere and then rolls about in its own urine. If the tirich does this, the person it has bitten cannot survive. If he has to survive, he must—before the tirich wallows in its own urine—take a dip in a river, well or pond or kill the tirich.

The second thing is that the tirich rushes to bite you only if you have looked into its eyes. If you happen to see a tirich, you must never look into its eyes. The instant that happens, it recognizes your scent and goes after you. After that, you may circle the whole earth, but the tirich will never stop chasing you.

Like many of the other children, I too was very afraid of the tirich. The two deadliest characters in my nightmares were the elephant and the tirich. The elephant would at least get tired after running for a while and I would escape by climbing a tree, or flying into the air but with the tirich I'd get caught in a web of sorcery. If I was going somewhere in my dream, I would suddenly come across the tirich, there was no fixed spot where this would happen. It wasn't as if I would only see it in the crack of a rock or behind old monuments or near some bush—it would appear in the bazaar, cinema hall, shop, or even in my own room.

In my dream I would try not to look into its eyes but it would gaze at me with such familiarity I wouldn't be able to stop myself and that was it, the moment my eyes would meet its eyes, its gaze would change—it would start running and I would take flight.

I would run in circles, take quick, small steps, suddenly jump long distances, try and fly, climb up to some high point, but despite a thousand attempts, it never fell for any of my tricks. It seemed very cunning, clever, wily, and dangerous to me. I felt as if it knew me very well. That familiarity shone in its eyes and looking at that glow I sensed that this was one enemy that was aware of every thought that entered my head.

This was my most terrifying, tormenting, fearful, disquieting dream. My body would be exhausted with all that running, my lungs would inflate, I would be drenched in sweat, become breathless, and a frightening, numbing kind of death would creep even closer. I would scream, start crying. I would call out to Pitaji, Thanu or my mother and then I would know it was a dream. But despite knowing this, I also knew very well that I could not escape this particular death. Not death—murder by the tirich—and that's why I would try my best to wake up from my dream. I would exert my full strength, open my eyes wide inside my dream, try to see the light and say something out loud, forcefully. Many times I did succeed in waking up at the last minute.

Ma told me that I had a habit of talking and screaming while dreaming. Often she would find me crying in my sleep. She should have woken me up in such situations, but she would gently stroke my forehead, cover me with the quilt and I would be left alone in that terrifying world. In my feeble attempt to escape my death—or rather, my murder—I would run, flee, scream.

But slowly, with experience, I worked out that making a sound in such situations was my only weapon to escape the tirich. Unfortunately, every time I would remember this weapon at absolutely the last minute, when it was *this* close to getting me. I could feel the breath of my impending murder actually touch me, I would be engulfed by a lifeless yet frightening darkness full of the intoxication of death, I would feel as if there was nothing solid beneath my feet—I was in the air and then that moment would arrive when the end of my life was near. At that point, in that infinitesimal and fragile moment, I would remember this weapon of mine and I would start speaking very loudly and I would come out of the dream. I would wake up.

Many times Ma would ask what had happened to me. At that time I didn't have enough command over the language to tell her the whole story, to narrate every single thing the way it happened. I was well aware of this inability of mine and that's why I would be filled with a strange kind of tension, disquiet, and helplessness. In the end, defeated, all I could say was, 'It was a very frightening dream.'

ᶜ

I don't know why I had this fear that the tirich that bit Pitaji was the same one that appeared in my dreams and whom I recognized.

But the one good thing was that the instant the tirich bit Pitaji and ran, he followed it and killed it. If he hadn't killed it immediately, the tirich would have urinated and then rolled about in its own urine. Then Pitaji could not have survived in any circumstance. That's why I was not overly worried about him. Instead, I felt relief and happiness because of that. One reason was that Pitaji had killed the tirich instantly and the second was that my oldest, most dangerous foe had finally died. It had been slaughtered and now I could go anywhere I wanted in my dream, carefree, whistling, without any fear.

That night, the crowd stayed till late in our courtyard. Charms, incantations, invocations were going on to cure Pitaji of the bite. The bite wound had been torn open and the blood drained out, it had then been filled with the red medicine (potassium permanganate) that was put inside wells. I was not worried.

The next morning Pitaji had to go to the city. He had to appear in court. There was a summons in his name. Buses travelled to the city on the road that skirted our village by around two kilometres. There were barely two or three of them in a day. Luckily, as soon as Pitaji arrived at the road, he saw a tractor going to the city from a nearby village. The people sitting inside were known to him. The tractor would reach the city in two to two-and-a-half hours. That is, much before the court was to open.

On the way, the matter of the tirich came up. Pitaji showed those people his ankle. Pandit Ram Avatar was also in the tractor. He explained that a specialty of the tirich's poison was that sometimes it would begin having an effect after twenty-four hours, exactly at the time the tirich had bitten the person the previous day. That's why Pitaji should not be entirely relaxed. The people in the tractor drew Pitaji's attention to another big mistake. According to them, Pitaji had done the right thing by killing the tirich immediately, but after that, the tirich shouldn't have been left like that. At the very least it should have been set on fire.

These people claimed that many insects and living things came alive again at night in the light of the moon. The dew and chill present in moonlight contains nectar and it has often been noticed that a snake left for dead and thrown away carelessly in the night becomes wet with the coolness of the moon, comes to life again and slithers away. After that, it is always on the lookout for revenge.

The people in the tractor were worried that the tirich, after coming to life again at night, would urinate and roll about in its urine. If that happened, then twenty-four hours later, at exactly that moment, the tirich's fatal venom would start taking its effect on Pitaji. Their advice was that Pitaji should go back at once and, if he found the body of the tirich where he had left it, he should burn it thoroughly and reduce it to ashes. But Pitaji told them it was important for him to appear in court. This was the third summons and if he did not appear this time, there was the possibility that a non-bailable warrant would be issued. The appearance in court was to do with the house in which our family lived. He had not been able to pay the lawyer his fee on two previous occasions and if the lawyer displayed the slightest carelessness and the judge decided to be whimsical, he could declare us bankrupt.

It was a peculiar situation—if Pitaji got off the tractor to go back to the village to burn the tirich's body, then he could be arrested on a non-bailable warrant and our house would be taken away from us. The court would turn against us.

But Pandit Ram Avatar was also a vaid. Apart from the astrological almanac, he had a deep knowledge of roots and herbs. He suggested that there was a way by which Pitaji could appear in court as well as save himself from the tirich's poison. He said that the essence of Charak was the formula that venom itself is the medication for venom. If he could get the seeds of a datura plant he could prepare the medicine needed to cut the tirich's poison.

The tractor stopped at the next village, Samatpur and a datura plant was finally found in the fields of an oil merchant. The medicinal extract was prepared by grinding the datura seeds and then boiling them along with an old copper coin. The extract was highly bitter so it was mixed in some tea and Pitaji was made to drink that tea. After that everyone was relaxed and reassured. The idea was to protect Pitaji from grave danger.

Actually, I knew a third fact about the tirich, which I suddenly remembered some hours after Pitaji had left. It was similar to that fact about snakes because of which the camera was invented.

It is believed that when a man kills a snake, the snake takes a proper, close look at the face of its killer before dying. As the man kills him, the snake looks at him fixedly, registering every minute detail of his face in the retina of its eyes. Once it's dead the man's picture is clearly imprinted on the snake's retina.

Afterwards, when the man has gone, a second snake, the partner of the dead one, peers into the latter's eyes and is thus able to recognize the killer. All the snakes start recognizing him. He can go anywhere after that, but they will forever be ready and waiting to take their revenge on him. Every snake becomes his enemy.

I was worried that Pitaji's face had been imprinted on the retina of the dead tirich. Some other tirich could come and peer into the eyes of the dead one and recognize Pitaji. I began feeling uneasy. Why had Pitaji not been more alert to this possibility? After killing the tirich, he should have taken a stone and smashed both its eyes. But what could be done now? Pitaji had left for the city and I was faced with the problem of finding the exact spot—in that vast, spread-out jungle near the village—where he had left the tirich after killing it.

Along with Thanu, and with a bottle of kerosene, matches, and a big stick, I stumbled around in the jungle looking for the tirich. I recognized it well. Very well. Thanu didn't have much hope that we would find it.

Then, all of a sudden, I sensed that I knew this jungle intimately. Every single tree looked familiar. This was the place where I ran in my dreams to escape the tirich. I looked around carefully—it was the very same place. I told Thanu about the narrow canal that flowed south a little distance from here. Above the canal, there were big rocks and an old keekar tree with massive beehives on it. They looked as if they were several centuries old. I knew that particular brown-coloured rock, which was half submerged in the stream throughout the monsoon, but could be seen fully after the rains, when mud and slush filled its cracks, and strange, weird-looking vegetation grew out of those cracks. The rock was covered with a layer of congealed moss. The tirich lived on the topmost crack of this rock. Thanu thought I had imagined all this.

But very soon we found the stream. And the aged keekar tree with its beehives, as well as the rock. The dead tirich was lying flat on its back on the grassy ground a little away from the rock. This was the very same tirich. A thrilling sensation of violence, excitement, and a kind of joy ran through me.

Thanu and I gathered dry leaves and sticks, poured a whole lot of oil on it and set it on fire. The tirich began burning in that fire. The smell of its burning flesh spread in the air. I felt like shouting at the top of my voice but I was scared I might wake up and all this might turn out to be a dream. I looked at Thanu. He was crying. He was a good friend of mine.

This was the place from where the tirich would emerge and chase me many times in my dream. I was surprised that I had known where it lived for so long, but I had never tried to come there during the day and finish it off.

Today I was recklessly happy.

Pandit Ram Avatar told us that the tractor passed the toll tax booth in the city at around quarter to ten. They had to wait for a bit while the toll tax was being paid. Pitaji got off the tractor to relieve himself. When he came back he said his head was swimming a little, by then it had been about an hour-and-a-half since he had drunk the medicinal extract of the datura. The tractor dropped Pitaji off in the city at five or six minutes after ten. According to Master Nandlal of Palra village, who was also travelling in the tractor, when Pitaji was dropped off at the crossing near Minerva Talkies in the city, he complained that his throat was feeling dry. He was slightly worried because he didn't know the way to the court and he disliked asking people for directions.

That was the problem with Pitaji—he remembered all the little paths in the village or jungle, but he would forget the streets in the city. He rarely went to the city. When he had to go, he would keep postponing the date of his departure till he could not delay it any longer. Many times it so happened that Pitaji left for the city with his luggage, but came back from the bus terminus itself. The excuse was that he missed the bus. Whereas we knew that nothing of the sort had happened. Pitaji would have seen the bus, but gone and sat somewhere—gone for a pee or to eat a paan. Then he would have seen the bus leaving. He would have waited a little longer. When the bus picked up speed—he would have run behind it for a short distance. Then his feet would have slowed and he would have returned, expressing annoyance and disappointment. By doing so, he would actually believe that he had missed the bus. We, who had assumed that he had left for the city, would be astonished to find him back home.

There is only a hazy picture of everything that happened to Pitaji in the city from seven minutes past ten when he got off at the crossing near Minerva Talkies, bang opposite Singh Watch Company, till six in the evening. This information was also pieced together after talking to people and making enquiries. You get such information after somebody's death, especially if that death has occurred in a very unexpected, unnatural manner. An accurate and detailed account of where Pitaji went and what happened to him on that day, Wednesday, 17 May 1972, from ten past ten till six in the evening, a period of about seven hours forty-five minutes, is hard to get. A rough idea of the events that happened can be gleaned from the information and reports that came in later.

Like Master Nandlal from Palra village saying that Pitaji complained of a dry throat from the point when he got off the tractor. Before this, near the toll tax booth, when he had come back after taking a leak, he had mentioned that he was feeling dizzy. That is, the medicinal extract from the datura was already having an effect on Pitaji. In any case, by the time he reached the city, it had been two hours since he had drunk it. I am guessing Pitaji would have been extremely thirsty by then. He would have gone towards some hotel or dhaba so that he could moisten his throat but, knowing his nature, he would have stood there for a while, unable to make the decision to ask for a glass of water or not. Once he had recounted how, a few years ago in the summer, when he had asked for water in a hotel, one of the servants working there had abused him. Pitaji was very sensitive, that's why he must have suppressed his thirst and left.

There was no information forthcoming from anywhere as to where he went between ten and about eleven o'clock, a period of around forty-five minutes. Nothing out of the ordinary happened in this period that anybody could say. It was difficult to find out whether any passersby on the street saw him or noticed him. My guess is that during this time he would have asked a few people for directions to the court and thought that once he reached there, he would ask his lawyer, S. N. Aggarwal, for some water. But either people didn't reply to his queries and walked past quickly or they replied so irately, and in such a rush that he would have been humiliated, upset, and distressed. This is usual in cities.

In these forty-five minutes, I suspect the effect of the medicinal extract would have become more pronounced. The hot May sun and his thirst would have made the effect worse. He would have stumbled a little and it is possible that during this time, he would have felt dizzy too.

At eleven o'clock, Pitaji entered State Bank of India in the city's Deshbandhu Marg. It is not clear why he went there. Ramesh Dutt from our village is a clerk in the city's Bhoomi Vikas Sahkari Bank. Maybe Pitaji just had 'bank' in his mind when he was walking by, so when he saw the words State Bank, he turned in there. He hadn't drunk water till then, so he probably thought that he would ask Ramesh Dutt for water, ask him the way to the court, tell him that his head was spinning and also that last evening he had been bitten by a tirich. According to the State Bank cashier Agnihotri, he was checking the cash registry at the time. There were bundles of approximately 28,000 rupees on his table. It was about two or three minutes past eleven when Pitaji arrived. His face was dusty and he looked ghastly and then he said something abruptly in a loud voice. Agnihotri said he got quite scared. Normally, such people don't manage to reach the cashier's table, which is set quite far inside the bank. Agnihotri also said that if he had seen Pitaji coming towards him a couple of minutes before, perhaps he wouldn't have got so scared. But what happened was that he was completely immersed in the accounts in the cash register when he suddenly heard Pitaji's voice, he looked up and, seeing him, got frightened and let out a scream. He also rang the bell.

As stated by the bank's peons, two watchmen and other bank workers, they were all startled by the cashier's sudden scream and ringing of the bell and ran towards him. By then the Nepali watchman, Thapa, had grabbed Pitaji and taken him towards the common room, hitting him all the while. Ramkishore, a peon, who was around forty-five years old, said that he thought some drunkard or madman had entered the office and because his duty was at the bank's main door, the branch manager could have chargesheeted him. But what transpired was that while Pitaji was being beaten, he started saying something in English. This made the peons even more suspicious. In the midst of all this, the assistant branch manager, Mehta, perhaps said that this man should be thoroughly searched before he was allowed to leave. Ramkishore, the peon, said that Pitaji looked frightening, in a bizarre kind of way. On top of that, he was covered in dust and smelt of vomit. The bank peons denied that they had beaten him up badly, but outside, right next to the bank was a paan shop and Bunnu the paanwallah said that when Pitaji emerged from the bank at about eleven-thirty, his clothes were torn and his lower lip was cut and bleeding. The skin below his eyes was swollen and blotchy. Such marks turn purple and blue later.

After this, that is, between eleven-thirty and one o'clock, there is no information to be had about where Pitaji went. Yes, the paanwallah Bunnu did say something, though he was not totally clear, or it could be that he was afraid of the State Bank employees and so avoided recounting everything clearly. Bunnu stated that after coming out of the State Bank, maybe (he stressed the word 'maybe') Pitaji had said that the bank peons had snatched his money and papers. But Bunnu was of the opinion that Pitaji could have said something else too, because he was unable to speak properly, his lower lip was badly cut, there was saliva dribbling from his mouth and he didn't seem to be in his right mind.

My own guess is that by this time, the effect of the medicinal extract had become quite pronounced. Though Pandit Ram Avatar doesn't think so. He pointed out that datura seeds are ground with bhang on Holi as well, but it never happens that a person takes leave of his senses. Pandit Ram Avatar believes that the tirich's venom had started making its presence felt in Pitaji's body and its disorienting effect had reached his brain. Or it is possible that when the watchman Thapa and the State Bank peons were beating him up, he might have suffered an injury to the back of his head which caused him to lose his mind. But I feel that till then Pitaji still had some degree of awareness and he was making every effort to somehow get out of the city. It could be that since his court papers and his money had been seized from him in the bank, he thought there was no point in him staying on there. Perhaps he thought he should go back to the State Bank and at least retrieve his papers. But he may not have had the courage to go back there. He must have been afraid. This was the first time in his life he had been beaten like this, that's why he hadn't been able to think clearly. He was very thin and since childhood, he had been troubled by appendicitis. It's also possible that at that time, the effect of the medicinal extract was so overpowering that he was unable to concentrate on any one thing and, in the grip of thoughts that erupted every second like tiny bubbles in his brain, or because of the recent shocks to his system, he kept stumbling about. But I do know, I can feel it very distinctly that the thought of leaving the city and coming home must have definitely been in his mind—a constant thought, emerging out of the darkness again and again, even if weak and muddled.

Pitaji reached the police station at around fifteen minutes past one. It is situated on the outer edge of the city, near the Victory Pillar that stands close to the Circuit House. The astonishing thing is that the court is barely a kilometre away from the police station. If Pitaji wanted, he could have reached the court in ten minutes. What we don't know is that though Pitaji had managed to reach there, was he still thinking about going to court? He didn't have his court papers with him.

The SHO of the police station, Raghavendra Pratap Singh, said that it was fifteen minutes past one at that time. He had opened the tiffin he had got from home and was about to have lunch. There was bitter gourd with parathas in his tiffin. He didn't like bitter gourd and he was irritatedly trying to decide what to do. That's when Pitaji arrived. He didn't have a shirt on and his trousers were torn. It seemed as if he had fallen somewhere or had been hit by a vehicle. At that time there was only one constable at the station, Gajadhar Prasad Sharma. He says that he thought some beggar had entered the police station. He even called out to him but by then Pitaji had reached the SHO Raghavendra Pratap Singh's table. The SHO said that he was anyway in a bad mood because of the bitter gourd. Despite thirteen years of married life, his wife still didn't know the things he disliked heartily, disliked so much that he positively loathed them. By the time he put a morsel of food in his mouth, Pitaji had reached very close to him. There was vomit on his face and below his shoulders, which gave off a strong stench. The SHO asked him what the matter was. Whatever Pitaji said in response was very difficult to understand. Later SHO Raghavendra Singh was full of repentance. If he had known that this man was the pradhan of Bakeli village and a former teacher, he would have made him sit in the police station for at least two or four hours. He wouldn't have let him go out. But at that time he felt that this was some madman who had come in because he saw him eating, and that's why he angrily called out to Constable Gajadhar Sharma. The constable dragged Pitaji outside. According to Gajadhar Sharma, he wasn't violent with Pitaji and he noticed that when Pitaji had arrived at the police station, he had a cut on his lower lip. There were scratch marks on his chin, as if he had fallen and scraped it against something, and the skin on his elbows was broken. He had definitely fallen somewhere.

No one knows where Pitaji wandered for about one-and-a-half

hours after he left the police station. It was difficult to know whether he had even had any water from the time he entered the city and got off the tractor at the crossing near Minerva Talkies at seven minutes past ten in the morning. It seems unlikely. It could be that by then his mind was in no condition to even register thirst. But if he managed to reach the police station, there must have been a thought in his head despite the intoxication, no matter how feeble and drowned in darkness, that he could ask the way home, or the whereabouts of the tractor or lodge a report about his money and court papers being snatched from him. It is deeply distressing to think that at this time, Pitaji was not just fighting against the venom of the tirich and the intoxication of the datura, but even in this state of groggy inebriation, he was worried about saving our house. Perhaps by then he had begun feeling that whatever was happening to him was nothing more than a dream, and he must have kept trying to wake up from the dream.

At about fifteen minutes past two Pitaji was spotted stumbling around the northern limit of the city, in its most prosperous colony— Itvari Colony. This was a colony of jewellers from the commercial and money markets, big PWD contractors, and retired bureaucrats. A few well-off journalist-poets also lived there. This colony was always peaceful and incident-free. Those people who saw Pitaji here said that by this time all that was left on his body was his striped underwear, and since its drawstring was probably torn, he kept trying to hold it up with his left hand. Whosoever saw him thought he was a madman. Some people said that every now and then he would stand and shout abuses. Later, a resident of the colony, retired tehsildar Soni sahib and a special correspondent and poet of the city's biggest newspaper, Satyendra Thapliyal, said that they had heard Pitaji clearly and in fact, he was not shouting abuses but he was repeating the words—'I am Ramsvarth Prasad, ex-school headmaster…and village head of…village Bakeli….!' The journalist-poet Thapliyal expressed his anguish. Actually, at that time he was going to a special party at the US embassy in Delhi to listen to music, he was in a hurry, so he left. Yes, the tehsildar, Soni sahib, said that he 'felt very sorry for that man and scolded the boys too. But two or three boys said that this man was about to assault Ramratan saraf's wife and sister-in-law.' The tehsildar said that after hearing this, he too felt that perhaps this man was actually a hoodlum who was just playacting. The boys were harassing him and in the midst of all this, Pitaji kept saying, 'I'm Ramsvarth Prasad...ex-school headmaster...,'

If you were to calculate, from the crossing near Minerva Talkies where Pitaji got off the tractor at seven minutes past ten in the morning to the State Bank on Deshbandhu Marg, then the police station near the Victory Pillar and Itvari Colony on the northern tip of the city, all in all, Pitaji had wandered for approximately thirty, thirty-five kilometres. All these places are not in the same direction. This meant that Pitaji's mental state was such that he couldn't think things through clearly and would start walking in any direction. As for the matter of him going to assault the saraf's wife and sister-in-law, which Thapliyal sahib thought to be true, my own assessment is that he had gone to them either to ask for water or to enquire about the road to Bakeli village. Pitaji must have been in his senses for that one moment. But they must have become frightened and started screaming, seeing a man with this sort of appearance coming so close to them. He got the injury to his brow, from which blood was trickling into his eye, at Itvari Colony itself, because later some people said that those boys began throwing stones at him.

The place where Pitaji received the most injuries is not too far from Itvari Colony. Pitaji was surrounded in an open space in front of a cheap dhaba called National Restaurant. The throng of boys from Itvari Colony that had started following Pitaji now included some older boys as well. Satte, a servant who worked at National Restaurant, said that the mistake Pitaji made was that on one occasion, he lost his temper and began throwing stones at the crowd. Probably one of the bigger lumps that he threw hit a seven, eight-year-old boy Vicky Agarwal, who had to get many stitches. Satte said that the crowd became menacing after that. They were creating an uproar and pelting stones at Pitaji from all directions. The dhaba owner Satnam Singh said that at that time Pitaji was wearing only his striped underwear, you could see the bones on his thin frame and the white hair on his chest. His stomach had shrunk. He was smeared with dust and mud, the white hair on his head was dishevelled, there was blood oozing out of his lower lip and from above his right eye. Expressing sorrow and regret, Satnam Singh said—'How was I to know that this was a simple, straightforward, respectable man and that a twist of fate had reduced him to this condition?' Though Hari, the servant who washed the cups and plates in the dhaba, said that in between Pitaji would hurl incoherent abuses at the crowd and begin throwing stones. 'Come you wretches...come...I will kill each one of you bhosdiwaalon... tumhari ma ki....' But I doubt whether Pitaji would have cursed in this way. We never heard him abusing ever.

I can say with complete confidence, because I knew Pitaji very well, that up to this moment, he must have thought again and again that everything that was happening to him was not real, it was a dream. Pitaji would have found these incidents absurd and meaningless. He wouldn't have believed them. He would have thought: what is all this nonsense? He has not come to the city from the village, no tirich has bitten him. In fact, there's no such thing as a tirich, it is a fabrication, a superstition...and all this talk of drinking a medicinal extract made from datura is laughable, that too after hunting for the plant in an oil merchant's field. He would have given the matter some thought and then discovered that, after all, why would anyone file a legal case against him? What was the need for him to go to the court?

I know that Pitaji too must have dreamt the dream that I did, a dream like a tunnel, long, hypnotic but scary. We had so many things in common. I believe that by now Pitaji would have been totally convinced that all that was happening was untrue and unreal. That's why he must have kept trying to come out of the dream. If he had started talking loudly, or perhaps shouting abuses, it was out of a desperate attempt to come out of the nightmare with the help of his voice. From what the employees of National Restaurant and its owner Sardar Satnam Singh said, it seems Pitaji sustained several injuries at this spot. Many stones and bricks hit his temple, forehead, back, and other parts of his body. Sanju, the twenty, twenty-two-year-old-son of Arora, the contractor who had the contract for that road, even hit him two or three times with an iron rod. Satte said that anyone would have died after receiving so many injuries.

I feel a strange kind of relief and my ragged breaths become normal when I think that at that point Pitaji would have felt no pain; because he would have become fully, deeply aware, with complete logic, that this was a dream and, as soon as he got up, everything would be all right. As soon as he opened his eyes he would see Ma sweeping the courtyard or see me and my younger sister sleeping on the floor...or a bunch of sparrows...maybe he would have, in the middle of it, even felt like laughing at this strange dream of his.

If, in his anger, Pitaji had started throwing stones at the boys, the number one reason was that he knew very well that these stones were being thrown in a dream and no one would be hurt. It could even be that after throwing a stone with all his might he would have waited eagerly and uneasily, thinking that the moment the stone struck some boy's head and broke his forehead, this nightmare would, with one jolt, scatter into little pieces and the light of the real world would come flooding in. Even his screaming was not out of anger. He was, in fact, calling out to me, my younger sister, Ma or anyone else that if he was unsuccessful in waking up from this dream, then someone should come and wake him up.

The most distressing thing happened at this point. Pandit Kandhai Ram Tiwari, the sarpanch of our village panchayat and Pitaji's childhood friend, went past the street in front of National Restaurant at about three-thirty. He was in a rickshaw. He was to take a bus from the next crossing to go back to the village. He saw the crowd that had gathered outside the dhaba and came to know that some man was being beaten up. He wanted to find out exactly what was happening. He even asked the rickshaw to stop. But when he made enquiries, he was told that a Pakistani spy had been caught trying to poison the water tank, and he was the one being beaten. Exactly at this time Pandit Kandhai Ram spotted the bus to the village and he asked the rickshawallah to hurry up and take him to the next crossing. This was the last bus to the village. If that bus had come three or four minutes later, he would have definitely gone and seen Pitaji and recognized him. The state roadways bus was always late by thirty to forty-five minutes, but that day, by chance, it was bang on time.

Satnam Singh said that the crowd in front of National Restaurant started drifting away and people began dispersing when Pitaji didn't get up from the ground for a long time. A big piece of a brick had struck him on his temple. Blood had started coming out of his mouth. There were injuries on his head. Satnam said that when Pitaji didn't move for quite a while, one of the boys in the crowd said that it looked like he was dead. When Pitaji didn't move even ten or fifteen minutes after the crowd had dispersed, Satnam Singh asked Satte to sprinkle some water on his face to ascertain if he had just fainted, in which case he would get up. But Satte was scared at the thought of the police. Afterwards Satnam Singh himself emptied a bucket of water on him. Because the water was thrown from afar, the mud on the ground got wet and stuck to Pitaji's body.

Sardar Satnam Singh and Satte both said that Pitaji lay there till about five o'clock. The police hadn't come by then. Then Satnam Singh thought that he could get stuck as a witness or become involved in the police panchnama so he shut his dhaba and went to see the film *Aan Milo Sajna* in Delite Talkies.

It was around six o'clock when Pitaji poked his head into the kiosk of a cobbler, Ganeshva, in a row of cobblers' shops on the pavement of the Civil Lines Road. By this point, he wasn't even wearing his underwear, he was crawling on his hands and knees, like some four-legged creature. He was covered with mud and black smudges and there were injuries on different parts of his body.

Ganeshva is a cobbler from our village, from the quarter beyond the pond. He said he got very scared and couldn't recognize master sahib. His face had become very frightening and you couldn't make out any distinguishing features. Terrified, he came out of the shop and began shouting. Apart from the cobblers, some other people also gathered there. When they peered inside the shop, they saw Pitaji crouching in the far corner amidst the broken shoes, scraps of leather, rubber, and other bits and pieces of junk. His breath was coming faintly. He was pulled out from there on to the pavement. That's when Ganeshva recognized him. Ganeshva said that he spoke into Pitaji's ear but he didn't respond. After a long time Pitaji said something like 'Ramsvarth Prasad...' and 'Bakeli'. Then he was silent.

Pitaji's death occurred at around quarter past six. The date was 17 May 1972. The tirich had bitten him in the jungle twenty-four hours ago, around the same time. Could Pitaji have predicted these events and this death twenty-four hours earlier?

The police kept Pitaji's body in the morgue in the city. The post-mortem revealed that he had many fractures, his right eye had been completely smashed, his collar bone was broken. His death occurred because of mental trauma and excessive blood loss. According to the report, his gut was empty, there was nothing in his stomach. This meant that the extract made from the datura seeds had already come out when he had vomited.

But Thanu says that it is clear now that no one can escape the venom of the tirich. It revealed its extraordinary magic exactly twenty-four hours later and Pitaji died. Pandit Ram Avatar also says the same thing. It could be that Pandit Ram Avatar says this because he wants to convince himself that the datura extract had nothing to do with Pitaji's death.

I think, I try and speculate that perhaps, at the end, when Ganeshva spoke in Pitaji's ear outside his shop, he would have woken up from his dream. He would have seen me, Ma, and my little sister—and then he would have taken his neem twig for cleaning his teeth and gone towards the river. He would have washed his face in the cold water, rinsed his mouth and forgotten this prolonged nightmare. He would have thought about going to the court. He would have been anxious about our house.

But I want to talk about my dream, which I get quite often. It is this—I have reached the jungle after crossing the mounds marking the boundaries of fields, and the rough, narrow paths of the village. I look at the stream of water, the keekar trees. The brown rock is in the same place, where it gets submerged in the stream during the rains. I see the body of the tirich lying on top of it. I am filled with joy. In the end, it was killed. I take a stone and start pounding the tirich with it, I keep hitting it with great force. Thanu is standing next to me holding kerosene and matches. Then, suddenly, I find I am not on that rock any longer. Thanu isn't there either, there's no jungle, instead I am actually in the city. My clothes are badly soiled, torn, and have turned into rags. The bones of my cheeks stick out. My hair is in a mess. I am thirsty and I try to speak. Perhaps I'm trying to ask the way to my home, in Bakeli, and that's when abruptly, a clamour rises from all around…bells start ringing…thousands and thousands of bells…I start running.

I run…my entire body is fighting for breath, my lungs start ballooning. I take short steps and then suddenly long jumps, try to fly. But the crowd is closing in. A peculiar hot, heavy wind makes me numb. The gusts of my own murder start touching me…and finally that moment arrives when my life is about to come to an end….

I cry…try to run. My entire body is drenched in sweat in my sleep. I talk loudly in an attempt to wake up…I want to believe that all this is a dream…and as soon as I open my eyes everything will be all right…. In my sleep I open my eyes wide and see…far away in the distance…but that moment does arrive in the end….

Ma is looking at me from the outside. Stroking my forehead gently, she covers me with the quilt and I am left alone. Struggling and fighting to escape my death, I become breathless, cry, scream, and run.

Ma says I still have the habit of mumbling and screaming in my sleep. But the question that constantly bothers me is—why don't I dream of the tirich any more?

THE LABYRINTH

SARA RAI

This is Banaras city, Kashi nagri. It stands on Shivji's trishul. Incomparable among the ancient cities of the world. From the beginning of time, the business of life and death has gone on here. Banaras is alive; it gives shelter to the dead and the dying. Crowds of people throng the maze of alleys. In Banaras, there is a sea of people living with the desire to die. They who die here will go to heaven, to paradise. This belief is as old as truth itself. Living in this place, I too have come to believe it. Belief is the ultimate truth.

City of ghosts. Women who died centuries ago silently spread their thick hair across the sky. The air is heavy with the breathing of shadows. In the glow from the setting sun, these shadows bend over spire, minaret, and dome. Steps of worn-out stone lead down to the tank, where the water turns from muddy to dark green; the stench of moss and sludge has been hanging in the air for hundreds of years. The boy flying a kite in the lane cuts his finger on its sharp string and the blood that flows from it is thousands of years old. Crumbling monuments stand in this century but their windows open to another sky. The spread of the ancient city, crowded with the people living in it, can be read like a history book. People drift across it with their own rhythm. The city has been written upon by time. And in the clamour of life stretching from one century to the other there are cracks in which ghosts dwell.

Amidst the crowd of ghosts, in my quiet corner, I am still alive and well. Perhaps I've been here from the beginning of time. I, Kulsum Bano, resident of Noor Manzil, 18/20 Ausaanganj, behind Kabir Chaura Hospital, in a straight line from the old peepul tree. Kulsum Bano, the eldest daughter of Sayyid Naseem Haider. Look, there's Abba huzoor's picture on the wall, clinging gently to a piece of decaying yellow paper. A Kashmiri fur cap, a jamawar shawl.

Shoulders like the walls of a fortress, grand moustaches. His forty villages and dozen kothis are not in the picture but the air of command on Sayyid Naseem Haider's face comes from them. The relict of a family that has lived in this ancient city for generations, captured in a solitary moment long gone. After him, the last fruit left on this old tree—me. No one after me. Because this tree bore no other fruit.

Yesterday that girl came to meet me, wearing men's clothes, slim, short haired, bespectacled, her face exactly like a sparrow's! She looked closely at my face, at the deep hollows on its old, yellow, papery skin and at the lustreless valleys of my eyes. As if I belonged to an extinct species. . Then she asked: 'How are you, Apa begum?'—in a familiar manner, as if she was an acquaintance of many years.

Like an animal who'd lived shut up in its den, I growled nastily, 'I am very bad, worse than bad, I'm dissatisfied with everything, rude, extremely ill-mannered, an infinitely troublesome old woman, continuing to live shamelessly, a burden on everyone, worth even less than dust, absolutely good for nothing, unendurable....'

I would have continued talking in this vein but seeing her look so taken aback I stopped. She looked out of her depth. Her mouth was open, but not a sound came from it. She was speechless.

Then she tried again, look at her nerve! She extended a hand towards me, and said, 'If you'll allow me, I'd like to talk to you for a bit....'

I asked, 'What do you mean by a bit? A quarter of a kilo, half a kilo, one kilo?'

Poor thing! Again, she stared at me, at a loss for words. I had slain her with just two sentences! My wrinkled face broke into a smile at the thought. Looking reassured, she too laughed a little. Just like a twittering sparrow!

'Actually, I'm writing an article on old houses and the people who live in them, for a newspaper. I wanted to ask you a few questions....'

It would not be easy to put her off. All right then, ask. Ask whatever you want, then go your way so that I too may breathe a sigh of relief. No one's coming here after that, and I'm certainly not going anywhere. End of story. No sooner had I spoken than she fished out a black box-like object from the bag slung on her shoulder and said, 'If you permit this imposition, may I record the conversation?'

So now this girl will trap my voice and take it away.

Haan bhai, I'm the last of my family. No, no one else is left. Can you see a crowd of people milling around me? My father had four children. Five, if you count Ali mian. He was just this high, three years old when he was struck down by cholera. I too fell prey to cholera. But I was tough, cholera didn't happen to me, it was I who happened to cholera. It ran away, tail between its legs! So, there were four of us left. I was the eldest, then Iqbal mian, then Tahira, then Sakina. They've all gone now, each one of them. Come, let's move on. You want to know what my father did? What a question! What indeed did he do? Well, he didn't go about selling curds, that much I can tell you! He was an aristocrat, do aristocrats have any profession? He walked with his head held high. Yes, there was a lot of coming and going in this haveli. It became an abode of ghosts much later. On festivals, relatives would turn up from everywhere. The house was always full. People like bunches of grapes in every room. Food being cooked in enormous quantities and the size of the tablecloth growing ever larger. There'd be twenty-two to twenty-five people at a time. Those secret meetings, the laughter, the whispers. The singers would come in the evening and the place would turn joyful with their music and dance. That's how I got obsessed with dancing, just by watching them. I'd dance all over the house, but despite my nagging, Abba didn't get me the ghungroos I needed. I was not one to give up. I got Yaqub to buy them for me from the bazaar. Such a passion for dancing! I'd dance all day but my feet never tired. It was these same feet that are now twisted like a witch's. Those days have turned to dust. Many are the flowers the garden brings forth, countless the changing colours of the sky!

Where was I in 1947? When the country was broken up into pieces? In hell! I was here, in my home, my own country, where else would I be? How could I leave my neem tree and go away? We heard that Pakistan was coming up across the border, but which border, where was this border? No, nobody went to Pakistan from our house, except for Iqbal mian. He was always faint-hearted and the riots scared him; he got taken in by what people said. And look what became of him. He left his heart on this madhumalti vine, yes, this vine that you see in front of you, with pink and white flowers. That didn't go with him. He died on alien soil, yearning for this madhumalti, for these wretched sparrows that live in it. After me? How do I know what will happen to this haveli after me? I don't waste my time thinking of such unnecessary things. The same that has been happening for centuries. The water drop is fated to be lost in the sea! The rooms on one side have already started caving in, the walls and the roof have long decayed. Getting them repaired is beyond me. Last month the fortified wall of the porch collapsed. And do you know what Halima brought for me from the rubble? Those wretched ghungroos that I'd asked Yaqub to get me almost eighty years ago, which had vanished.

Anyway, forget it, this story is very old and really long, like the entrails of a snake. End it here, just write down whatever you've heard till now. I'll say nothing more. The tale is over and done with, khuda hafiz.

What a relief that she's gone at last. With her black box and phone. Nowadays everyone you see has a phone in their hands, what do you call it? Mobile. The other day, Bittan mehtarani's niece, Jhallo, came and stood in front of me with a mobile in her hand. She asked me, 'Apa begum, do you know what this is?'

For God's sake! This is the twenty-first century. It's no joke. Not that I care! I live in my own time. My time creeps slowly alongside the swift current of that girl's time.

Whatever has happened in the past is not over, it grows and blossoms forever in my imagination. The shadows and the lights are still there. This journey, from noise to silence, life that starts suddenly and then pauses. The same labyrinth. Noor Manzil, lost in the fog of time, this is the same Noor Manzil. But Noor Manzil is not merely made of bricks and walls, beyond the reality of geography, it is spread out in the world of my mind, in my memories, where its likeness is set as though frozen in ice. So much time has passed. But I've got it wrong. Time doesn't pass, it's a constantly flowing river. Does it have a shore? No, I'm the one who's passing by. This monsoon, my bones will become ninety-three years old. By the grace of god, my hands and feet still function. I can walk without difficulty. If I live a little longer, I'll have been an eyewitness to an entire century. A whole century fallen from the tree of eternity!

That girl did her job and left but there is a clutter of images within me, a whole stack of them. And the pictures keep unspooling like a tape.

Abba's deep voice was heard in the porch, far away in the waiting hall. The buggy had just come and stopped in front of the house. The creaking of his leather shoes. The thak-thak of his ivory cane on the floor. Jerking my head away from Anna who was combing my hair, I swept aside the heavy curtains of the inner courtyard and ran out. The sunshine outside was blinding. In the distance, the well and along its edge a row of tall wild banana trees. Even taller was the silk cotton that stood alone like a sentry, in its full glory. Its bright red flowers stung my eyes. I ran like the wind. My long hair streamed behind me like the tail of a horse. I jumped up and swung on my abba's shoulders.

'Abba, I've been looking out for you for so long. Where were you? Did you get my ghungroos?'

He didn't say anything. There was a small frown on his face. Gently he disengaged me from his shoulder and turned his gaze to the syce, who was watching us attentively and listening to everything that was being said.

'Allahrakhe, go and put the gaadi in the stables.'

Then he addressed me, 'Come along child, come inside. What

was the need to come out in this wild manner?'

Holding my arm, he took me inside.

Abbajaan, the most handsome, smartest, strongest man in the whole world.

And I was madly in love with him. There could be no other person like him in the whole world. When I was younger, I used to say, 'If I get married it will only be to Abba!' How they would laugh at that! Abba loved all three of us very much. He loved Iqbal mian too but not as much as the girls. Intoxicated by his pampering, we were constantly preening, very pleased with ourselves. Who could put a stop to this strutting around? Anna would grumble to herself, 'I've never seen such attitude. These girls are really getting out of hand, they're up to some mischief or the other every day.'

Anna wasn't wrong. We were extremely naughty. When maulvi sahib came to teach us, we would study decorously for a while. Maulvi sahib used to consume opium. As the opium started affecting him, we would quietly tiptoe out of the room. We'd come out on the nearby veranda where the gong hung and we would bang it hard. Maulvi sahib would jump up, saying 'Hai hai!' and sit upright again. Then one of us would say, 'Maulvi sahib, you had dozed off. We've been revising our lessons for an hour.'

'So, is the revision done?' Maulvi sahib asked hestitantly.

'Yes, maulvi sahib,' we would chant together.

'All right, learn the lesson for tomorrow then,' he would say, as he slipped his feet into his shoes, and adjusting his cap, he'd step out into the alley. The entire study period would be over in just half an hour! And what after that! There would be mimicry of all the venerable elderly members of the household and general merriment on our part. We'd hide Anna's false teeth and go into splits at her toothless mutterings or, under cover of burqas in the afternoon, we'd frighten Anna's daughter, Suggan, by pretending to be ghosts. At other times we'd lock up Chachamian's younger son, Attu, in the hen coop and then run away. The sun never set on our mischief and devilry.

Even when complaints came in, Abba paid no attention. Secure in the circle of his love, we grew up wild. We'd do the mischief, and poor Iqbal mian would get the scolding. He kept a strict eye on Iqbal, to see he didn't get spoiled. But he wasn't prepared to hear a word against his daughters. When the topic of our weddings arose, he thought no boy in the world worthy of us. If one of them had a pedigree not quite up to the mark, the other was too short or too dark, else he was too arrogant or talked more than he should. Taking a cue from his attitude, we'd give the would-be grooms all sorts of nicknames. 'Shorty,' 'Monkey-nut,' 'Black face,' 'Arab horse' and so on. In short, he would reject any proposal that came on some pretext or the other. So we stayed on at Noor Manzil, at the height of our exalted family's fortunes, our impeccable pedigree, our beauty, and elegance. We didn't leave all of that to go anywhere. Look, Abba, I'm still at Noor Manzil. You won't have to ask for my address.

The sprawling grounds of Noor Manzil, where in the rains plants seem to grow at an incredible speed, and slugs and millipedes, red velvet-insects and newly born frogs celebrate joyously. Snakes that were imprisoned below the ground all year long slide out of their holes and welcome the monsoon, their supple bodies flexing, and tall grass spreads everywhere like green fire. Yes, these grounds are still there in the midst of all the hustle and bustle of Banaras city. You can still come here, slicing through the crowds.

Noor Manzil. Walls at least three feet thick of lakhori bricks, high doors, two massive gates studded with iron nails, a long curving entrance and in from the door you go down three steps to reach an enormous, open courtyard. In the middle of it, a water tank, from which a fountain leaps up ceaselessly, restless to touch the light. On both sides of the courtyard, two verandas with arches that had thick, heavy curtains in those days. In the winter the curtains would be drawn, ensuring that not a hint of cold entered, and in the summer they would be swept aside so that a rustling breeze could come in and cool down the place. Four madhumalti creepers climbed alongside the arches, whose stalks had grown so thick they'd have put any vine in a dense African jungle to shame.

Hundreds of sparrows lived in the vine.... At dawn and dusk their chirping created such a din you could hear nothing else.

In the rooms inside hung farshi punkahs whose cord, wound on the toe, was pulled by a servant sitting on the floor. Now that we have electricity those fans are of no use. But one of them still hangs in the hall. I remember the long summer afternoons when Suggan would grip the cord with her toe and pull it for hours on end. She'd doze off sometimes but her toe kept moving.

In one corner of the inner courtyard is a spiral staircase with wide steps that winds its way up to the room on the roof. Noor Manzil's sweeping, open roof. We would put out our cots on this roof on summer nights. The gleaming white sheets and pillows on the beds and the bela and chameli flowers placed at the head of the cots gave off such a heady fragrance! When it was suffocatingly humid and fire seemed to rain down from the sky, we would sprinkle water or rose and kewda on the charpais. If it rained we would drag the cots inside the room on the roof. And above the courtyard, in the eaves, were the pigeon cotes. Anna used to say that illness doesn't visit a house that has pigeons. Laqqa and Shirazi and Kabuli and that valuable Anardana, with eyes like those of Emperor Akbar.

Now more than half of the rooms are shut. One part of the haveli is open for my use. At the far end of the veranda four steps lead down to the basement which stays cool even in the summer; next to it the small courtyard in which I spend the winters and attached to it the little room that serves as my kitchen. Halima sleeps in front of it, with her daughter-in-law and grandchildren, while her good-for-nothing alcoholic son wanders aimlessly around the alleyways of Banaras. At night when everyone spreads out their bedding, the stale smell of fatigue and sweat that rises from there makes my heart sink. But what can be done? I am the one who told them to sleep here. I have no choice but to endure it. Were I to fall at an odd hour and break my leg, there should be somebody around to pick me up.

In fact, Halima leaves no stone unturned in looking after me. She nags me all the time, 'Will Apa begum have some tea?' or 'Apa begum, shall I bring the water for your bath?'

May God save me from this witch's attempts to bathe me. Do I roll in mud all night that I need a bath? But small mercies, it's a blessing that she's around. It's not as if I'm showering her with riches. Just a couple of rotis and dal to keep body and soul together. She's seen misfortune and that's why she's here, otherwise where do you get servants these days?

The rest of the house is shut. The curving stairway to the roof leads to a long veranda. Martyr's veranda is the name it has acquired over the years. When silence falls late at night, the Martyr comes down the stairs in his sandals made of wood. I can hear the knocking sound they make. But he never does finish coming down the stairs; he's been doing that for the past two hundred years. In fact, his coming down the stairs has become part of family lore. If you open the window of the room on the roof, you can see his grave right there. There's a difference of opinion on whether he's a good ghost or a bad one that's out to create trouble. You can't really tell, can you, with ghosts. Every Friday I send Halima to the veranda to light a lamp and incense sticks. Though what can the spirit do to me now? I am well on the way to becoming one myself!

I have said farewell to everyone. Abba, Ammi, Chachamian, Chachijaan. Then both my sisters and brother. All three were younger than me. In the left wing of the haveli, the four children of Chachamian. All gone. They sleep blissfully beneath the neem tree. Yellow leaves float and fall on the graves. Again and again, I sweep them aside, clear the surface. I scrape away with my nails the soil that has settled on the graves and come upon the names inscribed on the marble epitaph. Just the names, no other sign of the illustrious ones now gone. There's just me, with one leg in this world, the second leg in the other—straddling them both. I, Kulsum Bano. There is no one left to call me by this name. I've beaten everyone hollow, I just don't die! But I do tread carefully now. I saw what happened to Ammi, I learnt my lesson. I want to keep living; the desire to live is in every pore of my being.

Standing on the parapet of the roof blackened with moss, I'd flap my arms as though they were wings. A large moon, like a yellow plate, would be out in the sky. Making a loud flapping sound I'd rise in a cloud of dust. Bright moonlit monuments, trees, pillars, all would be left behind. Carving the air with my wings, I'd turn around and look back on Noor Manzil that kept receding into the distance. And the sense of freedom. Happiness, like a sparkler, would light up my heart. For years, this dream danced in my eyes. I'd go and tell Ammi about it. Ammi would be lying in bed. Forget flying, she couldn't even walk.

My Ammi. Even a wicked person like me once had an ammi. Nusrat Bano. She fell down in this very porch. She broke her hip bone and could never stand again. She'd lie all day on a large teak bed in the small courtyard. The seasons changed from summer to monsoon, monsoon to winter, then spring and fall and then summer again. There would be no change in her condition. The bed sagged because she was always lying on it. She was fading away. That fearless beauty of hers. Her eyes, like rivers of fire, the passion on her face. I've seen the light go out of those eyes. Ya khuda! Why did you give her that passion, only for it to be vanquished?

I'm saying this today, when her image is before me as I wander in the labyrinth of days gone by. Those days we had little awareness of how helpless she was. She would lie in a corner of the haveli all day while we rushed about creating a ruckus, like the still point of a constantly spinning world. She'd call out if she saw someone go by; they'd listen sometimes and at others ignore her and move on. What energy was it that swept us ever forward so that her voice never reached us?

Sometimes in the afternoons, when I heard her calling and went to her, she would gesture with her hand that I should come and sit down next to her. Then she would draw my attention to the sunlight filtering through the henna bush in a corner of the courtyard.

The gently swaying, tightly entwined twigs created a fine maze of shadows on the wall in front of us. Both of us would look at it, she lying down, I seated, till the light lasted. These continuously forming, changing, dissolving shadows would barely last a moment but in this play of light and shadow we would see islands, or grass and trees rustling in the wind, smoke rising from burning leaves, a caravan of camels that had been crossing the desert for many days. A finite world that would slowly vanish. She would whisper and ask me, 'Look, can you see that cluster of coconut trees swaying in the breeze? Those huge ships, the cactus trees in the desert?' There was the rustle of a moth's broken wings in her raspy voice.

But more often than not, I too would pretend I hadn't heard her, preoccupied as I was with myself. I was very busy those days.

Tahira bibi came running up to me.

'Apa! Apa! Come quickly. The kite has come again!'

Tahira, my sister, four years younger than me, my follower. The chicks had been released into the courtyard from under the bamboo basket which was their temporary home. They belonged to my Minorca hen, Kallo. For two days the kite had been circling over them; it carried off a chick yesterday and now it was back. Curse be upon this kite!

I leapt after Tahira like a streak of lightning, barefoot, without even the presence of mind to put on my jootis. The sky was stretched tight like a blue tent over the courtyard, on the tent were white clouds, like flags. No sign of a kite. But looking carefully, one could discern, high up in the distance, a miniscule black dot that kept growing. The kite was swooping down at great speed. My gaze went to the two little chicks, like balls of yellow wool, full of the innocence of their two-week-old life. Watching the kite filled me with rage. Suddenly the kite's shadow fell on the ground as she swooped down on the chicks. Then, in the blink of an eye I pounced on the kite, pressing down on it with my full weight. Its warm wings fluttered under my chest. They smelled of dust and heights.

'Suggan, Suggan!' I screamed. 'Quickly, get the big scissors.'

In a fit of rage, with the help of Suggan and Tahira, I cut off the eagle's wings. My bloodlust cooled only when I saw it walking with the chicks.

It is the same courtyard. I sit there till late every evening, watching the light change from muddy to grey to inky. All around me, solitude spreads like dense black smoke. Halima's goat is tied on one side of the courtyard, it is also black. It gazes at me with its blank eyes and I stare back at it like a fool. A curse be on this Halima. She could find no other place to tie the goat. One day it got free and chewed up all the gul-e-abbasi flowers. After being eaten by a goat, a plant doesn't thrive. And I get enraged if I see goat droppings. Tiny, disgusting black pellets strewn all over. The witch doesn't have the good sense to clean up after, just knows how to spread dung. But how many things can I yell about; I just sit in this garbage dump doing nothing.

Today when I was sitting in the courtyard, I heard Sakina bibi's voice coming from the hall. Sakina, my youngest sister. Her rounded voice, as though her throat was slick with a smooth string of mellifluous notes. Sakina's delicate face appeared in front of me. In her ears, dangling emerald earrings. Her turquoise dupatta fluttered in the hall, in the air that had hung still for ages. She used to put her head inside a copper pot and sing. Captured inside the pot, trying to find a way out, her voice would echo even more deeply. That pot would turn up in different places in the house, in the grain-store or in a pile of broken utensils. Then it too disappeared, like my ghungroos. Because of the good-for-nothing servants of this house, no household object ever stayed in its appointed place. I could hear Sakina's voice clearly. She was singing her favourite song–

Jhuki aayi re badariya sawan ki
Sawan ki manbhawan ki...

(The rain clouds of Saawan hang low
O so pleasing to the heart...)

Sakina and I would remain closeted in the hall for hours on end.

Her singing and my dancing! I swear, it never ended. What madness had me in its grip those days. I don't know where I got this craze for dancing from. Was it the gift of the singers who used to come to the haveli in the evenings, or did the roots of this passion go back to some other deeper hidden place? Could it be in my blood, passed on to me from a beautiful dancing girl who, by her art of offering fragrant paan had stolen into the heart of one of my ancestors? This boiling intensity in my blood must have come from somewhere, this intensity that cooled down only with the movement of my feet and the motion of my body.

Eyes closed, a smile on my face, my heart and mind in some other world, I would keep dancing. My feet got bruised but I never tired. Round and round I would go, twirling in perfect circles on the stone floor of the hall. Then, a hand holding on to the voluminous folds of my gharara, I'd stand completely still, like a top that stopped spinning. The whole time that I danced, I would be in some other place; it was as if I was another person. Finally when I stopped, out of breath, that other world continued to dance within me!

Far away, in some corner of the world, Sakina bibi is singing, her head inside that copper pot. Evening has fallen. Sakina's voice seems to echo from the rosy, golden sky. What a miracle that last month my ghungroos were found, lost for eighty years, hidden behind a wall. I take them in my hands and fiddle with them, turning them around. They were the same ghungroos; time and the humid atmosphere had imbued them with a green patina. With difficulty I bent my stiff back, and tied the ghungroos on my wooden feet. Then, like an ungainly bird moving clumsily, standing right there, I executed a shuffling, stumbling twirl. Something echoed in my heart, perhaps an old memory. A muted sound came from the rusty ghungroos, as though from far away.

NOTES ON THE AUTHORS

Agyeya (1911–1987) was the nom de plume of Sachchidananda Hirananda Vatsyayan, an Indian writer, poet, novelist, literary critic, journalist, translator, and revolutionary. He pioneered modern trends in Hindi poetry, fiction, criticism, and journalism. His novel, *Shekhar: Ek Jeevani*, based on his experiences in prison, is considered a literary masterpiece. He was fluent in many languages and was part of the underground activities of the Independence movement along with Bhagat Singh, Chandrashekhar Azad, and Yashpal. He won the Sahitya Akademi Award, 1964, for his collection of poems, *Prison Days and Other Poems*, and the Jnanpith Award, 1978.

Amarkant (1925–2014) was a Hindi writer who gained literary prominence in the 1950s during the peak of the Nayi Kahani literary movement in Hindi literature. Known for his pithy portrayal of rural life in the Hindi heartland, his stories such as 'Dopahar ka Bhojan', 'Zindagi aur Jonk', and 'Hatyaare' were part of a structural shift in Post-Independence Indian fiction. In 2007, he received the Sahitya Akademi Award for his novel *Inhin Hathiyaron Se* and the Jnanpith Award in 2009. His major novels include *Sukha Patta*, *Akash Pakshi*, and *Kale-Ujle Din*.

Asghar Wajahat (b. 1946) is a Hindi scholar, novelist, documentary filmmaker, and a playwright, best known for his novel, *Saat Aasman* (1996), and his acclaimed play, *Jis Lahore Nai Dekhya, O Jamyai Nai*. He has published twenty books including five novels, six full-length plays, five collections of short stories, a travelogue, a collection of street plays, and a book on literary criticism. Along with film scripts and short stories, he regularly writes for various newspapers and magazines. He received the Katha Best Novel of the Year Award in 2006 for his novel, *Kaisi Aagi Lalaee*.

Bhagwaticharan Verma (1903–1981) was one of Hindi's leading writers in the twentieth century. He gained prominence for his magnum opus, *Chitralekha* (1934), a historical novel which was adapted into two Hindi films, and wrote over seventeen novels during his lifetime. He worked as a screenwriter in Bombay and later edited a Hindi daily, *Navjeevan*. In 1961, he received the Sahitya Akademi Award for his novel *Bhoole Bisre Chitr* and the Padma Bhushan in 1971.

Bhisham Sahni (1915–2003) was one of Hindi's most iconic writers. Fluent in several languages, his body of work includes plays, short stories, novels, and essays. He received the prestigious Sahitya Akademi Award for *Tamas* in 1975. He was the editor of *Nayi Kahaniyan* from 1965–67 and the general secretary of the All-India Progressive Writers' Association from 1975–87. He was awarded the Padma Bhushan in 1998 and the Shalaka Samman, India's highest literary honour, in 1999.

Chandradhar Sharma Guleri (1883–1922) was an eminent Hindi writer of the early twentieth century. In 1915, he published 'Usne Kaha Tha', widely regarded as the first modern Hindi short story, in the renowned literary journal *Saraswati*. The story was adapted into a Hindi film produced by Bimal Roy in 1960. Known for his versatility, Guleri wrote several essays, three short stories, poems, plays, and translated Edward Arnold's *The Lights of Asia* into Hindi, entitled *Buddha-charita*.

Doodhnath Singh (1936–2018) was an eminent story writer, poet, and literary critic. Some of his best-known works include 'Sapaat Chehre Wala Aadmi', 'Dharmakshetra-Kurukshetra', and 'Surang se Lautate Huye'. He was awarded the Bharat Bharti Samman by the government of Uttar Pradesh in 2014.

Harishankar Parsai (1924–1995) is known as one of the greatest satirists in the Hindi language. Born in Jamani, Madhya Pradesh, he pioneered satire-writing as a distinguished literary genre. He wrote regular columns in various newspapers and magazines, most prominently in the Hindi-language daily *Deshbandhu*, called 'Poochho Parsai Se'. For his critical writings on the Emergency during 1975–77, 'Vikalang Shraddha Ka Daur', he received the Sahitya Akademi Award in 1982.

Kamleshwar (1932-2007) was one of post-Independence India's most prominent Hindi writers, having penned over thirty novels and several short story collections. He won the Sahitya Akademi award in 2003 for his book *Kitney Pakistani* and the Padma Bhushan in 2005. He was also editor of *Dainik Jagran, Dainik Bhaskar,* the now-defunct *Sarika,*and worked as a scriptwriter for Hindi movies and TV serials.

Kamtanath (1935-2015) was a prominent writer and playwright of the twentieth century. He gained literary fame for his unique depiction of class consciousness in newly Independent India. During his lifetime, he published over six novels and eleven short-story collections. To honour his extensive contribution to Indian literature, he was awarded the Yashpal Samman in 1994 and the Muktibodh Samman in 1992.

Krishna Baldev Vaid (1927-2020) was born in Dinga, present-day Pakistan. An acclaimed writer of stories, novels and literary criticism in both Hindi and English, he was known for his experimental, iconoclastic style. He translated many of his own stories and novels into English, including *Steps in Darkness* and *Bimal in Bog.*

Krishna Sobti (1925-2019) is regarded as the grande dame of Hindi literature. Her novels *E Ladaki* and *Mitro Marjani* are cult classics and known for their inventive formal approach and strong female characters. Her first short story, 'Sikka Badal Gaya', was notably published without a single change in the prestigious Hindi magazine, *Pratap,* edited by Agyeya. In her last novel, *Gujarat Pakistan Se Gujarat Hindustan (A Gujarat Here, A Gujarat There)*, she wrote about her painful memories of Partition. She won the Sahitya Akademi Award in 1980 for *Zindaginama* (1979) and the Jnanpith Award in 2017.

Mannu Bhandari (b. 1931) is an eminent Hindi novelist. She was one of the founders of the Nayi Kahani movement alongside Nirmal Verma, Rajendra Yadav, and others, and wrote extensively on the realities of urban life. Her major works include *Aap ka Bunty* (1971) and *Mahabhoj* (1976). Her short story 'Yehi Sach Hai' was adapted into a Hindi film entitled *Rajnigandha* in 1974, directed by Basu Chatterjee. In 2008, she was awarded the Birla Vyas Samman for her autobiography, *Ek Kahani Yeh Bhi*.

Mohan Rakesh (1925–1972) was an acclaimed novelist, translator, travel writer, and playwright. He played a significant role in the revival of Hindi theatre in the 1960s. His literary work includes novels like *Andhere Band Kamare* (1961) and plays like *Aashad Ka Ek Din* (1958) and *Adhe Adhure* (1968). His story, 'Uski Roti' was made into an eponymous Hindi film in 1971. He won the Sangeet Natak Akademi Award in 1968 for *Adhe Adhure*.

Omprakash Valmiki (1950–2013) is a significant figure in Indian Dalit literature. Born at Barla, Muzaffarnagar, Uttar Pradesh, he was among the first Dalit writers to gain literary acclaim in Hindi. As editor and publisher of numerous magazines, he played a key role in the pushing Dalit literature to the fore of the Indian literary scene. His memoir, *Joothan* (1997), a searing account of caste oppression in Independent India, is regarded as a literary milestone. He also won several awards for outstanding contribution to literature, such as the Dr B. R. Ambedkar National Award in 1993, the Pariwesh Samman in 1995, and the Kathakram Samman in 2001.

Premchand (1880–1936) was one of the earliest writers of Urdu fiction. His phenomenal output was marked by his passionate belief in the transformative agency of literature in ridding society of its myriad social and religious ills. He first wrote in Urdu, but later switched to Hindi in view of the poor market for Urdu books. He was the author of more than a dozen novels, over two hundred short stories, several essays, and translations of foreign literary works. Some of his novels and countless stories have been translated into English and other languages. His last novel, *Godaan* (The Offering of a Cow), that he finished just before his death in 1936, and the story 'Kafan' (The Shroud) rank among his most engaging and enduring works.

Phanishwarnath Renu (1921–1977) was one of the most famous and influential writers of the Hindi literary landscape. First published in 1946, he received major literary recognition for his novel, *Maila Anchal,*in 1954. His short story 'Maare gaye Gulfam' (The Third Vow) was adapted into an award-winning Hindi film entitled *Teesri Kasam* in 1966. He was awarded the Padma Shri in 1970, which he subsequently returned in protest of the proclamation of the Emergency.

Rajendra Yadav (1929–2013) was a leading member of the Nayi Kahani movement. He published extensively—short stories, novels, literary criticism, anthologies, poetry as well as translations into Hindi. He was the editor of *HANS*, the literary journal founded by Munshi Premchand. His literary oeuvre includes novels like *Sara Akash*, which was made into an award-winning Hindi film of the same title in 1969.

Sara Rai (b. 1956) is a contemporary writer, editor, and translator of Hindi and Urdu fiction. Born into an illustrious literary family, she published her first collection of short stories, *Ababeel ki Udaan*, in 1997. In her fiction, she explores the inner world and complexities of ordinary lives in modern-day India. She has won many awards for writing and translation, including the Katha Translation Prize in 1993 and again in 1997, the A. K. Ramanujan Prize for Translation in 2000, and the Coburg Rückert Prize in 2019.

Shaani (1933–1995) was a novelist, short-story writer, and editor. He founded literary magazines such as *Sakshatkar* and *Samkaleen Bhartiya Sahitya* and edited *Kahani*. Shaani became famous for his pithy portrayals of the Indian Muslim world in stories. His best-known novel, *Kala Jal*, was based on the conflicts and problems of a lower-class Muslim family, and went on to be serialized on Doordarshan in the 1980s.

Shekhar Joshi (b. 1938) is a distinguished Hindi writer of the Nayi Kahani movement. 'Dajyu' and 'Kosi Ka Ghatwar' are two of his best-known works, the former being made into a film by the Children's Film Society of India. Along with Sumitranandan Pant, he is regarded as one of the most influential writers of Uttarakhand. Several of his works have been translated into foreign languages. In 2012, he was honoured with the prestigious Shrilal Shukla Literary Award.

Shivani (1923-2003) was a prolific Hindi novelist and short-story writer. Her stories became massively popular following their serialization in magazines such as *Dharmayug* and *Saptahik Hindustan*. Proficient in multiple languages including Sanskrit, Gujarati, Bengali, Urdu, and English, she published over forty novels, several short stories and hundreds of essays and articles. Her most well-known works include *Chaudah Phere*, *Krishnakali*, *Lal Haveli*, among others. In 1982, she was awarded the Padma Shri for her contribution to literature.

Uday Prakash (b. 1952) is a Hindi poet, scholar, writer, journalist, teacher, and translator. Some of his best-known works include *Suno Kariger*, *Darayayee Ghoda*; *Abutar-Kabootar*, *Tirichh*, and *Palgomra ka scootar*. His major works of translation are *Romyo Rola Ki Diary* and *Lal Ghaas Par Neele Ghode*. He received the Omprakash Sahitya Sammaan in 1982, the Shri Kant Verma Smriti Sammaan in 1990 and, most recently, the SAARC Literary Award in 2009.

Usha Priyamvada (b. 1930) is a noted Hindi literary writer. Her writings depict the life of urban families in the 1960s and 70s, focusing on the role of women. She retired as a professor of Hindi at the South Asian Department at University of Wisconsin–Madison. She was honoured with the Padmabhushan Moturi Satyanarayana Award in 2007. Some of her best-known works are *Pachpan Khambe*, *Laal Deewaare* and *Zindagi aur Gulab ke Phool*.

Yashpal (1903-1978) was one of the most prominent Hindi writers of the twentieth century. A political commentator and socialist, he wrote an array of short stories, essays, novels, and travel books. An active member of the revolutionary movement, he was imprisoned by the British government and started writing while serving his prison sentence. He wrote more than fifty books including collections of short stories, novels, essays, a play, and memoirs of his revolutionary days. His two-volume magnum opus, *Jhootha Sach* (*This is Not That Dawn*) is considered the greatest piece of literature written about the horrors of Partition. He was awarded the Padma Bhushan in 1970.

ACKNOWLEDGEMENTS

There are many people who have helped me while I was working on this book. I must thank Alind Maheshwari of Rajkamal, Om Thanvi, Mrinal Pande, Ira Pande, Asghar Wajahat, Uday Prakash, Rachana Yadav, and Sara Rai for giving permission to translate the stories in this anthology. Thank you especially to Mrinalji, Sara Rai, and Rachana for all their help, warmth and patience. Vasudha Dalmia was always wonderfully supportive and encouraging; Francesca Orsini gave me excellent suggestions (at a lovely tea at Vasudha's). The ever helpful Akshaya Mukul was a phone call away whenever I needed to check anything. I will always be grateful to Shazi Zaman for his generosity, for sharing his knowledge of Hindi, for being there every time I called for help. Yasser Usman was a true friend, ever ready to take time out, drop in at home and pore over some of the stories with me. Rakhshanda Jalil was her lovely, erudite self, shukriya. Thank you to Kuldeep Kumar for our stimulating discussions and for his sharp insights into Hindi literature. I can never forget the kindness of strangers: Kanika Aurora, how much I enjoyed our conversations and your passion for Hindi literature. Balwant Kaurji, you made me see some of the stories so differently, in such a clear, sharp light. (And I owe a thank you to Vibhas Verma too!) Pranay Srivastava, you were kindness itself. I had the most fruitful conversations with Dinesh Kumar (and many thanks to my dearest dost Ashok Ganju, for introducing me to him). I'm grateful to Mihir Pandya and Suman Parmar for pointing me in the right direction when I embarked on this project. And thank you, Mita Kapur, for being there for me at every step.

My excellent editors at Aleph, thank you. I began this book with Simar Puneet, who had a real feel for the stories; we discussed umpteen longlists, then an equal number of shortlists. I was very sorry when she left Aleph, but then in stepped Pujitha Krishnan, calm, meticulous, with an unerring eye for what made a story, or a sentence work. It has been a delight working with her as she's steered the book through its many stages. Thanks also to Isha Banerji for her help with permissions and preceptive suggestions. A big thank you to David Davidar, who set me off on this enriching journey.

And as always, nothing would have been possible without my husband, Arun, who has been my staunchest supporter all through (not to mention my problem solver-in-chief when it came to my battles with the computer!). My son, Arjun, cheered me on from his home in New York. My parents wanted to know every other day: lekin kab aayegi tumhari kitab? Ab dekhiye, aa hi gayi.

NOTE FROM THE TRANSLATOR

Grateful acknowledgement is made to the following copyright holders for permission to reprint copyrighted material in this volume. While every effort has been made to locate and contact copyright holders and obtain permission, this has not always been possible; any inadvertent omissions brought to our notice will be remedied in future editions.

'Atonement' by Bhagwaticharan Verma. Reprinted by permission of Rajkamal Prakashan.

'Phoolo's Kurta' by Yashpal. Reprinted by permission of Rajkamal Prakashan.

'Gangrene' by Agyeya. Reprinted by permission of the author's estate.

'A Feast for the Boss' by Bhisham Sahni. Reprinted by permission of Rajkamal Prakashan.

'The Third Vow' by Phanishwarnath Renu. Reprinted by permission of Rajkamal Prakashan.

'The Soul of Bholaram' by Harishankar Parsai. Reprinted by permission of Rajkamal Prakashan.

'City of Death' by Amarkant. Reprinted by permission of Rajkamal Prakashan.

'The Times Have Changed' by Krishna Sobti. Reprinted by permission of Rajkamal Prakashan.

'Escape' by Krishna Baldev Vaid. Reprinted by permission of Rajkamal Prakashan.

'Where Lakshmi is Held Captive' by Rajendra Yadav. Reprinted by permission of the author's estate.

'Lord of the Rubble' by Mohan Rakesh. Reprinted by permission of Rajkamal Prakashan.